WINTER RAGE

CHARLES MCRAVEN

For information about this title, contact the publisher:

Secant Publishing, LLC
P.O. Box 79
Salisbury MD 21803
www.secantpublishing.com

Library of Congress Control Number: 2016952404
ISBN 978-1-944962-28-9

Printed in the United States of America

For Linda, who found me in these mountains

Chapter One

The old, heavy chainsaw snarled its way through the base of the towering white oak, blue smoke drifting the bone-chilling air as red-faced Uncle Charlie leaned into his work. Nate Prescott covered his ears, also red with cold, standing next to his tall aunt Andy, who kept glancing around them at imagined intruders.

Intruders, because not one of the three, despite assuring themselves of the rightness of this timber cutting, was really certain of it. The Mabrys claimed this land, although the spring, several yards up, had always been known as the boundary. No fence marked it, no stone piles or irons set, showed just where Prescott land ended and the wealthiest family in the county's spread began.

A light mist had become freezing rain and wind with the drop in temperature, and now the needle-like sleet drove the very marrow of the trees. Nate huddled in the ragged, oversize coat and tried to stay ahead of his running nose. The wool cap barely reached the tips of his ears, no matter how hard he pulled it down. Icy water seeped into his shoes, the sole of one bound up with baling wire.

By contrast, Andy seemed impervious to the cold, her angular, attractive face set almost in repose, despite the hawklike cobalt eyes. She, too, wore a threadbare coat and scuffed, mended shoes. Looking at her now, even with her having taken care of him for the past two years, Nate reflected that he never knew what she was thinking.

Nate could sometimes let his mind drift, usually while waiting, to a place he imagined, high in the sky, to look down upon himself in situations like this. Now he could see bent Uncle Charlie, Andy with her arms crossed, erect as always, and himself, standing back from the tree with her. The limbs below this sight cut the picture into shapes, their leafless branching patterning the scene they were a part of. He could imagine this place on the ground soon receiving even this weak overcast light after so many years of the tree's shade.

Finally, it started its fall, opening a space of that sky above as its almost-bare limbs caught others, bending, snapping them to fly back in what were known as "widow makers." All three lunged back as the giant crashed its way to the frozen ground, echoing through the still-standing forest. The chainsaw sputtered, then died, leaving an eerie quiet, with only a few drifting, dead leaves and twigs.

Some distance away, the mules, hitched to the worn wagon and tethered safely, had jumped in their patched harness, stared wildly around, then settled again. They'd grown accustomed to the family's timbering, back when Prescott land still had forest. *Crazy humans, goin' at it again.*

"Prime bourbon stave bolts," Charlie declared as he set the machine aside. Nate began measuring and marking with numb fingers for the saw cuts, using a length of sapling and a dull hatchet, while Andy cut away the limbs, far up the straight trunk with a double-bit axe. "Not one knot in fifty feet." He began pulling on the chainsaw starter rope with his stubby fingers, to no response. Finally, he threw the machine aside with a curse, strode to the wagon, retrieved the long crosscut saw.

Well, at least pullin' that thing will warm me up some, an' now th' sleet's quit. Uncle Charlie was so high on that chainsaw, said he traded for it, but I don't b'lieve it: prob'ly lifted it from a pickup bed somewhere. Nate grabbed the wooden handle, set the saw teeth on his mark, pulled the first stroke. Charlie settled his feet, bent, drew his own handle. Nate could smell the whiskey on his breath from six feet away.

The rhythmic travel of the saw was accompanied by outpouring white sawdust "worms" as the teeth bit, and a subtle metallic whang mingled with the distinctive sharp rumble. Nate tried to keep his end straight and not bear down: Charlie was always after him about that

("Can't pull you 'long with this saw, boy. Quit ridin' it: t'ain't a bicycle").

Nearing the bottom of the cut, long minutes into the frozen day, the log settled, pinching the blade. Andy set an iron wedge, hit it repeatedly with the flat face of a splitting maul, freed the saw. The brief respite let Nate straighten, easing the ache that had come into his lower back. Then he bent again, trying to count down the strokes till this cut was done.

After the first section, Andy took Nate's end of the saw and settled into a longer stroke, matching her brother's reach. Charlie appeared winded but wasn't about to quit this soon. His stubbled jaw tightened despite its chapped roundness, and he pulled determinedly.

Nate needed to pee, and used as an excuse a patrolling of the woods around them for anyone who might've heard the tree fall. *Nothin' to worry about: this's Prescott land. An' truth be told, it belongs to me now, since Pa bought it, an' Granpa really hasn't got a claim on it.* At this time, here in the icy woods, his muscles on fire, that fact didn't make him feel any better. And thinking about it brought back afresh the pain of losing his parents, the feeling that despite these relatives, he was really alone in the world.

Dave Prescott and his wife, Becca, had, two years before almost to the day, perished when their truck skidded on wet snow and went over a mountain precipice. They'd just made the last payment on their eighty acres, a GI loan he'd qualified for as a WWII veteran. The land was free and clear now, although timbered heavily by them to make those payments.

Nate was the only surviving child, having lost a brother and a sister in infancy. His widowed grandfather, Elijah Prescott, had not wanted to raise the boy, nor been able to, and since Becca's divorced younger sister, Andy, was already living with the family, he'd asked her to take him. Uncle Charlie sort of came with the package, whenever he managed to find his way back to the Prescott place after losing his infrequent jobs or disentangling himself from some woman.

Nate had always had a mixed admiration for Charlie, who was

never without friends. He was the center of every gathering, utterly without a sense of responsibility, but he drew people. Nate was by nature shy, and, at thirteen, tried without success to emulate his raffish uncle. Andy loved her brother, but alternately bullied him, covered for him, despaired of his ever amounting to anything. And couldn't seem ever to say no to him.

Her own ex-husband had been a handsome truck driver, but too ready to bed any other good-looking woman he found out on the roads. In or out of those emerging truckstops on the twisting highways before the interstates came. She endured him for almost three years, and was grateful to be well rid of him.

If Nate's idolizing his uncle had begun to wear thin, he wanted to do everything right for his aunt. He watched her now, bending over the saw, still somehow keeping those graceful movements as she did this man's work. Yes, in this his last remaining stand of timber.

So, I reckon I'm about th' youngest landowner around, much good as that's doin' us. No good trees left except this patch of oak, and the rest all stumps and brush. But these stave bolts should see us through th' winter, and we can put in a crop of sorts, come spring.

This plan, like every survival plan on these steep mountain hillsides, would depend on so many factors beyond their control—no late frost, sufficient rainfall, keeping foraging wildlife and pests away—that it was almost certain to fail. Plus the root-snagging, rocky plowing, the hoeing, fertilizing, weeding, before a single vegetable could be harvested. Bone-wearying labor, in an endless cycle that afforded nothing to look forward to.

By near dark, the three had sawed and cant-hooked a load of the short logs up skid poles onto the wagon and were headed home on the ice-slicked woods road. The mules knew the barn lay ahead, with what hay was left, and they stepped out with their burden, plumes of steam rising from their heaving breath. Even the slight wind generated by the wagon's movement seared Nate's face, and he hid it in the coat collar. It smelled of wood smoke. Andy and her brother walked beside the wagon to lighten the load.

Charlie Millard had chosen to do this timber cutting on the worst day they'd had for a reason. He knew Barry Mabry, son of the patriarch Montgomery, would raise hell over their taking these trees. More even than his stern father, Barry had always claimed that this strip of a few yards of land was theirs, although they'd never hired a surveyor to confirm it. And although everybody in this end of the county knew the spring had always been the boundary.

Down on th' likes of us anyway, them Mabrys. No sense givin' 'em 'nother reason t'put us down. Git our timber out, git through th' winter 'fore they even miss it. P'session's nine-tenths of th' law, way I always heard it, an' we got ourselves th' first load, an' more to come.

But it was four miles to the railhead where the timber buyer came on Saturday morning, and while everybody on the way would know about the stave bolts by then, they maybe wouldn't connect this with the property line. Dave and Becca had cut their timber for years; this would be just more of the same. And Charlie's plan was to sell the first loads for enough to put down on a cheap truck, then hurry the rest out of the woods before the Mabrys could even hear of it.

That was the plan. But mules are slow, and there are always holes in the best plans. On the second load, a wagon wheel collapsed, with no spare. It took two days to cut new hickory spokes, shave them with the drawknife, and hack out the curved felloes and bore the holes for the spokes. Then they took the assembled parts to Silas Greene, the only remaining blacksmith in the county, to have him heat-shrink the iron tire over the repaired wheel, tightening it for use.

"Oughta figger a way t'put car wheels on yer wagon, Charlie, rubber tires. These ole wood spokes, they ain't strong 'nuff t'carry a load lak you doin'." The man was ancient, but still practicing his craft sporadically here at mid-century in the Arkansas hill country.

Meanwhile, the load of bolts on its jacked-up axle was marooned alongside the gravel road in plain sight. And with the weight, the jack settled into the thawing ground, making it harder to attach the repaired wheel. Charlie and Andy hurried to dig out space for it, get the wagon back on the road, with Nate at school.

Granted, nobody but those who happened to pass there knew whose wagon that was for sure, but folks could guess. Seemed everybody knew everybody's business in Stark Township, and bad news traveled a lot faster than good.

But this and the next load finally got to the railhead on time, and Charlie collected over a hundred dollars for the prime bolts. They'd go to a distant mill to be cut and shaped into white oak whiskey barrel staves, charred inside to age bourbon. And of course Charlie would drink his share of that eventually.

He found a '37 Ford V8 flatbed truck that ran, albeit with a cloud of oil smoke following it and a thirst for 30-weight, for $150. Tires held air but were smooth. He knew he'd have to fashion chains for them to get over the snow and ice, but he could do that from scraps in the farm shop. *Haul four times a wagonload on her, and git in and out a lot quicker.* He talked the seller into taking $35 down and drove it away.

Just how he planned to make the payments for the truck wasn't a major concern of Charlie's. *Cross that there bridge when we git to it. Timber gone, won't need no truck anyway.*

* * *

The note on his desk had said simply that an old acquaintance of his wanted to get in touch with him. The retiring contractor had asked his secretary for the man's—woman's?—name, but he, a man, hadn't left it. *Well, with phasing the business out, I guess I can make time for renewing old relationships. Wonder who this is, though. College, maybe? Or even before? No, they'd surely all be dead by now, living on hog lard and bad whiskey.* Well, he had the number: he'd get to it maybe tomorrow.

Only he forgot. Seemed he was forgetting too many things lately, which was one reason he'd decided to close his successful contracting operation. None of the children or grandchildren wanted to continue it, although several of them had worked for him at different times. *Didn't really want to take it over: just a way station to bigger things, I guess.*

The builder was 73 years old. He hadn't thought much about retiring, since he enjoyed building these new architectural designs, the modern glass-and-stone houses that let in the outdoors, as well as the historic restorations. A classic plantation house here in Virginia still excited him: the patina of aged hand-hewn beams, the 200-year-old wavy glass in the mullioned windows, the generations of gentle wear. He still liked stroking that old wood.

It had been a good run. The only real regret was that his wife Audrey had died of cancer five years before, after sharing so much with him. That, more than anything else, was why he'd held on, dug deeper into his work, tried to lose himself in it.

It hadn't turned out that way.

But he'd kept on, not knowing anything else that might ease the emptiness, the reality of being alone. He worked with a dozen architects, and there was always one who had a new commission, and wanted him to build it. Or better yet, restore it. *I guess I've got that to be proud of at least: my following. No, I'm proud of my family, too, of course. Wish they weren't all so far away…*

* * *

Montgomery Mabry liked winter. He'd observed that most of man's achievements had been made when he'd been cooped up inside, free to think things out, work out solutions to life's problems. Summertime, everyone was out planting, harvesting, scrambling to lay up for winter. Dawn to dark for most folks; no time to figure better ways to do things.

And so now, after the war, new inventions were popping up, making farming more efficient, life more modern all around. Folks had electricity, even up here in the high hills. But the exodus was continuing, from the hardscrabble farms and log woods to the cities, where the fruits of all that wintertime-developed technology were waiting to be enjoyed. And selling out their old farms, several of which this lawyer'd bought cheap.

This was the time to hunt. Deer season had actually ended, but nobody in Everett County paid much attention to hunting seasons anyway, and this was his own land, to do with as he saw fit. And the now-rare whitetails stood out against the snowy fields and woods, targets for his fine Winchester rifle. A long still-hunt on a frosty morning was lawyer Montgomery's idea of a gentleman's pursuit.

Too bad his son, Barry, didn't like to hunt. *Never could stand the sight of all that blood, guts, the field dressing, the butchering.* He'd forced the boy to go along when he was young, certain he'd warm to the idea, but that hadn't happened. Barry had rebelled at this and most other directives his father had issued, and hadn't changed with maturity. *Not that he's matured much, even at thirty. Got a wife, son, but the judgment of an adolescent. Still, he's all we've got. Mama's boy, and Claudia always influenced him too much. Well, at least he's not queer.*

These thoughts and others of his late wife fled through the old man's mind as he tramped his acres toward home, after a fruitless hunt that had begun before daylight. The sleet and snow had largely melted in a freak thaw, but the air was still sharp, and clouds of vapor drifted from his breathing.

He was getting a bit winded, striding his bulk through the clinging snow. And since it was now downhill, he decided to reach the property line alongside the Prescott cut-over, then follow it homeward.

Mabry reflected that young Dave had done a thorough job of timbering his land. *Sound lad, that. Damn shame about the accident. Married into that no-good Millard family, though. They'd have mooched off him till he was broke anyway, I'd wager. Charlie Millard's not worth shooting.*

Then he saw the bare tops of fallen trees ahead, just down from the spring at the base of his hill. As he got closer, he could see the freshly cut stumps of old-growth white oak, the sheared limbs out onto the sprout-strewn Prescott side. He counted five new stumps, clearly on his side of the boundary, the logs gone.

Got to be Millard. Old Elijah would never allow this: crazy preacher, but no fool and surely not a thief. He saw tire tracks in the muddied, torn ground, and the distinctive imprint of tire chains. *But that's from a truck. Charlie hasn't got a pot to piss in: he'd have used Dave's old wagon.* He examined the stump cut, the top cut where limbs still protruded, too small for sale, saw the rough ridges the saw teeth left. *Chainsaw. Now, that boy couldn't afford a chainsaw. And five trees wouldn't buy any truck and that contraption.*

Montgomery straightened, surveyed the damage. Just this pocket of timber cut so far, but who knew what was next? Clearly the work of more than one man, and there was only Charlie's sister and that young boy at their place. Was someone else stealing his timber? If so, he/they were coming in over Prescott land, either with Charlie's knowledge or his involvement.

This had to stop. And yes, the sheriff should know of this. Prime white oak logs were worth money, whoever had taken them…

Oh, but it's about the boundary, for sure. Dave and I talked about that and didn't ever get clear about it. Should have had it surveyed, but he agreed to leave it as I know it's right. No need, with both of us knowing. And now Charlie's slipped in here, or helped somebody else, and stolen from me. And they've spent the money on whiskey and women, won't do a thing for that girl and the kid, who're probably near starving.

A wave of anger washed over the man, not so much at the loss of the trees as at the brazen, broad-daylight thievery by worthless men who envied him. Thought it was all right to steal from a man who'd built his holdings, his place in the county, by his own skill and hard work. *Damn worthless bastards. Won't lift a hand for honest work, but steal whatever's in sight. Well, you won't get away with this, Charlie Millard.*

* * *

There had been only two more prime white oaks in that disputed strip of land, the rest being hollow-center red oaks, hickories, black gum, and maple. Charlie had wisely stopped cutting, though, knowing that each trip to these woods pushed his chances of discovery farther. True, he fantasized about those last two trees, calculating how much the stave bolts would bring. *Pay fer th' truck, an' have enough t'git through rest of th' winter. But hell, don't need th' truck no more, an' it's a giveaway, now.*

He hadn't licensed the thing, or even registered it. Nobody would pay any attention to a beat-up heap like that in the dead of winter, and nobody had. He figured the $35 he'd put down on it had been a good enough investment, since he'd miraculously had neither a blown-out tire nor any major failure. *Reckon that can happen t' th' next feller.*

So he drove it across the county line in its accompanying cloud of smoke to an abandoned store building, parked it behind out of sight, and walked home. *Let 'em think whatever they wanta: coulda been stole from me.* He thought about selling the repaired chainsaw but knew people would likely remember that. Be handy for cutting wood, too, so he hid it under a wide, weathered barn board, under a pile of brush, not in the root cellar, the first place anybody'd look.

Later, at the ample stack of the resulting firewood behind the farmhouse, Charlie made sure the crosscut saw was close, leaning against the house under the porch roof. Anybody came nosing around, he'd have to look close to see what'd cut that wood.

"What happened to your truck, Uncle Charlie?" Nate asked him after school. "They repossess it?"

"Shore did. Figgered we need th' money more here, t' git through th' winter. Come spring, I'll see 'bout 'nother one, or a car maybe." That was all he ever said to the boy or to his sister. She, after all, had known he'd never pay it out: just wasn't the way Charlie did things.

Andy had done a big share of the timbering and had the calluses to show for it. She'd forcibly taken the money Charlie had brought home from the sales and hidden it in an envelope taped to a drawer bottom in her room. She was sure he'd kept part of it for alcohol and knew she couldn't do a thing about that. But she'd be switched if she'd let that labor and sweat be wasted, needful as they were.

Nate was her responsibility, and Charlie, although helpful most of the time he was home, was really excess baggage. He'd be off as soon as he heard of work somewhere, or some hare-brained adventure his buddies down at the store got him in on. She knew Nate and she would have to plow, plant, fence whatever they could to try to survive the coming year, without her brother.

And even with the timber money, these coming months would be tight. Becca and Dave'd had the land free and clear but hadn't saved a dime or laid in any long-term provisions. A few chickens, a couple hogs, and a milk cow, besides the two mules and wagon and the old shotgun, were their total possessions. They'd sacrificed everything to pay off the land, and she credited them for that now.

We'll live, Nate and me, long as we don't buy anything we don't need. And long as those Mabrys don't get after us. Seems the old saying's true: "Them as has, gits," and the rest of us just try to hang on.

Chapter Two

Barry Mabry was outraged. Here his father had discovered they'd been robbed of prime timber, and the old man wanted to go through channels to right the wrong. And he wasn't even sure it was that Millard bunch who'd done it. *Clear as mud: follow the money. Who's the kind around here would make his money from stolen timber? Who knows it's there in the first place? Who figures to get away with it? Got to be Charlie Millard, that's who.*

But, his father had argued, he was sure Charlie hadn't had a truck or a chainsaw to do that job. All right, maybe he'd had help, but that bunch he hung out with couldn't come up with a dollar among them. Could easily have been someone else, someone who maybe made this sort of thing the way he made his living and had the equipment to do it quick and dirty. Hard times, things got stolen. And even if the Millards had done it, how were they going to prove it? And on and on.

Barry wanted action. He'd resented Charlie Millard since grade school, when the younger boy had drawn the other children to him with his bragging and his way of winning games. The little girls had admired him, giggling at his exploits while he, Barry, older, much smarter, was ignored.

And years later, when Andy Millard had grown into teenage, disturbingly pretty, Barry, seven years older and out of college, had decided she would be his wife. Of course, the Mabrys were far above the girl's family socially, but she stood out from them all and from her classmates in high school. She never came to class in dirty or torn clothes, her black hair was always clean and shiny, her eyes sparkling that intense blue. And she was smart, had learned to speak properly, a rarity in the north Arkansas hill country.

Barry Mabry could offer her his family name, fortune, and an enviable place in Everett County society, such as it was. How could she possibly turn him down?

But she had.

Cold. And run off at the age of not quite eighteen with that worthless truck driver Cam Henry. The insult to Barry cut deep: the way she'd actually showed incredulity that he'd even *think* of courting her. As if she were more than an orphaned, dirt-poor farmer's daughter, or could even imagine she'd be *somebody* someday.

The attraction had turned to resentment, then to hate, which had grown with her brother's escapades, his drunkenness, his worthlessness, which in Barry's mind spilled over onto Andy. *Bunch not worth my time, none of them. What was I thinking?*

So Barry had immediately married Christine Baines, a blonde cheerleader in her second year of college over at Jonesboro. She'd been strangely shocked at her alcohol-fueled pregnancy, then outraged at Barry. But then she'd come to appreciate the obvious advantages of the forced union. And borne him one son, Giles, the heir apparent to the Mabry fortune.

Christine had quickly learned how to rule her immature husband, her surroundings, even her father-in-law a little, after his wife had died. And rule she did. Barry enjoyed, if that were the word, their relationship only on Christine's strict terms. She allowed him into her bed when she felt like it. She handled the money. She ran the household. She made the major decisions.

In view of his son's weaknesses, Montgomery realized that this woman was the only hope for the Mabry estate, and put his faith in young Giles as having some of her backbone. All in all, the future of the family seemed in acceptable hands.

But father and son butted heads often, despite Christine's trying to keep the peace and her source of wealth intact. There was the time Barry was positive the chicken broiler business was the financial wave of the future, and he'd tried desperately to make Montgomery see that.

"Old fool's so against anything I propose," he fumed. "War's over; people have jobs, money to spend, and now's the time to get in on the ground floor in this. Why can't he see it?"

"He's worked hard to build up his estate, honey, and won't risk it on something that could backfire." She'd witnessed this before: Barry with a new idea that demanded his father's money, and the lawyer's refusal to plunge in. And she knew her father-in-law was usually right.

In fact, the broiler boom *had* collapsed: too many of those big chicken houses going up, too many get-rich farmers and money men going after it all together. The market had skyrocketed, then nosedived just as quickly. Seemed the newly buying public wanted younger, tenderer chickens to eat. Or beef, now they could afford it.

Barry blamed that on poor management. If only he'd had the chance to use his knowledge, skill… Christine had secretly rolled her eyes.

Then there'd been the housing boom and the demand for lumber. Barry was so sure the Mabrys could harvest their extensive timber, make a fortune. His father pointed out that if they waited a few years while the trees grew bigger, they'd make even more. There'd be more people, more need for housing every year that passed. Barry argued that Dave Prescott was logging his place as fast as he could and making money at it, even on his small scale.

"True, but Dave's paying off his place: good plan. And he'll put it in pasture, probably go to beef, which we're already doing. No, we have enough fields, and folks have shown they want beef now that they have money in their pockets. Doesn't pay to jump into anything too quick, son."

And so it had gone. Christine knew her husband wouldn't be safe whenever he inherited the estate, so she'd have to insist on checking his financial balancing act constantly. Which meant handling the money, which she did already. Montgomery reflected that he and his daughter-in-law made a good team.

But this timber theft now. This was an outrage Barry felt he must handle, perhaps to prove to his father, his wife, that he was a man.

The man.

To hell with his lawyer father's approach. Okay, let the sheriff try to find the perpetrators. Let it go through the proper channels. He, Barry Mabry, knew who'd done it, and he'd take care of it his own way.

* * *

Reverend Elijah Prescott had prided himself on his son's grit. Served his country overseas he had, and earned himself those medals for valor. Then came home, bought himself that eighty acres, the old Putnam place, all grown up in good timber. Boy had determination and good sense, for sure.

That he'd married Becca Millard disappointed Elijah. That family had produced more than one black sheep, the latest of which was Charlie, who everybody knew could foul up a crowbar in a sandpile. And didn't one of them go to church, read the Bible, or even pretend to be God-fearing folks. That was Elijah's sharply judgmental line, and no Millard had come to the right side of it.

But Becca'd been good for Dave, and the old man had grudgingly come to accept what he'd termed an ill-conceived misalliance. True, he'd blamed the deaths of Becca's first two babies to inferior blood on her side, but he'd known deep down that wasn't her fault. And with Nate's healthy birth, it'd seemed God had indeed blessed the couple.

The aggressive way Dave had attacked the timber on his land impressed everyone in Stark Township, and even in the county. Wasn't easy, logging, and with just the one old truck, one of those new chainsaws, only mules to skid and load with. He and Becca had done it themselves, over fewer than five years time, and paid off the farm. Now that was a man to watch.

Until that day in December. The truck had plunged off the ledge road, smashed among the rocks below, killed them both, wrecked even that chainsaw. Left that one boy alone in the world except for that sassy Andy.

And she had that reputation. Well, just divorced from smooth-talking Cam Henry, but everybody knew a good-looking divorced woman must be playing around. Divorce was a scandal, any way you looked at it. *No better than she should be, that one.*

Elijah was a widower, living on the meager offering from his congregation at the little Holiness church up on the ridge toward the old state highway. He'd lost a leg in a car wreck when he was nineteen, T-model Ford head-on in a tight curve with a heavily laden log wagon. Still used a crutch with his wooden leg. He was almost a caricature of the backwoods preacher, aging, with that beak of a nose that arrived places well before the rest of him. To Elijah the world was etched in clear black-and-white relief, with no excuse for any grays in between.

He wasn't close to what was left of his family but did visit Nate when he could hobble his way or get a ride down to their farm. Andy he mostly ignored, though she treated him with the respect he thought was no more than his due. She brought Nate to see him, cooked for him, always cleaned his cabin while they were there, despite his grumbling. All in all, he supposed, Andy wasn't as bad as folks said she was. *Still, a divorced woman…*

Nate had told his grandfather about the stave bolt cutting, partly to reassure himself that this was indeed his own timber and they'd had the right to do it. The old man had simply nodded and offered no comment. Partly because, even though he knew there was some disagreement about the boundary location, it was a done deal, and no point in stirring up a fuss over a little thing like a few trees. Whole country was covered in trees after all, if not prime white oak, even after that first cutting two generations ago.

Elijah did know the Mabrys might contest the loss of the timber, more because Barry was so down on the Millards. It was common knowledge in the township that Andy had turned him down to marry that truck driver, and the boy'd never got over it. Married that Christine, who ran him like a toy train. *Well, Andy would've, too: boy's got no spine.*

But any money, wherever it came from, was sorely needed by the folks at the Prescott place, Elijah knew, and he just hoped no-good Charlie could at least pay his way. *Somebody oughta tie a can to that boy's tail, run him outta the county like a stray dog.*

* * *

Cam Henry had learned, on an earlier trip home to see his mother, that the very blonde cheerleader he'd met at the college in Jonesboro years before was now right here in Ridgeway. Married to that rich kid Barry Mabry. *Now ain't that a coincidence? Just run into her what, few years on back, when I d'livered that load to th' college dinin' hall...* He'd actually been almost knocked down by her that September day as he rounded his truck, clipboard in hand. She'd appeared suddenly out of nowhere, running with a bunch of other girls in the shortest shorts he'd ever seen.

The impact had knocked the wind out of her, and she doubled over, then fell. He'd thrown the clipboard aside instinctively and caught her before she could hit the ground, her blue eyes wide, her surprised mouth an almost perfect *O*.

Now, Cam had been blessed with that rare coming-together of genes that produce a child of uncommon good looks. From an early age, everyone who saw the boy remarked on what a handsome lad he was. So being told that continually from the time he could comprehend, he'd taken advantage of the gift. And his successes with the girls had given him a cocky assurance that'd made conquests easy.

"She's okay, girls," he'd told the other coeds. "Just needs a minnit t'git her breath." They'd milled around solicitously, then drifted away, since Christine, breath restored, hadn't been in a hurry to leave. He'd sat her down on his truck's running board and begun a concerned conversation that had lasted several minutes. During which she'd taken in his better physical attributes with what became interest.

"Be here till t'morrow," he'd told her. "Any chance I c'd see you again?" With his sincerest, practiced smile.

"Maybe. Got cheerleader practice after classes, around four." This man, so obviously more mature than the gaping college boys, intrigued her. And it was a dateless Friday, so just maybe...

"Okay, why don't I just drop by where? The gym? And we could go somewhere I could buy you dinner, maybe? Make up for nearly cripplin' you?" Both of them knew this game, and she thought *why not? Boring around here.*

Now, the dating philosophy among young males in the late 1940s was: some girls would and some wouldn't. But Cam Henry had learned that just about any girl, in the right situation, at the right time, with the right man, *would.* And, given that he was ready to spend his money and his charm on coed Christine Baines and did, resulted in learning that yes, she would. And did.

Later, he managed to have his trucking company dispatcher save the runs to the college in Jonesboro for him. Where he and Christine were able to contrive those always possible trysts college girls have consistently managed. This went on for nearly a year, a record for Cam Henry whose constancy had never been a characteristic he possessed.

And now, coincidence of the century, here she was just outside Ridgeway, with that loser Barry Mabry and apparently with his kid. *Or somebody's kid.* Well, he'd just hafta check in on that situation, see if the old flame could be relighted. After all, Cam had just the torch for such as that.

* * *

Eventually Everett County Sheriff Hal Burgess stopped by the Prescott farmhouse, saw Charlie in an open shed sharpening a crosscut saw. He got out of his battered '46 Ford the county hadn't replaced, and walked over. Burgess had graying hair but walked erect and had the local reputation of being a thorough but fair lawman.

"Hey, Charlie. B'having yourself?" Not unkindly.

"Tryin' to, Hal. Mostly just stayin' in, this weather, livin' on puddin' and wind."

"I guess. No work around, for sure. Heard you were over in Henderson County for awhile."

"Was, workin' in a warehouse, but they slacked off, come fall. Might git back on; weather breaks in March er so."

"Well, I gotta tell you, we got a complaint from old Mabry about some timber somebody cut on him, 'cross the line. Know anything about that?" The sheriff watched Charlie's face for a reaction. There was just mild surprise; Charlie had become good at this.

"Did? Wal, now. What part, y'know?"

"Down by that spring, head of th' little branch comes through below here. Said there were five big white oaks cut. Maybe logs, but looks like, from th' sawdust, it was stave bolts."

"Don't say. Bolts bring moren' logs, fer sure. No, don't know of ennybody comin' through here, but I been gone, lookin' fer work an' all."

"Don't see your car. Let it go back or sell it?"

"Had t'sell it. Gonna be a hard winter fer Nate 'n' Andy'n me, so yeah, I sold it over in Henderson. Catch a ride whenever I kin."

"I see. Okay, truck tracks come by down below, though; seems like somebody here would've heard anybody hauling timber out." Burgess suspected that Charlie Millard was capable of stealing anything that wasn't nailed down, but he needed some sort of proof. And a truck?

"Wal, I ain't been down there fer a spell. Know when this happened?"

"Back last of December, looks like. Montgomery just discovered it. Snowed on tracks maybe twice. You around then?" The sheriff was glancing around for evidence of a truck or of the chainsaw that'd left its marks on the stumps.

"Gone most've that month job-huntin'. Did make it back fer Christmus, but y'know we had that sleet, snow 'bout then. Holed up few days, then took off agin, got a ride over t'ord Everton. Heard old Martin Brady had his sawmill runnin' agin."

"Don't know him. No luck, there?"

"Naw, his boy was home f'm Deetroit, all th' help he needed, seemed like. Burnt trip, but I hooked up with a truck driver, went on down t'Little Rock, hopin'. Stayed with a cuzzin few weeks, then come on back. Did some shovel work down thar, but it run out." Charlie could lie smoothly, out of long practice. He knew Burgess wouldn't check that part of his story just over a few trees.

"You got a chainsaw? Good pile of firewood on th' porch, there."

"Not a chancet. Got some dead limbs a feller wanted trimmed, big ole oak he's 'fraid of fallin' on his house. Helped him cut 'em with his saw, hauled 'em over. Nate an' me, we cut 'em up 'th this ole crosscut, dulled it on thet hard stuff. Need more set to it: draggin' some."

"Yeah, you need a lotta set in those teeth or it'll bind up. That boy much for workin'?"

"He's a good hand, Hal. Helps m'sister Andy all round th' place. Mostly's got over losin' his folks, though that got to him bad. Off huntin' right now, rabbits."

"Okay, season's over on everything else. How's Andy gettin' along? Raisin' the boy, I know."

"She's doin' okay. Folks puts her down some, bein' she d'vorced that Henry boy, couldn't keep his pants buttoned. T'wan't her fault, that, but y'know, folks'll talk."

"They will. Good woman, Andy. I was a younger man, I'd come courtin'. She around?"

"Gone over to Miz Ed Carson's, quiltin' t'day. Tell her you ast 'bout her."

"Do that. You do know, though, I have to ask around about that missin' timber. Truck, dual wheels, looks like it had chains for the mud, snow. Bad weather for loggin'."

"I reckon. Funny how some fellers'll work harder stealin' sump'n than doin' 'n honest job, ain't it?"

"Is. Some folks just turned that way, though. We get a jail full of 'em, now'n then. Well, you keep an eye out while you're here, will you, Charlie? Probably somebody with a lotta help, slipped in quick and out, before anybody could spot 'em."

"Does seem odd, though, don't it? Nobody catchin' 'em? December, I'se gone mostly, but yeah, I'll ask Nate if he heered ennything, an' Andy, too. 'Course Nate, he'd of been in school, if t'wuz a weekday, an' Andy, she makes a little money helpin' clean house around, y'know, when she kin."

"I heard about that. Hard times for sure. Glad you can help out when you can, Charlie. They makin' it all right? Need any help?"

"'Preciate that sure, but Andy, she's got that pride, y'know, wouldn't take a thing 'less she worked fer it. An' I c'n leave 'em what I can, I'm sellin' m'car on back."

"By th' way, who'd you sell it to? Haven't seen it around the county."

"Told you, sold it over in Henderson. Feller name of Howard, worked at th' warehouse."

"Oh, that's right. Forgot. Well, you take care, Charlie, and stay outta trouble. Glad to see you're here helpin' out. Bad about that boy losin' both his folks that way." The sheriff opened the door of the Ford.

"Was. But Andy, she's took over like it's a job to do. Was real close to Becca, even bein' so much younger. Well, so was I, big sister an' all. Hate it, goin' that way, so young. An' after her'n Dave payin' this place off jist that day, y'know."

"Bad all around. Tell that boy hello from me, and Andy, too. Bye, Charlie." The Ford starter spun with that bee-sting sound, the flathead V8 fired, and the sheriff drove away with a puff of oil smoke.

Charlie spat, grinned. *Not no ev'dence atall. Not a smell. An' ole Montgomery c'n rant an' rave all he wants: nuthin' says we was anywhere near them trees. Ours, anyway, er Nate's. But I knew Hal'd be 'round, checkin'.*

So, reckon I c'n git on now, see what's out there, 'way from this hole. Git me a ride…

* * *

Nate had slipped home, spotting the sheriff's car just leaving. He hadn't bagged a single thing, but that wasn't what was bothering him now. *Sheriff here, we're in trouble, sure. Hope Uncle Charlie's headed him off. Reckon th' Mabrys called him in, accused us. An' right or not, they'll ride us, over those trees. Hope it doesn't come to anything big: make it hard on us. An' Charlie, he'll be gone off any time now, leavin' Aunt Andy'n me to handle it. Well, she's about as tough as anybody I could have on my side, so yeah, we'll take it on. Man can't cut his own trees, country's in a bad way.*

"What'd th' sheriff want, Uncle Charlie?" He broke open the old shotgun, extracted the shell. They both headed for the house in the slanting, weak sunlight.

"Oh, just askin' 'round about them trees. Like we figgered, ole Mabry, er maybe Barry, he's gripin' 'bout losin' timber that b'longed to us…you, anyway."

"Figured that. You explain it to him okay?" Nate avoided a melted puddle with its red clay mud that'd stain his new boots.

"Did. Nothin' atall t'hook us up with it all, anyway. No point in tellin' it around. Th' timber's yourn, but just stir up things more. We dunno nothin', didn't hear nothin'; must've all been gone when that truck come in an' left."

"Guess so. Glad we were able to bring in a little, get through th' winter. You plannin' on stayin'?" Nate liked having Charlie around: never dull with him here, telling stories of where he'd been, what he'd done. Even if, as Nate suspected, his uncle stretched the accounts outrageously. He'd catch his Aunt Andy rolling her eyes at some of his tales.

"Naw, not that long to spring now, so I reckon I'll git moseyin', see what's on over th' hill. Be back when I can, check up on y'all. Should be able t'put in a right nice garden, couple months or so. You'n me, we talked 'bout trenchin' th' little branch round th' hill to git some water on th' rows, y'know." He put a hand on the boy's shoulder.

"Oh, we'll make do, all right. Reckon I c'n do a man's work where it's needed. And Aunt Andy, she's a hand at 'bout anything."

"Is. Ain't worryin' none 'bout y'all gittin' by. Y'got th' money frum th' stave bolts t'carry you. Got wood cut. Yeah, I'm on m'way, guess in th' mornin'. When'd Andy say she was headin' back f'm Miz Ed's?"

"'Bout now, I'd say." The boy's eyes shifted to a spot well beyond the next ridge. "Wasn't needed so here, I'd like t'go with you one time, Uncle Charlie. Bet there's a lot goin' on, out in th' world." The blue eyes were wistful in the round face that would become sharper as he grew.

"Time 'nuff fer that, Nate, git a couple years on you. Yeah, we'll have ourselves a time 'fore long, out whar th' lights'er bright an' th' music's loud. Now reckon you'd best git th' kitchen stove goin', 'fore Andy, she gits back, starts supper. I'll go feed th' mules, patch that harness 'fore I leave."

Andy Millard's long legs ate up the few miles back from the quilting session with the other women of the farm settlement. She knew they viewed her with distaste, but she wasn't one to worry about what country tongues wagged about her. She and Nate needed new quilts, and she was glad for the community sessions that got so much more done than she could by herself.

They'd move the pews aside at the little Baptist church, hang the quilting frames from eye screws in the ceilings and gather around, stitching, basting, tying the colorful, salvaged pieces. Nobody here tried for the more complicated designs, anything harder than Log Cabin or Flying Geese. There were more Crazy Quilts around the settlement than any other non-designs, and they kept folks just as warm. And working side by side with her, some of these country women were losing a little of their disapproval of this newly single girl. At least while she was among them.

Andy worried, despite the money they still had from the timber cutting, about how she and Nate would survive long term. Sure, they'd put in the garden come spring, plant, weed, water from the spring branch, try to keep the pests out. And then a lot of picking, a lot of canning. And yes, now that the sow was bred, they could butcher the boar, raise the pigs for next year. They'd make it, God willing, as her sister's father-in-law Elijah would say, and she guessed that'd be enough.

And at going on fourteen, it wouldn't be that long till Nate would be grown and able to take over this, his place, be truly the man of the house. They could look forward to that time.

Well, they'd make it, that was, if those Mabrys didn't come down on them. Too many questions about just where that property line really ran, and they didn't need that kind of trouble. Nothing yet, but sooner or later Barry or the old man would find the stumps, probably raise a stink.

Andy knew her place was here with Nate. Old Elijah would've made a mess of trying to raise the boy, and so far she'd done all right, relentlessly teaching him proper speech, getting him to read books, go beyond the scant schooling here in the county. Teachers not much more educated than she was, and not being able to plant much in the kids' heads really, past the bare basics.

She wanted her sister's son to have a better life than she'd had so far, or any other young person in the township. Maybe eventually get off the place himself, make a name somewhere. Or at least become a man of importance here in Everett County: not the worst prospect.

So this life was okay for now, even with the clumsy advances of the local bachelors and some of the married men she'd had to put up with. They seemed to think she was ready to tumble into bed with any man with a pulse, her being divorced. And she'd had to use physical force a couple times to fend off a determined, usually drunk, would-be suitor. A stout piece of firewood had done it once, and the family 12-gauge shotgun another time.

Four or five years and Nate would come into his own here, and she could pick up her life again. Still be in her twenties, everything ahead of her. Get out of this hollow, find herself a decent job somewhere, make her own place. She hadn't any formal training, but neither did most of the women who were working, these days. Back during the war it'd been different, defense plants hiring every warm body they could, but all that was over, now.

Still, all those women hadn't just faded back into the woods. Taste of having their own money had opened them up mostly. No, women weren't going to go back to putting their feet under a man's table the way they had forever. And with Cam Henry just a bad memory now, she'd find herself a good man somewhere. Or maybe not; nothing said she needed a man to complete herself: do that on her own.

The house was warm, welcome, when she stepped inside, a finished quilt on her arm and her stitching bag in her hand. Nate was there near a window, reading a schoolbook, and the domestic sight gave her a flush of contentment. She guessed Charlie was out somewhere, and yes, he'd be gone soon, predictably. Or was he already gone? No matter, her brother would never change, never grow up, and the other two of them could/would do all right on their own.

"Charlie around?"

"Out feedin' the mules. How was quiltin'?"

"Fine. Look what I brought us." She unfolded the finished piece, with its scraps of faded fabric and some new bits. It was a comforter, heavy, a barrier against the mountain chill. A log cabin pattern, with its squares of stitched rectangles, lighter on one side of each diagonal, darker on the other.

"Looks good. C'n I have the one on your bed? Mine's thin enough to see through."

"You can have this one. I'll double with your old one. How was school?" She realized she sounded like a mother. *Well…*

"Oh, all right. Miz Morgan, she thinks we gotta spend all our time outta school on homework, but I'm ahead of most've the other kids, so far." He blushed a little at this brag.

"Well, that's good. And I just realized, you'll finish in May, be ready for high school come fall. Almost grown, Nate." She impulsively rumpled his thatch of hair she'd cut herself, which made him blush more.

"I wish. If I aim to run this place, let you go someplace nice, have yourself a life again, I need to git a headstart on it."

"*Get*, remember. Always work on your pronunciation, Nate. Nothing will hold you back more than backwoods talk when you're out in the world. My, the way Charlie talks, folks peg him as a know-nothing before he can show them a thing."

"You talkin' me down, sis?" Charlie came through the back door, held his hands to the kitchen stove.

"No need; you do that for yourself. Your own worst enemy,

brother." She smiled in spite of herself. Nobody could stay put out with Charlie. *He means well* was always what the kindest of his critics opined. She knew what the others said but didn't care: he was family. "Guess you'll be off down the road soon?"

"Matter of fact, I'm goin' t'morra. Oughta be some work some'rs soon. Maybe I c'n send y'all some money time to time."

"Be good of you. But Nate and I'll make it the way we did good on the stave bolts. Just hope that doesn't come back on us. Hard work enough, in the worst weather we've had."

"Wal, Hal Burgess, he did come by, this ev'nin'. Ast some questions 'bout just that. Told him we ain't heard nothin', seen nothin'. Best way, I figger." He looked to her for support. She was younger, but he knew she had a better head on her, always had. Gave him hell now'n then, but he reckoned he needed that sometimes. And she was his only close kin now.

"I guess. Doesn't matter if those trees *were* Nate's if that Barry gets on his high horse, comes after us. Been down on us ever since you outdid him in school, and more so after I sent him packin'."

"Didn't d'serve you, girl. Got hisself that stuck-up Christine, and lookin' t'git all th' fam'ly's money. And of course he'll manage t'piss it all away, crazy's he is. Shore glad you never hooked up 'th that'n."

"Cam wasn't any better, maybe even worse, but a girl's got to learn the hard way, I guess." She reflected, as she'd often done, on what her life could have been if she hadn't been so anxious to leave home, make a life for herself. Then roused to the matters at hand. "So, pack what you need tonight because you'll forget in the morning. I know you." She brushed a hanging strand of his dark hair from his red forehead, like a sister.

Nate tried to read on in the fading light, then gave it up, lighted a kerosene lamp for Andy, then another for himself. He hunched close, finishing the assignment. *Boring book: what do I care about the way the Government works, way up there in Washington? All they do up there is spend our tax money, and we don't get a thing back. Well, I guess the WPA did, and there's that Social Security thing when we get old. Not much use now, though, when we need it.* Nate didn't know—or had forgotten—the GI loan his father had bought the farm with.

After supper, which was another example of his aunt's skill in the kitchen, Nate did math problems for an hour while Andy knitted him a new wool cap, bigger this time. Charlie had nodded off in the one easy chair in front of the stove, his boots at first steaming from the outside wet down at the barn. *Probably dreamin' of his next wild scheme,* his sister speculated.

Nate scrubbed his upper body at a washpan, found a clean, patched shirt for tomorrow, took the new quilt up to his loft room with a candle, bidding his aunt goodnight. She watched him go, speculating on what it'd be like to have a son of her own. Might happen yet, but for now it was enough, as she'd told herself, to care for this boy her sister had birthed and raised. She was proud of him and hoped he wouldn't fall through the cracks as most of the youth did, here where joys were brief and times always hard.

Andy was continually glad she hadn't conceived a child with Cam. It'd surely be just as wild as he was, along with any others she'd have been saddled with. And surely no help from wandering Cam Henry. *That one's probably shacked up with some gullible, crazy woman somewhere, and no, I don't care. Can't believe I was fooled by all that smooth talk: promises never meant a thing, Cam's didn't. Just wanted another young piece, and green as grass, I didn't know any better. Well, like I said, you learn the hard way; don't forget for sure after that happens.*

She recalled a warning her sister Becca had given her about men, one of many, those years ago. She'd said that no matter what plans a girl had, or how independent she was or tried her best to be, the right/wrong man could get to her, given the hormones, the situation, the time and place, and she'd throw all those plans out the window.

And dammit, I walked right into that and didn't even realize it.

Now, Andy hadn't been able to suppress the natural desires of her body in this enforced life of abstinence, this nunlike dedication to the job of raising her nephew. She remembered Cam Henry's lovemaking that still could give her a shiver, his hot hands on her, his declarations of love, false and hollow as they'd been. And something else Becca had told her: *Once you get a taste of what it's like to be a real woman with the right man…*

And yes, surely there'd be the right man for her out there somewhere, once this time of denial was finally over. But she could and often did tell herself she'd never become another man's taken-for-granted convenience, no matter who he might be or how ideal he seemed. Given the trade-off, it just wasn't going to be worth it to give up whatever plans she'd make now or in the future, to fit somebody else's agenda. Plain and simple, despite the biological clock ticking inside her, Andy Millard would deny her natural need forever if that interfered with the woman she knew she could become.

And *would* become, no matter what.

Chapter Three

Montgomery Mabry's anger had cooled after he'd realized there was no way to prove Charlie Millard had stolen his timber. Sheriff hadn't come up with an iota of proof: Charlie didn't have a truck or a chainsaw, had supposedly been gone most of December, which was entirely likely, since he apparently came home to the Prescott place only to get fed by his sister.

Hal Burgess was of the opinion, at least to Mabry, that the theft had been by several men who'd been able to slip their truck in, race through the cutting and loading, and get out again before anyone saw them. Four men could manhandle the short stave bolts by hand, he knew. Privately, he was almost certain Charlie had been behind it, no matter how carefully he'd managed to hide any trace. And of course the truck tracks had obliterated any sign of the wagon's earlier passage that might have remained.

So the lawyer told his son not to do anything rash, certainly not to confront Charlie, who just might go crazy, drinking as he usually was.

"Not worth it, Son. Few trees too piddling to get yourself shot over. Sheriff doesn't think it was Charlie, and surely not old Prescott or that boy: too heavy a job for anything less than a crew, and no sign of a tractor or logging equipment."

"Dad, you know as well as I do that Millard did this. And it's not so much about the trees as his shoving it in our faces. He's slick enough to pull this off, no matter how he did it. Wouldn't doubt that sister of his was in on it, too, spiteful bitch."

"Now, let's not let our personal history into this, Barry. Everybody knows you'll never forget Andy refused you, so let that alone. Woman couldn't handle that size timber, and neither could that boy. Why, it'd take four good men at least, job like that." The old man shook his head. End of discussion as far as he was concerned. He totally discounted the possibility that boozer Charlie Millard could have recruited a crew, truck, chainsaw to log that timber. Boy just didn't have that kind of gumption. And mightn't even have been there.

The sheriff had neglected to mention that he thought the logs had been cut into short stave bolt lengths, easier to handle. Most timber went to the sawmills to be milled into boards and beams, and few people but loggers even knew what a stave bolt was. Barry certainly didn't; his privileged upbringing didn't include woodcutting in any form. And Arkansas wasn't a big distilling state, as was Kentucky or Tennessee, with a big market for the bolts.

Not that Montgomery had dismissed the affront; knowing the law, he simply wrote it off as not worth pursuing. No need to become a controversial figure or one who could be labeled as oppressing the little man. The lawyer had ambitions that included being elected to the state legislature or even the senate. Governor? Every vote would count.

But Barry had already been planning to avenge his family for this outright robbery. Never mind that his father opposed any overt action: the son would take this into his own hands, set it right.

And that meant a direct confrontation with Charlie Millard, man to man. He had no doubt that he could thrash the wheezing alcoholic if it came to that; he'd been on the boxing team at college, after all. And he was sure he'd find evidence of Charlie's involvement in the theft; the man just wasn't that smart. Underhanded but not smart. Expose him, get a warrant, get him thrown in jail. And just maybe kick his arrogant ass in the bargain.

So Barry laid his plan: he'd drive right up to the Prescott place, call Charlie out. But he'd have what the locals called a little "difference" with him: a .38 revolver, just in case things got out of hand. *Do the world a favor shooting that thieving bastard. Have to be sure to make it look like self-defense, though. Maybe get him to take the first swing.*

Behind his determination to eliminate Charlie was also a not-so-suppressed desire to remove any protection he might represent for Andy Millard. Ever since her return to the settlement, divorced, fair game, he'd wanted to avenge himself for her disdainful refusal those years ago. *Give that bitch a royal dickin', maybe slap her around some. She's no doubt bedded down with every available man she can find; everybody knows about pretty divorcees. And dammit, she's still too good-looking to go to waste.*

* * *

Charlie said goodbye to his sister and nephew early next morning and swung off down the road with his cheap suitcase toward the distant highway where he was sure he could catch a ride. He had enough money left for a couple weeks, from the sale of the chainsaw in the next county, and didn't plan beyond that. Something would come up; something always did.

Nate was sorry to see his uncle go for several reasons. First, he'd miss the company of the colorful man, his endless stories, his easy laugh. And he *was* a big part of the only family he had left. And of course then all the chores would fall on his own narrow shoulders, as they had whenever Charlie was gone. And of course, too, there wouldn't be any more adventures; those always revolved around his uncle's imagination and daring.

Andy didn't really like her brother's influence on Nate: too easy for the boy to try to emulate him, get into trouble. But Nate seemed to be a steady lad with no leanings toward the rowdiness that characterized most of the hill adolescents. *Real test will come when he's sixteen or so, want to join in on whatever sounds exciting. I'll have to keep him busy then, no time for foolishness.*

But she knew she wouldn't be able to shield Nate from the influences of the other boys, from the too-soon sampling of beer and moonshine, the too-fast driving, all the dangers. But with no car or truck, maybe she could keep him home, away from the worst of what awaited him. *Like being a mother, I guess. But I've taken on this job, and I'll see it through. Like to get him into college, but that'll take some doing. No way to save for such as that, living hand to mouth this way. Unless maybe he can win some sort of scholarship. Push him in that direction.*

* * *

It was that Friday afternoon that Barry Mabry drove up to the Prescott house, all primed for his confrontation with Charlie Millard. He'd tucked the .38 into his belt in back under his coat, within reach. He marched up onto the front porch and banged on the door.

Letting him in wasn't really Andy's fault: people just did that in rural Arkansas in the fifties. Unless it was the law, it was usually friends, kinfolks. Sometimes peddlers but not often. And banging like that, maybe somebody was in trouble. She laid the skillet on the kitchen table and went through, swung the door open. For an instant she didn't recognize Barry, only having seen him at a distance in the two years she'd been back.

"Where's Charlie?" Barry demanded, pushing inside.

"Barry? Oh, Charlie's gone, looking for work. Left yesterday."

"Gone where? Got business with him." Barry was checking out the room, not fully believing her.

"Wherever he can find work. Nothing hereabouts, so he's just gone." She didn't like his tone, cast her eyes about for…what, a weapon? Her eye alighted on the cast-iron skillet, but surely she wouldn't need that. Surely this post-adolescent would show a little sense and leave.

"Well, I know it was him, and maybe you, too, cut our timber down by the spring. Stole it outright. Now, nobody steals from the Mabrys. You help him, Andy?" He grabbed her arm.

"I don't know what you're talking about, Barry. If somebody cut your timber, it wasn't us." *Since it belonged to us.* "Nate and I've got no way to do logging. And you can let go my arm."

He shook her, grabbed her other arm, backed her to a wall.

"You're lying. You Millards always lie. And steal. Charlie's a worthless failure and a drunk, and you're no better, leaving your husband. What'd he do, try to keep you home from runnin' off to other men?" His face was one big sneer.

"You can't talk that way about my kin, Barry Mabry. You've always been jealous of Charlie. He was better than you, all the way back to grade school. Showed you up every way, and that's what's got you hating him. Besides, he's only been here a few days, so you're on the wrong track." She was thinking that Nate would show up from school very soon. She had to get rid of this man before then; the boy might do something rash. Her eyes roved for the shotgun leaning in the corner.

"Talk any way I want to, and it's true: liars, cheats, no morals, you and all your family. Outrageous, *you* raising Dave's boy. Have him rotten just like the rest of you…"

"Get out! *Get out!* What're you, drunk? Just *leave us alone, Mabry!* Go take your hatred out on somebody else, somebody who won't fight you, put you in your place!" Her eyes were blazing, just inches from his reddened face, she was that tall.

"Fight me, will you? You slut, you *whore!*" And he released one of her wrists and slapped her. Hard. The sound was sharp, like a gunshot. She screamed.

Her head swam. Things swirled in her vision. She realized for the first time that this was deadly serious: he could beat her, rape her, maybe even kill her in his rage. *Got to stop this, now.*

She lashed out with a knee to his groin, with a sound like slamming an icebox door. He let go, gagging on a roar of pain, staggered back. She shoved him toward the open door, punching him in the face with rapid-fire knuckles, screaming at him. The sound, combined with his groaning, was deafening.

He stepped back onto the porch, groped at his back for the gun. She started to slam the door in his face, race for the shotgun.

He was too quick. Still clutching his private parts with one hand, he whipped the gun toward her, and in that instant when she might have escaped, she froze. The muzzle of the .38 looked like a cannon, the spirals inside the barrel curiously clear, sharp.

"Now, bitch...*God, that hurts*...you're gonna get what you deserve. Fightin' me. *Me!*" He heaved a deep breath, steadied the gun on her heart, willed the worst of the fiery pain away. Then he reached, grabbed the front of her dress, ripped it away in a violent motion. The worn fabric parted, leaving her half naked. She tried to cover her breasts, backing against the wall. He hit her again, harder, with his fist. The pain was unimaginable. Her legs gave way; she felt herself slowly collapsing, sliding down despite herself, down the wall.

She couldn't see anything but a red blur, but she thought she caught more than the one contorted face, teeth bared like some wild beast, coming at her. *Was there another...?*

The sound was strange, a loud crack, as Elijah Prescott's crutch came down on Barry Mabry's wrist. Andy couldn't see what was happening, but the gun flew from his hand, he grabbed the ruined wrist and howled like a stricken animal. She covered her flaming, bruised face.

Elijah was raining blows on Mabry's head with the heavy end of the homemade crutch, bracing his hip against a chair, roaring at him like a lion.

"You scum! You d'praved, wuthless, low-down *bastard!* Whatta you *mean* here? Attackin' a *woman?* I'll *kill* you! Feed yore eyes to th' *crows!* The crutch splintered, and still the old man flailed the pieces on Mabry's bloodied head. He was bowed down, trying to cover his head with now-crooked, bleeding fingers.

Elijah threw the pieces of his crutch aside, balled both fists, and brought them down with a mighty thud on the back of Mabry's head. He went down with a grunt, and the old man grabbed for the chair to steady himself, then delivered a mighty kick to the man's head. He looked around for another weapon, saw the shotgun. Barry was a heap on the floor as Elijah began working his way toward the corner. Andy was moaning softly on the floor, blood spilling between her fingers.

"*Wait, Granpa!*" Nate raced in from the porch, around him, caught up the shotgun, held it away from the oncoming avenger. "Don't kill him, Granpa! What'd he *do?*" The old man stopped, gripped the back of another chair. Nate could almost see this scene from above: Mabry on the floor, Elijah primed for a lunge toward himself, holding the shotgun away. And there, on the floor, slumped against the wall…

"Tried t'kill Andy, boy. Done…tore her clothes half offa her. Caught him holdin' a…gun on her, yellin', hittin' her…" He paused for breath. And then Nate did see his aunt, clutching her torn dress to her, trying to stand. Barry Mabry didn't move.

Nate's mouth was open, his eyes staring first at the fallen man, then at Andy's efforts to rise, then at his grandfather, that face furrowed like a plowed field, the eyes a blazing fire. He set the shotgun back, went to help his aunt, who was trying to brace herself against the wall with one hand while clutching the torn cloth that barely covered her.

He lifted her, saw the bruised, bleeding face, clenched jaw, eyes shut in pain, and a wave of rage filled him. He wanted just then to blast Barry Mabry's head clean off with the 12-gauge, see his blood and brains spray the far wall. For a moment he tightened his hold on Andy as she regained her feet and let the anger consume him. *Now, while he's down. I c'n blow him all to hell, an' it's th' right thing to do. Just…*

"Take her upstairs, boy. I'll tend to him," Elijah's hand was on his shoulder, partly leaning for support. Nate glanced down at the wooden leg. The rage faded. A little.

"Yessir. C'mon, Aunt Andy. Can you walk?" He half lifted, led her toward the narrow stairs. She was so tall, but slumped over like that…

"I…I think so, Nate. So dizzy…can't see straight. Hurts…" But she managed a lurching step at a time, the boy holding her up, steadying her. As they were struggling up the stairs, she turned her head, saw through clearing vision her sister's father-in-law aiming the pistol at Mabry's inert, huddled body.

* * *

He didn't die; that was the part Andy regretted. Nate had run to the nearest house that had a telephone and called the sheriff. By the time Hal Burgess arrived, Barry was conscious, cursing, moaning, threatening every Millard and Prescott alive. Elijah was seated, still with the revolver, holding it steady on the man as he lay there. The old preacher's scowl told of his desire to shoot him dead if he so much as moved.

"Got a little trouble, I heard," as Nate closed the door after the lawman.

"Y'could say thet." Elijah nodded toward the battered and bleeding Barry. "Caught him holdin' this here gun on Andy, done ripped her dress most off, beatin' on her. I sorta put me a stop to thet." He handed the pistol to the sheriff.

"I see. Barry, you gone crazy? Drunk or what?"

"Lies, Burgess. All lies. I just… came to see Charlie, and… Andy started cussing me, hittin' me. Had to protect myself. Then this old fool… comes up behind me, broke my wrist, like to have… beaten me to death. Think he kicked me in the head." He was glaring through bloodshot, hate-filled eyes at the old man, gasping out his accusations.

Andy heard this, coming down the stairs unsteadily. She had washed, put on another dress, but still gripped the front of it reflexively as if to hold it together. She fixed piercing cobalt eyes on her attacker. All of them could see the bruises, see her shaking. Nate got her to a chair.

"Doesn't appear to me to be the case. Let's hear from her, now. You okay to talk, Andy?" Her lip was cut and swollen.

"I can talk, yes. And everything Elijah said is true. Barry attacked me, tore my dress open, started beating me, holding that gun on me. He'd accused us of cutting timber on his land or some such nonsense, was after Charlie. I told him Charlie's gone to try to find work, make some money to get us through the winter on, but he wouldn't leave."

"I see. Well, Barry, you're coming with me, now. Little time in jail maybe get your head straight. I know about that timber thing, talked with your daddy about it. And he told me he'd just let it go since nobody knows who cut those trees, and it doesn't look to me to've been these folks."

"It was Charlie; I know it was. He could've got help…"

"Don't think I wanta hear any more outta you, boy, unless this gets to court. That case, Elijah, Andy, you'll have the chance to tell it, too, and the judge will decide. Oh, Nate, you see any of this?"

"I heard Aunt Andy screamin', Barry hollerin', cussin' her, comin' in from school, and I saw Granpa come up the porch. Time I got inside, he'd knocked Barry to th' floor, was goin' after th' shotgun. Andy was down 'gainst the wall, all bloody an' cryin'. An' yes, her dress front was tore off bad. She was holdin' it t'gether, like." Nate had the image clear in his head, and a flush of embarrassment mixed with his anger, at the memory of seeing an exposed part of one breast.

"Well, Mabry, seems like you got witnesses. Now I know your daddy'll try t'get you off, an' maybe he can, but you'll have me to deal with, y'know? Right now you're going with me. Stick your hands behind your back." The sheriff produced handcuffs.

"Not goin' anywhere with you, Hal Burgess, till I get my talk with my lawyer, and yeah, that's Daddy. You got to get me to a phone so I can make the call I'm entitled to." He tried to sound outraged, but it came out through the blood as more of a whine. Burgess spun him around, reached, snapped the cuffs on.

"Phone's down at the jail, and yes, you get one call. From jail. Now move!" He shoved the man staggering out the door, the pistol pushed against his back. Turned.

"Sure sorry about this, Andy, Elijah. Hope you're not hurt bad, girl. And don't wash that dress: evidence. I'll let you know how this turns out." And he hustled Barry into his Ford.

"Now, gal, I know you never encouraged thet rotten feller, did you?" Elijah sat down to the supper Nate had put together.

"Elijah, I turned him down cold six years ago and tried my best to get away from him here. I think you know that."

"Shore I do. But y'gotta know, folks has their idees 'bout a woman's d'vorced, like t'was all her fault. Now I know Cam Henry, an' he's plain no good. Allus wondered you fell fer that slick talk of his'n."

"I was a fool, Elijah, a plain fool. And I know Barry's never got over me refusing him, for everybody to know. So full of himself, he's never forgot, and I guess he saw his chance to get back at me. What d'you reckon will happen to him?" She was having a hard time getting food in her swollen mouth.

"Oh, his daddy'll slip some money to where it'll do th' most fer him, an' he'll be out in no time. And I'm thainkin' he won't let this 'lone, now. Prob'ly come after me, 'long with you." The prospect didn't seem to bother the old man, who was putting away cornbread and blackeyed peas steadily.

"He better not," Nate said forcefully. "Reckon we can defend ourselves, can't we, Granpa? He comes 'round makin' trouble?"

"Y'd think so, but money talks, boy, an' ole Montgom'ry, he's got a lot of it. But I wanta know, whut's all that 'bout cuttin' timber on him? You told me 'bout some trees y'all cut down on yore part."

"Oh, well, Charlie an' us, we did cut those five white oaks, like I told you, our side of th' spring. Ever'body knows th' spring's th' line, but Charlie, he said t'would be best we didn't say a thing about it: just get th' Mabrys all riled up over nothin'."

"Um. Well, it done thet all right. But I thaink Andy's right: thar's more to this than a few trees. Y'git saw logs?"

"No, clear white oak, we cut it into stave bolts. Logs that big too much for us to handle anyway, an' th' bolts, they brought more at th' mill."

"Reckon so. Haul 'em on th' wagon? Heavy stuff." He speared a piece of ham.

"Took th' first littlest ones on th' wagon, then Charlie, he got this truck with some of th' money. Hauled th' rest on it. Rigged a cross-haul with the mules, to get 'em up skid poles. Too heavy to handle by hand."

"Fer shore. Wet down b'low th' spring. Y'git stuck much?"

"We rigged up some tire chains. That was Charlie's idea, an' it worked good. He let th' truck go back after."

"Still a lotta work. Glad y'got some outta it t'see you th'u th' winter. My church, it's done 'bout dried up. Good I git invited t'folks' places, er I dunno how I'd make it."

"You know you're welcome here anytime, Elijah." Andy put a hand on the minister's arm. "Just thankful you came this time when you did." He hadn't been exactly close to her, of course—had been to Becca—but she considered him family, even if he hadn't approved of her before. *Showed his true colors today, for sure.*

Supper done, Elijah rose, thanked Andy and Nate, looked around.

"Don't s'pose you'ns got a piece of hick'ry a man c'd split hisself out 'nother crutch, do you?"

* * *

Montgomery Mabry was outraged that his son was in jail. *Surely that rotten Charlie Millard did this. Boy was a damn fool to confront him, though, and look what's happened. But I'll get him out, see how bad he's bruised up. And yes, this has ratcheted up a big notch. Mistake, trying to ignore it. Barry was righ, in that part: should have taken care of it right at first. So now we will.*

"What happened, Burgess? And who did this? Although I know." His voice was a demand despite his resolve to keep it civil.

"Well, seems Barry went to the Prescott place, said he was gonna put it straight to Charlie about that timber thing, get it settled. Only Charlie wasn't there. His sister Andy said he'd gone looking for work like he's always doing. Next part's a little hazy, but the boy Nate says he heard the woman screamin', Barry yellin' at her. Then, before he got to the house, saw Elijah Prescott going in the door, fast as he could, with that wooden leg, crutch.

"Nate says, time he got inside, Barry was knocked to the floor, a gun lying there, and the old man was slamming him with what was left of the crutch. Andy was all beat up, bloody, lying over against the wall, dress half torn off her. Boy said he had to grab the shotgun before Elijah got to it, he was that mad. Now Barry, he tells it different, of course. Said Andy attacked him and he was just defending himself.

"It'll be for the judge to decide, Mr. Mabry, but from what I saw, even without anybody's story, Barry got way outta hand. Andy was still in a bad way, time I got there, maybe an hour later. Elijah says the boy about had to lift her, carry her out.

"Now, if you push this, I'll have to testify to what I saw and, of course, so will Nate, the old man, and Andy. Don't think Barry's got a chance, to put it plain."

"Burgess, I have no doubt Charlie Millard stole my timber. As you know, I let it go; didn't want to stir things up. But I see my son behind those bars, and he's still all bloody, looks like broken fingers and one wrist hanging, face and scalp all cut up.

"You can be sure I'll see those thieves in court, charged with criminal assault. You're talking about a worthless drunk, a crazy old preacher, and a divorced woman of questionable morals. And that boy will say whatever they tell him to." Montgomery's face had twisted in his anger.

"Well, sir, Charlie wasn't even there, so that part won't wash, no matter what might have happened before. Elijah acted to save Andy from a bad beating, maybe even saved her life. And I say you've no evidence of her *morals*, as you put it, because despite the gossip, nobody's ever learned of any misbehavior on her part. Woman's stepped right up to raise that boy, and I know for a fact she's run off one man came after her with a shotgun, and another with a stick of firewood. I think you have to be objective here."

"Hal Burgess, you're the one not being objective; you've always had a soft spot for that hussy, and everyone knows it." The man drew himself up with a triumphant leer. "I'd say any testimony you could give would be tainted, to say the least."

This made the sheriff angry. *Try to do my job, and this is what I hafta put up with. Old fool's got money, position, and wants everybody to eat anything he shoves at us. Well, Mister Montgomery, we'll just see what'll come of this. You might buy a judge, but you'll never have the support of folks hereabouts if you ever do run for that state job you're after. I'll see to that myself. Gossip? That can work both ways.* But he kept his outrage under control as he unlocked the cell.

"Take him outta here, sir, but this goes down on what I'd say was a common-law record, no matter how it turns out in court. If it gets added to, this'll count, and not in his favor." He turned and walked away.

Chapter Four

Now just what the hell has that fool husband of mine done, here? Gone after that Andy Millard is what. Got to prove what a stud he is, which he isn', by a long shot. Well, I'll play the faithful wife, stand by him. If I'm anything, I'm a damn good actress, to've managed all this so long.

Christine always picked up the entire family's mail at the village post office, being there as soon as the mail truck came from Batesville each morning. She needed to get out of the house as often as possible (away from Barry) and performed this little chore gladly. That way, too, her father-in-law could have his legal and other correspondence neatly right there and ready on his home office desk, which he appreciated.

Cam Henry knew this by now and sent Christine letters with no fear of discovery. More so since he used fictitious former sorority sisters' names and seemingly innocuous messages. The result had been a carefully managed renewal of their affair, interrupted those years before by her hasty marriage.

And just now, with this latest outrage of Barry's, she needed Cam. She'd resented his marriage to Andy, but knowing clearly just who and what this man was and would remain, had put that aside. *He's just entertainment after all, but damn good at it. Worthless, always will be, but oboy, does he know how to thrill a girl! Guess I'm due a little time for me about now.*

* * *

"But, Dad, I want *you* as my lawyer. I don't trust that DA or his assistant to handle this right. Surely there's another way to do this."

"Well, I can't prosecute a criminal offense, as I told you. The only way I can act as your lawyer is for you to file suit against those people. Sue them for damages. But, of course, the whole bunch won't have a dime among them. Not worth it."

"I don't care about any money. What I want is all this brought out in the open, the Millard trash and the Prescotts exposed as what they all are: liars, thieves, drunks, and that Andy shown for what she is, a slut and a whore. She tried to seduce me, Dad, then they ganged up on me."

"This should be a criminal proceeding, but if you're dead-set on my representing you, we'll do just what I said: sue them. I guess it'll prove the point, and I'm sure I can beat any lawyer they might drag up, if they even can do that." *I know this irresponsible kid of mine's not telling it like it was, but hell, he's all I've got, with Claudia gone. It'll be a hard sell, though, turning the whole thing around. I should talk him out of this, but that's never worked. With anything.*

* * *

There was one person besides the Millard/Prescott family who was certain Barry Mabry's version of the story, leaked from one community gossip to the next, wasn't true. And deep anger welled up in this mind. *Fool's gone out of control. High time somebody put him in his place. Afraid his kind will go on to worse, next time. Maybe this should be the time to start planning something serious to protect folks from whatever's wrong with him.*

But this viewer of events decided to wait on the chance the man would get over this, maybe just grow up like a civilized human being. If not, well, then perhaps…

* * *

The courthouse was packed, even in early April, when the people of the hill community should have been out putting in their gardens, planting their fields. That was what Nate was thinking as he and Andy entered. *Got our hands full, tryin' to get seed in th' ground, grow us a little to live on, and we gotta go through this. Oughta have let Granpa shoot that lowlife.*

Charlie wasn't there, not having returned or even sent a letter telling his whereabouts. So of course he knew nothing of the assault or this aftermath. Nate wasn't sure he was happy about that, even if his aunt was. *Afraid he'd go after that scum like somebody oughta.*

Elijah Prescott was already seated in the front row, having been brought by the sheriff, who was near him. *Said he'n Granpa'd be witnesses, 'long with Andy an' me. We oughta be able t'put that snake away for a long spell.*

He and his aunt sat. She wore a plain farm dress and a sun hat, low shoes. Nate noted that there was nothing flashy about her: she was in no way the picture of a...a loose woman the way he'd heard other kids giggle and knew the wives of the community gossiped. *Best woman here,* he told himself, scanning the crowd of eager spectators who were clearly looking forward to this juicy trial, as if it were some sort of entertainment or a county fair.

Again Nate seemed transported to some point above the scene, seeing it spread out under him, as if suspended up there. But he was there trapped in his seat, as were the others, in what was becoming a stifling, crowded gathering. He wished he could indeed somehow be lifted up and out of it. He shook his head to clear it.

The sheriff had not charged Barry Mabry with criminal assault, at learning of the father's plan to press civil charges of his own. But mostly at Andy's plea to get this behind them, not let it become a spectacle. It hadn't happened that way, of course, and now Burgess regretted his having held back. *Gonna try for their ounce of flesh, they are. Well, unless Judge Barnes has taken a bribe, which I seriously doubt, Barry's goin' to lose in front of everybody, and I guess she'll settle for that. She's not mean, but maybe she should be, a little.*

It had been difficult, but Sheriff Burgess had finally convinced Andy to hire a lawyer, knowing Montgomery, as his son's lawyer, would smear her publicly, destroy what reputation she still had. He'd persuaded Bobby Harcourt, a friend from two counties away, to represent her and Elijah, calling in an old favor and even secretly paying part of his fee. The man had agreed to take the rest in small increments. He'd wanted to countersue, at least, or try to get a criminal indictment against Mabry, but Andy had refused.

"I just want this to go away, Mr. Harcourt. More bad blood won't help. I don't think Barry will ever try anything like that again, once it's known all over."

Burgess wasn't so sure about that. Win or lose, he suspected Barry Mabry would nurse his hatred and find ways to destroy at least Andy. And if/when Charlie ever showed up again, he'd go after him, no doubt of it. Hill country memories are long, and despite social layers, these were hill people.

Burgess was a widower, having lost his wife, Lois, a smoker, to cancer four years before. No children, and he guessed that'd been good: he'd never have been able to raise them by himself. He was forty-five, still lean, still a vestige of the football player he'd been in college. He wasn't from Everett County, but he'd had a farm upbringing, worked in the mines down in Saline County, eventually earned his way through college. His mother had insisted on his learning proper English, much as he knew Andy had with young Nate. *Good thing, too: man labels himself a half-wit every time he opens his mouth, otherwise.*

The bailiff called the courtroom to order, said the obligatory *all rise* as Judge Benjamin Barnes entered, motioned everyone to sit. The judge took his seat, riffled papers.

"We have a civil suit for damages brought by Barry Mabry against Elijah Prescott and Andrea Millard before the court today. This is somewhat unusual, this type of thing normally being criminal assault, brought and prosecuted by the district attorney. But this is by request of the plaintiff so that his attorney, rather than the DA, could represent him. Are all present, bailiff?"

"They are, Your Honor. Both sides repr'sented b'counsel."

"Very well, let's proceed. Counsel for the plaintiff may present opening statement."

Montgomery Mabry rose, glanced at his son and the defendants, then faced the judge. He wore his usual black hard-weave three-piece suit, spit-shined shoes, and exuded an air of authority lacking in young

Bobby Harcourt, his opposite, who looked like a disheveled college student.

"Your Honor, plaintiff charges that he was attacked without provocation by one of the defendants, Andrea Millard, that woman there," and he pointed at Andy, who returned his look with an icy stare, chin firm. "This happened February ninth at the Prescott home where the defendant lives.

"Plaintiff states that he went to this house to confer with one Charlie Millard, suspected of stealing timber from his—our—property. Defendant, his sister, made advances toward him, then when he rebuffed her, became outraged, violent, and attacked him. In trying to defend himself, he inadvertently inflicted minor injury to her. You can see, Your Honor, that Miss Millard, formerly Mrs. Cam Henry before her divorce, is quite tall and perfectly capable of doing physical damage. Among other things, she kicked him in the groin." A tittering among the spectators. Judge Barnes slammed his gavel, glared.

"Further, during the altercation, the other defendant, Elijah Prescott, entered and attacked plaintiff with a heavy crutch, breaking his wrist, then proceeded to strike him repeatedly until the weapon shattered. This attack resulted in multiple cuts and broken fingers as plaintiff tried to shield himself. Defendant then knocked him senseless and apparently kicked him while he was down. We will produce the doctor who treated him as witness to these assaults. A clear case of unrestrained violence by unruly people against an innocent man." Montgomery sat, stone-faced.

"Noted. Counsel for the defense?"

"Yes, Your Honor. We will prove beyond any doubt that the plaintiff, Barry Mabry, did enter defendant Andrea Millard's household, where she is the guardian of young Nate Prescott, her nephew, with intent to defile. That he first asked for her brother, Charlie Millard, who was absent. That he then turned on her, accused her of the theft of certain timber, assaulted *her*, ripping her dress away..." There was a concerted gasp from the spectators, which the judge again put a stop to. "He began beating her. She admits to defending herself, and yes, did kick him in the groin in an effort to protect herself and get him out of the house.

"We will further prove that plaintiff then drew a revolver, held it on her while he resumed the attack. At this juncture, her screams of pain reached the other defendant, Reverend Elijah Prescott, who came to her aid. The court will note that Reverend Prescott is not a young man, has one wooden leg, but he nevertheless, despite the danger of falling, and facing that lethal weapon, used his only option, his crutch, to defend Miss Millard's honor and her life.

"We will call witnesses, including Nate Prescott, who heard his aunt's screams of pain while returning from school, as well as plaintiff's angry cursing and defaming defendant. He heard blows and sounds of a body slammed against a wall. He then saw his grandfather, the other defendant, enter the dwelling, and heard more blows. He, too, entered, to witness plaintiff on the floor, his grandfather struggling to keep his balance, and his aunt in a bloody heap also on the floor against the wall, obviously the victim of the attack.

"We will also call Sheriff Hal Burgess, who was summoned by Nate Prescott, who ran a half mile to reach a telephone to call him. The sheriff reached the scene an hour later, and he will describe what he saw." Harcourt favored the Mabrys with a disdainful, challenging stare and sat. The judge pursed his lips, paused as if to absorb these opening statements.

"I see. Prosecution, call your first witness."

"Call Dr. Aaron Blake, Your Honor."

The bailiff swore the physician in. He was an elderly, stooped man with a wisp of white hair, a rumpled gray suit, and scuffed shoes. Everyone in the courtroom knew him: he'd delivered most of the babies, many now grown, who were there. And patched up cuts, broken bones, stitched up gashes and treated every malady. Aaron Blake was a man everyone could believe.

After he was sworn in, Mabry approached him, with the requisite saddened countenance.

"Dr. Blake, did you treat my son, Barry, on the morning of February tenth of this year?"

"I did. You brought him to my clinic early."

"And could you describe his injuries for the court, please."

"Yes. I treated him for a broken wrist, three broken fingers, lacerations to the face and scalp. There was also a bruise to his rib cage."

"Would you say these injuries were consistent with an attack, sir?"

"Objection!" Bobby Harcourt had risen. "Calls for speculation on the part of the witness."

"I believe, as a medical man, the doctor may offer his evaluation, Counselor. Overruled. The witness is instructed to answer." Harcourt sat.

"Well, certainly: a man doesn't beat himself over the head, and all the broken bones were accompanied by bruises."

"So you could say definitely that the plaintiff was attacked?"

"Not necessarily attacked: beaten, yes, but I couldn't speculate on what the provocation was."

"Your Honor, I move that this last part be stricken from the record: this wasn't asked."

"So ordered: jury will disregard. Continue."

"Would you say plaintiff's injuries were the result of an exceptionally *violent* beating, Doctor?"

"Well, you could say that. A fight, probably, with the defendant. As I said…"

"Thank you. Nothing further, Your Honor." Mabry sat.

"Your witness, Mr. Harcourt. I will remind you, Doctor, you are still under oath."

"Dr. Blake, can you say for certain, from your medical experience, that the plaintiff's injuries resulted from an unprovoked attack, or could they have been in *response* to such an attack by *him*?"

"No way to tell. Only one who could testify to that would be the defendant or another witness."

"And that testimony is to come. Thank you, Doctor. Nothing further, Your Honor."

"All right: your next witness, Mr. Mabry."

"Call the defendant, Andrea Millard. And she is to be entered as a hostile witness, Your Honor." A loud buzz from the courtroom. *Andy. Now it'll git intr'stin'.* The judge rapped his gavel, restored quiet.

Andy rose, confused. So did Bobby Harcourt, who wasn't.

"I must object, Your Honor. This witness was not on the list plaintiff's counsel submitted."

"I agree. What do you have to say to that, Mr. Mabry?" The lawyer hadn't wanted Harcourt to prepare Andy in advance.

"Your Honor, counsel for the defense raised the question of this defendant in his cross examination of my witness; she's fair game." He'd counted on that.

"I believe Dr. Blake raised that issue, sir, and I must deny your calling of this witness. You may sit, Miss Millard. Next witness, Mr. Mabry."

He hadn't been able to go after Andy, catch her off guard. *Well, no matter: I'll tear her apart on cross, anyway.*

"Call the plaintiff, Barry Mabry."

After he was sworn in, the witness glared at his quarry. *I got the best lawyer here, Andy Millard, and we're gonna win this. Your kid Harcourt's outta his league, and we'll make you and the old man sorry you ever tangled with a Mabry.*

"Mr. Mabry, will you tell the court what actually happened on February ninth at the Prescott house?"

"Well, I went there to talk to Charlie Millard. I suspected him of stealing prime timber from our land, across the boundary near the spring down beyond Prescott's house. Andy came to the door, said Charlie wasn't there, invited me in. I didn't want to go inside, knowing her reputation: divorced woman and all…"

"Objection! Defendant's so-called reputation has no bearing on this case."

"Upheld. Leave that alone, Mr. Mabry."

"Uh, okay. But well, I did go in, thinking maybe Charlie was really there, that she was hiding him. I was sure he'd cut that timber: been just like him…"

"Objection! Charlie Millard is not on trial here in this case, Your Honor."

"Upheld. Don't try to drag him into this. Get on with the relevant story, sir."

"Well, she started coming on to me, right off. Now, I'm a married man, Your Honor, and I didn't want any of that. Everybody knows what kind of woman…"

"Objection! It's been established that gossip about Miss Millard is inadmissible, Your Honor." Outrage showed on Andy's face at Mabry's blatant lie.

"Sustained. If you can't stick to the story, Mr. Mabry, I'll have you removed from the stand."

"Yessir. Well, I tried to push her away, get back out the door, but she just kept coming. I told her I wasn't interested, and that made her mad. She started scratching my face, beating me with her fists. I had to defend myself. She even kicked me in my…private parts." Again the titter from the spectators. A stern look from the judge.

"Then old man Prescott came up behind me, hit me with his crutch, broke my wrist. He used that crutch on me, wouldn't stop. I couldn't get away. I was head down, trying to cover up, and he was hitting my hands, broke my fingers. Then he must've hit me with something else because I went down, lost consciousness. And he must've kicked me, the bruises…"

"Objection! Witness was by his own admission unconscious and couldn't know what happened after that. Calls for speculation."

"Sustained. Continue."

"What did you see after you regained consciousness?"

"Elijah Prescott was holding a pistol on me. Nate Prescott was helping Andy up…"

"Helping her up?" This came as a surprise to the lawyer, whose son hadn't remembered to leave that part out: *He's put his foot in it. Everybody will wonder how she got put down.* Barry realized it, too.

"Well, I guess I got that wrong. It was all blurry: I was hurt bad."

"Understandable. Then what?"

"They left me there on the floor, bleeding. Didn't do anything for me. About an hour later, the sheriff came, took me to jail. Me, not them."

"So you went there peaceably, were subject to unwanted attention by Miss Millard, were attacked by her, then by Elijah Prescott. Then arrested, is that correct?"

"Yes, but the sheriff said I wasn't under arrest exactly, but he locked me up in jail."

"Which sounds like a violation of your rights, doesn't it?"

"For sure." Barry turned his glare on Hal Burgess.

"Your witness, Counselor." *Maybe we've blackened the woman enough for the judge to believe our story. And I'll really go after her, later. Now let's see how good this Harcourt boy is. Probably one of his first trials…*

"What was the reason you went to the Prescott home on February ninth, Mr. Mabry?"

"I already said, it was to talk to that thief Charlie…"

"That testimony was stricken from the record. He has nothing to do with this case. Now, *why* did you want to talk with him?"

"Objection! Counsel has just stated that information relating to Charlie Millard has no bearing on this case." Montgomery wanted the focus kept on Andy.

"Sustained. Proceed."

"So I may assume, since mention of Charlie is off the table, you went to confront his sister, Andrea Millard. Is that correct?"

Montgomery Mabry saw he'd been tricked. *Damn kid's better than I thought. Be careful here, son.*

"No, I… Ugh, I… Well, I guess I didn't find the person I wanted, so I…"

"So you went after his sister, is that correct?"

"Objection! Counsel is leading the witness, Your Honor."

"Overruled. You've agreed that defendant's brother is out, Counselor, so that leaves it open as to why plaintiff went to the house."

"No! She came on to me!… I mean…"

"But you went into her home, uninvited, since you've just stated that the person you wanted wasn't available."

"I…You're confusing me."

"No, you're confusing yourself. We want the truth here, and it appears you had your own motives for entering the house after being told the person you wanted wasn't there. Why did you go inside?"

"I *said* I thought she was hiding Charlie. Woman like that, she'd have lied..."

The judge interrupted, banging his gavel so hard everyone jumped.

"I've ruled that speculation about this defendant's character is out of order. No more of that."

Harcourt continued. "So, as defendant can testify, you forced your way into her home, didn't you?"

"No! She invited me in... She..."

"Knowing you were after her brother? Not likely, is it?"

"She didn't care about her brother: she wanted me. She..."

"Really? It's common knowledge that she had earlier rejected your courtship, Mr. Mabry. Why would..."

"Objection! Hearsay, has no bearing on this case."

"Oh, but it does, Your Honor: establishes why the plaintiff started the fight. But I'll withdraw the question." Of course the point had been made.

"Hmm. All right: clerk is ordered to strike the question. Proceed."

"So let's get this straight, Mr. Mabry. You had a compelling reason to go to the Prescott home, whatever it was, and also reason to go into the house after a woman, who'd previously rejected you, told you the person you were after wasn't there. A woman who clearly didn't want you there, correct?"

"She did want me there! I didn't want to be there..."

"But you did go there. Doesn't make sense. She overpowered you, dragged you inside against your will?" Here the courtroom burst into giggles at the image. Despite the gossip, the news of Andy's driving horny men away was in everyone's minds.

"And isn't it true you were on the boxing team in college, sir?"

"I...yes, I was."

"Nothing further, Your Honor." Harcourt sensed he'd gotten all he could out of this witness. He'd bolster his case with Andy's testimony, if necessary.

"Call Sheriff Hal Burgess, Your Honor."

The sheriff took the stand, reflecting on how many hundreds of times he'd sat in that chair over the years, how he'd seen all sorts of chicanery. How he could only state what he'd seen, how he must keep it objective.

"Now, Sheriff, would you tell the court what you saw when you were called to the Prescott house on the evening of February ninth?"

"I entered the dwelling after receiving a call from Nate Prescott that there'd been a fight, and that two people were injured. I saw the plaintiff on the floor, with Reverend Prescott holding a pistol on him. Barry was bloody, obviously in pain, holding an injured wrist, cuts on his face and scalp. A broken crutch was on the floor. While I was trying to determine what had happened, Miss Millard came downstairs, also showing bruises to her face, one eye swollen shut, with a severely cut lip, and limping.

"I was given the pistol without having to ask for it, and I asked whose it was. Reverend Prescott told me it belonged to the plaintiff, Barry Mabry, and that he'd threatened Miss Millard with it."

"Hearsay, Your Honor. Move to strike."

"Sustained. We will no doubt hear that testimony from the other defendant, sir. Continue."

"Pursuant to assessing the situation: a woman beaten and bruised, and a man, also beaten, who is, however, a known former boxer, I also saw a bloody dress, ripped down the front. I took him into custody." *Good: we both got that about the boxer past him.*

"And did you or did you not immediately call for medical assistance?"

"I did not. I allowed him his legal telephone call, which he could use however he chose."

"But you gave him no treatment, nor did you call for a doctor?"

"That's correct. It was by then late, the only clinic nearby being closed. I also knew you, sir, would take care of it, being the man's father."

"I submit that you were derelict in not providing medical care, Sheriff. Why did you take only the plaintiff into custody? Why not the defendants?"

"My assessment of the injured woman, the torn dress, and the fact that Elijah Prescott is a minister, elderly, crippled, with only one leg, led me to believe the attacker was Barry Mabry."

"You said there was a gun, being held by Elijah Prescott. Wasn't that gun obviously his or Miss Millard's?"

"I can't speculate on that, sir."

"But it could have been?"

"It's possible. But it hadn't been fired."

"Irrelevant. Now, Sheriff Burgess, it's been rumored that you have a personal stake in the welfare of Miss Mil…"

"Objection! No relevance and mere gossip, Your Honor."

"Sustained."

"All right, then, could your assessment have been somewhat slanted, Sheriff?"

"No, it couldn't. I've reported the facts as I saw them, which is my job. And I resent the implication that I would twist any facts, as you are doing, sir."

"Move to strike, Your Honor."

"Sustained. Is that all, Counselor?"

"No further questions at this time but reserve the right to recall."

"Your witness."

"Yes. Now, Sheriff Burgess, you testified that the defendant, Elijah Prescott, was holding a gun on the plaintiff when you arrived. Has that weapon been impounded?"

"It has, yes. It went under lock and key."

"And you also testified that the other defendant, Andrea Millard, came down the stairs as you arrived. Could you, with your extensive background and knowledge of injuries, describe them for us more fully?"

"Objection! The doctor has already done that, and this witness is not an expert."

"Overruled. The doctor only described injuries to the plaintiff. Besides, the sheriff has without doubt experience in such contexts."

"Thank you, Your Honor. Now, Dr. Blake testified that he could not tell whether these injuries to plaintiff resulted from an attack by defendant or a defense against an attacker; is this correct?"

"Yes." *Where is this going?*

"But she was clearly beatenl everyone agrees to that. Now, the plaintiff told us he was defending himself against an attack by this woman. Were the visible evidences of her injuries, in your already established judgment, consistent with an attack by her on the plaintiff?"

"Objection! Speculation."

"Overruled. The sheriff's qualifications to comment have been established. Proceed."

"To be more specific, sir, you observed that her eye was cut and swollen shut. What could that have been caused by?"

"Well, if plaintiff had pushed her away as he claims, that would hardly have produced a cut and an eye swollen shut, inflamed. That would suggest a blow—a hard one."

"And would her lip being cut and puffed up be consistent with someone pushing her away?"

"Not at all. I'd say that was caused by another blow."

"And plaintiff himself testified that he saw her being helped up by her nephew, so in your opinion, had she been knocked to the floor?"

"I'd say so, yes."

"Yes. And about that bloody, torn dress. To what would you attribute that?"

"Obviously ripped off her, and the blood would have come from the cuts. There were also scratches at the base of her throat, consistent with fingernail gouges."

"I see. Again in your opinion, could the defendant have torn her bloody dress herself?" Harcourt wanted to preempt Mabry's expected redirect.

"I don't see how. The reinforced collar was torn, which would have required a very strong pull, consistent with the scratch marks as it was grabbed."

"Objection, Your Honor! This speculation has gotten out of hand."

"Sustained. But it is an intriguing observation. Is the dress in evidence?"

"It is, Your Honor." Harcourt produced it, entered it into evidence. The judge held it up, examined it. Although the fabric was worn, the collar in question was quite strong away from the tear, as he saw, testing it. The bloodstains were now a dull brown. He nodded at Harcourt to continue.

"Now, Sheriff, do you have anything to add to your testimony?" This was shaky ground, this being a cross-examination.

"Only that Barry made no mention at the time of Andy's having allegedly pushed herself on him. He made that up later…"

Objection!" The lawyer was plainly enraged.

"Withdraw the question. Nothing further." Harcourt sat.

"Call your next witness, Mr. Mabry."

"Call Elijah Prescott."

The old preacher hobbled to the stand, was sworn in, not even trying to suppress a glare at Barry Mabry and his father.

"Now, Mr. Prescott, the plaintiff has testified that you beat him with your crutch, breaking his wrist and several fingers. That you struck him with some heavy object, knocking him unconscious, then kicked him repeatedly as he lay on the floor. Then you held him at gunpoint until the sheriff arrived. Is this correct?"

"It is, only that I used m'fists: they was th' heavy objeck. Kicked him oncet. And I'd do it agin. Harder." The glare was intense, as if Elijah were indeed the modern version of that raging Biblical prophet who'd slain Queen Jezebel's pagan-worshipping sycophants.

"And was that your gun?"

"Naw, I knocked it outta yore boy's hand, where he had it coverin' Andy while he wuz beatin' on her."

"Not yours. Did it belong to Andrea Millard?"

"Naw, I jist told you…"

"Or did it belong to Charlie Millard?"

"No! Th' gun wuz in Barry's hand, an' I knocked it away."

"Can you tell us why you attacked my son?"

"I done told you: he wuz beatin' on Andy."

"Did you actually see this? Or did you come inside afterwards and just think this was what was happening?"

"I saw it. Heered her screamin', him cussin' her first, then saw he wuz hittin' her with his fist an' backhandin' her up agin' th' wall, callin' her a thief an' a whore."

"Which hand was he holding the alleged gun in?"

"Which han'? Lessee, he wuz hittin' her with his right, so must've had th' gun in his left."

"Must've had? You don't remember? What else don't you remember, Mr. Prescott? Didn't you actually make up what you just described to protect Miss Millard? Didn't you lie?"

"Naw, I didn't lie. Barry Mabry, he lied. Still pissed 'bout Andy turnin' him down…"

"Move to strike, Your Honor. I'm done with this witness."

Harcourt let the courtroom settle down, taking his time.

"Reverend Millard, how would you describe your memory?"

"Sharp. I don't even hafta write m'sermons, son. I 'member th' Scriptures: don't take no notes neither."

"I see. Would you agree with Sheriff Burgess's observations about Miss Millard's injuries?"

"Yes, only I seen 'em fust hand. Seen thet Barry hittin' her, seen th' blood m'self."

"Did you see him tear her dress off?"

"Naw, he'd done already done thet, 'fore I come in. She wuz tryin' t'cover herse'f up an' couldn't pertect her face, whar he wuz bustin' her."

"Do you own a gun, Reverend?"

"Naw, I don't. Had a shotgun, but hadda sell it last year, when th' church, it couldn't pay me 'nuff t'live on."

"Do you know whether Andrea Millard or Nate Prescott owned such a gun, the .38 pistol?"

"Doubt it. They's poorer'n me."

"No further questions." He sat as the old man rose, still glaring, and limped back to his seat beside Andy and Nate.

"Recall? Recross examination?"

"No, Your Honor."

"Very well. Any other witnesses?" the judge asked Mabry.

"No, sir. The prosecution rests." *Until that boy manages to call that woman, then I'll cut her to pieces on cross.*

"Very well. Any other witnesses for the defense?" He looked at Harcourt.

"Yes. Call Montgomery Mabry."

"Plaintiff's attorney? You didn't specify him on your list, Counselor."

"That's correct, and if Mr. Mabry declines to testify, I do not object." This was a gamble, but the young lawyer was certain the desperate man would take the bait. The crucial bait.

"I'll testify. Willingly." And the elder Mabry rose, strode to the witness stand as if he owned the courtroom.

"I'll allow it. Proceed, Mr. Harcourt." *Now, what's this all about?*

"Thank you, Your Honor, and Mr. Mabry. Now, I'm entering this .38 revolver as evidence. Do you recognize it, sir?" To Mabry.

"Never seen it in my life." After a cursory glance.

"It has a serial number, sir, and it was registered to its purchaser by name. Do you still say you don't know whose it is?"

Mabry's face went white. *The damn gun. How did I let that get past me? And that sneaking kid of mine took it…*

"I'm waiting for an answer, Mr. Mabry. You testified that you don't know whose this gun is, correct?"

"I…I must've made a mistake. That…that could be…"

"No, that 'couldn't be'; that *is* your .38 revolver, Mr. Montgomery Mabry, purchased by you, registered in *your* name. You've committed perjury, sir, before this court. Now didn't your son take your gun from your house when he went to confront Andrea Millard?"

"I…I don't know why he took it, but…"

"And so it *was* he who held it on her, which allowed him to beat her, wasn't it?"

"I…can't testify to that."

"But I'd suggest that it's highly unlikely that either Andrea Millard or Reverend Prescott secured *your* revolver from your house and threatened your son with it at their home. No further questions."

Mabry couldn't take his mind off the business of the gun. That wasn't like him, to let that crucial evidence sneak up on him. *Am I slipping here? That's lost us this case, and I let it happen. Have I been so blinded by all this, I'm not thinking right? Got to get a grip on myself, stay objective. Not that it'll do me any good, now. Damn!*

The judge rapped his gavel to quiet the courtroom.

"Any further witnesses for the defense?"

"Yes, Your Honor. Call Nate Prescott." He took the stand, was sworn in, trying to keep his voice from going into falsetto.

"Now, Nate, can you corroborate Reverend Prescott's and Sheriff Burgess's testimony? That is, agree with it?"

"Y…yessir, what they said was right."

"What did you hear as you neared the house, coming home from school?"

"Well, like you said at first, I heard Andy cryin' out, Barry shoutin' at her, callin' her names. An' I heard hittin'."

"You heard hitting. What did that sound like?"

"Like somebody punchin' a sack of feed, sorta."

"And did you see Reverend Prescott enter the house?"

"Yessir. He pulled himself up onto th' porch an' got inside, quick."

"And what did you hear after that, before you went inside?"

"Sound was more a crack, an' I heard somethin' hit th' floor, somethin' hard. Then there was more cracks."

"And what did you actually see when you entered?"

"Saw Aunt Andy kinda slumped down, against th' wall, tryin'

t'cover herself up, cryin', groanin'. Granpa was slammin' Barry with his crutch, holdin' onto a chair. Then he got Barry's gun, held it on him. Him an' Aunt Andy, they were all bloody."

"Then what happened?"

"I helped Aunt Andy up, 'bout had to carry her up, laid her on th' bed. Then I ran back down, told Granpa I was goin' for a telephone t'call th' sheriff. I ran to Clemsons' and called him."

"And when the sheriff came? What then?"

"It was just th' way he told it, an' there wasn't anything atall said about her invitin' Barry in."

"Thank you. Do you know why Barry Mabry came to your house with a gun?"

"No,sir, I don't. Figure he was either after Uncle Charlie, or maybe he wanted to get Aunt Andy alone. He'd bad-mouthed her before."

"Nothing further."

Montgomery Mabry didn't even cross-examine the boy.

"Closing arguments. Mr. Mabry."

"I…well, I decline to close, Your Honor." He was visibly rattled, beaten.

"Very well. Mr. Harcourt?"

"Yes. It's clear that, for whatever reason, the plaintiff went to the Prescott house carrying his father's gun, obviously bent on a violent confrontation. Whether or not he, as he testified, was after Charlie Millard for alleged timber theft, or whether he was determined to attack and defile Andrea Millard, we'll never know. We do know, since it's common knowledge, that gossip has painted her as an immoral woman, with absolutely no evidence. That she divorced Cam Henry is also common knowledge, and there is an unfair stigma attached to divorced women. Not, I would add, to divorced *men.*

"You have heard the testimony of four witnesses pointing to Miss Millard's being attacked by Barry Mabry, a former boxer, well able to take care of himself. And further testimony that Reverend Prescott, a man of God opposed to violence, nevertheless came to her rescue.

Given the circumstances and the evidence, Mabry's insistence that she tried to seduce him is ridiculous.

"The facts of the case are clear, Your Honor. We ask that the defendants be judged not guilty and acquitted. They have not chosen to bring a countersuit against Mabry, however, although I would gladly represent them in such an action." He sat.

"It's late. I will pronounce my decision at nine o'clock tomorrow morning. Court adjourned." His Honor rapped his gavel, rose, and retreated into chambers.

The curious onlookers filed out, talking excitedly among themselves. Harcourt suggested that his clients wait to follow them, knowing they'd be bombarded with questions, once outside.

"How do you think the judge will rule?" Andy asked. She did not appear overly concerned, but the anger at Barry's lies still sparked in her eyes.

"I don't see how he could possibly decide against us," the lawyer replied. "His gun, your injuries, our witnesses. I didn't want you subjected to Mabry's insulting examination, which he wanted to spring on us, confuse you. That's why I pressed that legal point, and why I didn't call you to the stand."

"I'd have told the truth."

"I'm sure of it, but he'd have twisted it, managed to paint you as black as possible, and planted the idea that anything you said was false. That's what lawyers like him are good at. I'm just glad that about the gun shut him up."

"Mabrys all thaink ever'body oughta jist let 'em have ever'thaing, not put up no fight," Elijah groused. "Thet Barry oughta be hung."

Nate had taken it all in, following as best he could the ups and downs, recognizing all the lies, seeing the sheriff's objectivity, surprised that his aunt hadn't taken the stand in her own defense. *Granpa said he heard Barry callin' her a whore; didn't hear that myself. But that'd sure be th' way ever'body'd see her, way Barry lied about her throwin' herself at him. She couldn't stand that man before; can't stand him now.*

"I'll stay over to hear the verdict, of course," Harcourt assured them. "It's not like a sentencing or anything that vital, but it will mean a lot to let everyone know you're innocent, Miss Millard. The Mabrys clearly set out to destroy your good name, and I'm sure the judge sees that."

He left them, returning to the old brick hotel in Ridgeway for the night. *Shouldn't be a thing to worry about: clear case. But Mabry's got money, and despite his wanting to run for office, I'd almost bet he's tried to bribe the judge. Don't know enough about His Honor to guess how that could've gone.*

Well, waiting for a verdict is always hard. I'll just have to try and push it all out of my mind, get some sleep.

Chapter Five

Two months after the judge pronounced Andy and Elijah not guilty of attacking Barry Mabry, she turned a corner in Ridgeway, carrying a few purchased groceries, salt, sugar, and spices, and almost ran headlong into him.

"Well, if it isn't the triumphant bitch," he snarled. "Proud of yourself, Andy?"

"You're lucky we didn't countersue you, you piece of pig shit. But as long as you keep away, leave us the hell alone, we'll let your cowardly attack go; we're a lot bigger than you and your father." She moved to go around him.

"Not so fast." He grabbed her arm, causing her to drop her sack of groceries. Something broke. "So the judge believed you instead of me. That doesn't change the fact that you're shacking up with half the county, you whore."

People were stopping, staring, but nobody was close enough to hear. *Now what're them two doin' t'gether? Makin' up, er makin' out? Don't look like neither…*

With her purchases on the sidewalk, Andy's right arm was free, and she swung it, hard, to land an open palm loud and hard against his cheek. The onlookers grinned as Barry staggered, let her go. There was a sudden movement past her.

"You *ever* use that kinda talk about my aunt again, you're a dead man, Mabry." Nate's words cut through the air, even from his just-growing fourteen-year-old-frame. He took a step closer, fists balled, as Barry rubbed his inflamed cheek. "Only I won't stop th' way Granpa did. Now, you git on back an' hide b'hind your wife's skirts, you *pervert!"* This time every spectator heard this and laughed out loud.

"Why, you little…" Barry reached for the boy, who stood his ground, cocking his right fist.

Andy had stooped quickly, grasped the neck of a bottle of soda pop she'd bought as a treat for Nate, which had broken against the concrete. She stepped beside her nephew, glaring at their enemy, the jagged neck of the dripping bottle thrust at him. He stepped back, his eyes riveted on the weapon. She turned her head partially but kept her own eyes on Barry, called out.

"Now, you all saw this man grab me, knock my groceries outta my hand, call me a filthy name. I'm defending myself like I tried to do last time he attacked me. Just you remember this if he ever tries it again."

Barry backed away, his entire face now red with anger and shame. He turned and strode away. Andy watched him go as Nate bent, gathered the rest of the fallen purchases. The onlookers drifted away in little knots, talking excitedly among themselves.

"Reckon he's ever gonna let you alone, Aunt Andy?" Nate was still trembling from the confrontation.

"Doesn't look like it. His kind just can't accept anything that goes against what they want. I just hope he doesn't try anything worse than confronting me. Have to make sure I'm not alone, I guess. Glad you were here, Nate."

"What gets me is th' way he just walked right up and insulted you, front of all those people. Got no shame." They walked to the edge of the village where the mules and wagon were hitched, climbed on, headed the miles home.

But halfway there, they heard a car behind them, coming fast down the narrow gravel road. Nate was driving, looked over his shoulder as the mules reacted to the loud sound. He saw the ditch to their right wasn't deep, and just before the speeding car reached them, he slapped the reins hard against the already spooked mules. They lunged off the road, snatching the wagon after them.

The car, a big Hudson, barely missed the rear wheel of the wagon.

Nate had all he could handle, hauling on the reins. But Andy had seen, through the cloud of dust, that the driver was Barry Mabry. *Fool was willing to trash his car to hit us. This's serious.*

"Who'd run us off th' road like this?" Nate gasped, having finally controlled the mules. "Somebody drunk?"

"No, that wasn't a drunk, Nate; that was Barry Mabry in that car. And I wouldn't put it past him to try that again. Turn off onto that log road ahead; he won't be able to drive up it in that low-slung car. We can connect to the other track through the woods, get home that way, off the main road."

They had gone only a hundred yards up the rocky, weed-grown trace when they heard a vehicle coming back down the county road, fast. It stopped at the mouth of the log road: the Hudson again. And Barry Mabry shook his fist at them, yelled something unintelligible. Nate whipped up the mules again, fearful that the man might have a gun. The car spun its wheels as it roared away.

"That's scary," Nate managed, again slowing the spooked mules. "Will he ever give up?"

"Doesn't look like it. And now we have to watch close, in case he tries to come after us at home. Without Charlie, it's going to be hard to watch all the time." She was replaying in her mind Mabry's charging into the house, clearly bent on attacking her. *You know, I think saying he was after Charlie was just another lie: he's set on punishing me, raping me, I'm sure of it. Well, he'll face a loaded shotgun next time, even if I have to sleep with it.*

For his part, Barry Mabry's rage only increased after the public confrontation. He'd never forget the laughing, even jeering of the Ridgeway spectators. He'd given in to the need for some action, some way to strike out at Andy and her nephew, actually trying to smash into their wagon with his car. *Not the smartest thing I ever did: they'd know it was me, and things would only get worse. No, I've got to plan something they can't link me to…*

That night Andy tried to stay awake, the shotgun cradled across her knees, watching the moonlit yard out her window. Hours passed with no disturbance, and she finally succumbed to the drowsiness and slipped into sleep.

Morning showed everything to be normal, and she dismissed her fear; there was work to be done before Nate would be ready to go off to the county high school in a few weeks. He'd have to walk a half mile to the paved road bus stop, then ride the remaining eight miles. *Not much time to help with chores then. Wonder where Charlie is? Well, he'll show up sooner or later, but we could sure use another pair of hands right now.*

So as the days, then weeks passed with no further trouble, she almost forgot about Mabry's attack. *Must've shamed him enough he'll stay away. I hope.*

* * *

Young Giles Mabry was often confused at his father's behavior. Usually Barry was all right to be around, play with, and like any six-year-old, the boy loved his father. But there were times the man would yell at him, or at his mother, over something that didn't seem important. And more than once, he'd thrown things, broken things in his anger.

At these times, Giles would run to his room, bury his head in his pillow to shut out the loud voices of his parents. Usually these outbursts didn't last long: his father stomping around, cursing, sometimes loud sounds as he slammed objects, his mother standing with arms crossed, waiting for him to calm down.

But at other times, she shrieked at him, forcibly grabbed his wrist to keep him from smashing a vase or picture or something else she wasn't about to let him destroy. Then it'd all die down, and Giles would peek from his hiding place and eventually creep back from his bedroom, look from one parent to the other to see if the war were over.

As the boy grew, he realized that his father's outbursts followed a pattern: they were always touched off by his not getting his way in something, usually denied him by his own father. Giles felt he ought to be on Barry's side in these situations, but he also loved his grandfather, and this confused him more.

Also, Christine almost always agreed with Montgomery, pointing out the obvious flaws in her husband's reasoning or the lack thereof, which of course enraged him more.

Barry never struck his wife. She'd made it clear from the first that she wasn't going to be his doormat, no matter the unpleasant details of their marriage. And that she would gladly shoot him dead if he laid a hand on her. She later amended that promise to include the protection of Giles.

This warning probably wouldn't have deterred the man if he hadn't been totally convinced that she meant every word of it. Christine had a rocklike resolve about her that said simply*: I will do whatever I must in any situation to win.*

Most of the time Giles felt safe in his home, but there was always an uneasiness about the place, which he supposed was normal, not knowing otherwise. With an animal instinct, he'd race for cover at danger and emerge when that seemed past. So if that was life, he accepted it. Only as he came to know other children did he begin to realize that his father's behavior wasn't the way other dads acted.

He became closer to his mother as a result of Barry's lack of control, relying on her good sense much as his grandfather did to keep sanity in their home. Christine Mabry, like Andy Millard, was capable of sacrificing whatever was necessary to survive and see to it her son was not warped by his father's immaturity.

Psychologists have written reams of opinion about how this kind of divided loyalty harms a child, but all agree it isn't good. That Giles was able to grow normally was a tribute to his mother's devotion, which nonetheless never crossed over into smothering. In that way, Christine could be said to be the ideal mother.

Which Montgomery recognized, much as he'd seen the girl's potential when she'd first come to him forthrightly, pregnant with Barry's child. While another father would surely have sent her packing, perhaps with a dismissive payment, the old man in his shrewdness saw in her the salvation of his fiefdom.

Giles knew no more than that his mother and grandfather were closer than in most families, and he gradually realized that his father was the outsider among them. That the family continued to function didn't cause the boy undue alarm, just a necessary shifting of loyalties.

* * *

Charlie Millard was washing a car at a small service station in North Little Rock, owned by one Chester Peaks, an aging, stooped refugee from a Delta farm. The job paid less than a dollar an hour, but it was all he'd been able to find. And no, he hadn't saved any money to send his sister after paying for a room, trying to feed himself, buying a faded '48 Chevrolet coupe for $225.

With the end of summer, though, he began to worry about how Andy and Nate would manage; not that far till winter again. And as always, when he reflected on how he seemed to spend whatever money he made on drive-in food, women, and beer, he felt ashamed. *Only fam'ly I go, an' I oughta help 'em out more, I know. Nate'd be better off sellin' that wore-out place, git away f'm there. Only…lessee…fourteen, though. Be a couple years b'fore he could git enny kinda job. Guess things just gotta work out more 'fore ennything like that c'n happen.*

He'd had no word and finally realized his sister and nephew didn't know how to get in touch with him. Now, how had he let that happen? He resolved to send a note right then, just as soon as he finished the glass on this car. *Fifty Olds Rocket; wish I c'd afford one like it, only I'd want a convert'ble top, an' blood red.*

It was lunchtime, and he tore a sheet off a notebook on Chester's desk, scrawled a message: "Sorry I haven't wrote, Andy. Let me know what's happened up there since I been gone. Get up t'see y'all soon's I can. Stay sweet, Charlie." He found an envelope and a stamp of Chester's, walked down to a mailbox, and posted the letter with his return address on it. Then dropped into a nearby café where a shopworn redhead he knew greeted him with a weary smile.

When the letter arrived two days later, Andy was taken aback by the realization that her brother could know nothing of the attack, the trial, and certainly not of the more recent brushes with Barry Mabry.

Should she tell him? She knew he'd drop everything and rush up here, probably get himself and all of them in trouble with some rash, even violent scheme for revenge. *No, plenty time to tell him, whenever he shows up.*

She showed Nate the letter, and his reaction was immediate. He was sure his aunt would let things slide the way she usually did: no sudden moves till she'd thought it out. So he resolved to write his uncle, telling him of events and the continuing harassment by the Mabrys.

But it was late after he'd finished his chores by lantern light, then his homework. High school sure took a lot more of a fellow's time, he reflected. Well, maybe he'd have time for that letter, lunchtime at school tomorrow.

It was around midnight that Andy smelled smoke and awakened to see an orange glow out her window. She jumped out of bed, ran to a window to see the barn ablaze. Then she heard the screams of the mules, which were inside the burning structure. She threw on a tattered robe, shoved her feet into her shoes, yelled for Nate.

"Barn's afire!" she shouted as she ran down the stairs. She grabbed a bucket, worked the pitcher pump by the sink frantically, looking out at the roaring blaze. *No use, this. Try to get the mules out, then.*

She raced, the terrifying animal sounds raising the hair on her neck, feeling already the scorching heat from the blaze. Nate was suddenly right behind her, then past her, racing toward the barn door. That door was beginning to burn, too, and the closer he got, the more intense the heat. He had to stop, shield his face with his arm. Despite this, he thought his hair was beginning to burn.

"Can't reach 'em," he almost sobbed. Andy grabbed him, pulled him back as a section of the haymow above crashed down on the stable. The dry hay ignited in a fireball, and the mules gave out last, horrible, dying cries.

The man parked well down the road saw the eerie glow of the destroyed barn from his car. He flipped his cigarette out the window, started up. and drove away.

* * *

Nate's outrage at the loss of the mules and the barn consumed him. It had to be that Barry Mabry, he was certain. Nobody else had it in for his family, and this was just the low-down kind of nastiness the man would pull. He called the sheriff the next day from the nearest phone, having stayed home from school.

"Killed both our mules, Mr. Burgess, and burnt th' wagon, too. Hogs were out in their pen, and chickens okay, but hay, feed, harness, everything…gone." He could not keep the anger out of his voice. "Had to be th' Mabrys."

"Any evidence of them? Anybody see a car?"

"Don't know, but was back in th' summer, he jumped Aunt Andy in town, knocked her groceries outta her arms, grabbed her, an' was cussin' her when I caught up. He went after me, but Aunt Andy, she held him off with a broken bottle. Ever'body there saw it. Called her a…a whore, he did."

"I didn't hear about that. Anything else?"

"There was. We were drivin' the wagon home, an' here he came, almost run his car into us. I got th' wagon up a log road, an' he stopped, cussed us. We've been lookin' out since, but he got to th' barn while we were asleep."

"I'll be out directly, Nate. Where are you?"

"I'm at th' phone at th' Clemsons'. Stayed home from school."

"I'll pick you up there. Wait for me."

The sheriff was angry, knowing that Nate and Andy had no other enemies, but he hoped to find real evidence against Barry Mabry before charging him. He reflected that barn-burnings were as old as feuds, a way to hit out at someone without actually attacking him. He was surprised that he hadn't heard the gossip about Barry confronting Andy those days ago. But then, most country folks avoided any police if they could. And despite his years here, he knew Everett County would never fully accept him, let him in on all the gossip.

At the Prescott place, the smell of burned flesh was strong in the smoke still rising from the few charred beams in the ashes. Nearby trees were scorched. He hoped for an empty gas can, tire tracks, boot tracks—anything at all. But there was only the burnt-out space where the barn had been, with the smoldering humps that had been the Prescott mules.

Andy came down from the house, her mouth a tight line, her eyes ablaze at the destruction. Burgess tipped his hat to her, expressed his regret.

"Everything we had, gone, Hal. And no way it could have been an accident: no electricity there, no fire we might have had. Old forge hasn't been used in a year at least. Of course we suspect Barry Mabry, after the way he's treated us—me."

"I'd have to agree, but there's not a shred of proof, Andy. He's not left as much as a footprint here. I'll ask everyone on the road if anyone saw a car or even a man on foot, but I must tell you, this is the hardest thing to prove there is."

"He's gone over the edge here, Hal. Called me a triumphant bitch and a whore, right there on Main Street with people watching. Grabbed me, but Nate and I drove him off."

"What Nate tells me. Then tried to run you over on the road?"

"Yes. Would probably have wrecked his car, but he didn't seem to care. I tell you, the man's crazy."

"Well, I can confront him about the car thing, even arrest him if you'll press charges. He'll deny it, but we can tie it in with what people saw in town."

"Oh, I just want him to leave us alone! Bobby Harcourt wanted us to sue him, but I wouldn't take a cent of that man's money." She spat, then her expression changed to one of hope. "Do you think he'll quit, now he's about burned us out?"

"I'm afraid not; he's escalating this. People like that don't like themselves, always want to blame somebody else for everything that happens to them. I hate to suggest this, Andy, but do you and Nate have anywhere else you can go? Anybody to stay with?"

"You mean run from him? You mean we're not safe in our own

house here in America? There have to be laws to protect us, Hal, some other way to keep us safe. No, this farm is all we have, and now we can't even work it. And winter not that far away…"

"I could check by often or send a deputy, but there's no way to know when he'll take the next step. Well, I'll go over, get after him with what we have. Now, you two be on the watch. Heard from Charlie?"

"We did get a letter yesterday. He doesn't know about the other—the attack, the trial—any of it. I'm afraid he'll come back, go after Barry, get himself in trouble or even killed, he'll be that angry."

"Maybe. I wish there was more I could do, Andy, Nate, but I'll do what I can."

"Thanks, Hal. And I suspect you've already helped us out: I know Bobby's fee had to be more than he charged us. You helped, and yes, we thank you." She clasped his hands for a moment. A warmth ran through him. *Damn, if I was just ten years younger…*

"No problem there. I'll be in touch." He turned awkwardly, walked to his car.

Nate surveyed the ruin of the barn for a moment, then ran to the house, got paper and pen, and wrote his letter to his uncle. In it he poured out all the facts, all his frustrations, anger. He ended with a plea for Charlie to come home, help them put their lives back together somehow.

Nate didn't show the letter to Andy. He found an envelope, stamped it, and walked out for the second time that day to mail it. *Can't waste time here: don't know what will happen next, but have to do somethin', quick.*

Andy could easily guess about the letter, but she said nothing. She took a sweater against the early evening chill to come later and told Nate to stay, keep his eye out. He didn't ask where she was going, and she didn't tell him.

The miles were long to Elijah Prescott's little cabin up in the mountains. Hours later, Andy passed the closed church, looking lonely in its clearing by the dirt track. A quarter-mile beyond she saw Elijah splitting firewood in his front yard. He'd balance himself on his wooden leg, swing the maul, then quickly use it as a crutch to steady himself. A small pile of wood showed his work. He saw her.

"Evening, Elijah," she greeted. She was breathing heavily from the last climb on the stony trail, and her feet hurt. He nodded in response, wondering why she'd come alone. Of course something was wrong.

"Nate all right, girl?"

"He is, but we've had trouble, Reverend. Lost the barn, both mules, and the wagon in a fire last night." They both stepped up onto the porch, she setting a small bag down. He sat.

"Mabrys. You call th' sheriff?"

"We did. No evidence, but Barry jumped us in town on before, grabbed me, cussed us out."

"Rat there in town?"

"Front of everybody. We held him off, but then he tried to run us down on the way home. We've been watching, but he must've sneaked up, set the barn afire."

"And Charlie, he's still gone, I reckon." A statement. She only nodded. He ruminated for several minutes, then stood up from his old rocking chair, stumped inside without another word. She waited.

"Got ever'thaing I need. Let's us git goin', girl." He had a small knapsack.

"Now you wait. I've brought a little something to eat, and it's a long walk back. Almost dark anyway, so no hurry." She brushed past him, lighted a candle, went to his stove. There was kindling next to it, and she lit a fire. He watched in silence as she put water on for coffee, began heating a thick soup she'd brought. Then she turned to him.

"We want you to move in with us, Reverend Elijah. You've no way to live up here, what with the church closed and all. You're family, and we need you. I know you see it that way, all packed up, but it's not for just a few days. I know Nate's written Charlie, and we'll all be together, work it out amongst us. Sheriff thinks it'll get worse, and we want to be ready."

They ate quickly in silence, then she closed up the stove, extinguished the candle. The half moon was up in a clear sky, and they started out, she carrying more of his scant belongings. The old man swung along, his wooden leg making a sort of double clicking sound with his crutch as they struck the stony trail, then the road that passed in front of the church.

"We'll send somebody up for whatever you need, soon's we can, or come ourselves. Charlie'll have a car, for sure. Been gone since winter, and he's surely managed that."

"Hope so. He sent enny money to he'p out?"

"No, and we didn't know where he was to let him know about things, but now we do. He'll come; always has."

Elijah didn't say out loud his thought that Charlie Millard only came home when he was broke or running from the law. But Andy was right: time to hunker down, all of them, see this through, try to build back whatever they could. It'd be hard, no timber left, no way to plow and plant, no way to get around. But the four of them would manage, he was as sure as he was of God's care. *Won't let us starve, He won't.*

Chapter Six

"You say their barn burned? That's too bad." Montgomery Mabry sat in a wooden armchair on his front porch, the sheriff standing. "Nate and that girl won't have much left. Get the livestock?"

"Did. Lost both mules and their wagon, all their hay, feed, harness. And with no electricity, no fire of theirs, it wasn't an accident. No, they've nothing left to live on, Mr. Mabry. Your son around? Wasn't at his house."

"No, he's not here. And what does he have to do with it?"

"That's what I have to ask him, sir. Did you know he accosted Andy Millard in town the other day, grabbed her, cussed her in front of several onlookers?"

"Boy's got a temper, all right. Hasn't gotten over losing the court case, of course. That girl came on to him, Burgess, provoked him, and you and I both know it."

"Judge ruled differently, and I agree with him. Anyway, that's history, but both Andy and Nate say Barry tried to run them down with his car on their way home. That's cause enough for me to follow up on it."

"Their word against his, and I wouldn't give you a nickel for Andy Millard's word. She's no doubt got that boy to swear to anything by now. Travesty, woman like that raising Dave's kid."

"You tell Barry I'll arrest him unless he comes in, Mr. Mabry. Charge will be attempted murder."

"Now that's a little harsh, Sheriff."

"What's harsh is that your boy's gone over the edge. Barn-burning's just one step; next one might be a lot worse, and I'm not going to let that happen." Burgess turned, left the sputtering lawyer.

* * *

Cam Henry pushed the long-nosed White tractor-trailer up the twisting hill on U.S. 65 north out of the tiny village of St. Joe. The big Mustang engine, with its thirsty four-barrel carburetor, bellowed the rig around the tight curves with the driver split-shifting the transmission and the two-speed rear axle expertly. The cab grew hot, and he cranked a window down.

He was ahead of time on this load, bound for Springfield out of Bastrop, Louisiana. The thought occurred to him that this time he had time for a quick run over to Everett County to see his folks. *Been most a year, an' Mama, she'd like t'see me, I know. An' maybe git another shot at Christine, while I'm there.*

This got him thinking of his ex-wife, Andy, and for probably the thousandth time, he regretted losing her. *Shore ain't found 'nuther'n as good, but I guess I just hadda try, see what else's out there. Damn fool, really. Ennyway, she wouldn't give me th' time of day, after all's happened. Thought I c'd keep m'runnin' around f'm her, but that woman, she's just too sharp. Well, th' judge done said I gotta stay away f'm her, an' if I wanta keep m'ass outta jail, reckon I'll do it.*

He'd hoped to catch sight of her on his infrequent trips through Ridgeway, but he'd heard she stayed on that old farm of her sister's, taking care of that boy. Well, seeing her would just make him feel worse, he knew, so he'd just have to forget it.

But visit with Mama a bit, sure, and just maybe… Layover in Springfield anyway, and he could even be a little late; nothing in this load needed that bad. So he eventually reached the turnoff at the little general store, headed the nose of the White toward Ridgeway. And the familiar miles rolled past under his wheels, and he turned the radio on to hear Tex Ritter singing that song from the movie *High Noon.*

He parked on the wide street several blocks from the courthouse square, seeing the old family Dodge in the driveway. His mother had learned to drive after her husband had died, so yeah, she'd be home. He walked whistling up the steps, knocked.

"Who's there?" came from inside. He could imagine his mother bent over the kitchen stove and did note it was almost midday. *Good, git fed right for a change; been missin' good cookin' ever since Andy left.*

"Well, well, look whut th' cat drug in. C'mere, boy, an' git a hug; been missin' you somethin' awful. Y'got enny time off?" His mother wrapped his spare frame in a huge bear hug. "Y'ain't eatin' right, I c'n tell that fer sure." She stood back, looked him over.

"Naw, gotta git on up th' road, but wasn't that far, so thought I'd make time t'come see m'favorite girl. You been all right?" He was searching the familiar room, remembering growing up there.

"Makin' do. Arlie an' Sarah, they come 'round when they can, but t'ain't often enough. Little Calvin, he's growin' like a weed, an' they got 'nuther one on th' way. Come set y'self down; I'se just 'bout through cookin' dinner." She kept up a steady stream of news while she bustled about the kitchen, a sight and sound he hadn't realized he'd missed as much as he did.

"Big news 'round since I seen you." She paused, a big spoon in her hand, her eyes on his. "That no-good Barry Mabry, he went an' tried t'rape yer ex-wife, hadda big trial." She watched to see what the effect of this news had on her son.

"*Did?* That low-down critter! Whut happened?"

"Well, way I heard it, there was somethin' 'bout Charlie cuttin' some trees Mabrys thought b'longed t'them, an' Barry, he went over t'settle it. Took his pa's gun, turns out. Charlie, he wasn't there, an' th' boy, he just jumps Andy, beat her up bad, tore her dress most off'n her…"

"He *whut?*"

"Did. Only old 'Lijah Prescott, he come along 'bout then, an' he beat th' devil outta Barry, broke him up bad. Sheriff took Barry t'jail, but old Montgom'ry, he got it turned around some way so they sued Andy an' th' preacher. She was let off, but Barry, he couldn't let it 'lone, seems like."

"What happened after that? More cussedness?"

"Well, th' word 'round town was he jumped her'n young Nate right on th' street, grabbed her, cussed her, then tried t'run 'em down on th' road home. An' 'twas a few weeks on, th' Prescott barn got burned plumb down, got th' wagon, kilt their mules, lost ever'thing inside.

"Now, I ain't been high on Andy ever since she left you, Cam, but such as that, it just ain't right. Folks been talkin' her down, but she's done took care of Nate right along, since his folks died. An' she's took old Elijah in, too, after his church, it dried up on up th' road." She raised her hands.

"Now, I done kep' outta yore business with Andy all 'long, but th' way I see it, th' Mabrys has got way too big fer their britches, an' made it harder on that girl. An' I'm 'fraid that Barry's got a screw loose er somethin' an' I'm just that scared fer Andy."

"Well. That's some news, all right. She ain't took up 'th nobody else?"

"Don't seem t'of. Don't come t'town much atall, just works that pore ole place with that boy. And Charlie, he don't come 'round much, help out. Y'know, I'm not so down on Andy as I usta be…"

"Havin' it rough, for shore. Well, we couldn't make a go of it, y'know, an' no use goin' into th' reasons why now. But yeah, that's lowdown. Mabrys think they gotta right t'throw off on ennybody gits in their way. 'Course it all goes back t'when Andy dumped Barry fer me." He remembered the striking girl he'd met when she was in high school, and the twinge of regret returned. Along with a darker emotion.

The anger that burned inside Cam Henry stayed with him, even as he headed the rig back toward 65, not having connected with Christine. Didn't matter that much, though: the way north was where that new red-headed woman waited for him.

But that bastard Mabry oughta be hung an' jist left up there to rot. Slick, lettin' some time pass, figurin' that'd keep folks f'm thinking he done th' barn. But I reckon ever'body knows he did. Time for somebody to lay for that'n, now.

And of course, that would make Christine available. *Yeah, grievin' widow, need a man aroun'.* Cam Henry grinned.

* * *

The '48 Chevrolet coupe eased to a stop in the side yard, and Charlie Millard got out, stretched. It was late afternoon, the shadows lengthening. The place was quiet, only the ticking of the cooling car engine audible. He looked around, then saw Andy and Elijah down past where the barn should have been, the two of them feeding corn to the hogs, talking, laughing. He took that sight in for a moment, reflecting that the preacher'd never liked him. They saw him, and Andy waved. *Old man's here, though, and I reckon that's good. Beat th' shit outta that Barry agin, he comes around. I'se worried, just her an' th' boy here. Shoulda shot that bastard while he had th' chance, way Nate told it. Guess he's in school.*

"Got that car an' thirty dollars, Sis, Elijah. Reckon that'll help some. Y'all been able t'put up much f'm th' garden?"

"Some." She hugged her brother. "And we'll butcher, first cold spell. But it'll be a hard winter, I'm afraid. Elijah's church closed up, and we've brought him here now, been helping right along." At the house, Andy set about putting supper together, glancing at the battered clock. Nate was due soon.

"Well, you know Nate wrote me, why I come home. What'd Sheriff Hal say 'bout th' barn, th' other stuff?"

"Said no evidence, but he's gone after Barry about that scrape in town and trying to run us down. Witnesses in Ridgeway, and he said he could put it together, maybe do something about it. 'Course his daddy'll fight it. Hal said he thought next time would be worse, though, like one of those serial killers they talk about, crazy people." Elijah sat quiet, watching to see how Charlie would take this.

"Well, Barry Mabry needs killin', beg pardon, Reverend. He's left y'all—all of us, I reckon—'thout a thing here. Man's meaner'n a snake, an' y'don't let a snake bite you if y'git him first." He looked to his sister, busy at the stove. She nodded grim agreement. Then he looked at Elijah, whose mouth was one straight line, his jaw clenched. "Not that we oughta go that far or anything, but that's whut oughta happen."

Just then Nate clattered up the porch steps, entered. Saw his uncle, and his eyes lighted up.

"Hey, Uncle Charlie. Saw your car. Been here long?"

"'Bout half 'n hour. Jist catchin' up on stuff. Ennything left t'do in th' field?"

"Taters yet to be dug, some carrots, some late green stuff. Few apples, pears. Aunt Andy's canned a bunch as it came in, an' we got three pigs come cold weather."

"Won't hardly be enough to git th'u th' winter though. Reckon there's deer up on th' mountin?"

"Most hunted out, I hear, but a feller could get lucky."

"Th' Lord will pervide," Elijah intoned. "He takes keer of His chillun."

"Yeah, I reckon. But I allus heard His children gotta help Him out some, now'n then, if they're gonna git by." Charlie had avoided churches and preachers all his life, and now here was one, right among them. Of course the old man'd proved he could deal out justice when needed, he remembered.

The four of them talked through supper and afterward about their situation, mostly about the fear that Barry Mabry would do something else to them, especially if he found out Charlie was home. That didn't seem to bother him a lot.

"Have that shotgun handy is all we c'n do. Man tries anything like he done b'fore, he gits hisself shot. Plain self d'fense." He spread his beefy hands.

"Don't b'lieve he'll try ennythaing like that agin," Elijah said. "Prob'ly come up 'th some new craz'ness we ain't thought of. Dunno whut, but wouldn't put a thaing past that'n."

Nate took this in, imagining putting the bead of the old shotgun on Barry Mabry and pulling the trigger. Yes, he could see that scene, from up at his vantage point in the sky: the two of them, faced off. With himself quicker, deadlier. *Wonder what that'd be like? Bible says not to kill, but if th'other man's comin' after you, what's left to do? And if he gets after*

Aunt Andy again, killin's too good for him...

Then the talk went back to preparing for winter. Charlie brought up the two prime white oaks left down at the spring and calculated what those stave bolts were worth. But of course they had no chainsaw now, no mules or wagon, and sure no truck to get in and out quick.

"Best leave that alone," his sister warned. "It's what started all this."

"No, that snake's been lookin' for a chance to git at you ever since you come back. He's plumb eat up with hate for all of us, goin' on back t'when we were kids. Timber's jist 'n excuse. B'sides, ever'body knows them were Nate's trees."

"Doesn't seem to make any difference to those Mabrys, Uncle Charlie, they bein' mine to cut. Y'know, this is gettin' to be like one of those old-time feuds you read about back in Kentucky. Like the Hatfields and McCoys. Only nobody's been killed."

"Could've been, easy," Elijah pointed out. "Andy fightin' him lak she wuz, he might've jist shot her, crazy's th' man's got."

"Well, I'd say, folks," Charlie began, a bemused smile on his red face, "we jist do like Elijah says, an' trust in th' Lord t'take care us through th' winter, do th' best we can, an' maybe git a headstart on next year. I'm sure I c'n trade fer 'nuther mule or two, anyway put together a slide fer firewood an' all, put in more of everything come spring, and we'll make it okay."

"I guess that's best, yes," Andy agreed. "And of course all of us watch out for each other. I fear you'd be his next target, Charlie, once he hears you're back."

"Reckon I c'n take care myself, Sis. Always been able to, even if 't seems like I 'tract trouble some way." He grinned, also imagining a confrontation with Barry Mabry, man to man. *Wouldn't run from that neither, come to it.*

Lying in bed, staring beyond the ceiling of the farmhouse, Nate felt a new closeness with what was left of his family. They'd survive, as they'd said, and that created a picture in his mind: the four of them against a hostile world. *All been so much easier if Mama an' Daddy were here.*

Dear God, take care of them there with You. An' us, too.

* * *

The leaves were heavy on the November ground, the trees mostly bare after a storm. It was cold now, and smoke wafted from the scattered chimneys of rural Stark Township. No one was about, it seemed: suppertime.

The woods trail was an abandoned forest road that led past the remains of an ancient cabin, said to be that of the first settler in the county, back in the early 1800s. It had fallen, decayed, now mostly a heap of rotting debris with the jagged base of a stone chimney jutting.

The bundled figure was engaged in a curious task, dragging the broken-off top of a fallen tree across the path, pausing often to catch its breath. A handmade wooden ladder lay nearby. After being satisfied with the result, whoever it was scuffed aside the leaf cover, tramped a new route nearer the cabin remains, right to an old caved-in well. The ladder was lowered into it, and the hooded shape climbed down.

There was little water down there, the fallen dirt having turned the bottom to mud. *Now, I can make this look like an accident, but I've got to make sure. Fall in, yes, that's taken care of, but could someone climb out again? Caving in, nothing to grab hold of, but somebody could hear yelling, and I can't afford that.*

So, have to go through with the plan, the thing I read about in the National Geographic *about ancient hunters. But God, this is a line I'm crossing, and there's no going back…*

The climber returned to the surface, moved away to a dozen or more sharpened sections of small trees, maybe two inches in diameter. These were taken two at a time down into the well and pushed deep into the mud, with their spiked ends upward. They presented a closely spaced, deadly reception to anything falling into the old well, much as those pitfalls fashioned by primitive tribes in hunting large game.

Which was exactly the intended purpose. Next, the shadow figure pulled the ladder up with a sucking sound as it was freed from the muck. Then, slender dead tree branches were laid across the top of the well to form a tight screen. Smaller twigs followed, then several layers of the newly fallen leaves, from the broad oaks to the long hickories, the occasional sycamores. This part of the operation was carefully attended to so when finished, no eye could detect the trap.

Finally, the hunter, for that's what this actually was, brushed out all tracks, and cleared just enough forest duff and leaves to create a believable path straight across the well instead of around it as the original had been. To any creature traveling the old track, this would be the route.

It was still daylight but just barely. Satisfied, the hunter carried the ladder out of the woods toward the boundary that marked the Prescott property, leaving no tracks on the leaf carpet. It was left partway up toward the distant house to be retrieved on what would be the return trip. The hunter knew Nate Prescott couldn't afford a dog there that'd sound an alarm.

The next step was for this mysterious figure to head through the forest toward Montgomery Mabry's fields and his big house, almost a half-mile distant. Darkness settled as the lone figure moved quietly along, unhurried but with purpose. The moon rose, now a lopsided, reddened shape, past full.

Nearing the Mabry farm, the hunter slipped soundlessly to the gate of the cattle pen where Montgomery's prize bull was kept separate from the cows. It was perhaps the lawyer's most treasured possession, sire of his herd of Herefords, which generated a sizeable part of his income.

The hunting hounds were quiet up by the house as the gate swung open, and the slight breeze was from there and carried no scent. The hunter presented a handful of feed to the bull, which came forward eagerly. A quick snap, and a nose clamp with rope was attached, and the bull followed the figure out the gate. Turning, the hunter jerked hard on the wooden latch, springing it with a little sound.

The big animal left clear tracks across the field, despite the thick, browned grass and stubble; the figure leading it left none. The way led straight toward the Prescott holdings, and the bull plodded obediently after its leader, who offered additional handfuls of feed for the beast's eager tongue.

Reaching the forest at last, the bull was led through the trees in the dappled moonlight, toward the ruined cabin and the camouflaged well. Finally they reached it, and the hunter led the animal around the pitfall and on, following a route that veered well away from the Prescott place. Then, tying the bull to a tree, the hooded figure went back, brushed out the tracks circling the well, and scattered leaves over the ground. Even in the moonlight, it was obvious the animal had continued straight across the pitfall.

Satisfied again, the ghostly figure slipped back to the prize bull, untied him, and led him on at a right angle from the old homestead. They went on for nearly a mile, then to another farm field with its ragged fences halfway down where the bull was turned loose, the remaining feed left on the dead grass for him to scavenge as his leader slipped away.

Nearing midnight, the ladder was retrieved and carried quietly up to the first Prescott shed and hidden behind it. Then the shadowy figure faded into the scrub woods.

* * *

Montgomery Mabry was an early riser. He enjoyed tending to his own cattle each morning, letting them out to pasture or forking hay down from the loft, watering them, checking on their condition. He'd built up his showplace farm over many years and prided himself on keeping up with the latest beef production trends. And with that registered bull, he now had the best herd in the county, perhaps in the state.

And surprisingly, his son had lately taken a real interest in the cattle operation, so much so that the old man had eventually turned much of it over to him. It became one of the few things the two of them could enjoy doing together. Barry even began affecting a ten-gallon hat, cowboy boots, and rode an aging paint gelding out after the herd at every opportunity.

The first thing Montgomery noticed, tramping out toward the

nearest barn, was that the gate of the bull's pen was open, the wooden latch pried open on its bolt. The bull was gone, and he surmised it must've pushed against the gate hard enough to spring the latch.

Or, by God, somebody's stolen my bull. He saw the tracks clearly, pressed deep into the ground by the heavy animal through the brown grass. He searched for human tracks but found nothing. *Wouldn't show anyway, this heavy fescue.*

The lawyer stood back, sighted along the tracks he could see. They led straight toward the Prescott place, and alarm mounted inside him. *Could those white trash have stolen my bull? Surely not Nate, but that Andy? And oh my God, Charlie could be back. Just like him, after stealing my timber, to do something like this.* He looked at his watch.

"Dammit," he said aloud. "I've got to be in court in two hours: no time to track that bull. Well, Barry can find him. Must caution him against going to Prescotts', though, he might run into Charlie." *Should I call the sheriff on this? No, not just on a bull's getting out. Maybe smelled a cow in heat somewhere, took off on his own. Well, call my boy then, leave it up to him. Probably enjoy riding that horse out after him, round him up.*

"Son," he said into the phone. "Bull's got out, and I've got to be in court. Can you track him, bring him back?" He didn't want to suggest that the animal had possibly been stolen, knowing the immediate assumption Barry would make about the Millards.

"Oh, we were going up to Branson today. But sure, won't take long: we'll go later on. You see his tracks?"

"Clear, heavy as he is. Should be able to find him soon. None of our cows in heat now, and he probably got the wanderlust. Or some other lust." He grinned into the telephone, heard his son chuckle on the other end. "I'll be back by five or so." He hung up. Gathered his papers, went out to his car, the aging '47 Chrysler he still kept.

Barry told Christine to take her time getting ready for their trip, that he'd surely be back in a couple of hours. Still plenty time, since they planned to stay over, see at least one of the local music shows that were beginning to pop up at the mainly trout-fishing resort. Branson was also the first place north that wasn't alcohol-dry, and there was always something to do there.

She was okay with that and watched him drive the Hudson off on the mile toward his father's farm. *No problem: I've got my car if I have to go anywhere before he gets back.* And yes, the housekeeper was there to watch Giles.

Barry reached Montgomery's farm, got his saddle from the barn, and whistled to the paint. The old horse pricked his ears and came, eager for an outing. He liked to carry his rider across the fields and along the forest paths, a welcome change from the paddock.

The man cinched the saddle, taking his time as he reflected that all this—the horses, the house, farm, timberland—would be his after a few years. And he'd do a lot more with it than his cautious father had, for sure. *Just let me get my hands on this place; I'll make it a gold mine.* He swung up onto the horse, guided it over past the cattle pens, then along the line of the bull's distinctive tracks, out across the big fields. He saw no other impressions, and at first assumed, as his father had said, that the bull had just pushed his way out the gate.

Then, as it became evident the direction the animal's path had taken, toward the distant Prescott place, suspicion mounted inside the man. *Now what the hell? You don't suppose one of those thieving rednecks has stolen Dad's bull? Be just like that Charlie, if he's back, to do that out of spite. And nobody's tracks would show on this fescue stubble. Damn, have we been robbed again? Maybe should've brought a gun with me.*

Well, go on, see where this leads. If it is *to their place, I can come back, get firepower.* The thought of another confrontation, this time with Charlie, gave him a thrill. *Settle this once and for all. And open the way for another shot at that bitch Andy. Boy will be in school, and chances the old man's around this time about zero. Or maybe he will be there: get two birds at once, like Dad's always bragging.*

The tracks led into the woods, still visible where the hooves had cut the fallen leaves. Eventually they led onto the old trail that had been the wagon road to the settler's cabin. Here the ground was harder, from those long-ago iron-shod wheels and the washing away of the soil to leave stony ground in the old ruts. Several times Barry had to dismount, scrutinize the ground closely where leaves had obscured the tracks, and there were stretches where they didn't show at all.

This made him feel like a Western cowboy, trailing lost stock, and, well, he guessed that was really what he was doing. He got a mental picture of himself, broad-brimmed hat, boots and all, riding some imaginary range on the frontier a hundred years before.

Fallen trees had opened this forest to sunlight, and undergrowth had sprung up, making it difficult for the horse to follow the trail. Barry dismounted, tied him to a tree, went one careful step at a time, the brush tearing at his suede coat. The worst were the greenbriers, called locally *sawbriers*, that could rip a man's arm deep, like a natural version of barbed wire.

He soon saw the tracks did not always follow the old trace. The bull appeared to have wandered this way and that, for some reason. *Surely not been stolen then, or the thief would've wanted to get away, quick, straight line. Or maybe that thief Charlie just wanted to make it seem like that. He's not smart at all, but he's sly, always figuring a way to cut corners, get away with stuff anybody else'd be caught at.*

Finally the bull's trail appeared to go back to the old road, where he had to circle, look closer. Then the hoofprints veered off the trace onto softer ground again, this time around a big fallen limb. He followed, still on foot, looking ahead. He saw the old chimney remains and figured the bull would follow the old road where it was clearer now, not toward the Prescott place but to the next farm where there were more cattle. *Yeah, well, just goin' after company then, I guess. So maybe Millard didn't steal him. Might not even be around, but that Andy's capable of it: probably desperate now, got her just deserts for the way she treated me.*

He thought he caught a glimpse of movement behind the ruined chimney. But before that could really register, the earth beneath him suddenly gave way, and Barry Mabry plunged, amid a shower of twigs and broken branches, screaming in shock.

Chapter Seven

The news spread fast. By the next afternoon, hardly anyone in Stark Township was unaware of Barry Mabry's grisly death.

Charlie had been to the village to see about trading for a mule the day before, which was before anyone knew about it. But back home, passersby had stopped and excitedly reported bits of the tragedy to him.

"Plumb stuck through," he told his sister later. "Fell in that ole well at th' settler's cabin, onto some stakes somebody'd set up down there. Must've covered th' place up, or maybe he got pushed in. Somethin' weird." He shook his head in disbelief.

Andy was horrified. *What an awful way to die; nobody deserved that, even if he was a pervert. Of course we're only hearing gossip: wait till the facts get straightened out. But this is barbaric.*

Nate, home from school, and Elijah were at the hog pen dispensing corn, talking about how this murder would change things.

"They's gonna come after us," the old man predicted. "I reckon that Barry hadda lotta enemies, but y'can bet ole Montgom'ry'll git th' law on us fust." He turned gloomy eyes toward the distant spring and the Mabry land beyond it.

"Why us, Granpa? And couldn't it have been an accident?"

"No acc'dent, naw. Don't nobody set up sich as that nowadays t'git deer er even a stray black bear. Somebody after Barry, fer shore. Thet about th' bull gittin' out, thet wuz t'git th' feller to foller it, lead him rat to thet ole well. An' we're th' likeliest ones th' law'll come after, bein's we busted him up b'fore."

* * *

Montgomery Mabry had received the news with a shock that threatened to fell him. *My boy. My only boy, killed like a wild animal. Somebody will pay, and pay in blood. Horrible way to die, and it will be avenged. My boy…*

Christine Mabry was stunned also, the realization coming over her face when the sheriff told her the bad news. She seemed at first not to comprehend, then gradually her eyes focused, and the horror of it registered. *Barry gone? My husband gone? Murdered? Who…what… Oh, my God!* She turned, caught up her young son, hugged him to her fiercely. *What'll become of us?*

* * *

The next morning the Prescott house was visited by Sheriff Burgess and a deputy named Cale Wilcox. It was just after breakfast, with Nate gone to catch the school bus and Andy washing the dishes in a battered pan. The two men had not gone out yet to cut firewood, were drinking coffee Charlie'd brought with him, with feet to the stove, going over yet again the scant information they'd heard.

"Mornin', folks," Burgess greeted after being invited in. "Guess you've heard about Barry: everybody seems to've." He took an indicated chair, as did the deputy, who looked around, fixed his eyes on Andy. *Dunno if what they're sayin' 'bout her's true lately, but that little girl's grown up to be one fine-lookin' woman. No, she was fine-lookin' back in school.* For her part, Andy vaguely remembered this man from years ago. She managed a smile of greeting to them both.

"Heard the gossip is all." Charlie moved reflexively aside so he could see both lawmen better. "Prob'ly about twenty percent true, lak always."

"Well, the gist of it is that the Mabry bull got out sometime before morning yesterday and Barry tracked him to the old settler's cabin. Fell down the old well onto sharpened wood spikes. Couple of them went right through him, so of course he's dead. Wife sent a neighbor looking for him when he didn't come home, knew he'd gone after the bull. Man found his horse tied to a tree, then finally came to the well. Called it in. Christine's about gone crazy over it. Bull was at another farm, in with their cows."

"Well, three folks stopped by, told us three very different stories," Andy said. "But anyway you look at it, that's a terrible way for anybody to die."

"Sure is, and somebody had to plan it all out: how to get him there first. That is, if he was even the target, which he probably was. Then rig that pitfall so he couldn't see it. Must've taken awhile to disguise the hole, put all those stakes down in there.

"What scares me is that anybody could've stumbled into that trap: some hunter, even a kid out in the woods. Or of course, the bull itself, if somebody wanted to get at the Mabrys that way. Could've just shot it, though. Unless the killer did use him to lure Barry there."

He paused, looked from one face to the other. Elijah Prescott looked grim, but that was his normal expression. Charlie's head was cocked sideways, as if waiting for more information. Andy just looked sorrowful. The sheriff couldn't read anything into any of their faces.

"Well, bad news all 'round," Charlie finally said. "Old Barry was a little crazy, way he's bin comin' after us, but lak Andy sez, don't nobody wanta end up thataway. Got enny clues to who dunnit?"

"Working on that. Got an expert tracker up from state police in Little Rock, try to see if there was somebody got the bull out, led him. Tracks hard to see on that fescue, but everybody makes a mistake sooner or later." He expected some reaction to this, if indeed the guilty person were one of these. He didn't get it.

"Wal, y'd shorely find a track er two at thet well, Hal," Elijah pointed out. "Feller hadda spend rat much time thar. Now, one th' neighbors said seemed lak it happened fust thaing in th' mawnin', so reckon whoever done it worked at night? Be hard t' wipe out ever'thaing in th' dark." His mind was working.

"Of course it could've been laid out the evening before, late, I guess, but with this being such a complicated operation, the killer must've been really careful: tracks, any trace at all, any connection to him."

"Well, Hal," Andy spoke up. "You're not here just to tell us about it: I know we're suspects with the bad blood between us and him. If you can find out when it must've happened, we can tell you where we were. Just ask us." There was no challenge in her eyes, no defiance: she knew Hal Burgess was a fair man.

"I'm afraid Barry may have had other enemies, Andy, but yes, we'll have to question you all and everybody who might've had a gripe or even a connection. Montgomery Mabry's fit to be tied over this, understandably, but it's not just him. The newspapers all over have gotten wind of it, and Everett County's big news on account of it. I'll get pressure from the governor even before it's over, so anything you all might've seen—car alongside the road, somebody walking or riding by, anything that could help—I'd appreciate it.

"And much as I hate it, we'll even have to question Nate. Gone to school, I guess?"

"Yes. Gets home around four-thirty. Charlie's been doing his chores for him since he's been back, or Elijah has. You must know, Hal, we're looking at a hard winter here. Charlie hasn't been able to find mules or wagon we can buy, and of course all our hay's gone in that fire."

"I know it, and I wish I could help, someway. But this murder's going to have me going night and day till we catch whoever did it. Well, I guess we better get started whether I like it or not. Charlie, where were you, last couple days?"

"Wal, y'prob'ly know I been back few weeks, after gittin' a letter f'm Nate, tellin' me what all Barry done. I cut a trail back home, jist in case I'se needed, y'know. An' just so you know, I don't think he come here that time t'see me atall, Hal: was after Andy. Ain't never fergot bein' put in his place, that'n.

"Been tryin' t'figger a trade fer at least one mule, but don't wanta give up m'car jist yit. Will, though, if we hafta have th' cash. But y'said last couple days. Wal, me an' Elijah, we been cuttin' farwood steady, now it's got colder. Did go t'town day 'fore yestiddy, tryin' t'find some sorta trade er work. Figgered somebody'd need some he'p, y'know, whar I c'd pick up few dollars. Didn't work out, so we cut wood yestiddy. Slow goin' thet ole crosscut saw, but pore folks got pore ways."

"Who'd you talk to in town?"

"Wal, old Matt Kindridge, fer one. Thought he might need a hand, them horses an' all. Allus gits somebody t'muck out th' barn, y'know, but he done hired some kid. Then…lessee, saw Miz Ed Carson, thought mebbe she'd need a hand, her a widder an' all. Then there was…"

"Okay, easy enough to check that. Not that I doubt you, Charlie, but I'm gonna have to answer to folks up the line, you know. Andy, you can verify Charlie's statement, too, of course."

"Yes, I've put him to work whenever I can catch him, Hal. And of course Elijah's been here all along, been a lot of help."

"All right; I'm satisfied, but like I said, I should look around some, just so I can say I did. Mind if Deputy Wilcox and I just take a turn around?"

"Help yourself. Barn's gone, of course, but sure, go ahead."

Outside, Burgess directed Wilcox to check the sheds, see if he saw anything suspicious.

"Like what, Sheriff? Dunno what to look for."

"Oh, I don't know. Won't be any extra sharpened stakes for sure, but you might just measure some of Charlie's boot tracks, and I guess Elijah's, too—real stretch, that—just in case the tracker comes up with anything to compare with."

"Okay. What about Andy's? Though I doubt she was in on anything. Can't afford to count her out, the big boys come down on us."

"Sure, okay. Guess I've been thinking too small, here. Go ahead."

Wilcox headed for the sheds, and Burgess walked out to the first place he knew Dave Prescott had logged, the steepest part of which had unfortunately grown up in sprouts and undergrowth later. The killer stakes had been small red oak, and in the years since the cutting, they'd be about the right size. Most of Mabry's land was in big timber.

He didn't expect to find freshly cut green top wood that wouldn't burn in the stove to hide it, but there just might be a suspicious stump or two. He took his time, threading his way around and through underbrush, looking for small branches and maybe a sapling top left from such a cutting.

The flatter places Dave had meant to plant and had actually put in some fescue, so there wasn't much new tree growth to see. And no, he didn't find anything incriminating.

He headed back, hearing the rhythmic strokes of the crosscut saw as Charlie and Elijah cut a dead oak into stovewood blocks. He marveled at the old man's ability to balance himself, partly on the saw he was pulling, and do this job. *That man'll do whatever it takes to make it, always has. Andy's got good help there, with Charlie apt to drift off anytime he feels like it.*

Wilcox signaled to the sheriff from behind the farthest shed from the house. He had something, or thought he did. Hal strode over, a question on his face.

"Ladder here, Hal. Got mud on th' bottom end. Now whatta you s'pose they been usin' it for? House is on high ground, no mud up there, if they were patchin' the roof or somethin'." He had an expression that was both puzzled and a touch triumphant, obviously putting things together in his mind.

The sight of the mud jolted Burgess. Ladder was just about long enough to have reached the bottom of that old well. Handmade, old but solid. Hickory, so it was tough, and the uprights had been made narrow: lighter to handle. *Not hard to carry, even from as far as the old settler's place. Damn, this could be the break we need, and right here, not hidden at all. Which doesn't make much sense: almost too easy to find.*

"We'll take it with us, Cale. Tie it to the top of the Ford: some rope in the trunk, I think. But first, bring it up to the house: somebody's got some explaining to do."

They stopped at the firewood operation first, backtracking to the near woods. Charlie and Elijah were bent low, just completing a cut through the big log section.

"Got something we need to ask about, men," Burgess told them. "This your ladder?"

Charlie straightened, as did Elijah, who caught a sapling for support, now that the saw wasn't solidly in the cut. Both of them looked at the ladder, and both looked puzzled. *Could Charlie be that good an actor? Lies easier'n telling the truth, though. Doubt if Elijah could carry this thing that far and back…*

"Not ours, Hal," Charlie shook his head. We got one 'bout that size, one Dave put together, up b'hind th' house where Nate an' me was nailin' on a few shingles blowed off. But that thing don't b'long here: sorta lightweight. Where'd y'git it?"

"Behind that far shed. Didn't find any tracks there, and doesn't look like this mud's from around here. And it's about long enough to get somebody down into that well, Charlie, where there is mud." It wasn't an accusation, but it might as well have been. "Got any idea whose it might be?"

"Don't. Don't atall. Yours, Elijah? You bring it frum your place?"

"Didn't, and couldn't of. Andy an' Nate got a ride up t' he'p me move jist whut little I got, an' no, I ain't clumb a ladder since I wuz a kid."

"Oh, of course not," Burgess said hastily. "Why don't we just go up, check on that other ladder now. You gotta know, Charlie, this looks really suspicious: kind of thing that could be really important in this case."

"I reckon. An' somebody's put thet thing here, Hal; ain't mine, never seen it, an' thet just leaves whoever done it pointin' a finger at us." He was growing angry at this realization. Somebody'd… Wilcox moved his hand to his holstered revolver. *If he tries anything…*

But Charlie knew better than to turn this into a fight. *Cards stacked agin' me; somebody's put this on me, an' I gotta go slow, figger whut t'do.* He led the way up and around the house, where his late brother-in-law's wooden ladder still leaned against the roof overhang. It was a little heavier and of course had no mud on it. Burgess examined, compared it.

"Well, on the surface of it, looks like it's somebody else's ladder, all right. But it *was* here and that looks bad, Charlie. In fact, it'll be just what the district attorney will use in court against you. That and the fact that you and Barry were enemies. And your reputation shouldn't make any difference, but you know it will. Now, before we get really serious here, try hard to think of anybody else who'd kill Barry and plant that ladder here, put the blame on you folks."

Andy had come outside, hearing their voices, and saw the muddy ladder. She knew immediately what it meant.

"Hal, where did you get that?"

"Afraid it was down behind that last shed, Andy. Know anything about that?" He tried to keep it from sounding like an accusation.

"No. You see ours there. That one's about the same length, so of course we wouldn't have two that much alike." She looked at her brother. *Could he have found another ladder, easier to carry, and killed Barry? No, I won't believe that. And why would he leave it out where anybody could find it? No.*

"So," she continued, her mind working, "somebody else put it there, and there could be only one reason for that: to frame us."

"Or mebbe th' feller jis' shoved it b'hind thet shed, fust place he come on, t'git rid of it," Elijah speculated.

"He could have ditched it anywhere, even left it near the well," Burgess pointed out. "If it doesn't belong here, it was put here. But who'd have done that? That's what we have to find out. Any ideas yet, Charlie?"

"Wal, I'd say Barry Mabry hadda buncha enemies, way he wuz allus lordin' it over ever'body, clear on back t' school days. But kill him thataway? Thet's more 'n ennybody d'serves. There's gotta be somethin' big b'hind this whole thing, Hal. Maybe hooked up with some sorta crime thing, like we hear about?"

"Not likely, here out of the way like we are. Now, people kill other people for just a few things: money first, and that doesn't figure here. Or revenge, which is a lot more likely. Or to protect themselves or others, and if that was the case, it'd go lighter on whoever did it. *Yeah, plant that idea, let it work.*

"This was thought out carefully, I'd say; not just chance it was Barry who fell in that trap, which means the killer *did* let that bull out, knowing he'd be the one to go after it. Montgomery was due in court that morning and not everybody knew that, knew he wouldn't be the one. Of course, there was the chance that a hunter, someone lost, or a stranger would fall in, so I'm thinking the killer may have hidden, watched, maybe to warn anyone else away. What do you all think?"

Sharing his speculations with these people who were indeed prime suspects wasn't the way a lawman was supposed to proceed, but Burgess had a purpose: maybe one of them would let something slip, incriminate himself. *Or, omigod* her*self; can't let myself rule Andy out here. She's maybe the likeliest, after what Barry did to her.*

He didn't like that thought.

"Wal, if he laid th' trap that night, then went right off an' got th' bull 'fore ennybody'd be up an' about, long chance fer 'nuther feller t' stumble on th' well," Charlie reasoned. "But I been thinkin', Hal, 'bout other folks as would've had it in fer Barry. Way I heard it, he was th' one th' ole man put up to collectin' rent an' all, them houses on th' other places they owned. An' jist about ever'thing else th' ole man didn't wanna do fer hisself. I'm sayin', couldn't somebody carry a grudge, 'count of th' boy comin' down on 'em? Lak mebbe th'owin' 'em offa the place?"

"Possible, but again, that's a little strong. People who don't pay their rent or trash a place, get thrown out, usually get over it, just go somewhere else, do it again. Now, if maybe Barry assaulted another woman, maybe somebody's daughter, that'd be more in line with this. Know of any other things like that he'd done?"

"I wouldn't put that kind of lowdown attack past him," Andy responded, a glint in her eye. "But I haven't heard of anything like that in the time I've been back, and I don't get included in the general gossip. Elijah, you hear things from the folks at your church?"

"Naw. They's talk a foot deep 'round thar, 'bout ever'thaing frum whut sours milk t' who's done run off. But 'cept fer goin' on 'bout how th' boy's wife Christine run him lak a toy train, I ain't heered a thaing."

"Now that's somethin'd point t' Barry's maybe jumpin' th' traces with 'nother woman, I'd say," Charlie volunteered. "She puts him in th' doghouse, he mebbe run off t' the cathouse. Sorry, Sis." He wasn't sorry, of course.

"How'd that come back on him, though?" Deputy Wilcox joined in the speculation. "Oh, like you said, maybe somebody's daughter. Or wife, maybe? I know that goes on, always has."

"Again, possible. We'll look into that, certainly. But I have to tell you all, on the surface of it, you're the first people everybody will look at here. Now, I'm not arresting any of you, mostly because the ladder thing just doesn't fit, and I want to talk to Nate soon's I can, but don't even think about leaving, or that'll label you guilty. Do I have your word you'll stay put?" He fixed Charlie with a stern eye, then Elijah, and even Andy.

"Ain't got no place t' go," the old man stated the obvious.

"Neither d' I," Charlie said.

"Hal, I think you know my place is here with Nate, and even if I did murder Barry, which I've considered doing, I can't leave my nephew alone. Which, of course, would be the outcome if I'd done it and got jailed. Yes, we'll all be right here; count on it."

"All right. But I'm going to make myself unpopular, Charlie, and take the distributor rotor out of your car. Or I could leave Deputy Wilcox here, but I need him. And cuss me if you want to, but not arresting you on suspicion will put me in a bad light already, understand?"

"Oh, I know you gotta do whut y' gotta do, Hal. Was t' other way 'round, I'd chain you to a tree."

There was an almost tension-relieving laugh all around. Burgess and Wilcox took their leave after the sheriff told them he'd be back to talk to Nate later in the day. The incriminating ladder rubbed the already scraped Ford, tied onto its top, the muddy end wrapped in cloth.

"You got somethin' in mind, Hal," Wilcox probed as they drove the gravel road toward town. "Leavin' it wide open so maybe Charlie could run."

"Maybe. He'll need a little time to figure a way out without the car, though, and you're gonna bring your car back, keep watch from somewhere. He does run, we'll know, and we've got our man. And that'll cover us if—no, *when*—the higher-ups come after me for not taking him in."

"Well, I knew there was a reason you're th' boss an' I just work for you."

Chapter Eight

"We's under th' gun, folks," Charlie declared. "Don't matter what else Hal turns up, that ladder'll git me hung." He was casting about for a way out.

"Not necessarily: you didn't do it, and I don't think Hal believes you did. I'm sure he'll find out the real killer, and it'll all blow over." Andy wasn't as optimistic as she sounded. *Here it all comes again. Is this family under a black cloud? First I go off the rails with Crazy Cam, then Dave and Becca die, then Barry's assault, then the barn, his death, and now we're headed for jail? Or worse?*

"Naw, Andy, Charlie's right: law allus wants t' settle sich as this quick, an' it's done all set up agin' us. I'd say run, but we ain't got a way to." The old man shook his head in resignation.

"You mean that? Run when we haven't done anything wrong? When you *didn't* kill that scum, which he deserved, when Charlie *didn't* go after him, when all we did was cut a few trees that belonged to *us?*"

"Won't matter none. Hal, he won't come down on us s' much, but he's gotta bunch he hasta answer to, an' they'll want this took keer of fast, an' thet means us, one way er t' other." The old man stared sadly out a window.

And their mood hadn't lifted by the time Nate came home, not that long before dark. He could see at a glance that something was troubling his family.

"Sheriff's been by," Andy informed him, "and found a ladder with mud on it down behind the far shed. Thinks it was used to set that trap for Barry, and we think somebody's planted it here to point to us."

"Why, that's crazy. We didn't do that! What'd he say?"

"Wal," his grandfather answered, "he don't really seem to b'lieve enny've us done it, bein's we already got a ladder 'bout th' same size, an' bein's it warn't even hid good. But lak I'se sayin' awhile ago, Hal, he's got them 'bove him pushin' him, an' I'm 'fraid th' law's gonna come down on us hard."

Nate took this in. He'd known, of course, that the feud with the Mabrys placed the family directly in the spotlight as suspects, but the fantastic circumstances, the weird way Barry had died, had made it all seem unreal, not a direct threat. Now stark reality did set in.

"Hal wants t'talk t' you, too," Charlie told him. "Guess he's gotta cover ever' poss'bility. Boils down to all of us s'spected, fer sure." He gazed gloomily at the crackling stove.

Just then the sheriff's Ford drove up, and Andy went to open the door for him and Wilcox. The ladder was no doubt secure somewhere. *Of course they couldn't take the chance we'd make that thing disappear. Hal's no fool.*

"Evenin', Nate. Just gotta ask you a few questions; be able to say I didn't leave anybody out." Burgess took a chair but Wilcox stood near the door, watching Charlie.

"Sure, Mr. Burgess, but I don't know what I can tell you." He turned his palms up.

"First thing would be whether you might've heard or seen anybody around, maybe doing your chores down at the sheds, or out in the woods, or going across your fields? I'm thinking Barry's killer planted that ladder to incriminate you all, and we really need to know if *anybody* else's been poking around."

"Nossir, I don't remember seeing anybody. We're off the road, y'know, even though folks stopped by, told us about it, so anybody else around close would be sorta out of place, y' know. I'd remember." He was aware he'd said 'y' know' twice, nervously. Would that make him a suspect?

"All right. Now we've seen the ladder your dad made, and I can't figure you folks having two of them about the same size; doesn't make sense. But like I've told the others, finding it here with mud on it that matches what's in the bottom of that well has to look to anybody else like somebody here's the killer." He watched the boy's face.

"So if you don't find anybody else with maybe a grudge against Barry, we're the prime suspects, like they say in the crime novels, right?"

"Afraid that's the way the DA will see it, with the…things that've happened with him here before. Now I'll say I'm leaning hard toward somebody putting the blame on you people: ladder just wasn't hidden, and it'd have been really dumb for any of you to leave it down there. I just need all the help I can get to find out the real killer."

"Yessir. Well, looks to me like whoever did it had a real big grudge against Barry. Okay, it looks bad for us, but none of us did it, so who else would go after him like that?"

"That's what we're looking for. And we'll keep looking, but I have to tell you all, I won't be able to avoid an arrest with the pressure on me. Everybody's heard about it now, and I'll have to push ahead with any and all suspects." He looked apologetically at Andy.

"You'll take us all to jail?"

"No, and right now there's not enough cause for singling out any one of you, and maybe there won't ever be, but I want you to know the facts." He rose, put on his hat. "So I'll leave it at that for now, but you all ask around, keep your eyes open." The two lawmen took their leave. Deputy Wilcox hadn't said a word, Andy noted, but she'd seen his eyes on her more than once. And now she remembered him better: the shy boy back in high school who'd sort of followed her around.

"Wow," Nate breathed. "We're *all* suspects? Even you, Aunt Andy? Me?"

"Afraid so, Nate. Charlie's the one they'll go after, just because the folks around here have always talked about him. Well, me too, I guess. So maybe the two of us will be sort of the targets they'll try to hang this on. And we were just discussing whether we'd ever get a fair trial, with Mabry's connections."

"And you bein' th' one he come after," Charlie told her, "they'll think either you got your r'venge on him, or I took up for you: got to him 'fore he could do worse. 'Spite of th' way that trial went, folks don't trust neither of us."

"So what's to do, then?" Nate knew they couldn't just wait for the axe to fall.

"I say run," Charlie declared. "Dis'pear to somewheres they cain't never find us, take new names, start over way away from here." For him that was the only way out.

"I'm not in favor of that," Andy objected. "First of all, that'd make us look guilty. Second, they'd find us. Why, the four of us showing up somewhere, people there would talk, word get around, and the police would surely have pictures of us up: wanted killers." That just wasn't the way, in her judgment. "But what do you think, Elijah?"

"Wal, I bin kickin' it 'round ever since thet ladder thaing. An' I gotta 'gree with Charlie: we ain't got a chancet, Andy. We stay, I'm shore Charlie er even you, will end up in jail er wuss. Th' law, it ain't gonna stop till somebody's done got put away. Th' cops, thet's jist thar way." He shook his wizened head.

"All right then. Nate, this is your place. You'd stand to lose the most if we even *could* get away, go into hiding the way Charlie says. Could you do that? It's all you have. And I don't think you or Elijah would really be the suspects in this."

"Now you just wait a minnit, sis. Why couldn't Nate here, since he was so close t' what Barry done to you, an' then that other stuff, why wouldn't they think he could've done it, same's me or you? Protectin' you?"

"I've thought of that, too," Nate answered him. "I think I'm just as likely to be charged as any of us. But back to what you asked me, Aunt Andy: you've always said you wanted me to get an education, move up to some better life. Now, I don't want to leave here; this is home. Mom and Daddy, they worked hard to pay for this place, and it was for me—I wasn't big enough to help much—and yes, it means a lot to me, what all we've planned for it.

"But that doesn't matter if I lose it anyway and maybe go to jail for something I didn't do. And I just now realized I couldn't even work to send money to keep the taxes up, or they'd find me—us. I'm afraid, from what you all have said, and from what I see, I will lose the place, one way or another.

"So I'm thinking maybe you're right, Uncle Charlie, Granpa. But really, where could we go? And how? No money, and we couldn't take your car. They'll be watching us like hawks for just that: running." There didn't seem to be a way out.

"Well, I'd say we got a day er two maybe," Charlie speculated. "Gotta be a way; people dis'pear all th' time. I heard there's thousands of unsolved mys'tries, folks jist vanished, never heard of agin. I say we all put our heads on it, figger a way, then jist do it. We c'n land on our feet anywheres. I done it a lotta times."

"We're broke, Charlie," his sister reminded him. "Got *nothing*, and no way to get anything. And I'm not giving up on Hal; he'll find out who did this, and we'll be okay."

"Whut if'n he don't?" The old man's eyes held no hope.

"Well, he's not arresting any of us yet. I say wait and see."

"Won't work, Sis. Ever' day passes he don't nail th' real killer, we're th' ones they'll look harder at. Now's th' only time we got to git."

"Okay, Uncle Charlie, how do we do it?"

"Been studyin' on it all along and right hard since t'day. First thing, we gotta strike out. Now. Hal, he's done took m'car outta th' picture, an' it'd be too easy t' spot anyway. So we jist head off up th' mountin while it's dark, put as many miles 'tween us an' here as we can. Don't think anybody'd miss us fer a day er two 'cause we don't git comp'ny anyway. Then we git just whatever rides we can to as far as we can git."

"Four of us? That's ridiculous, Charlie. Daylight, everybody'd see us, remember us. Four people hitchhiking? Make sense, here." Andy shook her head.

She was right, Nate saw, and really, so did the others. It was well enough that Charlie was also right. Now was the time to disappear if that was the only option, but so far nobody had an idea how. Suggestions continued however, late into the night.

"I could slip off, git us a distrib'tor rotor fer my car outta a junk-yard, an' we could be on our way," Charlie proposed. "Mebbe by dark t'morrow."

"I already told you, they'd have us in a flash, Uncle Charlie. Car'd be th' easiest to spot."

"Okay then, maybe paint it 'nother color? They got them spray cans now, y'know?"

"Charlie, we all know there'll be a deputy parked out at the road. Hal Burgess didn't just leave us here, trusting us to stay put." His sister was shaking her head.

"Hmm, yer right. But maybe I could slip off afoot, make us a trade fer somethin' older, git th' buyer t' come out, maybe git a few dollars boot?" His mind was racing from one dead end to another. *Somethin' hasta work, here: never been stopped clean b'fore.*

"Sight unseen trade for your car? That's not even a possibility," Andy pointed out. "You could talk most folks into just about anything, Charlie, but a used car dealer? They get rich by being slicker than everybody else."

"Wal," the old man spoke up. "It's gittin' late. An' one thaing we ain't done, we ain't prayed 'bout this mess we's in. Let's us jist bow our heads 'n ast th' Lord t' show us th' way." He looked out of his red-rimmed eyes from one to another of them. They nodded.

"Lord, reckon Yore th' only way outta this'n. Whatever we done, er ain't done, we're astin' fer You t' guide us in th' way You want us t' go. Fergive us, Lord, fer th' things all of us has done an' th' times we've done fergot You. We need You bad this time, Lord, so please show us th' way t' do whut You want. Amen."

They went to bed then, all with thoughts, ideas, fruitless speculation rampaging inside their heads. There didn't seem to be a way out of this, except maybe Elijah's way, to trust God, but none of the others really believed He would intervene. Seemed nobody else ever had, for the Millards or the Prescotts.

The old saying, "Them as has, gits" echoed in Nate's mind as it had many times before: poor folks just always got trampled in this life. *Well, maybe not. Barry had everything, and somebody made sure he didn't just keep on with his meanness. Does that mean the killer was maybe doing God's work? Not what the Bible says.*

Elijah tried to hush his worries and let God handle them, as he'd advised, as he'd prayed for. He did believe the Creator would take care of this family, but he'd had enough experience to know that deity would do so in His own good time. *Looks like we sorta need it now, Lord.*

Andy had the illusion that a giant hand was closing around them. She'd had this feeling before when it seemed there was no way out of her hopeless marriage to Cam Henry. She'd been trapped. Divorce had been a last resort. *Unless I'd shot him.* And here it was again: events ballooning out of control, her little family—what was left of it—threatened, and nothing but crazy schemes that wouldn't work.

It came to Charlie around midnight, after he'd tried unsuccessfully to sleep. *I'm th' one they're after. If I was gone, they'd be sure I was th' killer, and yeah, they'd stop lookin'. Andy an' Nate would be safe, an' so'd Elijah.*

So, I gotta be gone.

He dressed quietly, pushed the door open a crack, listened, looked in on his sleeping sister a last time, then did the same with Nate. He could hear Elijah's snoring from the back room as he slipped downstairs. *Miss 'em, all of 'em. But best thing I can do is get outta their lives.*

He took only what he could stuff into his coat pockets, along with three biscuits left from supper. He had four dollars in the world. They could get the part for the car some way, drive it or sell it. He found the title to it, scribbled his name on it by the faint light from a window. Yeah, they'd make it through the winter like they always had. He wasn't so sure about his own chances. He closed the door soundlessly behind him.

Charlie knew most folks on the run headed for Detroit or California. Or in his case, maybe down to Little Rock, where people knew he'd often gone. He also knew he had little time, was on foot, and had to beat any pictures of him that might be posted on the walls of every public place in the state. And a lot of other states.

He headed up the hill through the woods toward Elijah's distant old cabin, intent on circling it and striking the highway that wound east/west across northern Arkansas toward the Mississippi River. With any luck, he could catch a ride with a trucker going that way, away from where the law would expect him to run.

* * *

Andy woke Nate next morning to get him off to school. Elijah was already up, had the cookstove going and the chill off the air in the kitchen. He had the short sleep of old men, balanced usually by a nap after the noonday meal. Since Charlie had been home, the two of them had worked together, which had kept Andy from worrying overmuch about the minister's losing his balance out alone, getting hurt.

Not seeing Charlie anywhere, she knocked on his door, but there was no answer. She pushed it open and instantly knew he'd left them. *Just like him: do something even if it's wrong. Now, could that really mean he killed Barry? No, I won't believe that.*

Then she noticed a note he'd left for her:

"Dear Sis: I've decided the best thing for the family is for me to leave out. I've signed the title to my car over, and you can keep it or sell it, maybe trade it for mules and a wagon. I won't be coming back ever, I guess. Love, Charlie."

She hurried downstairs to tell the others.

"Gone on foot. An' he'll git away clean, I'd wager," Elijah said. "But th' law, they's gonna be all over ever'body 'n' everywhar, tryin' t' find thet boy." He did not seem overly troubled.

"So," Nate asked, "this'll make the sheriff sure he's the killer, Granpa. You don't believe that, do you?"

"Naw, I don't, boy. But thaink about it: he's done run off, an' thet'll do jist lak you said: make 'em thaink he's th' one done it. An' shore, oncet they figger thet, they'se gonna do two thaings. Fust one is, they'll let th' rest of us 'lone, which'll be jist whut yore uncle meant t'happen. Thet's th' good part. But then they'll stop lookin' fer who really done it, an' thet's th' bad part."

"I hadn't gotten that far, Elijah," Andy admitted. "And I was guilty of thinking he was just saving his hide: knew I didn't want us to run so he just left. Now I see what he's done for us. Only that means he's gone for good, can't ever get in touch with us."

"Unless Sheriff Hal really does find out who killed Barry," Nate pointed out. "But how'd Uncle Charlie ever know if he can't reach us?"

"Wal, boy, lak I said, ain't no lawman gonna try too hard t'git th' one done it, now. An' shore, it'll th'ow a bad light on us, bein' Charlie's family, but reckon we c'n stand thet. Whut folks thainks don't bother me th' way it usta."

"That's right: people talk about me since my divorce like I've got the plague, so it won't make much difference. Oh, I just wish they'd all leave us alone, let us be."

"Hope t'won't come down hard on you, Nate, 'mongst them young uns in school an' all. Kids c'n be meaner'n growed-ups. Jist don'tcha let it git to you bad. Gotta jist keep on keepin' on. We'll git th'u it all right, Lord willin'."

Nate didn't see why the other teenagers would blame him for what they thought his uncle had done. The ones he'd talked to were about evenly divided on their opinions of the outcome of the trial. And surely, since the Mabrys had lost that one, this shouldn't make things worse. Or so he imagined, in his 14-year-old naivete.

He was troubled mostly by the realization that his uncle could never come back, that he'd never see him again. Oh, they'd get by here, just barely. And yes, Charlie's car was still here. They could come and go if they could buy gas at 28 cents a gallon. *No, be best to sell the car, get another team, wagon. Maybe one with rubber tires. Car oughta be worth a couple-three hundred. Well, we can talk about that when we got time. Right now I need to go catch that bus…*

* * *

Cale Wilcox had been spelled by another deputy at his lookout post about the time Charlie had slipped away. He'd gone home to sleep, then reported in to Hal Burgess next morning.

"Nobody came or went, boss. Heard from Jim?"

"No, all quiet when I sent his relief. I think Charlie and the others will stay, hope we find the real killer. Don't see how they can run, even if one or more of them are guilty."

"And you don't think Charlie did it, sounds like."

"He's got an alibi, but of course so far it's mostly only the family that can verify it. We've found folks who saw him in town, but the problem is we don't know when the trap was set. To be truthful, Cale, I just don't know who did it. Hadn't thought Charlie was sharp enough to plan it out that way, and the ladder thing looks like a frame-up. But he's wiggled his way out of trouble so many times, he could've done it. Think about it: if your sister'd been attacked like Andy was, you'd be boiling, right?"

"Well, yes, but I don't think I'd go kill th' man. Maybe beat hell outta him, cripple him up some. And I don't think th' average man would do that either, even 'round here where we both know tempers get hotter'n they oughta."

"Exactly. And I just don't think Nate would do it. Grisly business, and the boy's never shown a nasty side. I guess he could've gone over the edge after what happened, sort of a temporary out-of-control thing, but no, that just won't wash. And physically, Elijah's almost an impossibility."

"So what about Andy? You leaving her out? Seems she'd have th' strongest motive." He felt he had to ask this, as part of his job, despite the way he, too, felt about her. And there was more to that feeling than the young deputy let his boss or anyone else know.

"Not really. If she'd been a mean woman, she'd have countersued Mabry; their lawyer wanted her to, and Mabry's money would've looked good. She just wanted it over with is the way I see it. Could be wrong, of course, and no, I won't rule anybody out till we find out more. And on that, the tracker hasn't found a single footprint: the killer was good, I think better than Charlie or his folks."

"Maybe so. Any progress on th' other—th' idea Barry might've got into hot water with 'nother man's wife or daughter? I know he's married to that knockout blonde, but I hear she ruled th' roost, maybe not a real happy home, and th' man could've strayed onto strange territory."

"Nothing so far. Christine is certain her man didn't slip around, but of course she wouldn't know unless he was really careless. And if he was, we should have found out about it by now. No, she seems devastated by Barry's death, sure Charlie Millard did it, or even Andy. And Montgomery's high on the woman, says she's the best thing ever happened for Barry."

"So we got nothin' real, except that ladder an' our s'spicions. I've known about Charlie, how he's been in some sorta trouble all his life. Nothin' that bad, but like you said, his sister an' all…

* * *

Cale Wilcox had secretly admired Andy Millard since they'd been in high school together, several years behind Charlie. Cale'd been super-shy, intimidated by her careful use of the language, her always looking her best, even her independence, not following the herd to the latest fad. He noticed she read a lot, and that got him to doing the same. He fantasized being able to hold an intelligent conversation with the dark-haired girl on any topic she could bring up. *Yeah, show her I'm not just 'nother dumb-ass, tongue-tied redneck.*

But Andy hadn't seemed even to notice him back then. True, she didn't give any of the boys in school the time of day, which had intrigued him more. But that was all right; let the ballplayers go after the bright ones, the silly, giggly girls. He could see there was so much more to Andy, and he wanted to find out what was there, share with her, get close. He knew he could do this, if only she'd respond a little, encourage him. *Give me an inch, girl, an' I'll take me a mile.*

Andy may have remembered Wilcox years later, in that crowded courtroom, but again, he'd hardly registered. No wonder: she was so wrought up, so angered, so humiliated, that just another face in the crowd went unnoticed. And of course she could never have sensed the outrage the man was feeling, seeing, listening to Montgomery Mabry vilify her, paint her as an immoral woman who'd tried to entrap his son.

Cale Wilcox had regretfully witnessed Andy's blindness in being seduced by Cam Henry, that womanizing truck driver. He'd expected so much more from her, the girl he'd idealized, fantasized about. As a country boy of little experience with women, he couldn't have realized the effect a clever, even smooth Romeo could have on even a sharp girl like Andy. And when she'd thrown him out and moved back to the county, he'd rekindled a hope that there might be a way he could become the real man in her life.

The problem was, Wilcox had married another woman, a waitress at the local diner whom he'd met on his regular stints as a deputy sheriff. Gracie laughed a lot, flirted a little, and always had a smile for him. He'd started dropping by often, drinking more coffee than was good for him, just to be near her.

And things had progressed rapidly with her, with no other woman around who'd interested him. Andy Millard's absence had left a hole in his young life, and now he realized he needed to fill that hole. Gracie was willing, having grown tired of the grind of being on her feet all day, putting up with groping farmers, salesmen, other predators.

So when Cale asked her, she'd said yes. They'd moved to a little cottage just out of town, and by the time Andy returned to take over raising Nate Prescott, there were Wilcox twins. So the deputy put his former idol away on the shelf of his memory and did his best to stay away from her. Being a father affected the young deputy's sense of loyalty more than marriage had, even.

But he'd never forgotten Andy. And seeing her smeared, degraded in that courtroom and in the community in general, set off a smoldering anger deep inside him. He was never again able to view Barry or Montgomery Mabry as quite human from that point on. Putting in his time at the firing range, Wilcox had often found himself imagining the target as Barry's heart. And now that he was gone, the image shifted to that of the man's father.

Chapter Nine

With no other leads, Hal Burgess drove out to the Prescott place again two days later. He decided to send the watchers home, since apparently nobody had tried to run away from there. But leaning on Charlie seemed the only course left; maybe the man would let something slip this time.

The Chevrolet was right where it should be, and he could see Elijah surprisingly urging an old wheelbarrow of firewood up toward the house. He watched for a moment, noting how the old man used the handles to brace himself, even while pushing it. *Guess he could've managed to set that trap, but no, not that hike all the way to the bull pen without leaving a mark. Wooden leg's got a small cap on it, would've pushed into the ground.*

Andy was hanging washing on the clothesline to catch the sunlight, although it was a chilly day. Burgess took in the sight of her, still beautiful even at this homely chore. He parked the Ford, greeted her.

"Everything all right here, Andy?"

Now, do I lie to him about Charlie? Maybe just tell him he's out hunting? No, he'll find out soon enough. But I wasn't about to let him know he's gone before I had to; let him get as far away as possible. But then I don't want to be seen as an accessory here either.

"Come in, Hal; there's something you have to know." She carried the empty basket up the porch steps, set it aside. "Have a seat. Coffee?"

"Sure, thanks. Didn't see Charlie outside. Amazing how Elijah can handle that wheelbarrow. Guess Charlie's busy at something else?"

"That's just what I have to tell you. I'm afraid Charlie's gone, or something's happened to him." She poured the coffee with a hand that did not shake, looked him in the eye.

"Gone? How? Okay, tell me." He leaned forward.

"Said he was going hunting a couple days ago, needed to get out, not be cooped up. Didn't come home by dark, and I worried a little, but thought he must've gone farther off: not much game around here. And I have to tell you, he's hunted at night before, which might not be legal, so we didn't worry; all just went on to bed.

"Next morning, the shotgun was back here, so I didn't check on him, let him sleep in. Then I walked over to Miz Ed Carson's, where we gather to do quilting. Stayed till almost dark, trying to help one of the women finish, you know.

"Well, I got home, and Charlie wasn't here. Elijah'd been down with a cold, in bed mostly. Said he'd seen Charlie in and out, not clear on just when, so again I didn't worry much. But he didn't come home for supper, and he's been gone ever since. Now I realize I haven't seen him in two days, and I can't say just when he left." She spread her hands. *Maybe not completely true, but most of it is.*

"I see. So he could've just now gone, or has been gone two days?"

"I guess so. He's been restless, pacing around. All of us are worried with all that about Barry's death, and the idea that we're probably the prime suspects."

"So what do you think? He just walked off, and nobody knows exactly when? That's hard to believe, Andy."

"I'm sorry, Hal. We didn't know, and I suppose we should've checked closer. And I guess, called you…"

"Yes, you should have. This is serious, Andy. But you say the shotgun was back here yesterday morning, but what, nobody actually saw Charlie?"

"That's right, and I know it doesn't sound logical, but like I said, things are crazy around here. We just don't know what to do, and it's as if we're almost prisoners here, just waiting for you—the authorities—to come after us." She twisted her hands in her patched apron.

The sheriff felt a pang of sympathy for her. *Damn, she's caught in the middle of all this, with that no-good brother, having to raise the boy, provide for old Elijah, and surely dead broke, with no way to earn money, except for that little house-cleaning, and not many folks hire that done.*

"Okay, you realize this makes it almost certain that Charlie killed Barry Mabry, don't you?" What other conclusion could he draw?

"I know it does, but he didn't do it, Hal. Somebody's framed him—us—with that about the ladder. I was just hoping you'd find out who really did it. But yes, Charlie should've stayed. I guess he just reasoned he couldn't possibly win, so he ran."

"All right. I have to get on his trail right now. I don't think any of you helped him escape; how could you? But we'll have to hunt him down; you know that. State police, law enforcement in other states. It's going to be hard, Andy." He looked into her eyes, saw the anguish there. For an instant, he wanted to take her into his arms, hold her, calm her.

He rose instead, walked out the door to his car, got on his radio. Elijah Prescott watched him drive away from his window, his wrinkled face inscrutable.

* * *

The only thing that'd kept him sane, Montgomery Mabry thought, was the certainty that Charlie Millard had murdered his son and would be tried, convicted, and die in the electric chair. He was outraged that Hal Burgess insisted that he didn't have enough evidence to arrest the man. He was having him watched, he'd assured the lawyer, but covering all other possibilities at the same time.

Damn Burgess won't move on this, when it's obvious. Millard's heard about Barry's anger, believes he burned that barn, accosted his sister. Plain case of revenge, envy: goes back for years. I'm a half-inch from just going over there and blowing that bastard all to hell. He's ruined my life, Christine's, and left little Giles with no father. Damn him! Damn his soul!

Despite her evident grief, Christine Mabry worried about her father-in-law: this was breaking his heart. She took her son to his house, dismissed his aging housekeeper, set about cooking dinner, making the place more welcome. She'd have to be a strong pillar for him now. Yes, and he could help her cope with the horror of it, too.

Giles was now six but hadn't fully realized that his father was gone and would never come back. He kept asking for him, watching out of the window, sure he'd see the Hudson coming up the drive any time now. Christine brushed away tears. *No, I can't give in to this; I have to be the one to hold us all together.*

* * *

When he'd accepted the fact that Charlie was now out of their lives, Nate Prescott tried to envision what lay ahead for the family. If they could make it for say, two more years, he'd be sixteen, could drop out of school, find work. It was well enough that they could—had to—scrape out an existence trying to farm the place, but with no income, no timber, nothing they could sell except that car, there was little to look forward to.

All right then, just take it a day at a time, trust in the Lord the way his grandfather had insisted. *But what if He doesn't think it's that necessary to take care of us? I can see getting by this winter, and maybe next summer, with the crops. But what then? Granpa's old, won't be able to do for himself much longer. It'll be just Aunt Andy and me, and what'll we do when we need shoes, clothes?*

And she won't let me leave school, find work; wants me educated, be able to have a decent life. This place won't ever let us do anything more than barely live. I see too many old people chained to their farms, worn-out lives and worn-out places.

He didn't want that for himself either. All right then, he'd just have to buckle down and do the best he could. Right now the three of them were free—his uncle had seen to that—and it was up to them to work out whatever they could. Couple of years it could all change, and he'd try hard to make that happen.

Nate was growing now, seemingly inches every month. That helped at school when one of the kids or another made some snide remark about his having an outlaw for an uncle and a fallen woman for an aunt, and maybe they even had something to do with Mabry's death. He'd tried to ignore these jibes at first but soon saw they weren't going to stop.

Nate wasn't stupid; he wouldn't get himself into trouble if he could help it. He confided in the school's principal, a young man recently from Memphis who'd known nothing of the gossip about the family. At this school, the superintendent actually ran everything; the principal was in reality the chemistry teacher, and his title was almost honorary. But Nate knew he'd get no sympathy from the real boss.

"Mr. Mann, I'm in an…awkward position, I guess you'd say. I need to talk to you about it."

"All right, Nate, what's troubling you?" He indicated a chair.

"Well, you may have heard some talk about my Uncle Charlie, who's never held a job for long. Just sort of comes and goes when he wants to, travels a lot. You know my parents died three years ago, and my Aunt Andy came to take care of me. She had to divorce her husband when he cheated on her, and people talk her down for it.

"Well, the kids here throw that up to me, more so since Barry Mabry got killed. You might've heard about a court case on back, when he attacked my aunt and my grandfather beat him up protecting her. She'd turned Mabry down years back when he wanted to court her.

"So now Uncle Charlie's gone off again, and the law seems to think he's a suspect in Barry's death. Now, I don't like the kids putting me down, and I've taken it best I could. But it's getting worse, and I really want to punch a couple of them out, sir. I know that's not the way to handle it, and I don't want to fight. I guess I just want you to know what's happening. I can't help who my kinfolks are, but I'm not ashamed of them, either.

"Thing is, I don't think I can just roll over much longer. They'll think I ran to you like a sissy, and I'm no sissy. What do you think I should do?"

"Um. Well, no, you shouldn't fight them, Nate. And you shouldn't have to put up with taunts and cruelty from the other young people. Now you know the superintendent has this leather strap in the drawer there, and much as I hate it, I've even used it myself when I've had to, when there's the need, to keep the discipline we must insist on around here.

"Now, you're the one who'll have to decide how much you can allow yourself to be bullied. But I must go on record as saying I won't tolerate fistfights in this school, no matter the cause. So if there appears to be no way to avoid a confrontation, it can't happen on school grounds. That's all I can say."

Okay, that means I can beat hell out of Mark Reid next time he insults me, but I have to do it somewhere else. I can do that. But of course the Bible says to turn the other cheek. Seems like that just lets the enemy get a better shot at you. Gotta think about this some more.

He wouldn't go and whine to his aunt about this. No, a man had to handle situations like these himself. But maybe his grandfather had some advice.

"Nate, yer right: th' Bible, it sez don't hit back, an' thet's hard t' do, when t' other feller's onto you bad. Now, ever'body s'pecs a man t' stand up fer hisself an' his fam'ly, an' thet's th' diffrunce: th' fam'ly. You kin take whatever ennybody dishes out to you—thet's gotta be yore d'cision. But standin' up fer somebody else, thet's 'nother thaing alt'gether. Seems t'me, th' minnit enny kid starts in on Charlie er Andy, y'c'n see yore way clear t' defend 'em."

That made sense. And during his chores Nate began to strike a boxer's pose, jabbing, dodging, punching the air like it was an antagonist's face. He even hung a burlap sack full of sawdust from a barn beam and used it to practice on. In the 1950s, boxing was still a favorite spectator sport, with immortals like Joe Louis idolized. It was supposed to be a sport, yes, he reasoned, but it was defense, too.

Look out, Mark Reid. I'm ready for you.

* * *

The killer had had good and sound reasons for the elaborate trap that killed Barry Mabry. Of course, the obvious method would have been just to shoot him down after stalking him somewhere remote at the farm. *But what if I'd missed, and he'd somehow survived, maybe galloped out of range on that horse of his? Sooner or later, what he could've told might lead to me. No, this way, it could've been just a pitfall for deer, an accidental death. And if he had survived, no one could ever have connected me with it.*

Of course, nobody has been able to do that, anyway.

The motivation for the murderer's actions was deeply buried and would remain so, despite the sheriff's digging, the father's and the wife's frantic demands for justice. *Rant on, people, lawyer; you'll never know the real story.*

And he never would.

* * *

Hal Burgess had his private thoughts about why Charlie Millard had run. Despite the clumsy evidence of the ladder, he didn't think the man was the killer. As he'd told Wilcox, Charlie just wasn't that sharp or that patient. But who was? Who, with a motive, could plan and execute that complicated a trap? He cast about for the hundredth time for a suspect.

And he didn't like what that led him to.

Andy could plan that. Andy pretends she's past the insult, the assault, the shame, the gossip, the humiliation of the trial, even though she won. But I know that girl. I've seen those eyes go hard. Hate to think it, but yes, she could have done it.

But why would she leave the incriminating ladder right there to be found? After the rest of the detailed, careful execution? No, that just didn't make sense. Still, it'd maybe be worth it to talk to her again, probe some more, not take for granted that she was innocent.

He didn't want to do this. But yes, the higher-ups—and they were swarming nowwould take him to task if he didn't. Turn over every rock here, keep after every even remote suspect, that was what he must do.

So he drove the smoking Ford up the dirt drive again. He had nothing new to tell her, no trace of her brother, which would, of course, relieve her, but also nothing on the real killer. If there *was* another real killer. She had the hood of Charlie's Chevrolet up, head under it.

"Hello, Hal. What part did you take out of this thing? Charlie left me a note and signed the title over to me, so I guess I'll try to get it going. Maybe trade it for a couple of mules if I can."

"Here, Andy, this is the distributor rotor. It goes in here," and he bent, removed the distributor cap with its seven wires, and slipped the part back on. "Should be okay, now. Try the starter."

She climbed in, started the engine, and for the first time, looked around inside the car. *Not bad, really. Be nice to have, if we could buy gas for it.* She shut it down, closed the door after her.

"Thanks, Hal. I don't think Charlie would've dared fix it and drive it away, but then I didn't think he'd just walk off, either. Any news?" She led him up the porch steps, out of a faint drizzle that had begun.

"Nothing at all. Wherever Charlie went, he's disappeared completely. Now, I don't know if you'd tell me if he'd contacted you, but I don't believe he would anyway. Just so you know, I think he ran so we *would* think he was guilty, take the pressure off the rest of you."

"So you really don't think he did it?" She was eyeing him closely. And as always, he reacted, at least internally. *Damn, she's a fine-looking woman.*

"Just doesn't make sense: that ladder in plain sight, and not one you all would have had. And we've talked to two people who can verify he was in town, but that doesn't help much, since we don't know when the trap was set. But my gut feeling is, no, Charlie didn't do it. Motive, yes. Maybe even opportunity, but no."

"But, of course, you're getting pressure from everybody on up to the governor to arrest somebody. And the obvious target is my brother, no matter what you think." It was a statement. Andy was pinning her hopes on the police never finding him. *Better though—no, perfect—if they could find the real killer. Then we could have a life again, although Charlie'd probably never find that out: stay gone.*

"That's the problem all right. And I've got to go over again and again the ground we've covered. Ask more questions, push people harder, try for any clue at all to what really happened—well, we know that—*who* made it happen."

"And that's why you're here, isn't it? Well, Elijah's coming up from the potato shed now," looking out the window, "but Nate won't be home for another hour or so. So if you want to give me the third degree now, go ahead." She crossed her arms. She was wearing a patterned dress that Burgess guessed was made from printed flour sackcloth and old high-top men's shoes. But that didn't make her any less attractive.

"H'lo, Hal. Enny news? Er are you jist come callin'?" It was meant to be light banter, but it took the lawman back a beat. *Did I really just want to see Andy again? Got to watch that, stay objective. I'm here to decide if she's a suspect.*

"No news, I'm afraid, Elijah. Charlie's got away clean, and I was just telling Andy I think I know what he had in mind: knew it'd take the heat off you all if he ran. But nothing on anybody else, either; no suspects." He spread his hands.

"Wal, we done figgered thet out 'bout him goin', 'cause no, he ain't th' one you want. But shorely thar's *somebody* had it in fer Barry. Somebody thet's better off 'ith him daid." The eyes looked keenly at the sheriff.

"Got to be, but just *who* is the big question. Man must've had enemies we don't know about. If so, I'd guess his dad or Christine would at least suspect that, but neither of them can think of a soul. Or at least that's what they're telling me."

Andy took this in. *And as long as they can pin it on Charlie, they won't try very hard to help uncover anybody else.* She knew it was entirely possible that the immature Barry could have gotten into something shady. More so since it had become common knowledge that he and his father had been at odds over some investment schemes he'd wanted to pursue. *Probably wanted to show the old man he could be a big dog, too; prove himself in some twisted way. Maybe borrowed money from the wrong people; couldn't pay it back? Or maybe gambling? Don't see how he could've kept that a secret.*

Hal Burgess was watching Andy's face. He reflected that he seldom knew what a woman was thinking—any woman. And he guessed that this one could bury what was going on in her mind so deep nobody could suspect it. *That's why she may be the one: never let on. Maybe even has shoved it away so far it isn't even real to her any more.*

After some further speculation and small talk, she surprised him by inviting him to supper, since Nate was due and it was getting dark.

"Well, I…that is, I was going on back to town, but thanks, I think I will. Mighty nice of you to offer." He knew it would be simple fare, and as he often had, now wondered how this family was surviving. But here was a further chance for some stray bit of information to surface. *Yes, and I have to realize that even Nate could be part of the whole thing, unlikely as it is.*

That young man climbed the porch steps, unsure still how he'd explain the bruise above his left eye. *Well, just tell the truth: best way. Sheriff's here again. Hope they haven't found Uncle Charlie.* At that thought, he forgot about the bruise.

"Sheriff Burgess is staying for supper," Andy told him, then saw the discoloration. "What's happened to you, Nate?" She stepped close, examined his forehead.

"Just a little…disagreement, I guess you could say. Mark Reid's been spoiling for a fight for weeks, and I guess I just finally obliged him." He blushed uncontrollably.

"What was it about?" the sheriff asked, although he thought he knew.

"His big mouth, mostly. I got him off school property, told him he had to shut up about us, gossip an' bad-mouthing and all, and he took a swing at me."

"Looks lak he done c'nnected," observed his grandfather wryly. "Whut's he look lak? Enny better?"

"Some worse, matter of fact. I knew I'd have to stand up for us sooner or later, and today was just sooner, I guess." He was rubbing a scraped knuckle.

Andy said nothing. She wasn't going to scold the boy for what he'd done, shame him. Growing up in these same Arkansas hills, she'd seen enough fights to know some couldn't be avoided. Maybe this would hush some talk up, and maybe it wouldn't.

"Enough said," she declared, putting the subject to bed. "Let's eat, shall we? Nothing fancy, Hal, but we grew it all ourselves except for the biscuit flour, and we're a little proud of doing it."

"You should be, Andy; you all are making do where most folks couldn't, and I know it's been hard. You okay for the winter?" *Don't step on her pride here; wouldn't take a dime of charity.*

"We'll make it if we sell the car, and that's probably why Charlie left it for us. Won't be going anyplace fancy, but we'll manage." He couldn't tell if she was put off by his concern or welcomed it. "Now, Elijah, if you'd ask the blessing." They all bowed their heads.

Of course the talk centered about the murder investigation and the lack of clues or facts. Having expressed his doubts about Charlie's guilt, Burgess joined in on his hosts' speculations. *No you and me here: it's all we.* That realization and the fact that he'd been invited to stay warmed him.

"How're you doing in classes, Nate?" he asked. "Homework getting you down? It always did for me."

"Oh, I'm not having much trouble, sir. Since Aunt Andy's been here, she's been helping me with grammar, writing and stuff. Math isn't hard for me or science, but English doesn't come easy. I have to watch how I talk all the time if I'm ever going to be anything but a farmer." He was repeating what Andy had said so many times, and the sheriff suspected her influence would make a lot of things possible for this young man.

Sure cuttin' herself off from a life of her own, though. I admire that a lot: sees her duty and she's doing it. Good woman. He found himself calculating how much longer Nate would need her, when she'd have some choices again. *He gets a scholarship to college, be less than four years till he'll be gone…*

"You thainkin' somethin' y'kin tell us 'bout?" the minister asked. He'd noticed Burgess's faraway stare.

"Oh. I was just thinking, from what Nate said. There are college scholarships, some of them nobody ever applies for. Get one of those, Nate, and you'd be on your way. Given any thought to what you'd like to do later on? You mentioned math, science."

"Got a cousin's an engineer, went to Tech over in Russellville. He's got on with an oil company out in Tulsa, making good money. Maybe that. I like biology, too, and they're letting me take the class with the sophomores. I hear that could be the start of medical training. Might be I could study to be a doctor, but that's really aiming high, I know."

"Not necessarily. And the doctors I know all see it as a sort of calling, you could say, more than the money. What do you think about that, Elijah?"

"Wal, doctorin's good, way folks allus needs patchin' up. Be somethin' all right, iff'n a Prescott got into thet. But I hear they's years've studyin' on past college, 'fore they's enny money comin' in. Dunno how we'd manage thet." He thought a moment. "But iff'n th' Lord's willin', it could come about, fer shore."

"There's nothing wrong with being a good farmer either," Andy pointed out. "I think it's really about what you want to do. And somebody's got to feed the world, so many people going off to work in factories, businesses, seems to me there's a lot of opportunity right here on the land. Of course, you'd have to have a tractor, machinery, fencing, maybe hired help. I guess it's really going to be a sort of business enterprise nowadays, like everything else." She wanted her nephew to make up his own mind what to do with his life instead of having no choices.

"Yore right, Andy," the old man agreed. "Folks all goin off t' th' bright lights an' all, churches closin' up, seems lak they's worshippin' machines 'stead of th' Lord. Changin' world, fer shore, an' a lot of it's fer th' wust. But don't reckon a feller'd oughta try t'live in th' past, git old an' sour on th' way thaings is."

Burgess found he was enjoying this family talk, being a part of it. He admitted to himself that he'd welcome a relationship with Andy, but as always, the difference in their ages ruled that out. *Coming home to that woman would be about as good as it gets, though. Let's see, she'll be about 24, and I'm 46 and counting: too much difference. Just have to let that idea go.*

His stay with the family confirmed in his mind that none of these three could have had anything to do with the murder of Barry Mabry. Nobody was that good at acting, not even Andy Millard. He said goodbye convinced that this was a dead end. And he found himself actually hoping they'd never catch Charlie, even though he was the prime suspect and the pressure was on. But if that happened—his staying hidden—the man could never be a part of this clan again.

Chapter Ten

Christine Mabry eventually moved into her father-in-law's house with six-year-old Giles. The loss of his son had aged the man: he'd become forgetful, spending long periods gazing off into the distance. She knew he was reflecting on the waste of it all, the ruin of his dream for his estate, his legacy. Being there with him helped him realize that Giles would eventually carry on his grandfather's work, and she hoped the boy would help draw him out of himself.

"It's just us now, Pa," she told him, bringing him his favorite bourbon and lemon toddy. "You'll have to be father to Giles now, and I'll depend on you to do that." She squeezed his hand, then sat across from him to read her son a children's book.

Now, that's a picture, all right: Barry's girl and my grandson. And she's right: it's just us to carry on, be a family. I'm grateful she's come; could've chosen not to.

But that bastard Charlie Millard; he murdered my son, and now he's gone. Off to some end-of-the-world where he'll never be found, and I'm helpless to right this outrage. I'll keep trying, though; he'll surely contact his sister, and she's the key. Maybe even helped him do it; she's that sort. Night and day difference between her and Christine.

Of course, his daughter-in-law's move put her in a better position to enjoy the old man's wealth, but he was too torn up over his son's death and too grateful for her presence and apparent good sense to take note. And if he had, he'd surely dismiss the suspicion as groundless. She *was* the mother of his only heir.

* * *

Charlie Millard had walked briskly the rest of the night, reaching the east-west highway where he caught a ride a few miles to a small town. There he got a cup of coffee and two donuts, knowing his little money would have to last till he could find work somewhere.

His next ride took him a few miles up into Missouri toward West Plains, but his hitchhiking luck ran out there. Hour after hour he walked east, but for some reason the traffic was light, and cars sped on past his upraised thumb. Finally a farmer gave him a lift to a turnoff to his fields, and Charlie was afoot again. Eventually another farmer in a gaudy handpainted orange and pink pickup truck picked him up, and he rode a few more miles. The man had a stutter, and the conversation was mostly one-sided.

He walked on more hours until he reached a wide place in the road with nothing but a gas station/country store and a junkyard behind the station.

It was nearly dark now, and he was footsore. Nobody was at the junkyard and the station was closed, so he slipped back among the relics to find a place to spend the night. Eventually he located a car with no engine, but it had unlocked doors and all the glass in the windows. He bundled up on the back seat and tried to sleep, despite being hungry and cold.

Next morning he bought two candy bars from the store and set out again, not knowing what lay ahead. The world right then seemed hostile to a man with no money, hungry and with no prospects, but he plodded on steadily, sure his luck would change.

And it did. With no cars in sight, his eyes were on the ground ahead, his mind back on the Prescott place and his sister, when he spotted a wristwatch, just lying there. He stooped, retrieved it, and noted that it looked expensive. Sure enough, the lettering on it said 14-karat gold.

Well now, look what I've gone an' found me: somebody's lost watch, an' just when I need help th' most. Git to a town, I c'n pawn this, or sell it, be on m'way.

Dunno how much futher I got to go, but I think m'luck's maybe changed.

And the very next car stopped for him on the way—eventually all the way—across the Mississippi River. The driver was a mill supply salesman, headed on east toward Kentucky. He was talkative, and the miles fell away behind them as the two exchanged stories. Charlie had always been able to open up to people, usually get them to do the same.

"Yeah, I'm 'bout broke," Charlie confided. "Only got this watch left, an' reckon I gotta sell it, git on down th' road." He showed it to the other man, hoping he'd maybe want it.

"Looks like a nice watch. Where you headin' anyway?"

"West Virginny; wanta git into minin' if I can. No money in farmin', and I'm sure I c'n land somethin', workin' on 'quipment, runnin' machinery, whatever's t'do."

"Lot of mining there, for sure. My old territory was out of Charleston, but my wife didn't like living there. We're in Paducah now. She likes those old plantation houses and all the horses."

The salesman had calls to make in eastern Missouri, so he dropped Charlie in Poplar Bluff. He found a pawnshop there and came away with forty dollars after hard bargaining with the watch. He treated himself to a pair of hamburgers, a two-dollar motel room, a shave and shower and a good night's sleep.

The world looked better to him next morning as he sipped coffee at a café, but he knew he had to make this money last, no telling how long till he could find that job. So he decided to hike to the edge of town and stick out his thumb again.

But before setting out, he got into a conversation with a cross-country trucker at the gas pumps who was heading east and wrangled a ride well across much of Kentucky. Past the Mississippi, the miles rolled away beneath them, each one putting him farther from the reach of the law. Many hours later, arriving at Bardstown, he began to breathe easier, but he wanted to get farther on into the backwoods.

After another night spent on the backseat of a rusted car on the back row of a used car lot, he ate a spare breakfast, walked to the edge of town, and thumbed a ride across the rest of Kentucky on into West Virginia. *Wrong place t' find work, I'm hearin' now, but I know pore folks're more likely to help a man than rich ones.*

It was indeed a depressed state he found as he hitchhiked for another two days toward the capital, Charleston. But there were chemical plants there and mining operations out in the hills: apparently all the industry there was in the state. The air smelled bad, and he figured any work would be nasty, but he needed a job—any job. *Only thing is, a big outfit'd maybe have folks that'll want papers. Gotta git way out in th' woods, stay there.*

Charlie's checkered work background had been mostly hand labor, and here as elsewhere, there was too much competition. The only other thing he knew was farming, but most of this land wasn't fields: steep mountainsides with creeks between, narrow roads and cheap frame houses up on stilts where the slopes rose.

He recalled the wisdom of the saying that a poor man couldn't hire help, no matter how he might want to, so he knew he'd have to find some sort of operation that generated cash. He'd seen rich horse spreads in Kentucky, but that'd been too civilized: too likely places to be found. *Some'ers around here there's gotta be a shirt-tail coal mine, or mebbe a feller's got him a big farm, needs help. Keep lookin', but m'money won't last, an' I don't look like nothin' but a bum.*

He climbed up a narrow canyon with a small stream plunging down it to a little hidden pool. It was cold, but he shucked off his clothes, scrubbed up quickly, shivering violently. He had a change of jeans and a wool shirt, which he got into after a halfway drying-off. After he'd stopped shaking, he managed to scrape off most of his stubble by feel and decided that was all the sprucing up he could stand.

He slipped back down to the road, resumed walking deeper up into the backwoods. Eventually, much higher up, the land flattened somewhat, and small fields appeared. The farmhouses were little more than board shacks, the horses and mules lean, and an air of neglect pervaded. He strode on, confident that things would get better.

Always somebody slicker'n th' others t' take advantage of 'em, git land, cattle, timber. Back in here's where they'll never find me, an' I'll just hafta take whatever I c'n find. He'd always been able to talk himself into work of some kind and still felt confident that he could do it this time. *Gotta happen soon, though, er things gonna git thin.*

A car approached from behind, and turning, he saw a green Cadillac. He stepped aside and watched as it passed. The driver was a gray-haired man with a younger blonde woman as passenger. *Now, that's somebody's got money, an' he's goin' up this little road. No tellin' how far, but I'd say he's got a big place up ahead. Shore not much b'hind.*

So, coal mine? Cattle farm? Or maybe another town ahead, and the man could be just a lawyer or doctor. But the sighting encouraged Charlie, and he strode on. *Got a good feelin' about this. Looks like a rich man with a young wife, if that is his wife. Could be his daughter. But if he was headin' fer a town, wouldn't be on this twisty road…*

He was right. Two miles farther on, well-kept farm fields opened on his right, ranging up the now-gentler hillsides. A tall, white house appeared, with barns, stables, and machinery sheds. This place would surely need farmhands unless they were already full up.

And then he heard the distinctive sound of chainsaws beyond the fields in the heavy timber up the slope, and the occasional crashing of falling trees. A logging operation was going full force, and he saw a laden truck easing down a woods road and between fields toward the road he was on. Another possibility, for sure.

* * *

Hal Burgess had finally admitted to himself that he wanted to court Andy Millard. All the reasons not to had almost convinced him to stay away, especially since she could be a suspect in Mabry's murder. Could be, but he was 100 percent sure she hadn't done it, or even participated in its planning.

The trap itself was just too complicated, too many chances for it to go wrong. Anyone could have stalked the man and shot him with a rifle, then hidden the gun. The whole thing about the pitfall, leading the bull into the woods, chancing it all on Barry's being the one to go after him, counting on his not seeing the covered well: it hadn't made sense from the beginning.

Had to be some twisted mind at work. A genius? Or maybe just some old boy thought he'd try that old pitfall way to take the rare deer. Maybe no gun or too broke to buy cartridges. *Or maybe he was really after old Montgomery, got the wrong man?* But again, there were surer ways…

But back to Andy: he thought he knew the girl well enough to be sure she wasn't guilty. *Or could I just want her not to be?* But he dismissed that thought immediately, seeing her now more clearly as his possible future wife.

Still, that difference in their ages was like a barrier: he couldn't imagine her pushing his wheelchair in thirty years. *But that's a whole generation away.* If she'd consider him, they could have that long together. And she surely didn't seem interested in anyone else, so maybe he had a chance.

This almost-fantasy got shoved aside often as the sheriff wrestled with his feelings, the lack of their logic, the real likelihood that she'd reject him. *I'm easy old enough to be her father, and this doesn't make sense; oughta just forget it. But there're couples making it work, no matter their ages. And she's no silly young thing, even if she did go off with that worthless trucker.*

But he knew he had to let this whole unsolved murder thing fade away before he pursued Andy. He was mature enough to realize she'd have to get past a lot of the obvious obstacles too, and that'd take time. *Well, got time enough, I guess. Looks like we'll just have to give up on Barry's killing: no clues, no information, no breaks. Unless Charlie really did it after all and we find him.*

Time: that was what it always entailed, no matter what the plan or the situation might be. Patience was the only way to go here. Andy would surely stay with Nate until he was out of high school, another three-plus years. So unless some knight came riding in on a white horse, he could start making sure he slipped into being the only eligible man in her life.

Just how to go about that was a problem, with the necessity of appearing objective regarding the case. And he couldn't visibly give the struggling family much help for two reasons: her pride and that conflict of interests. *But I can maybe shoot a deer and share it with them. Be har, with so few of them, though. Could maybe go and help cut firewood, but that'd be pretty obvious. Well, anything I do would be obvious.*

He finally decided an occasional visit to report progress wouldn't be out of line. If he could make any progress with things at a standstill. *Only thing that'd sour this whole plan would be to find Charlie, have him stand trial. And with nothing to defend him, he'd be convicted, and I'd shoot myself down with Andy forever.*

So, bottom line, it didn't make a bit of difference whether he'd decided to pursue the girl or not. He just couldn't do much at all till the case resolved itself one way or another. He didn't like that, but knew he'd have to live with it. And the images of his coming home to her, to a cozy room and her good cooking just served to torment him.

Well, only thing I can do reall, is to work harder to find the real killer, go over everything we've got again, see if I missed anything. Maybe that would keep the girl he was coming to love out of his mind a little.

* * *

Gracie Wilcox had been through a bad day. The kids had broken dishes, thrown things at each other, whined and pestered her till she couldn't see straight. She'd swatted both of them, which had worked for a while, but then here they came again. So now Cale was due home, and supper not started, the house a mess, and she had the king of headaches. She just wanted to disappear, escape for just a day, an hour, any break at all.

But here he came, and yes, that frown meant he'd had hell at his job, too. But she couldn't bring herself to care that much. *Man's got an office to go to when he comes in off the road. Or he can drop in at the café, like he used to do. I've got nowhere when it gets too rough. And he's about to gripe; I can tell it. Well, dammit, I've been through the wringer all day, and I can't take any more.*

"What the devil's happened here? Looks like a war zone, Gracie. Can't you make these kids behave? Damn place looks like a tornado hit it." He bent, started picking things up from the cluttered floor. His wife just stared at him, hands on her hips, while the twins, sensing the tension, retreated toward their bedroom.

"Cale, I've had the worst day I c'n remember. Nothin's gone right, an' I'm about to pass out on th' floor. Just give me a minute t' get myself together, an' I'll get onto supper…"

"Supper's not ready yet? Damn, woman, what you been doing all day?" Then, seeing her face, he backtracked, held up his hands. "Okay, okay, sorry I said that: just had myself a bad one, too. All this about that Mabry gettin' killed's got us all crazy." *Not that the bastard didn't deserve it.* He hugged her, kissed the tousled hair as she clung to him.

"Here, let me help." Right then, his wife looked like a mangled rag doll, and for a fleeting instant, he wondered why he'd ever thought she was cute. And the image of Andy Millard flashed in his mind. The way she always managed to look good, no matter the patched clothes, the scuffed farm shoes, the reddened hands of the man's work she had to do.

The road not taken. A line from a poem they'd had to read back in school. *Yeah, and here I am, and here we are. So just swallow it, Cale old boy; you play the hand you've been given. Or dealt yourself, I guess is closer.*

But he was never, ever able to get the image of Andy out of his mind.

* * *

With cold weather, the little family got onto hog-killing. In past years, all the neighbors would've gathered at one farm, bringing their animals in wagons, carts, and everybody pitched in together. That had been a more or less social gathering, with the children running around, getting underfoot, the women visiting, making the noonday meal.

The men and some of the women would kill the hogs, sometimes gut them first, then immerse the carcasses in big old cast-iron pots of boiling water to scald and loosen the hair, which would then be scraped off before the butchering began. Now slanted oil drums with tops cut out were used, and two men could lift and lower the hogs into the water.

But since the war, it seemed the entire aspect of such gatherings had faded, with most families having cars or trucks, more working away from home, buying more of what they consumed. So the three at the Prescott place tackled the chore themselves one chilly day into winter.

Elijah had Nate straddle one of the now-grown creatures, holding it immobile by the ears while he slashed its throat. It lunged out of the boy's grasp, but soon fell over, its throat gushing. A few twitches later, the old man opened it up, pulled out the entrails, making the carcass lighter to handle. Then Nate and Andy dragged it to the barrel, heaved it up and into the boiling water. This was when they missed the absent Charlie most. Elijah waited with his treasured, hand-forged knives ready on a low work table they'd constructed out of old barn boards that'd somehow survived the fire.

They kept the edible organs—heart, liver—and buried the rest. The old man was proficient with the razor-keen blades, slicing seemingly slowly but steadily. The pile of hams, side bacon, fatback, roasts grew steadily under his practiced hand.

Much of this would be cured, hung in the smokehouse, but Andy would can a great deal of it, too, in boiled glass Mason jars with their purchased lids. They'd render out the lard, strain it for frying, baking, and whatever their needs. What was left from that, the cracklings, she'd bake into cornbread or set aside for snacks.

Most of their neighbors now took their field-dressed hogs to the locker plant in the village, to have the meat cut up and packaged, then frozen. For a fee, they'd then pick up what they needed, most not having a way to keep it frozen at home.

Elijah knew the secrets of curing pork and worked his magic on both the hogs, smiling his satisfaction at the meat in the smokehouse. And Andy would grind sausage from the bits cut away from the larger pieces. Little was wasted in this whole operation, simply because they couldn't afford that.

Finally, as a sort of celebratory treat, she'd make doughnuts, which they'd deep-fry in the new lard. Nate always ate more of these than was good for him, and always got a stomachache from it. He guessed he'd never learn.

* * *

Elijah Prescott wasn't completely convinced that Charlie hadn't killed Barry Mabry. He, too, was mystified about the complex trap that'd been laid for the man and had doubted the not-bright Charlie could've planned and done it. But with no one else to be found, he admitted to himself the possibility. *Guess we're better off ennyway, with him gone. Boy never could leave th' likker 'lone, an' whut help he wuz here, little's he wuz around, we c'n do 'thout him. Andy, she's allus took keer've him, stood up fer him, an' shore don't b'lieve he done it. So I'll jist hafta keep m'idees to m'self, see how it all turns out.*

He liked being here with his grandson and this woman he'd come to respect, if not approve of completely. They were family, and that was a comfort to the old man. He did what he could around the place, given his crutch and the aches of age, and it seemed they'd get by, if barely.

Andy had driven the car to town, with a *For Sale or Trade* sign in the window. Eventually she'd bargained hard for a good gelding workhorse and cash. Most of this she put aside, and the family agreed that one good horse could handle the farm work, with no more logging.

Elijah had spent time with Silas Greene, the blacksmith, at his old shop, and the two had put together a two-wheeled cart from wood and the iron remains of the wagon. Nate helped with shaping the shafts, altering second-hand harness, and fitting junkyard automobile wheels and tires to it. This work was complicated, but another step up in their make-do existence.

The cart allowed them to make trips to the village, and that and a hand-built sled hauled firewood from the woods. This looked like the best they could hope for, given their poverty, but it was enough. In fact, the old man realized their situation was better than that of a number of families he knew of farther back in the hills. As far as he was concerned, the newfangled offerings of the towns were for other folks, anyway.

Elijah was a bit afraid Andy might find herself another man and go off after him, leaving Nate and him alone here. But so far the girl had proven to be steady, refusing every clumsy advance.

Except for Hal Burgess. The old man could tell the sheriff was drawn to her, but he couldn't say what her feelings were. Didn't matter the age difference, he knew: right two people'd be able to handle that. In fact, the preacher had been fifteen years older than his own wife. And their life together had been wonderful, till that heart thing.

But it'uz th' Lord's will, I reckon, t'take her th' way He done. Hard way t'go, but I don't doubt fer a minnit she's with Him now. So, if it's His plan t'git Hal an' Andy t'gether, He'll git it done, one way or t'other. And not the worst pairing in the world either, he reflected. But he also knew the sheriff couldn't very well launch a courtship with the cloud of Mabry's death over the family. *Git that cleared up, reckon he'll start comin' 'round serious. If he don't, thaings'll jist hafta go 'long lak they are.*

As the months passed, Nate observed that the family's life was sort of hovering in midair, with no clear direction to go, no resolution. *Sort of like those visions I get from up above. There's just us three down here, goin' at it, doin' what we gotta, gettin' by, a little like ants.* He guessed they'd just have to hang on, take it one day at a time. As winter deepened, then eventually lessened, he was surer than ever that Charlie had escaped, and he was relieved. That it also meant he'd probably never see his uncle again caused him regret, but there was enough to do around here to take his mind off the man.

Nate continued to do well in high school, tutored by his aunt, whose determination for him to succeed never flagged. She took on more of the chores around the place so that he'd have more time for study. She checked books out at the village library for him to read, as well as broadening her own knowledge, snatching late hours by lamplight for her own reading.

Nate was fiercely proud of Andy, and having established the fact that he'd tolerate no criticisms of her, rarely had to enforce his defense. He still practiced his boxing, worked hard at home, grew alarmingly, and going on fifteen, seemed to mature quickly.

The three of them would often go over their finances, prospects for the spring planting, fencing, and that proposed irrigation Charlie had suggested. Andy budgeted little for shoes and clothing, somehow creating shirts and dresses and even coats from fabric she managed to acquire.

Nate, too, knew his aunt would eventually leave the farm: good-looking women just didn't stay hid, dry up and get old alone. He'd often gone over in his mind the available men in the region but always concluded that none of them was man enough for Andy. Except yes, maybe the sheriff, Hal Burgess. But he hadn't shown much interest beyond politeness, the boy thought, and there was that…shadow, he guessed he'd call it, over them.

So for now, they'd just go along, manage. He'd finish ninth grade in May, be fifteen. Come spring they'd try to plant enough to maybe have some to sell in town, bring in a few dollars. And despite the general poverty around, there were little jobs to be had now. The widow Jenkins, farther up the road, wanted her barn roof fixed, and she got a regular government check of some kind, could pay a little.

"She c'n buy th' tin, but it'll be rough, puttin' it up by y'self," Elijah told Nate. "Whut I seen a couple times, a feller'd git short pieces he c'd handle, lappin' 'em over one 'nuther, an' didn't need no help. Her barn ain't got a steep roof, so I reckon it'd be safe 'nuff. I'd go talk to her 'bout it, I wuz you. Couple Sat'dies oughta do it, 'pendin' on th' weather."

Saturday, not the Lord's Day. The family didn't go to church, but Elijah insisted on a Bible reading every Sunday, which he presided over. And he frowned on the idea of doing any but necessary chores: milking the cow, feeding the stock, getting in firewood. So if an occasional Saturday bit of work would bring in some money, he was all for it. Also, he wanted Nate to learn to price jobs, get proficient at any and all work that came his way. The next years would fly by, and the boy, whether he got into college or not, would have to be able to make his way.

So, by the time early spring came, the barn roof had been repaired and Nate had twenty-five dollars to add to the remaining cash from the car sale. Feed for the horse, cow, pigs, and chickens had taken its toll, however, there being little hay and grain harvested from the limited fields.

Corn required a lot of space, but it was the staple crop. They'd planted much of it by hand the year before, among the decaying stumps of the cut-over land. During this winter, Elijah had piled brush on these and burned more of them out, an ongoing job he could and did handle.

This meant they could plow and harrow more ground than before, put in more corn and other crops. A one-horse operation wasn't that much, but if they worked it right, that one horse could take care of their little farm.

Andy started seeds in little paper cups inside the farmhouse windows and took care to keep the stove warm as they sprouted. Summer here was dry past June, and the earlier the seedlings could be put into the ground, the better. That often meant piling leaves over them to ward off spring cold snaps, but it was a necessity. Farming to any degree had always been a chancey thing, with little room for mistakes.

* * *

It was as if something had clicked in Montgomery Mabry's mind one sunless day that winter. He'd grown suspicious of the police efforts being made to locate Charlie Millard and decided to go on the attack himself. Christine saw the change that morning: her father-in-law wore a determined look rather than the defeated countenance that had followed the death of his son. It scared her.

"That Hal Burgess isn't doing a thing to find Barry's killer," he told her. "I'm going to see to it that he's not re-elected, first of all." He paused, drank coffee. She waited: there was more. "And I've got contacts all over, men who know how to track a man down, and I'm going to use them."

"Won't that be terribly expensive? You're talking about private detectives?"

"And any others I can enlist. I haven't been in law all these years without making some friends, Chris, and now I'm going to call in some favors. Detectives yes, among other things. And as for the expense, what's more important than finding justice for my son?" He rose, patted his grandson on the head, and went to get his coat.

She watched him drive away. *Well, bankrupting yourself and us for revenge seems a little crazy.* She had come to know approximately what the old man was worth, and yes, it was a lot. But she could also envision him becoming obsessed with this project, paying out a steady stream of money to anonymous men in trenchcoats who could find out nothing more than the cops. That worried her. *There's a time to put some things behind you, get past the grief and take care of business. Barry's gone, Pa: don't let this avenging angel thing ruin you.*

* * *

This life wasn't bad, Charlie Millard reflected. Sure, logging was hard work, but with these chainsaws, a tractor with log forks to skid and load with, late-model trucks that weren't about to fall apart, it was okay. Sure beat bending over a dull crosscut saw all day. And now as Charlie Barrett, he'd started a new life.

He'd shown up at just the right time, when one of the loggers working for Donald Lemons had suffered a broken leg when a falling tree back-jumped onto him. Lemons was the landowner Charlie had seen in the Cadillac, and he was having a big tract of his prime timber logged. The man also had cattle, horses, that expensive house, and a feisty young second wife.

He also had a grown son, Ronnie, who liked to oversee all the work on the place. Just out of college, the boss's son wanted to establish himself as the hard-driving right hand of his father: on the way up to bigger things. The men tried to avoid him.

Charlie was philosophical about his situation: *Jist do m'job, don't screw up, an' don't trouble trouble.* He was glad for the pay, at a dollar an hour, the room he'd rented for twenty dollars a month, and this place he was sure he could remain anonymous. He did wish he could send a little money to Andy but couldn't take the chance the authorities would track him down if he did. More and more, he realized he'd never see his sister or the others again.

This attitude of just getting along would have worked well if young Ronnie Lemons hadn't taken an instant dislike to the cheerful, red-faced Charlie. Perhaps it was because the other workers were all local men, had never left their West Virginia environs, while this man was obviously a drifter. Charlie talked of other places, things he'd seen and done, and while his embroidered tales of exploits were probably harmless, the boss's son interpreted them as sowing discontent.

Or perhaps Ronnie just wanted to exert his authority. There was a popular theory among business executives at the time that dictated the necessity of this. One had to take some drastic action right at the first: say, fire someone to nip any possible future insubordination among the rest of the work force.

Charlie knew this. Charlie had seen this. Charlie had experienced this. So he was extra careful not to tread on Ronnie's sensitive toes. He always addressed him as "Mr. Lemons, sir" and was superdeferential.

But the young man thought he saw a bit of sarcasm in this, a touch of a smirk on Charlie's face, which might or might not have been there. Charlie was always grinning, after all. It was going to be a little challenge to get rid of this guy, but Ronnie knew he could find a way.

Charlie had also observed the way the senior Lemon's young wife flirted with the men. There was a white-haired logger in his sixties named Theo she always teased, who always colored, stammered at the attention. *Prob'ly thinks he's too old t'count.* And Jeannie, the wife, had taken to giving a little swing to her hips whenever she passed Charlie.

Now, this wasn't anything new, since his past had been littered with waitresses, farm girls, and even the occasional nurse down at Little Rock. Women had always liked Charlie, his ready laugh, his easy ways, the boyish enthusiasm about him. But he realized from the first that Jeannie Lemons was trouble. He vowed to stay as far away from her as possible, going directly to the woods in the mornings and staying off away from the big house.

Which again should have worked. If he hadn't had to go back to the workshop that day after a new chain for that chainsaw.

That's when he caught sight of Ronnie Lemons and his stepmother behind a tractor in a groping, panting embrace. He tried to ease back out of sight, chain in hand, but stumbled over a hammer on the concrete floor, making a noise.

Ronnie wasn't sure that what he saw was a man—just a flick of disappearing movement beyond the corner of the shop—but he was instantly alert. Jeannie pulled him to her fiercely, demanding all his attention, but he knew he had to be sure. He stepped back, pushing her away.

"Somebody's here," he whispered. She straightened immediately, brushing her dress, smoothing her disheveled hair. *God, don't let it be my husband; he's s'posed t'be in town.*

But by the time her lover reached the corner, there was no one in sight. He circled the workshop, saw nothing. His father was away today, the men on the farm crew were at early plowing, and the loggers were… He couldn't hear the usual distant chainsaws. *Okay, they're taking a break, but one of them could've slipped down here.* And he instantly suspected Charlie, the smart-mouthed new guy.

Just to be sure, Ronnie got into the farm's Army surplus Jeep and drove up to the logging operation. The men were rolling logs out of the tangle of cut limbs with cant hooks so that the tractor could get at them, pull them to the trucks.

Except for Charlie Barrett, who was at a big stump putting a new chain on his chainsaw. But nothing looked suspicious; they were all at work, not slacking off. So he'd just imagined seeing someone: guilty nerves jumpy. *Or maybe it was one of the farmhands. We've gotta be more careful.* Ronnie turned the Jeep around and left without a word. *Never hurts to let them know I'm watching them anyway, checking up on them.*

Charlie's mind was racing. He'd run most of the way back to the woods, dodging down a deep ravine, and when he'd seen the Jeep coming, he'd carried the chainsaw back farther, hoping Ronnie wouldn't see him. And he'd hurried the job, cutting a finger on a sharp saw tooth. But it was okay; the man hadn't singled him out. He breathed deep, partly to get air after the run back up the slope.

So. Ronnie might've thought he saw Charlie, but obviously he wasn't sure, or he'd have said something. Now the question was, what was he to do about this, if anything? Tell the boss? Nah, he wouldn't go against his own son on the word of a hired hand. *Just keep quiet: none a my bizness, none of it. Pr'tend it didn't happen, an' I git to keep m'job. Gotta stay clear of that woman, though, er she might jis' take it into her head t'rub up agin' me. That'd git me shot, fer sure. Ole man didn't do it, that boy would, sure's hell.*

But although Ronnie Lemons had no real reason to suspect Charlie of spying on him, he still just didn't like the man. Too cocky, too glad-hand, always with that silly grin on. Oh, he worked hard, the other hands said, and they liked him. But hell, a drifter like that, no telling when he'd just not show up for work, be gone the way he'd come. And probably steal whatever wasn't tied down.

It was a few days later that Ronnie was in the workshop, talking to one of the farmhands who was tinkering with an ailing tractor. He happened to look on the wall where spare chainsaw chains hung on a hook. Something about a chainsaw… *Yes, that Charlie was putting one on that saw up in the woods. He was here to get it, and he saw us. So he thinks he's got something on me now. Well, you sneaking bastard, you won't get the chance to tell Dad. I'll see to that.*

He had to get rid of the man. Could just fire him, make up an excuse, but his father would want to know why, and Charlie might find a way to tell him the truth. It didn't help that he worked hard, got along with the others. There had to be a way to set something up.

Chapter Eleven

"Here's what I've found out," Montgomery told the two men from Springfield who'd come to his office in Ridgeway. "The sheriff had a deputy watching the road to the Prescott place where Charlie Millard was staying with some of the family. He got away on foot: car was disabled. He surely headed north through the woods so nobody would see him. He'd gone south to Little Rock often, so would've avoided that way. Now east-west Highway 160 cuts across up here, you know, through Forsyth." He pointed to a map. "And the question is, which direction would he go in once he got there?"

"Well, we know most men on the run head for California, or up to Chicago or Detroit, where they think they can find work, disappear," the man called Crandall pointed out. He was tall, a little gawky, but with intense eyes. "Probably clear out of the country, and if he hitchhiked, there'd be no trace." This wouldn't be easy.

"Well, I thought about that, but the trap he set for my son was pretty elaborate: maybe the man's not as dumb as I thought. He'd have thought of the obvious places to head for, and maybe do the opposite." Mabry cocked his head for an answer.

"Maybe. But as far as you know, he was broke, no car, never had money? So could be he didn't get far. Nowadays most folks won't pick up rough-looking men on the road the way they used to. But if he got lucky, if he changed his name, he could disappear anywhere, close or far.

"But his picture is in post offices all over this region. Here's a couple of copies. It's been months, and with the police dragging their feet and no reports of sightings anywhere close, I think he did get a long way off."

"So we don't have anything to go on?" Atkins, the other man, shorter but with a chiseled face, asked. "Looks like you'd be wasting your money hiring us, Mr. Mabry. We can try, but it'll be like looking for the needle in the haystack; he could be anywhere." He spread his hands.

"What I have is a strong feeling that he went north, then either west or east. Now somebody will remember him, somewhere. What I'm asking you to do is start with Highway 160 and go both ways at least to the next state line, asking at every gas station, café, town."

"That's still a huge part of the country, sir." Crandall pointed out the obvious. "You sure you want to spend that much money?"

"I want Charlie Millard. Now I'm willing to pay for a month's work: thorough work. After that, if you haven't found anything, no trace, we'll reconsider. And just maybe the sheriff here will turn up something in that time, too. Maybe Millard will contact his family."

Both the detectives knew this would be a near impossibility, but what the hell, this old guy was willing to pay. Their ten bucks an hour each would build up on him quickly, but this was what they did, so okay: go after that needle. And sure, they *could* get lucky, unlikely as that was.

With ear pressed to the closed door, Christine Mabry had heard most of this. She'd begun going into town to her father-in-law's office to help his secretary who, at 74, didn't put in a full day lately and was off today. She stepped back, sat quickly, and was shuffling papers as the two detectives filed out. Atkins ran his eyes over her as he put on his hat. *Good-looking woman, the dead man's widow. Wonder if she could have some connection to this Millard: always more to a pretty woman than what you see. But the old man's convinced he knows what happened, so off we go.*

Christine, too, noticed the sharply dressed Atkins and had caught his eyes on her. Well, she'd give this all a few necessary years and maybe she'd start looking around again. Why not? Have to be extra careful, though: the old lawyer was sharper than his son had been. She wondered where Cam Henry was just then.

But this worried her: Montgomery sending this high-priced team out on a dead-end road with absolutely no clues to follow. *He has a feeling? Where'd that come from? He's grasping at straws. Millard could have caught a freight to Canada or South America. Is he losing his mind?*

She thought about this later as she picked up her son at school. They had a good home with the old man, and she'd listed her own house for sale; she'd have that money. Their future looked secure enough. But if the Mabry family fortune was about to be squandered, that didn't look good.

* * *

Sort of like a pet dog, Charlie was: somebody always had to look after him. Would've been all right if he'd just stayed around. Or stayed gone, made a life for himself. But I guess I just took on the job of big sister, even if I was the youngest. Becca didn't have much patience with him, but he got along with Dave all right. And Nate's always mistakenly idolized him. Well, he's gone, and I guess it's for good; he won't risk writing us, since he'll suspect the police will go through our mail.

But Andy missed her brother. It wasn't just that he had worked his share while he was here—more than his share. He'd just always showed up, grinning, after months, even years, and the place had always brightened up those times. Now the three of them here seemed to spend all their time working, and there wasn't much laughter at the Prescott place.

She encouraged Nate to go to school activities, get involved in sports. At the rate he was growing, he could make the basketball team next year for sure. And there were still pie suppers, square dances in the local community, the traditional places for young people to gather. The churches here were mostly Baptist or Pentecostal, neither of which approved of any other kind of dancing. There were probably youth group projects, but he hadn't shown any interest in them. When she'd suggested he get out more, he'd dismissed the activities as "full of giggly girls nobody wants to be around."

Well, I've said it before: we'll just keep on like we are till things change one way or another. Hal Burgess won't find Charlie now, and he's not located any other suspect. It'll all blow over in time, and as long as nobody comes after us here, I guess we'll be all right.

Andy was well aware of the sheriff's interest in her; women just knew these things. And yes, she'd considered him as a possible future man in her life, despite the years between them. He was certainly the best-educated available specimen around Ridgeway, having, as she knew, a college degree. And yes again, she did get lonely for a man of her own, but things were still too much up in the air. *I'm surely still a suspect, even if they're sure Charlie did it. Gosh, even Nate's probably one, too, in the eyes of the crazy law.*

Whoever had killed Barry Mabry had certainly done her a favor: no more assaults, nastiness. From him or any other man since. And yes, Charlie could have seen to it she was protected in just that violent way. *But why the elaborate trap? He could've just shot the man out in the woods. Or maybe he thought that'd be too good for him.* She shuddere; the image of her tormentor impaled on sharp oak spines had never left her. In fact, it was so vivid she sometimes felt she'd actually seen it.

* * *

"Thought I'd let you know, Burgess, I've hired detectives to track Charlie Millard. You don't seem to've made any progress, and I want the man." Montgomery Mabry stood before the sheriff's desk, declining a seat.

"Your decision, sir, but it's a waste of money; we've got the state police on it, with the cooperation of the Missouri people, and they've even contacted the Tennessee and Oklahoma forces. There are pictures of Charlie on post office bulletin boards for two hundred miles in every direction. He might change his name, but I doubt he'd be in any sort of disguise."

"How about any contact with his sister? I'm not convinced he was sharp enough to dream up that complicated trap; she's always been the smart one."

"We've intercepted all mail going to their house, and they don't have a telephone. I doubt if he'd trust anyone to take a message to them by hand either."

The lawyer was past patience with Burgess. The man wasn't really trying here.

"Not to put too fine a point on it, Sheriff, but could you be letting your personal feelings for Andy Millard keep you from a serious effort here?" He knew he'd insulted Burgess, but he didn't care. "She could have done it herself, you know: motive."

The sheriff didn't rise to the bait. Pompous lawyers always bullied, and he'd weathered many of them. They *did* sometimes make him wonder why he'd chosen this profession.

"She is a suspect, sir. So is Elijah Prescott, and even young Nate, though I doubt either of them was involved. Everybody's a suspect until proven otherwise. But yes, Andy Millard had the strongest reason to kill your son: she couldn't know when he'd attack her again."

"He didn't attack her, Sheriff: you know she tried to seduce him. Why isn't she in jail?"

"You seemed certain Charlie was the guilty one, more so since he ran. What, are you grasping at any straw you can find, Mr. Mabry? Andy Millard was acquitted. She hasn't gone anywhere: she's still raising Nate, taking care of his grandfather. And with absolutely no evidence, there's no reason to arrest her. You're a lawyer; you know that."

"All right, but I'm also certain she knows where her brother's gone. Surely there are ways to get her to tell. We're talking a depraved murderer here, and I can't see why you haven't gone down every avenue, turned over every stone." He glared at Burgess, who ignored him.

"Thanks for coming by, Mr. Mabry. Now, I have work to do, and good luck with your detectives." He took the lawyer by the elbow, ushered him out the door. He'd liked to've thrown him bodily out.

* * *

Sam Carmody, the mill supply salesman, knew he'd be a few days more in Missouri, so he wrote his wife a letter, something his kids always liked to see, too. He'd gone out of his way to follow up on a message from near the town of Doniphan about a hammermill, and he stepped into the first post office he passed on the way there.

The posted pictures of wanted criminals were the usual: poorly reproduced photographs probably well out of date, and he stepped past the bulletin board to the window.

"Need a stamped envelope," he told the clerk, who began rummaging through a drawer for it. While waiting, the man noted one of the posted pictures, and it triggered a memory. Hadn't he seen that man? He moved closer. Name was Charlie Millard, but that didn't mean anything. He saw a lot of people on his territory, and despite a memory for names, which helped a lot in his business, this one didn't ring a bell. Still…

His letter sent, he got back on the road, calculating his commission for the hammermill, assuming the miller at Doniphan would buy it. He always assumed this, since that positive approach usually worked. Not "Do you want this?", but "Let's talk about how much money this machine can bring in for you."

But the face on the wall kept creeping back into Carmody's mind: he didn't like not being able to put a name to a face. Then he remembered the hitchhiker but couldn't remember if he'd even given a name. Hitchhikers usually didn't. *But wanted for murder, that's serious. Let's see, what did he say about himself… just that he was headed for West Virginia, and I told him I'd worked out of Charleston. Probably doesn't know much about that state, way he talked.*

Charlie's round face came back to him, the way the man grinned, seemed pleasant enough. *But a murderer? That's scary. Did I help a killer escape? Maybe, but nobody'll ever know about that. Keep quiet I guess, and it's a long shot, anyway.*

He drove on, trying to put the man's face out of his mind. Once in Doniphan, he hunted up his potential buyer and focused on the desired/needed sale. A hammermill was a machine that had swinging cutters inside to reduce grain to, first, livestock feed, although it could be used to produce finer meal. The machines were much faster than the old millstones, even those now run by engines instead of water wheels. Or even the serrated steel rollers most mills had switched to.

"Now, Mr. Halleck, this mill is good as new and half the price. I know you've gotta cut your expenses here, and this little mill will make you more money than anything you've got here." The miller sat behind his scarred desk, stone-faced, clearly a man who drove a hard bargain. The salesman liked them that way: each one a challenge.

And it was only 45 minutes later that, the order in his pocket, he shook hands, promising the machine in five days. He drove away, smiling at the final price: $25 profit above what he'd expected. He'd be able to buy his wife a little something, maybe in Sikeston.

Carmody's favorite hotel nearby was a little one at a wide place in the road that was formerly a thriving village. With the drying up of small grist and flour mills in the region and related businesses, the place had become seedy, but salesmen still gathered there when in the area. He might see his old friend Jackson Ames, an office supply salesman and a notorious ladies' man. Ames had cut a swath among the secretaries and telephone operators thereabouts and was always good company for a drink or two.

The village now had boarded-up storefronts and a closed cafe, and the hotel's sign was a little askew, but the proprietor welcomed Carmody like an old friend. He reported that he'd heard from two of the regulars, but not Ames.

"He'll come swinging in here any day now, I reckon, Sam, maybe with a jealous husband after him. Dunno how he gets away with some of his shenanigans."

"Moves fast and never looks back. But that man could sell office machines to an Eskimo; won't take no for an answer." He took his suitcase upstairs to his usual room, got out of his suit, took a shower.

Later at dinner in the peeling dining room, Carmody was talking to another salesman about politics, the economy, the rising price of cars, and, of course, women. The other man was single and sold aluminum cookware at parties hosted by former buyers. His prospects were usually girls just out on their own, settling into apartments with their first jobs. His face resembled that of a horse, but that hadn't hindered his success with the young ladies. Carmody was considered handsome, but he was faithful to his wife. Almost always.

The conversation began to drag, when he remembered the face on the poster, and wondered if his friend had seen it. Idle question, but it wouldn't go away.

"Well, yeah, I did see that on a post office wall: feller wanted for murder down in Arkansas. Amiable-looking sort, but y'can't tell about people, can you? They say Billy the Kid was th' kind you'd wanta buy a drink for."

"Yeah, funny. Thing is, I might've given that very fellow a ride back a couple months. Sorta gives me the creeps, thinking I maybe had him right there in my car." He took a sip of his beer.

"Really? Wow, wouldn't that be somethin' now. You sure?"

"Oh, not that sure, no. Just tuggin' at my mind, y'know; won't go away."

"Well, why don'tcha just call that in to whatever cops are after him. Might help, even if it's been awhile."

"Should, I guess. He did say something about going east to West Virginia. I was on that territory, few years back. Maybe give 'em a direction anyway."

Next day, Carmody visited the village post office, and sure enough, there was the picture of Charlie Millard, with requests to contact the Arkansas State Police or the sheriff's office at Ridgeway. He jotted down the numbers, got change for a pay phone.

"Don't know if this'll be any help," he told Hal Burgess, "but I may have given a ride to this Charlie Millard back a few weeks." He actually felt a little silly: this was a stretch, to say the least.

"Anything helps, sir. Where was this?"

"I was heading for Poplar Bluff on a sales call on U.S. 160. Fellow didn't give me his name but said he was getting out of farming, heading to West Virginia to work in the mines. Now, I used to be on that territory, out of Charleston, so I suggested he go there to see what was available: lot of mining, chemical plants, and such there. Anyway, I know this is a long shot, but I just thought…" his voice trailed off. *Waste of time, but I've got it off my chest, anyway.*

Burgess questioned the salesman as to time and any other details he could remember. Carmody prided himself on his memory and gave the sheriff all he could recall.

"Pleasant fellow actually, not the type at all, but I guess that's why criminals get away with stuff, isn't it? Anyway, hope this can help."

At his end, Burgess got out a map, calculated the route Charlie could've taken, north maybe as far as U.S. 160, then east toward the Mississippi River. West Virginia was a long way, but it was as underdeveloped as the Arkansas mountains: "Fight for last place in th' Union, those two do" was a standing joke.

Well, now. I guess if I wanted to disappear, that'd be about as deep a hole as I could find. He'd guess we'd start with California or up north and go a long way from there. Charleston…I'll get the state boys to contact those folks, get Charlie's picture up. Never been there, but everywhere's got post offices.

* * *

Charlie never could keep his mouth shut. He enjoyed talking with everyone, about work, cars, the weather, and any other topic that might come up. He was careful not to mention anything specific about his past, just where he was from, anything that might give a hint to connect him with the manhunt he was sure was still going on.

But the natural talk at the West Virginia Lemons farm inevitably included the boss and his family, particularly the lively Jeannie. The men speculated about the older husband and younger wife, as gossips have since the world began.

"That gal, she don't care who she teases," old Theo observed, watching from a distance as at that moment she was visible downslope laughing with one of the farmhands. "Git that ole boy hotter'n a pistol, then leave him with his face jist hangin' out," he grinned.

"Wonder if it's all tease," another logger mused. "Might jist be spreadin' it aroun' 'mongst a lotta guys."

"Oh, I'd say it's a littla both," Charlie put in. "Kinda woman does jist what she wants to, an' don't care who knows it. Wouldn't mess with th' likes of us o'course, but mebbe some slick salesman, er lawyer, doctor. An' y'know, where there's honey, there's gonna be flies."

"Didn't know no better, I'd s'spicion that Ronnie might jist be gittin' him a little of that when Daddy ain't lookin'," Theo ventured.

"Oh, I know…" Charlie stopped himself. *Better keep that quiet, now. Come back on me fer sure.* "What I mean, I know that's mebbe likely, him here right in her face, y'know. 'Course I wouldn't be one t'say so." He managed his trademark grin.

"Wal, I seen 'em up close t'one 'nuther plenty times," Theo went on. "Man'd hafta be made outta arn, he didn't give that a try."

"Stepmama, but that don't count none," the other logger observed. "She ain't real kin, an' I wouldn't doubt thet boy, he wouldn't keer, neither. Be 'bout like yore dawg'd keer, Theo."

Charlie knew more than he was about to let on with this subject. Another time, he'd seen Jeannie and Ronnie leave the big house in the Jeep when the senior Lemons was absent and head in the opposite direction across the fields. *Not my bizness. Don't care what they's doin', but sure, they's doin' it. Jist gotta stay outta their way, an' I c'n save me up a little, prob'ly move on. Ronnie, he don't like me, plain, an' if he ever gits ennything on me, he'll come down on me. There's other farms, other loggin', an' them mines I heard about.*

The lady who was the object of this speculation took care to keep her husband satisfied between the sheets, ensuring, she hoped, that he wouldn't suspect her of any infidelity. She was a good cook, and with the part-time kitchen help, provided a rich table and saw to it that he stayed happy. Which, of course, allowed her to stay happy, also.

It was actually the father, Donald Lemons, who noticed the posted picture in a Charleston post office on a trip to town. It looked familiar to him, but at first he didn't make a connection. He was one of many thousands who never registered those pictures; they'd become almost invisible to the general public.

Then as he paid the men off that Saturday, he noticed the resemblance to Charlie Barrett. *But that poster said Arkansas. Other side of the country: coincidence. He's one of the best men I've got. Still, that man's name was Charlie Millard. Easy enough to change a name. And I didn't ask for a Social Security card, paying cash. Damn government takes too much of what we make anyway.*

But it was enough to cause Lemons to check the closer post office in the next village, which displayed the same picture. It read: *Wanted for Murder and Flight to Escape Prosecution.* Well, if that really was their man, he'd certainly fled a long way. He resolved to have a talk with his logger, find out more about the man.

He started with his son, Ronnie, who'd worked closer with the hired help than he had. Surely he'd have noticed anything amiss with the affable man.

"Ronnie, you getting along with those boys in the log woods all right?"

"Sure, Dad. They work hard, earn their pay. We've about finished with the close stuff, though; need to move them on over the big hill into that white pine now. But is there a problem?"

"Not really. How about that Charlie Barrett? He seem okay?"

"Well, now you ask, there's something about him that rubs me the wrong way. He works hard, sure, and the other men like him. But he's sort of a smartass, always joking, and I don't know, maybe sticks his nose into things that aren't his business."

"Like what?"

That had slipped up on Ronnie. He'd seen Charlie watching him, particularly when he was with Jeannie, and he was sure about the chainsaw chain incident. *But be careful, here.*

"Oh, just that he talks too much, in general. I know for a fact all the men gossip about us. Jeannie can't walk past without all of them ogling her, more so that Charlie. I guess I sort of resent that: rednecks."

Donald Lemons wasn't blind; he'd known from the beginning that his new wife was a head-turner. And he also knew his son was also attracted to her: how could he not be? But had this Charlie, who just might be a wanted criminal, gotten out of line with her? Surely not, or she'd have said something. Still…

"You know anything for sure?"

"Well, no, I guess not. It's just that I don't think like those guys who work for us. Jeannie's a good-looking lady, and she's your wife, and I just don't like loose talk about her—us." That was weak, but it was as far as he would go toward an accusation. Let it work in his father's mind, and maybe he'd be rid of Charlie, one way or another.

And it did. While he didn't say anything to his son about the post office picture, Donald Lemons found time to talk with the logger next payday. *Just find out a little more, that's all.*

"You're doing good work, Charlie. Be moving you all on over the hill next week into that white pine. Oh, where'd you say you were from, by the way?"

"West, other end of Kentucky, an' spent some time 'cross th' big river in Missouri, on back. Raised on a farm up in th' hills, nothin' but rocks t'bust yer plowpoint an' cut-over timber."

"So, what brought you here? This country's about as poor, except for this steep hillside timber."

"Oh, like t'travel some. Met a feller usta be a salesman outta Charleston, told me about this country. I'se thinking minin' but always liked th' woods, an' you treat us fine, sir. 'Preciate th' work, an' it's somethin' I c'n do all right. Git along with th' boys okay: tight crew." *Where was this going? What did the boss suspect here?*

"Well, Ronnie hard to work for? Give you any hassle?"

"Ronnie? Aw, no, he don't hardly come around much, leaves us mostly alone. Theo, he's th' man in charge, an' we do what he sez."

Charlie was nervous, and Lemons could see that. Still, this didn't seem like a murderer. Was Ronnie just imagining things? And did it matter really? The logging was going well, making money. Of course there were lots of available men out there looking for work…

"So, you planning on staying with us? Or maybe seeing more of the country?"

"Mr. Lemons, sir, long's I'm welcome here, I'm yer man. If

m'work don't please you, jist you send me along. Ronnie, he ain't satisfied with me er somethin'?"

"Oh, not at all. Just like to know more about the men working for us. My wife ever go up, visit with you all?"

"Oh no, sir. Dangerous, y'know. Tree's liable t'come over back'ards er send them broke limbs flyin'. No, Theo, he's told her polite-like she oughta stay back."

"Well, that's right, and I'm glad none of you has been hurt, like that other man. Well, you just keep on like you have been, and I'd say you've got a job here till the timber runs out. Like in a couple of years." He smiled, clapped Charlie on the shoulder.

Now there's somethin' tall standin' up b'hind all that. He ain't just askin' t'be polite. Wonder if that Ronnie's planted somethin' in th' ole man's head now. Don't think I oughta hang around much longer, git bit by somethin'.

So Charlie's next move that same Saturday afternoon was a ride into the village, where an enterprising garage owner there fixed up mountain-ravaged cars and trucks to resell cheap. Mostly to the local boys who went to him when all they could afford was wheels for their short-term needs. Like just until the next Saturday night's antics. He was suspected of packing sawdust into howling differentials and building up rusted-out holes with Bondo, but some of his offerings weren't totally useless.

Charlie bargained for a dented '41 Ford with the flat-head V8 that didn't smoke too much. The tires weren't great, but he knew he could always pick up a used 600-16 tire anywhere for a couple dollars. And a dollar tire pump only cost $1.75 now, and inner tube patch was cheap.

He didn't want to register the car, but he needed current license plates, and managed to lift them off a newly wrecked car there at the garage well after dark.

And he was on the road. That very night. Which happened to be the same night Donald Lemons told his son of the post office picture that could easily be their Charlie Barrett.

"I knew it! I knew he wasn't all he appeared to be. Well, we'll just call the sheriff, let him question this guy. And either way, I want him gone: plenty other men can cut our trees."

"Well, I didn't find out anything useful about him, but yes, I'd say let the police deal with this. No use putting ourselves at risk in any way. Yes, I'll call in Monday morning."

Charlie wasn't really dumb, even if he'd fumbled a lot of his life. He realized that the cops might have somehow tracked him, or why had Lemons suddenly questioned him? And it wouldn't take them long to check for ways he might've left the Arkansas country. The garage owner here could and would surely give them the description of the car, too, so yes, he needed to do something about that also.

He drove south all day Sunday on that pair of license plates, then found a state park where he could sleep in the car. He was headed that way for no particular reason. He'd saved as much as he could, uncharacteristically staying off even beer, which had been tough. So even if he didn't have much money left, he could stretch it a long way.

Monday morning he stopped at a hardware store for paint, sandpaper, and two brushes. It was a clear day, and he drove down a country road, then off on a logging track to a wide place. He went over the exterior of the car with fine sandpaper to remove the shine; thinned paint, a dull light blue, and began applying it to the Ford. It was the new latex kind that was water-based and dried faster than the oil-based, and he needed it dry soon.

The big brush covered the major expanses, and he used the finer one around the chrome and up to the windows and tight places. The brushes left little streaks, but he'd done a lot of painting in the past, and the finished job would require a close eye to detect it. With sanding off the gloss of the original black, he knew the new paint wouldn't peel.

This took most of that day, and he ate what he'd picked up at a grocery store, drank water from a small spring nearby. He didn't look forward to another night in the cramped backseat of the car, but he could stand it.

The thing that worried him most was how Lemons might've learned who he was. Or maybe he hadn't, maybe he could've just stayed. *Naw, I got th' feelin' that Ronnie knew I saw him an' Jeannie, an' he'd of come after m, one way or t'other. Thing t'do is t'keep movin' b'fore things gits hot.*

Then he remembered that the police often sent pictures of suspects to post offices to help them find them. *That'd maybe done it, but way out here? Some way they must've got somethin' t'go on.*

And it really didn't matter: another place, another job, maybe without such as that trash at the Lemons place. He'd miss old Theo a little and a couple of the others, but, well, his life held a lot of goodbyes. Good folks everywhere, and this traveling wasn't that bad. Have to stop at a cheap motel, get cleaned up before he tried for another job, but he was better off all around than he'd been back when he'd left Arkansas.

* * *

The detectives had split up, Atkins going west on 160 back toward the distant Oklahoma line and Crandall headed east toward West Plains. Earning their pay, they checked cafés, roadside gas stations, and grocery stores for traces of the man in the pictures they carried. A few people recognized Charlie's face from seeing it in post offices, but nobody had seen him in the flesh.

Both men knew this was a wild goose chase, but it was money—they had their advances—so they kept at it for a week. Boring, tedious, but that was the nature of detective work, despite the image in movies and paperback novels. They checked in twice a day on pre-arranged pay phones with each other, just in case of a lead, but they knew there wouldn't be any.

Crandall speculated on whether their employer was crazy or just grasping at straws. Didn't matter, but this would get old really soon. He decided this wasn't what he wanted to keep on doing and told Atkins that on the phone from his motel that night.

"This isn't my thing, buddy; whattya think?"

"I'm with you on it, but we do need the bucks. Wanta pull off?"

"Thinking about it, yeah. Gotta use up the advance dough, I guess, but no, I'm already sick of it."

"Okay, let's call the lawyer, see if the cops down there have found any leads. Anything to narrow it down some."

"Sounds good. I'll do it now: not too late. Call you back either way. I'm headed for Poplar Bluff, for all the good it'll do me, and I think I oughta stop at the Mississippi. Where are you?"

"I'm west of Joplin, close to nowhere Kansas, land flatter'n a New England spinster. Yeah, call me at this number."

* * *

Montgomery Mabry had known Hal Burgess didn't owe him progress reports, or if he did, he suspected the sheriff wouldn't share them. But the lawyer had helped get one of the deputies off on a minor alcohol charge and had made a cash contribution to the man to let him know anything he thought might help in the search.

And yes, it seemed the police had heard from a salesman who said he thought he'd given Charlie a ride east on the very U.S. 160 his detectives were on. He couldn't wait to hear from them, to direct both eastward. The source had said their quarry had mentioned Charleston, West Virginia. Long way, but if it led to the killer's capture…

So when Crandall called in that night, Mabry told them of the tip. The detective didn't seem too enthusiastic.

"You want us to go there? That'll make this a high-priced project, sir."

"I don't care. Just do it. You should have enough to get you there, and if not, I'll make arrangements to get you more. My feeling that he'd gone north onto 160 was right, and with this, I think you'll find him. Maybe employment office in Charleston. I imagine the police have contacted law enforcement there, and maybe his picture is up around the region. But again, I want you to find him because they just won't try very hard. Catch a bus, train, whatever; I'll pay."

Crandall Called Atkins with the news, which excited neither man.

"Long way, surely a dead end, and I just don't wanta go," he said.

"Maybe we can say we did when we didn't?"

"Nah, the old guy will wanta see receipts. So I guess the choice is jump ship right now or go ahead, see if this leads us to anything."

"Well, I'll head back, meet you somewhere, and we'll talk about it more. Say back home in Springfield?"

"Sounds okay. Yeah, meet you at the office tomorrow. We both know the guy's crazy, but you know we don't have a whole lot else going on right now. And he's willing to keep pouring dough into us. But I get just as tired spying on unfaithful husbands as I do this stuff. So think about it, anyway."

* * *

The contractor found the note about the stranger who'd called, one day when he'd put on the jacket he must've worn that day. *Now, what was that all about? Don't remember. Well, he didn't call back so must not've been too important. And I'm trying to shut things down; don't want any more business. Or maybe it's not business. Okay, I'll call, see what this's about.*

He dialed the long-distance number, and it was picked up two rings later. A voice like any other answered, but he could tell this man was old, too.

"This's Nate Prescott. I got a note to call you back some time ago, but I'm afraid I misplaced it: just now found it. What can I do for you, sir?"

"Mr. Prescott, I'd like to meet with you, whenever you say. I heard you're closing your business down, and this doesn't have anything to do with that, anyway. It's about something that happened when we were both young, back in Ridgeway, Arkansas."

"Who is this? I haven't been to Ridgeway in forty, fifty years."

"This is Giles Mabry. You surely remember me, Barry Mabry's son?"

There was a moment of silence as Nate's mind ran over the name. So many names…but Ridgeway? It took a moment to register.

"Oh yes, certainly. Well, this is a surprise. Yes, we can meet if you'd like. When suits you? I'm free most afternoons, after I check in with what's left of the business."

"Saturday? I can fly in to Charlottesville then. I'm in Dallas."

"Saturday's okay. Sure. But that's a long way just for a visit, Mr.

Mabry."

"Oh, I think it'll be worth it. Call you when I land."

Nate punched off, wondering what in the world Giles Mabry wanted to tell him. He hadn't seen the boy—well, old man, now—since he'd left the place. *Let's see, he'd have been what, maybe eight years younger? That'd make him about sixty-five, sixty-six now. Retired, surely, from whatever he's been doing in Dallas. He should have inherited the Mabry place, all those acres, from his grandfather, but that didn't happen, I remember. Now, where'd I hear that? But must've moved on to greater things. Yes, those terrible killings*: it was all coming back to him now.

Well, this is news, I guess. And of course she'll want to hear about this, whatever it turns out to be. The woman in his life was eighty-three, but still sharp, still very much involved with Nate's pursuits. She'd been his guide, his mentor, his motivating force for almost all his life, and the two were still close.

Nate had installed his aunt Andy in a restored cottage from the late 1700s outside Charlottesville many years before, after she'd retired from the interior design business she'd owned soon after college. And now, after his wife's death, she'd picked up looking after him as she'd done sixty years before.

He thought about that now, how she'd denied herself, worked at everything she could find, sending him money from her first real job through his college years. And how he'd then insisted she go herself, then in her thirties, supported partly by his earnings.

That had been first in Springfield, then Memphis, before he'd left his engineering job, married Audrey. And before coming here, where he'd acquired his taste for restoring historic houses in the area that included most of Virginia, North Carolina, Maryland, and Kentucky.

That was all so long ago, all of it. And nobody in Everett County would've guessed I—we—could ever work our ways out of that poverty. Grace of God, that miracle. With a lot of help from Aunt Andy. He didn't know or care much what might be going on back in those mountains today. Both of them were in comfortable circumstances now, and for that he thanked that same God.

Nate had combined his skill as a craftsman, learned from his grandfather and in that work-for-tuition college, with a practical business knowledge and had succeeded after a slow start. He'd given up his engineering job in order to pursue what he really wanted to do: build places for people to live. He'd learned the most important lesson early: to go after the money first, although he'd always enjoyed the actual hands-on work itself, and that had been the winning formula.

But Giles Mabry, coming all the way from Dallas; must be more to this than two old men going over memories. The feud's what it must be about, and I guess you could say we're still sort of enemies, though I hope not. Buried all that long ago.

Nate got the mental picture of himself and an aged Giles Mabry from that old perspective in the upper air. He was here below, and the other man, indistinct now, across the states in Texas. There were masses of people, places between, but the two of them stood out, clear in some sort of…destiny?

Chapter Twelve

Montgomery Mabry hadn't wanted the police to find Charlie Millard before his detectives did for a very specific reason. He knew the evidence against the man was circumstantial, and while there appeared to be no other suspects and he was certain in his mind Millard was the killer, he might just be acquitted. He'd seen that too often as a lawyer: the gross miscarriage of justice.

He wasn't going to let that happen.

Not to the murderer of his only son. No, even in the supposedly enlightened 1950s, there were still ways to see that Millard did not continue his dissolute, evil life. Montgomery Mabry would hire an assassin, located for him by one of his associates in the inner cities: Memphis, Springfield, St. Louis. Through enough intermediaries, for enough money, this would be possible—even a certainty.

Mabry had all but abandoned any hope of running for public office: his grief, his thirst for revenge had shifted his whole outlook, priorities. And he was beginning to sense that he was possibly losing some of his edge. He could never forget that about missing the obvious connection with that gun at the Millard trial, among other slips.

So what if perhaps some rumor began after Charlie was killed: nobody could ever connect him with the deed. And even if it left a stain on him, a doubt, forget the need to curry voter favor. This needed doing.

So much so that he contacted Crandall again, raising the price by half. This was unheard of at the time: fifteen dollars an hour each when grown men were struggling to make a dollar and a half. That decided both detectives, and they were on an eastbound train toward Charleston the same day. *Still a long chance they'll find him, but the field's narrowed a lot, now. And I still have the feeling they'll get him, if he runs to the ends of the earth.*

Atkins and Crandall weren't sure at all, but the lure of the money was too much to ignore. So, go to Charleston, make a few inquiries, spend a reasonable amount of time there, then go home and collect. And okay, something *could* turn up: a clue, a trail. The man would, after all, feel he was buried so deeply he wouldn't try very hard to stay hidden. The men had learned that the farther a wanted man ran, the more careless he became. And people always let things slip, things others remembered later, things that could leave a trace.

In Charleston at last, they rented a '55 Chevrolet and checked in with the state employment office. Their spiel was that they were hired to locate this Charlie Millard to inform him of inheriting an estate back in Arkansas. He was known to have come to this city looking for work, and could any of the staff here recall seeing him?

None did, although one remembered seeing what he thought might be the same man's wanted poster at a post office branch. No, the detectives assured him, this man was just an ordinary citizen, unaware that he'd come into money.

Atkins and Crandall had been warned to stay away from any law enforcement wherever they went: Mabry wanted his man for himself. Both manhunters suspected the old man had serious plans for their quarry and agreed they would stay totally hands-off if they ever located him. That sort of deal could get them burned badly, they knew.

"Well, if I was looking for work and trying to stay outta sight," Atkins speculated, "I wouldn't stay here in this town. I'd go out into the mountains, maybe try one of those smelly chemical plants or a mine? Too many chances somebody'd remember seeing his picture here, y'know?"

"Yeah, and there's 360 degrees out from here, and no way to know which way to go." He thought a moment. "No, according to this map, there aren't that many roads outta here. I guess we could ease out a couple of them, ask around, on the off chance. Man was trying to get lost, and what a state for it this is. Look at these empty places on the map."

"But he was hitchhiking, so somebody'd remember him, sure. Problem is, we don't know which road to take. Wanta flip a coin?"

"Makes about as much sense as any of this. Okay, let's spend a week, like we said. Take this first highway out of town, then work our way around like a clock, all right?"

"Why not? Old man might just check on us if we try to pull the wool totally over his eyes. Maybe crazy but not dumb. Yeah, let's head out, ask around. Looks like most of the side roads dead-end, and I hear it's poor country, not much going on. One thing we haven't found is any evidence he's stolen anything: car, stuff to sell, or broken into anybody's house. Would've been some word somewhere."

"So he's gotta be either honest or just being careful not to leave any trail, which we knew to begin with. But with no dough, how's he living? Somebody's gotta have hired him somewhere. I doubt he's got a rich uncle back in one of these hollows."

They drove. They stopped, asked. They tried any business they passed. Soon the locals would be talking about the lucky guy nobody could find who'd inherited big bucks somewhere. The gossip grew, got outsize, provided a half-day's speculation along the back roads. After all, what else was there to talk about on the front porches, the benches at the courthouse squares, the country store seats around the wood stoves?

* * *

Charlie was in north Georgia in mountains that looked a lot like Arkansas to him. And the place was about as poverty-stricken. But he'd scored that job in West Virginia, so maybe his luck would hold here. No place had offered work along the way, and this was about as far as he wanted to stretch his limited money. He'd had to buy two tires so far, and his generator had gone out. He'd parked the car on hills wherever he could, to roll-start it and save his battery, and never used his lights.

But here, at a place called Roswell, he'd had to pay for a junkyard generator, planning to stay till he'd scoured the whole region for work. Any work: mucking out stables, digging ditches, driving a truck, farm work, since it was now well into spring. As a last resort, he'd have to sell the car, which had also made it necessary to replace the generator.

But Charlie was an optimist—always had been. Something would turn up. Again. He figured he had two weeks if he continued to sleep in the car, eat crackers and cheese, and not buy even one beer. In that time he'd be able to drive out along all the roads from this town, see what was out there. Then walk, if it came to that. He was hard to discourage.

He did miss his family a lot. He'd really enjoyed Nate's looking up to him, eager to hear his tales. And of course Andy had always taken care of him: little sister but like a mother, too. And even old Elijah had finally come around, at least to tolerance, and the two of them had done the farm work together like real family.

It'd been so much better before, being able to get back home, broke or otherwise, see them, help out, reconnect. Of course, his sister always rolled her eyes at his escapades, but she'd never turned him awa and wouldn't, ever. Wasn't that what family was all about, after all? You took care of your own, no matter what, and they took care of you. The world didn't, that was for sure: let a man starve if he had no place to go.

But now he couldn't ever go back there again. Or risk contact, even with using another name. Cops would jump on any letter from any place strange coming to the Prescott farm. He regretted not having sent a note from that West Virginia place since he was leaving anyway: at least let them know he was okay. Wouldn't tell the cops anything, that. But no, they'd probably sweat Andy and Nate, thinking they'd somehow helped him escape. *No, best th' way it went, all told.*

So, make another life for himself, here where they talked different but acted like poor folks everywhere. He thought about that some: how the old idea that folks were different off away from home was just wishful thinking. *Ever'body's gotta eat, have hisself a place to be, some kinda work t'do. Don't matter whar he lands: prob'ly even rednecks like me in New York, feller get outside that big town.*

He'd struck up a conversation with the junkyard owner as he took the generator off a wrecked Ford. Asked about work, of course, but old Lurvy hadn't known of anything.

"Wisht I c'd afford you: gittin' too old t'fool with this stuff," the stooped, white-haired native had told him. "No money in it, way ever'body's buyin' new cars 'n pickups. Cain't afford 'em, but y'know, on credit, an' a lot of 'em's havin' t'let 'em go back when they gits laid off er come up short."

"Well, I could maybe help you 'n hour or two, y'git in a bind, if I don't find m'self 'nuther job. I'll check by, time to time, y'don't mind."

"Naw, not that much happenin', but sure, we c'n pass th' time, I reckon, watch th' rust spread." He guffawed, slapped Charlie on the back.

And as the days passed with no prospects, the fugitive did stop by, bring the old man a nickel Coke or a pack of cigarettes. They'd sit on the tattered car seat in the shack office, talk about politics, women, the usual topics. It got so, too, when somebody actually needed something, a part or some old iron, Charlie would go with his new friend Lurvy and help him.

"'Preciate it, but y'cain't do this fer free, Charlie. Here, you take this five now. Git y'self a good night's sleep over t'th' boardin' house yonder. Livin' in yer car make you mean." He laughed at his own humor.

"Aw, well, thanks, Lurvy. Fact is, ain't a thing turned up. If I c'n help a bit, glad t'do it."

And as these things sometimes went, the old man found things Charlie could do: heavy stuff like pushing the worthless hulks off the hill behind the place, pulling the usable engines out, prying the worn-out cars up on their sides to remove axles and springs. He couldn't pay much, but his new helper was used to bare subsistence.

And now and then somebody would junk a car that had been in

an accident or maybe had a bad engine he didn't want to spend money on, that the old man just happened to have the right replacement for. He and Charlie would work on the revived vehicle, fix whatever else was the most trouble, and put a' *For Sale* sign on it.

"Way I see it, y'git th' wust whar it'll work, an' that's whut a feller'll thaink's all thet's wrong 'th it, Charlie. He won't mind th' wipers don't wipe, er th' dash lights don't light up, er th' seat's tore. Long's he kin git it down th' road t'his woman's place an' back, he'll spend ennythaing he's got on it. These young'uns got th' idee a car's th' most important thaing in th' world, an' they'll go 'thout groceries t'git thar hands on one ever' time."

And there were always farmers, loggers, poor folks who'd buy anything that ran, and with literally no overhead, these sales were almost pure profit. And Lurvy was generous in sharing these occasional windfalls. After all, this boy had done all the heavy work and wasn't the world's worst mechanic.

So it looked as if this would be as good as it would get for Charlie, at least for now. And the old man eventually even let him have a room in his sagging house, since he'd been widowed many years before. The two became a team, albeit a ragged one in a ragged enterprise, subsisting on the scraps of trade, the rare sales, the cobbling together of more or less mobile vehicles.

Charlie had purposely gone into the local post office early on, suspecting a possible picture of himself there, but none was visible. *No reason for ennybody to s'spect I'm down here: guess I'm as lost as I'll ever be.*

* * *

Nate and Andy plowed, planted, irrigated, weeded as they had every spring and summer. Old Elijah was less and less help, arthritis compounding the difficulties of having only one leg. But he'd taken on another job: teaching Nate woodworking. The two of them spent long hours in Dave's old shop, shaping tables, chairs, even doors and windows for people in the area.

With school out for the summer, Nate treasured the time working with his grandfather. Andy watched them out her window, a new one they'd made, with fondness. Elijah was being father to her nephew, as she was being mother. It made her warm inside. The boy would go on to become a competent carpenter in time, she could tell.

Three years now, and he'd be off to college. They'd talked about that a lot, and all agreed they should sell this marginal farm, which now without timber, could not produce quite enough to survive on. Surprisingly, Nate, as its owner, now seemed to have no qualms about parting with the place. It wasn't as if it had been in the family for generations, and he knew the value of it spent on his education would clearly be much greater.

Meantime, he was getting closer to sixteen, the age he'd formerly looked forward to, the age he'd planned to drop out, work somewhere. Thanks mostly to Andy's influence, his viewpoint had changed radically, and he read more, studied hard, even in summer, to keep his grades at the top of every class. Maybe even some scholarship would be within reach. If so, he meant to get it.

Elijah Prescott saw the changing world as a dizzying place, with that new television, regular airplane transportation, the lessening of rail travel, and the beginnings of the interstate highway system. It was happening too fast, and he was just as glad not to be out in it. Here was his family, all of it that mattered. Any reservations he'd had about Andy were long gone: he admired the woman, now viewed her as one of God's children.

But Elijah was no fool: he knew deep down this dedicated, decent woman could easily have been the one who'd planned and executed Barry's murder. The man had deserved it, and killing had probably been too good for him, even if that didn't square with what the Good Book said. He studied about this for a long time, finally concluding that it just had to stay between Andy and God, and he wouldn't judge. No, not judge at all: God'd do that.

He did wonder when she'd want to go off and find herself another man, which would leave him pretty much hanging, but he reckoned God would also take care of him, one way or another. In his opinion,

God did that, although not always the way a fellow might want. Didn't matter, though, that: he could tell his old heart was failing and knew he might not live to see the family scattered. *His will, whatever He's got planned, an' it's fer me t' foller thet plan, best I kin. Meanwhile, I c'n teach Nate all I know, set him up fer whutever's t'come.*

Hal Burgess came around from time to time, with no news whatsoever about Charlie. The West Virginia tip hadn't panned out, although that Lemons family there had called the local sheriff, sure that their temporary employee was Charlie. By the time the lawman had come to that farm, Charlie—if it was indeed Charlie—had gone, in the manner of so many backwoods drifters.

And of course the detectives Montgomery Mabry had hired hadn't found a trace of their quarry. After the planned week in the area, they'd contacted their boss and told him that there'd been no sightings. Mabry's contact in Burgess's office had told him of the Lemonses' suspicions, however, which that sheriff had relayed back to Ridgeway. So the lawyer had urged his men to keep on the trail. Except now there wasn't a trail. None at all.

Ronnie Lemons had insisted the police try to find how the man had disappeared, but they dismissed his suggestions that they could learn that he might've gotten a car, somehow. The sheriff there had better things to do than chase temporary help that'd wandered off and didn't follow up, other than to report the supposed sighting. *Dunno what's got Ronnie so pissed off, anyway. What'd this Charlie do, shoot him down with his pa's young wife? Pushy bunch, anyway.*

* * *

The summer wore on, and Montgomery Mabry seemed to diminish, with no progress toward finding his son's murderer. He became sloppy in his work, forgetful, sometimes snappish, which he always tried to curb around people who mattered. He spent a lot of time with his grandson, now seven, mirroring what Elijah Prescott was doing with Nate: being surrogate father, trying hard to keep the lad from becoming a mama's boy.

He was concerned that Christine would surely begin casting her eye around for another man. That was to be expected, he'd known, *but surely not this soon. Why, it's only been…* He couldn't let that happen, or she'd take his grandson away with her, of course, and with who knew what kind of jerk? He cast about for a suitable local match for her, one that'd keep her close, but none of the men he knew would measure up. *Damn, I hope she doesn't run off with somebody like that Andy did: worthless truck driver. No, she's got more sense. I hope.*

He'd hectored Hal Burgess about not arresting, or at least harshly questioning, Andy Millard about her possible role in helping her brother with the killing, but the lawman insisted he'd taken that as far as he could. Always the same reply: no evidence.

So as he'd vowed, the lawyer began undermining the man as election time drew nearer. He admitted to himself that this was revenge, maybe even cheap revenge, but he needed someone to blame for his misery. He began bad-mouthing Burgess, exaggerating any weaknesses he thought he'd uncovered in the man's conduct in office.

It backfired, as his accusations became more transparent: the Everett County folks just knew better. Nobody really liked a lawman, but if you had to have one, Hal Burgess was about the best you could hope for. The man was fair, you had to give him that, even if sometimes he stepped on some toes. Anyway, they weren't about to throw him out, get somebody in there a sight worse.

With the wearing-out of time and its dimming of hurts, Burgess gradually increased his visits to the Prescott farm, making time to lend a hand when he could at whatever chore needed help. He wanted to make himself the obvious man in Andy's life, both to bring her around to his planned courtship and to discourage anybody else who might have that in mind.

She always seemed glad to see him, but there was a reserve about her, a little distance that he sensed. *Not ready to think about such as that yet, I guess, worried about Charlie, got that murder hanging over them all. Just have to keep on taking it slow, I reckon; don't push her.*

For her part, Andy regarded the sheriff as a sort of friend, but she knew he had his job to do, and he *was* hunting her brother. Her innocent brother. And she had no illusions about his coming after her, Nate, or Elijah if some clue should surface that implicated one of them. After all, somebody had planted that ladder, clearly to point the finger at them.

No, the status quo would just have to do regarding Mr. Burgess. And maybe he wasn't the right man, anyway. There was the age thing, first of all. Then, being married to a lawman, she'd never know when he might go out on a case and not come back alive. *Wrong man, wrong situation, wrong time, and I guess I'm just the wrong woman.* She effectively put the sheriff out of her mind again, at least in the context of suitor.

Besides, with their plans to sell the farm, there'd be no reason to stay around here. Elijah would need her help for a while, but the way things were going with him, she had to face the fact that biology would take its course. *Not being cold-hearted here, but it's a fact that he's not got a lot of time left.*

She'd come to have a genuine affection for the old man, his clearcut right-vs.-wrong attitude, his generous heart, the help he was able to give. And most of all, the way he was helping prepare Nate for whatever lay ahead for him.

Being a carpenter wouldn't be bad, and it was a good skill to have. But she knew her nephew would aim higher, do more with his life. She'd seen too many country boys settle for subsistence, slowly growing older while still talking the lie of somehow growing rich. Reminded her too much of Cam Henry, who'd never be anything but a cheating, lying truck driver, never thinking of anything beyond his truck and the next woman. She didn't like remembering.

* * *

Charlie Millard would have been safe if he'd just stayed there in north Georgia, subsisting, in hiding. But Charlie just couldn't see spending his life that way. There were no attractive women here available to a penniless shirttail mechanic, and he missed the old freewheeling lifestyle he'd managed. And he was getting older, not the kid he'd been, never thinking about tomorrow, or really beyond the next Saturday night, with its honky-tonk sounds, beer, and good-time women.

But most of all, Charlie missed his family. As fall deepened, he thought more and more of the Prescott fireside, his sister's cooking, young Nate, and even old Elijah, with his fire-and-brimstone proclamations. He'd sit and daydream when nothing was happening at the junkyard, which was most of the time, about what family he had left back there.

Be time t'git firewood in. Nate'll be in school, tenth grade now, or is it 'leventh? An' Andy, she'll need help. Wouldn't doubt but Elijah's some laid up, old's he's gittin'. Sure wish there was a way I c'd go on back. This prospect of hiding for the rest of his life had never looked good, but now it was downright depressing. He knew he could never return to Everett County, but there had to be some other way to live. Some way to have a little fun at least, and surely a chance at some sort of contact with the family.

But there wasn't, and he knew it. The problem was Charlie had never been good at figuring things out, long term. He knew that, too, and had admitted long ago that good people like his sister had always done the heavy thinking for him, appreciating his help, his good humor, his company. As long as he hadn't pushed it too far. And he thought about the murder, and whether the law had found another suspect. *That'd mean I could go on back, git me some sorta life agin.*

But he knew better, deep down. So he moped, so much so that old Lurvy noticed.

"Got yerse'f 'n'ole gal some'res yer pinin' fer, Charlie? Er jist not sociable t'day?"

"Oh, just missin' some of th' folks, I reckon. I wanted t'see more of th' country, y'know, but I guess I done that already now. Sorta wishin' I c'd git on back, least for a visit."

"Y'never said whar yer from, an' t'ain't my bizness. Long ways?"

"Yeah, too far. Well, I guess I c'n stand it awhile longer, though. Things slow down much more, y'cain't 'ford my help, an' I guess I gotta be thinkin' 'bout movin' on, sooner er later." He looked at the old man fondly. He'd become a good friend and now depended on him for more than just the heavy lifting.

"Wal, hate t'see you set on leavin', but yer right: bizness slow, an' no tellin' when it'll pick up. Seems lak ever'body's got money 'nuff fer new cars er jist makin' payments. Wreck now'n then, but no, it don't look real good down th' road with winter comin' on."

And November did come, with its flurry of fallen leaves and sharp nights and its homesickness. Work slowed to the point there wasn't really any of it.

And Charlie made up his mind.

He'd thought this out as much as he thought anything out: he'd slip on back to Arkansas and just hide out at the farm. They always knew when somebody came up the long woods road to the house, and he could hide in the root cellar till they left. He'd even thought about his clothes on the line: Nate'd be about his height by now, and nobody would suspect the added washing.

He'd not be able to go out where anybody could see him, ever. But he could help with chores by lantern light when he couldn't be slipped up on. And no, he wouldn't be a drag on the family: do his part, even if it meant housework so as to stay inside, let Andy out more. Hell, he could even learn to sew if he had to, help her at home with quilting and such.

It was a ridiculous plan. Stupid. Bound to backfire. He put it out of his mind again and again, even after he'd made up his mind to do it.

Then he did it.

Lurvy paid him a fair price for the Ford, out of a sack of accumulated dollar bills he had hidden. Then Charlie rubbed black walnut juice on his face, neck, arms, backs of hands, tickled at this idea. When he looked into a mirror, he saw a black man, with only his blue eyes to give him away. So he bought a cheap pair of sunglasses and wore them around town. Nobody gave him a second glance, even people who'd come to know him. *Now that's somethin', ain't it? I'm just a black feller t'all of 'em, not fit t'speak to, even t'notice. Now, this's gonna work, fer sure.*

He bought himself a ticket west and when the bus came, he went dutifully to the back, sat with a brown sack of bread and bologna and a warm Pepsi-Cola. There would be changes in Tennesee, then again in Little Rock, but he'd be home in two or three days, depending.

He had to wait at a couple of back doors to cafés for the food he'd paid just as much for as the "white" folks inside, and that was a revelation: he'd just taken for granted that black people were different—never really thought about it—but here it was, and yeah, it was wrong. *Hafta maybe think 'bout tha, some; most places back home they don't even get t'vote.*

He missed the connection in Memphis because he wanted to stroll around, see the sights. Biggest town he'd ever been in, even with his roaming around the past few years. Lots of black people here, but still not treated anywhere near equal. And things cost more here like they did in any city, so he was glad to be moving on.

He knew Little Rock well and didn't pause there since he was afraid, even with his disguise, somebody he knew might recognize him. He hadn't been able to find out if he was still a wanted man but suspected he was. So he changed buses, headed north on U.S. 65 toward Harrison and the Missouri line, his concern growing as he got closer to home. But again, nobody seemed to pay him any mind there at the little junction where he had to wait for the eastbound bus.

There wouldn't be that next local run till the following day, so he bought himself an additional secondhand coat the store owner let him have, and hiked out into the woods to spend the night.

It was cold, but he piled dead leaves, burrowed into them, and slept fitfully, dreaming alternately of the homecoming ahead and of waking up in jail. When the sun finally appeared, he rose, stiff and chilled, shook off both the leaves and his misgivings, walked back in time to catch the smaller bus.

There were almost no blacks in Ridgeway. That part of north Arkansas was just that way; had been since the last lynching of one in Harrison in the late 1890s. So Charlie couldn't ride the bus all the way into the village without causing a minor sensation. He'd get off a few miles out, hike through the woods and across fields to the Prescott farm.

Then he'd surprise the family because black walnut juice didn't wash off; just have to let it wear away in a few weeks. He could picture old Elijah, confronted by what he'd think was maybe a runaway slave from another age. He looked forward to his reception with a touch of glee.

Once off the bus, he hurried across the road and into the sheltering oak forest. He knew where he was and set off in the midmorning chill. It'd take him just an hour, he figured, plenty time for noonday dinner. He was hungry, and the thought made him walk just a little faster.

Nate was at school, it being a Thursday, not yet Thanksgiving. As Charlie approached the farm, he saw Elijah trying to balance a small block of oak so he could swing the splitting maul at it. It fell over twice, and Charlie could see he was having trouble righting it, bracing himself on a fencepost each time. *High time I was gittin' here: th' folks needin' help.*

"Howdy, sir," he greeted the old man with a grin he couldn't suppress.

"Howdy yerse'f." Elijah straightened, stared at the sight. Was this a hobo, way off from any road, any railway? He started to question this man.

"Y'don't know me, do you?" Charlie asked, almost laughing out loud.

"Naw, cain't say's I do. Whatcha doin' off out here, feller?"

"Figgered I'd hit y'all up fer a bite if I could..." Charlie then saw Andy coming down from the high porch, a question on her face.

"Wal, I reckon..."

Then Charlie couldn't hold it any longer. He burst out laughing and even being turned away from Andy, she knew instantly who it was. She came running down, grabbed him, turned him around to hug him. Then she saw his face.

"Oh! I thought...I... *Charlie?* Is that you? It *is* you! What in this world...?" and she did hug him, hard.

"It's me all right, an' nobody ever s'spected it, all this way I come. Elijah, I fooled you good, didn't I?" He laid a hand on the old man's shoulder, careful not to tip him over.

"Wal, I never. You don't look a thaing lak yerse'f, Charlie. Shore did fool me. But whutever made y'thaink y'could git away'th comin' back? Y'know th' law's still huntin' you hard, ain't never slacked off." He was still scrutinizing this man, not totally sure yet.

"It just got so I couldn't stand hidin' any more, bein' away f'm ever'body. I been all over, workin' when I could, but it all just went so sour I hadda come on back."

"Charlie, you know you can't stay..." She was shaking her head, afraid for him. And glancing down the drive toward the road, afraid somebody passing would see.

"Think I can if I stay outta sight, stay inside, help you there, do chores b'lantern light. C'n hide in th' root cellar when ennybody comes. This'll wear off in time; be worse if somebody did see me black, cause s'spicion." She didn't look like she believed him.

"We'll just have to see then. Come on up, food's ready. You eaten lately?"

"Bite here'n there. I got a few dollars saved, too, he'p out some."

No one visited the place the rest of that day, and sure enough, Charlie helped Andy clean and even asked her to show him how to sew. He was predictably clumsy at this, and she shooed him away after he'd stuck himself with the needle for the third time.

"Wal, I c'n cut wood come dark, anyway. An' whatever else comes up. Won't be a drag on y'all."

Nate came home, stopped stonelike at sight of his uncle. Only it couldn't possibly be his uncle. Not a black man at the kitchen stove, stirring a pot of black-eyed peas. With the widest grin on him the boy had ever seen.

"What's going on, Aunt Andy? Who's this?"

"Well, look close. Ever see that grin before?" She had a big smile on, too.

Nate stepped closer. Drilled Charlie with his eyes. Then gradually his face relaxed, and he grabbed his uncle in a bear hug. He was as tall, if a lot thinner.

"Uncle Charlie! Wow, you sure fooled me. How'd you get all black?"

"Walnut juice. It'll wear off, few weeks. I couldn't stay 'way, Nate; got to missin' y'all too much. Figger t'stay hid, do what I c'n get away with, layin' low. Andy tells me there's no change, nothin' new on th' killin'. But I see they've left y'all alone, busy out huntin' me."

"They have, and Hal Burgess doesn't think you did it. He comes around, but I think it's more to see Andy. Even helps out some." He glanced at his aunt, to see her color a little, shake a finger at him, despite her smile.

"Feller's a bit old, I'd say. You like him, Andy?"

"Not really. Don't dislike him either, but I have to remember he'd put us all away in a flash if he found some crazy evidence that we'd done it. No, men are staying away, and I'm that glad of it." She rescued the peas before they could burn.

Charlie wasn't so sure; good-looking girl like his sister wouldn't stay hid much longer. But for now, this situation was better than anything else he'd come up with. Long as the law kept looking somewhere else for him, they'd keep leaving the family alone, and if he stayed hid, it'd work.

He hadn't, of course, thought ahead to how hard this would be. So Hal Burgess would come around some, and there were always the neighbors, though they were few; gradually folks were getting over Andy's supposed stigma. More so since she'd stuck with raising Nate and taken Elijah in. There just wasn't new fuel for their gossip fires any more.

And of course he'd get deathly tired of staying inside. Sure, he'd go out at night, do what little he could with hand tools in the shop, cut wood and anything else he could manage, but anybody passing, even on the distant road, would see lantern light, grow curious in time. He hadn't thought of that either.

Andy was still dubious but couldn't turn her brother away. Okay, they'd try this for a while. And if she got the slightest hint that someone suspected, she'd send him off on his own again; she wasn't about to allow him to stand trial as the only suspect: a sure death sentence.

So the first weeks passed, with Charlie's having to dive for the root cellar trapdoor only three times, once for Burgess, once for Miz Ed Carson, once for a random traveling Watkins salesman. Nobody'd stayed long, and he could stand it. The last time, however, he'd had a cold and had to bury his head in several layers of old quilt down there to keep his coughing quiet. Andy had given him the old home remedy of onion juice and sugar, which helped some.

But she knew his chances were going to diminish the longer this hiding went on. They talked about it, of course, but Charlie was unconcerned: he was getting away with it, he was here where he'd rather be, and sooner or later it'd all blow over.

"How?" Nate asked one evening. "Long as th' sheriff doesn't have anybody else to go after, you'll never be able to go out and be seen."

"Well, I guess I could black my face agin, but I figger that'd just bring more 'tention to us. And Hal, he'd get s'spicious 'fore long."

"Wal, I dunno ennythaing else y'cn do that'd make it better, Charlie," Elijah mused. "When you wuz gone, th' law left us alone. Yer here, an' th' law's leavin' us alone jist th' same. But if they ketch you, we'll all git charged with har'brin' a wanted man, so thet's gotta be part of it. Now, ain't nobody gonna try to run you off; this's home fer all us. An' I reckon we c'n all stick t'gether on this all right. Thaing t'do is t'make shore y'don't git caught. Enny little slip-up an' don't matter Hal don't thaink y'done it, he'll be here 'fore y'c'n say scat."

"What I'm worried about, Uncle Charlie, is that you'll get real tired of bein' cooped up here, inside all the time. And even if you keep on working by lantern light, somebody just might get suspicious, sneak up to see what's going on." Nate had thought about this a lot and was becoming more concerned, like his aunt.

"Could happen, I reckon. An' yeah, I ain't havin' much fun neither. Guess I could go back on th' road: done it b'fore. But fer now, winter an' all, I'd jist's soon stay hid. Come spring, t'would prob'ly be best I moved on agin. Could always black m'face again, slip in t'see y'all, time to time. Thing is, though, like always, I'd hafta scrape up a few bucks t'be able t'do it." That reality always raised its ugly head.

"You did it before," his sister pointed out. "We don't want you to leave, of course, but if the itch gets too bad, you'll do it; I know you. So I guess we'd better just accept it, and be working on just how to handle making it happen."

Chapter Thirteen

It was late December again, almost two years to the day after the timber cutting that Charlie finally had to get outside. It was a bitter, windy morning, the kind that kept every living thing inside: the air felt as if it would tear the skin off your face.

Wrong kinda day, but I gotta git shet of this place fer a spell. Ain't nobody out, this weather, an' I'll just take th' old shotgun, do some huntin'. Been missin' that bad, an' for too long. C'n see a long ways, leaves all off, an' won't nobody sneak up on me. See 'em first an' just slip on away. Wrapped up good, won't look nuthin' like m'self anyway."

He didn't tell the others, just quietly eased out of the house before they were up. The icy air cut at him, but it held a sweetness he hadn't remembered. Maybe it had a taste of freedom in it. The ground, with its half-melted snow refrozen, felt good under his worn, high-topped shoes. He stuffed his hands into coat pockets, the shotgun cradled under his right arm.

Down by the spring, he stared at the two remaining tall white oaks, regretting not having cut them. *Wish there was some way t'do it now, when we need th' money. But that'd be pushin' it too far, an' with just th' one horse, couldn't haul much. Still, that cart'd take maybe two bolts at a time…*

Charlie actually believed he was destined to land on his feet every time he got into a bad situation. He always had. And with the whole country out looking for him, here he was, home, safe, well fed, warm and cared for. *Don't get enny better'n this.* And he would find at least a little money somehow, and yeah, hit the road again come spring, keep his family safe. *Think they call it aidin' an' abettin'—somethin' like that—but they won't be, once I'm on th' road. Yeah, an' I c'n black up agin, like I said, come home some.*

These thoughts occupied him as he tramped into the Mabry woods, scanning the bare trees for whatever game he could find. Squirrels would be out, bad as the weather was. Almost no deer, hunted till they were rare. It took a really stealthy hunter to slip up on a buck or wait in an elevated stand to bag one.

* * *

Montgomery Mabry had a serious case of cabin fever, too. He told Christine he just might take a walk outside, stretch his legs a little. He hadn't slept well: had been sitting for hours, going over legal papers, concentrating till his eyes were sore.

"In this cold? Why, the wind's up: you'll get yourself chilled, Pa. Why don't you teach Giles to play chess instead? Barry had just started showing him the moves when he…you know. Don't go out; you'll get pneumonia. Besides, it's not that long till lunchtime." Christine refused to refer to the midday meal as dinner, as the locals did.

"Just for a few minutes. This place has gotten claustrophobic. I'll wrap up good, just go down, check on the horses, cattle. Be back in maybe twenty minutes, okay?" He liked her concern for him: like a real daughter. She'd sure taken over running his house, and yes, some of the paperwork, too. He felt a surge of affection for this mother of his grandson. She'd resisted any urge to go out after another man, wisely choosing instead to devote herself to raising Giles, and taking care of him, too.

And now she insisted on wrapping a wool scarf around his neck, found a bright red knit cap for his balding head. This was for visibility, since there could be hunters out, even in this weather. She kissed him on the cheek as he headed for the back door. Giles looked up from a book he was reading, said goodbye.

Mabry had so appreciated Christine's devotion and her concern for him that, the night before, he'd rewritten his will, which he'd never gotten around to since Barry's death. Lately he'd been feeling physically ill, with some dizzy spells and that poor sleeping. The doctor had found nothing wrong, advising him to slow down. After all, at his age…

In the new will, he'd left everything he owned to his daughter-in-law, with the exception of half a million dollars he'd put into a trust fund for Giles. He realized that this, payable to his grandson when he reached the age of twenty-one , would not be available for most of his college expenses, but that was part of his plan. *His mother will surely pay for that, but if by some accident she doesn't, I want him to learn the work ethic: work his way through, just like I did. Make a man of him.*

On the way out, he decided to take his deer rifle. *Might just get lucky: venison would be really fine, this weather. And I've already got the red cap on.* He stepped out into the icy morning.

Boy, it is cold out here, but bracing. Get the kinks out of my legs, then back inside, forget about hunting; she's right, I don't want to get sick. Just go on down, check on the barns…

But once there, he thought he saw the outline of a big rabbit out in the field beyond, and the idea of a short hunt resurfaced. He didn't want to shoot the rabbit with this 30.06: tear it to bits. But maybe just beyond that low ridge, he could sweep the downslope with the scope, see if maybe a buck was browsing the frozen grass.

Just past the rise, he was sheltered a little and resolved to go on farther where he could see into the open woods. That's actually where deer would be, he was sure, out of the wind, now that it was well into the morning. *But I'll want to be back in time for dinner—won't keep Christine waiting. Just a quick look. Walking's warming me up, anyway.*

He reached the shelter of the first trees, noting how they'd grown last couple of years. Maybe Barry had been right about timbering this part: about time for him to harvest them. He leaned against a big hickory, searched the woods.

And saw the distant shape of a man. Instinctively, he slipped behind the tree.

* * *

Gone, an' out in this weather. Now whut's thet fool boy gone an' done? The old man had risen early as always, was kindling the fire in the big cast-iron stove, the hungry wind tearing at the eaves of the farmhouse, trying the cracks. *Lak some critter, er a lonesome ghost, wants in.* He'd seen Charlie's muddy shoes were not where he always left them by the back door. And the shotgun was gone, too.

Too much wind out fer huntin'; reckon he jist hadda git outside fer a spell. Little lak bein' in jail I reckon, cooped up in here all th' time. Don't bother me none: let 'er blow all she wants. I'm here by th' far, an' thet's jist whar I'm gonna stay. Boy oughta be okay: ennybody else out t'day be plumb crazy. Git th' cookstove goin', too, 'fore Andy, she comes down. She'll git th' boy up…

Elijah could remember the time a little thing like the weather couldn't slow him, or keep him from morning chores. Now he was all aches, and huddled close to the warming fire. He could hear the sounds of his people now moving about above him, and reflected on how God had so provided for them. *Warm house, coats on our backs, 'nuff t'eat fer now, an' we got one 'nother. 'Bout's good as it gits, in this life.*

He remembered winter days like this, when he'd come in from chores to the glow of his little snug cabin, the smells of cooking, his young wife at the stove, a smile of joy on her sweet face at sight of him… So very long ago, all that. He let his mind play over these memories with a honeyed sadness.

Andy came down, put a hand fondly on the old man's shoulder, grateful for his having fired up both stoves.

"How you feeling, Elijah? Bitter out. Charlie should've lit the fire."

"Charlie's gone, Andy. Took th' shotgun; reckon he hadda git outta th' house fer a change. Cabin fever, y'know."

"Oh! Well, I hope he'll be careful. Somebody see him… But bad as it is, surely nobody else will be out." She hoped so, fervently. Starting breakfast—some bacon left, and yes, grits—she couldn't help worrying. And she'd have to send Nate to do the chores now before school. Couldn't let her brother be seen out in daylight when he got back. *Or I can handle that; not a big thing. Elijah's right: this house can hem you in, no sunlight for days on end…*

* * *

Charlie Millard thought he'd caught a glimpse of movement over toward the Mabry field, but just there was brush grown up in the woods edge where the sun would hit. *Maybe a buck, headed out to graze? Can't see good.* But he broke the old single-shot open, extracted the birdshot shell, replaced it with double-aught buckshot. And began to move stealthily through the trees to get a better line of sight. Venison from a buck or, more likely, a doe would stretch a long way to help the family through this winter, cut down on what they had to buy, be good all around…

Of course, Mabry hadn't recognized the bundled figure easing through his woods, all muffled up as he himself was. He ran a list of neighbors through his head, wondering which of them would be out on such a day. *Well, I'm out in it, so I guess somebody else couldn't stay inside any longer either.*

His land wasn't posted against hunting because everybody knew it was his and respected him. He didn't mind the occasional hunter, long as they all stayed far from the house and barns. Montgomery Mabry prided himself on never locking a door; didn't need to. So okay, he'd just stay behind this tree, let the bulky man go on with his hunting, then head back. Sudden move might spook the fellow, make him think he was a deer. Of course, he had the red cap on the way you were supposed to, to avoid that sort of thing. *Bless that Christine; she thought of everything.*

The hunter would move on, he'd go on back home, eat with the family as planned. *Been out longer than I meant to, already.* He removed the red cap, peered around the tree trunk to see the man not moving on, but coming directly toward him. And he wasn't that far away. He started to call out, announce his presence, but something about the figure seemed almost familiar. *Neighbor, of course, but…*

Then in his mind, a sudden bolt of lightning crashed. *That looks like Charlie Millard. No, couldn't be…* But he called up the image of the man, his red face, chunky body. He may not have realized it, but he *wanted* that to be the murderer of his son. *Charlie Millard, that bastard, right here, hiding in plain sight where nobody'd ever think to look for him.* And cold resolve filled him: he'd kill the man right here on his property, execute justice when he couldn't get it any other way.

No, wait: I can't make a mistake here, have to be sure. But he's got a gun, and if it is him, he'll shoot me. Could he be stalking me here? Oh, my God, he's come after me! He has. A fleeting thought of self-defense flickered in his lawyer's mind as he muffled the sound of chambering a round under his coat.

He couldn't risk another look; the man was too close. And he couldn't ease around the tree, stay out of sight as he came past. And he couldn't call out if that really *was* Millard, warn him. No, this couldn't be a Western shoot-out. This had to be fast, accurate.

Deadly.

He waited till the man was maybe thirty feet away, by the faint sound of his tread in the crisp snow, then he lunged from cover, raising the rifle while focusing hard on the face now showing shocked surprise. *It's him!*

And Montgomery Mabry shot Charlie Millard through the heart.

* * *

Nate and his aunt talked about the call from Giles Mabry, there in her cottage in Virginia over a dinner she still enjoyed preparing to share with him. He was trying to remember anything about the boy/man that could be of significance, but it was all so long ago. Andy, on the other hand, had several things to say.

"He'd have inherited everything the old man had put together, but Christine wanted to sell out, leave the country. She always thought she was cut out for better things; after all, she'd been a *cheerleader.*" It wasn't said with respect.

"But Giles would've been just a kid when it all happened. Why would he want to contact me now? I'd just as soon it all stayed forgotten."

"Some people carry secrets so long, that when they're old, they want to clear up loose ends, I guess. He'd had his young world so upheaved—if that's a word—that it must've changed his life a lot. So I guess whatever he's got to say to you must mean a lot to him, if not to you."

"Another time, another life really. I have trouble keeping it all in sequence now. But it did all start with our cutting that timber: I can see that clearly still. And of course Uncle Charlie, shot dead that way."

"Yes, that was the worst. He never did any harm to anyone, just kept blundering into situations that got him into trouble. Tried his best to keep the rest of us safe, and even that backfired." She was remembering the young Charlie, his round, red face, that persistent grin. Big brother who'd always acted like the younger one who needed constant rescuing.

Nate was remembering, too. *Good-time Charlie for sure*, the man he'd so looked up to when he was young. But all that about the feud, the killings, had changed everything for all of them. And in retrospect…

"But we never really knew, did we, Aunt Andy, for certain, I mean, whether he actually could've killed Barry Mabry." It was a statement. "He was so set on protecting you—well, so was I. And so was Granpa."

"Oh, yes we did know about Charlie. Or maybe I should say *I* did. I knew absolutely."

"But the sheriff never found anybody else. And with him dead, it was a closed case. And then Granpa died, too. Oh, it's troubled me from time to time, part of that stupid feud between us and them, but no, I never believed he did it, and Granpa just couldn't have."

"You never know what's deep inside anyone, Nate," she said, as if still teaching him, and with more force than he'd expected. "There's a secret place all of us keep locked up, hidden from even the closest other person. And it's who we really are, what we believe, what we're capable of, when it comes down to stark choices."

He remembered that after he'd driven home. *So forceful, the way she said that. So what's she got stored away inside? What haven't I seen all these years? One thing for sure, when that woman locks something up down deep, it's gonna stay there.*

* * *

At first, Montgomery Mabry just stood there, his rifle pointed at Charlie's shuddering body, and he realized he was shaking, too. Then the man went quiet, his eyes staring up into the bare limbs, and the shock to his own system lessened.

I've done it. I've killed Millard, that murdering bastard. But now I've got to salvage this, think this out. All right, he's got a shotgun: clearly stalking me. Self-defense, no doubt of it. But what if Burgess reads it the other way: I was stalking him*? I'm the one with motive. Have to make this clearer…*

Calm returned, and his icy will matched the chill of that lifeless day. He took the shotgun from Charlie in his now-gloved hands, aimed it at the hickory tree just off-center, and pulled the trigger. The buckshot blew a sizeable chunk of bark and wood off the tree he'd been hiding behind. *So far, so good:* To anyone, Millard had evidently fired first. Then he thought to eject the spent shell, shove another halfway in, leave the gun broken open.

And the tracks in the scuffed, crusted remains of the snow? Well, surely he'd gone to the dying man, made sure: *anybody would have done that, Sheriff.* Then he realized he hadn't chambered another round. *Should've done that right after the shot. What if I hadn't killed him? He could've still gotten me.* He'd leave the brass by the tree, make it look as normal as possible: defending himself against a killer who'd stalked him.

Then, satisfied, he left the body, its blood staining the snow, and tramped home. The thought came to him of the unbelievable coincidence of running into just the man he was hunting, out of the billions of people on the planet. *No, this wasn't coincidence: it was justice, fate. If there's a God, He must've used me as His instrument.*

Yes.

Feeling returned to his stiffened legs and feet, and eventually he reached the barns, then the house. He remembered to stamp the snow from his boots before he entered. His mind was clear, seeing every detail. He was in total control, or so he was convinced.

"What's wrong, Pa?" Christine saw that he was shaking as he unwound the scarf, began taking off the coat, cap.

"I'll tell you later, honey. Let's eat now. Sorry I was out so long: thought I saw a deer, went after it." He sat at the laden table, managed a smile at his grandson. And by a mighty effort, shelved the events of the past half hour completely.

Afterwards, he went to the telephone in his study, closing the door behind him, dialed the sheriff's office.

"Burgess here. What can I do for you?"

"Mabry, Sheriff. I've just defended myself against none other than Charlie Millard, out in my woods. He was coming after me, and got off the first shot, but I managed to kill him. You need to come on out and I'll show you."

There was a long beat of silence, then:

"You're sure it was Charlie? Yes, of course you are. I'll be there in twenty minutes. Don't clean your gun, don't touch anything." He hung up, got his coat and hat, then remembered to call an ambulance. He and Deputy Wilcox drove toward the Mabry place.

As they rode, both men were thinking how this would devastate Andy Millard. *Her brother killed. And by the very man who had the strongest motive. She's had so much to fight her way through: this'll kill her.* Burgess's reaction was sadness; Wilcox's was deep, deadly anger.

"Now this'll be a shock, Christine," the lawyer prefaced his account. Giles had gone to his room to read, and the two were in his study. "Not to sugar-coat it, I ran into *Charlie Millard* across the fields, and he was coming after me with a shotgun full of buckshot." Her hand went to her mouth; her eyes widened.

"Yes, and he even got off a shot, but there was a tree between us. I had to kill him, self-defense. Sheriff's on his way now."

"Oh, my God! But you're okay?" She grabbed his sleeve as if to spot holes from the buckshot.

"Yes, he didn't have time to reload, or I'd be dead." He watched for any sign of disbelief: there was none. "It's a mess, all of it, but it's over now. We can be sure justice was done for my son. Finally. Not the way I'd have wanted it, but it's done. Hope it won't go too hard on Giles. You better tell him, however you think best." He put a hand on her arm affectionately, managed a wan smile.

Burgess and the deputy drove up, came inside as Christine opened the door for them. She was still reeling from the news, but automatically greeted them, led them to her father-in-law's study. The old man rose from his desk, welcomed the lawmen.

"Nasty business, Burgess, but I had no choice. He was reloading when I stepped out from behind that tree, would've killed me for sure." The lawyer was completely in control, as if he were cross-examining a felon. And he wasn't completely sure he *hadn't* been the victim here. He'd make the sheriff believe he was, at any rate.

"Well, we'll go see, sir. You show us the way, or come with us. You say it was beyond the fields in the woods? Which way?

"I'll come with you. Christine, I guess there'll be an ambulance on the way, so direct them by the upper field road so they won't get stuck, all right?" He was getting into his coat, *yes, completely in control.*

"Of course. Mr. Burgess, this is just awful, that man trying to kill Pa, after what he'd done…before. Please tell us it's all over now, the bad blood and all." Her eyes were pleading; if she felt any satisfaction at Charlie's death, it didn't show through the concern.

"I'll know more after we investigate this, ma'am, but yes, I'd say this sort of puts an end to…as you said, the bad blood." He and Wilcox followed Mabry out the back door.

"Bad day to be out, sir." Burgess pulled his coat collar up, his hat down onto his ears against the wind.

"It is, only I'd been cooped up with paperwork so long, I just had to get some air. And you've probably heard I like to hunt when it's cold. Didn't figure anyone else would be out, but there he was, coming this way." It was important to plant as many points as he could in the lawman's head from the beginning.

"Well, we had no idea he was even back here. Must've just gotten back, but why go out on the worst day of the year? Doesn't make much sense." Burgess shook his head.

"Nothing that man's ever done made any sense. All that elaborate trap he set, and before that, stealing my timber. Whole life was crazy."

Hal Burgess's mind was whirling. *Charlie was back. Did he really come after Mabry? Stupid. He couldn't have known the man was out here in this miserable weather. What? Was he planning to go right up to the house, force his way in, kill him there? And what about Christine and the boy? Doesn't make sense. Had he maybe even called Mabry, drawn him outside to settle this? Too many questions here.*

And oh, my God, what if Andy has harbored him, was somehow in on it? Okay, it's been less than two weeks since I was out there. So just a few days, maybe only one, he's back. Why go after Mabry first thing?

It was just too much of a coincidence for Burgess to take, both men out in foul weather, running into each other by chance. No, in his experience, things just didn't happen that way.

So there must've been some sort of contact between the two, unlikely as that would be. But Mabry going out alone against Charlie? What, acting out some sort of television Western gunfight? Surely not. Mabry would certainly have called in about any contact with his enemy, stayed safe. Or would he? Of course, he had a scoped rifle against Charlie's old single-shot. Or had Charlie used a different gun? Too many questions. *Just have to let it unfold, one step at a time, and here's the first step, that body lying over there.*

***

The worse part, Burgess realized, was going to be confronting Andy Millard. Charlie had surely gone home first, and she hadn't notified him. *Well, don't guess I'd have done that either, if it'd been me.* But he'd obviously taken the shotgun from the house, gone after Mabry. Or could he have gone out for some other reason? The sheriff plotted the direct route from the Prescott place toward Mabry's house: it would have been across the cut-over land and into the woods, and it should have been, yes, direct.

But it hadn't been. The shooting had taken place well off a

straight path; out of the way, and on such a foul day.

As usual, he'd go to the farmhouse alone, not wanting the family to be further embarrassed by the presence of a deputy. Wilcox was taking care of Charlie's remains, and yes, he'd have to ask how they wanted that handled. This with Andy wasn't going to be easy: an obvious accusation, along with the dreaded news.

Nate would be in school, not scheduled home for another two hours. Elijah could take any shock; the old man was made of iron. Andy would go to pieces at word of her brother's death, something he could envision with regret. But she'd have to face the fact that Charlie had been there, been harbored, had taken the old gun on whatever mission that had driven him.

She heard, then saw his car, and the dread that had filled her since discovering that Charlie was gone swept over her again. *Dear God, don't let this be bad news, even if I know it is.* She opened the door as Burgess stamped the snow off his shoes, let him in. He didn't look happy.

"Hello, Andy. Afraid I've got something bad to tell you. Where's Elijah?" He looked around for the old man.

"He's in bed, Hal. Won't say so, but I'm afraid his heart's giving out: I see him clutching his chest a lot. Been down since early. You want coffee? We got some from the sale of one of the pigs."

"I guess so, thanks. But Andy, the bad news first…" He looked around again, hoping for some way to cushion this. There was none. "Charlie's been shot, Andy. He's dead." *Get it out: she's got to deal with it.*

"Charlie? Charlie's *dead?* Where, Hal? Where'd this happen?" She had rehearsed just what she'd say if anyone learned of her brother's presence here, and she'd stick to that, no matter what. So would Nate, if questioned. They'd known this time would come eventually—not the death, though: *God, not that!*

"Right here, Andy. Montgomery Mabry shot him just this morning, over in the woods on his place. Said Charlie was coming after him with a shotgun." He looked into her inscrutable eyes, then glanced around. The shotgun wasn't in its accustomed corner.

"Here? Charlie's been *here?* We haven't heard from him in a year,

Hal. And you say…you say Mabry *shot him?"* She steadied herself with a hand on the back of a chair, her other covering her face. *Not dead. No, not Charlie. Dead, and by Mabry's hand. How did this happen? What made Charlie go out? Hal said in the woods; how could they have run into each other, nasty day like today?*

Nothing made sense, and her mind wouldn't settle down, accept the fact. She knew, on some level, that she had to be really careful, here: the sheriff could trip her up easily, in this state. *Charlie dead…*

"He called it in just afterwards. Said he had to get outside for a bit, took his rifle with him. Now, I don't believe in coincidences, Andy. Why would Charlie take the shotgun and head for Mabry's place?" It was time to start pushing while she was off-balance. But she fixed him with a direct stare.

"Hal, I didn't know Charlie was anywhere near here. He left last year without a word, hasn't contacted us at all. And I don't have the faintest idea why he'd go after Mabry. Look, Barry was killed: Charlie had no reason to try to kill his father. This just doesn't make sense." She shook her head as if to clear it.

"Well, where it happened wasn't on a path from here to there, but that's gotta be a minor point. Charlie's gun had been fired: took a chunk out of the tree Mabry was behind. Had to've fired first." He spread his hands.

"And I have to ask: where's your shotgun? He surely came here, got it."

"Hal, we had to sell that old shotgun—let's see—about two weeks ago, to buy groceries. Elijah knew one of his church people who wanted one, a friend of the man who bought his from him, on back. He came here for it, all packed up, going west, he said. Elijah will remember his name."

Could that be true? Could what appeared to be fact in actuality be something else? Or is she that good a liar? Did Charlie really slip back, go after Mabry first thing without contacting his family? That'd be a stretch for simple Charlie. No, Andy is covering for him—for herself, Nate, and Elijah.

And the old attraction for this woman fought with his duty as a lawman. After all, *she* hadn't stalked Mabry, Charlie had. Or had he? Wait, could Mabry actually have stalked *Charlie?* But again, how could he have known his quarry was back here. Unless—that idea again—a meeting was set up beforehand. *Omigod, this could cut both ways.*

"I'll have to talk with Nate, you realize," and this was déjà vu from a year ago—two years ago, with the timber thing. "Not to contradict you, of course, but something's very wrong here, you realize, aside from his getting shot. He didn't even contact his *family* when he got back? That's unbelievable, Andy."

"Hal, he's not been in touch since last winter, I told you. Whatever was between him and Mabry, and I have no idea what that could've been, must've been his top priority. And consider this: he left here to protect us, knowing you lawmen would conclude he was the guilty one, and that you'd leave everybody else alone. That's in keeping with his coming back secretly, not telling us this…whatever it was. Surely you can see that?"

"Well, I'll admit I never thought of it that way. And this so-called coincidence of both men just happening to run into each other: I just don't buy that. I'm thinking they may have set something up between them: exact time and place. Nothing else makes sense."

"That I can't speculate on. Look, Hal, this has me reeling, as you can imagine: my brother killed, my brother who was innocent of killing Barry. Surely after all this time, and with absolutely *no* motive for his stalking Mabry, you can find out what's behind this." It was a plea, a tear-streaked supplication.

"Andy, I'll try my best. It's another situation that looks obvious on the surface but has a lot down under it, out of sight. Tell you what, I'll leave now, come back tomorrow, Saturday, talk to Nate then. You say Elijah's down; can he talk all right?"

"I suppose so, but yes, Hal, I need to be alone, just now. Go on in, see what Elijah has to say. I've got to go up to my room." She turned, went up the narrow stairs, gripping the worn railing for support.

Burgess knocked at the old minister's door, got a reply. He went in to see the man lying in bed under several patched quilts, seeming shrunken, diminished. *Oh, bad: it's been only a few days.* He drew up a chair, sat.

"Elijah, you hurting?"

"Reckon so, Hal. Tried t'brush it off, but truth be tole, I'm thet porely. Thaink it's m'heart, givin' out." He rolled partially over to face the sheriff. "Heered y'talkin' t'Andy, 'bout Charlie, only I din't hear th' fust of it. Whut's happened to him?"

"Well, Charlie's dead, Elijah. Came back, some way he and Montgomery Mabry ran into each other in the woods, and Mabry shot him. That's the gist of it."

"Charlie's back here? When? Why ain't we heered? Thet don't make no sense, Hal. He's been gone a good year, he has. An' gone t'Mabry's? Whut's th'sense in thet? It'd be plumb crazy, an' Charlie ain't crazy, whutever he is…wuz." He shook his head. If the rehearsed story bothered the old preacher, he wasn't going to let it show. *Perfect th' fam'ly fust off: God an' me'll hafta work that'n out 'tween us later.*

"Well, I'm not saying it all happened just the way Mabry told it, but the bare fact is, there were at least two shots fired. Charlie's missed, and the lawyer's didn't."

Elijah didn't dwell on the lie—*well, almost lie.* But he also knew how hard it'd be if the law knew that boy had been here all along; they'd talked about it enough. And Elijah Prescott had assumed the role of head of his family, and he'd stand up for them while he still had breath. He'd have to stand by that version of events, of course, and for now, Nate and Andy needed him.

Burgess couldn't tell if the old man was telling the truth or not, but he'd need to push this. If he could catch these people mixing up their stories, he'd know more.

"Andy tells me you all sold your shotgun," he ventured.

"T'warn't mine. Dave, he left it. Hadda sell mine long time ago, but yeah, we's real short here, Hal. Feller I knew needed one, give us fifteen dollars fer it, an' Andy, she sold it."

"Who was that?" He had his notebook out.

"Name of Shad Harlow. Wuz headin' out west, he sed, an' figgered thaings'd be higher-priced out thar."

"I see. Know how to get in touch with him?"

"Naw, th' whole fam'ly left out, few weeks ago. Some of m'church folks, they might have 'n'idee, but I shore don't." That part was true, at least, the Harlow family heading west, and easy to check.

"We've got the shotgun Charlie used, Elijah. Surely you could identify it, if it was the one."

"Don't see no way it could, bein's th' one Dave left here's gone some'rs else. But you're tellin' me whut? Some way Charlie went up 'ginst Mabry? Whut'd *he* have?"

"30.06 scoped rifle. Claims Charlie shot first." He was watching the old man's face closely.

"Thet ain't no match, Hal. Charlie, he wouldn't have no chancet 'ginst a gun like thet. Sounds lak murder, t'me." The shaking head again.

"Well, Mabry says it was up close with him behind a tree. Says Charlie came after him, blew part of the tree off, and he had to defend himself."

"Wal, thet's jist his word fer it, ain't it? Not lak Charlie's around no more, c'd tell us diff'runt."

"Right. But what worries me is how'd they meet on a bad day out in the woods? And why? I'd say Mabry had motive, but not Charlie. Like I told Andy, I'm leaning towards maybe they got in touch some way, wanted to settle up."

This intrigued the old preacher, he could tell. New idea, no matter how far-fetched. He watched as Elijah processed this conjecture. Then he shook his white head again.

"Come up agin' Mabry when he knowed th' man wuz out t'kill him? Thet don't wash, Hal, 'less he had some way *t'prove* somebody else done it. An' if he did, he'd of come t'you with it, shorely.

"An' I heered y'sayin' t'Andy out thar, 'bout why Charlie, he didn't come here rat off: lak she sed, he wuz still pertectin' us lak he done when he run off, makin' you'n ever'body else thaink he wuz th' one killed Barry. Naw, last folks he'd let know he wuz hereabouts'd be us: thaink about it."

Yes, that did make a convoluted kind of sense, and it tallied with what the sheriff had guessed earlier. So all right, Charlie *hadn't* come here at all, had found another shotgun somewhere in his travels. Easy enough, that. But that still didn't explain why he was on a collision course with Montgomery Mabry, who had every motive for killing him.

He left the old man with a promise to tell Dr. Aaron Blake to please come out and check him over. He knew Elijah had surely refused to let Andy take him to the clinic. *Stubborn old coot: won't fight it, 'cause he'll say it's the Lord's will. Well, maybe it is…*

But during this time, Burgess had realized he couldn't wait to talk with Nate Prescott. Andy would fill him in to the smallest detail as to what she'd told him, and the two would hone their stories about Charlie, his being here, the shotgun. No, he'd have to wait a little over an hour till the boy got home from school.

He climbed the stairs, knocked, told Andy this, and she just replied that he could do whatever he needed to. So he went back down and outside to wait and check around for footprints that might tell him more than he knew now. If Charlie *had* been here, either hiding or to sneak the gun, he'd surely have left tracks.

But the snow, partially melted then refrozen, showed such a muddle of indistinct footprints, he could tell nothing. The hard freeze of the night before wouldn't show any recent tracks: the crust was solid over the bare, iron-hard ground, not broken through leaves or grass, just here. As he strode thoughtfully around, he processed what he knew.

Charlie could and probably had gotten the shotgun from somebody else. Old thing like that, it'd have been cheap. And yes, to protect the family, he could've come back, but not let them know he was around. So where'd he have spent last night? Surely not out in the woods; freeze to death, unless he'd had a fire, some sort of shelter. And he wouldn't have shown himself to anybody—wouldn't have dared. Had he camped in a tent then? And if so, for how long?

That was a good question, now. Could he have been hidden for long enough to spy on Mabry, even maybe wait till he saw the man leave his house, then head him off in the woods? Let him get close enough to blast him with buckshot? That would explain some things, if true. The whole settlement knew the lawyer liked to hunt and didn't avoid bad weather for it.

So, if there could be a camp of sorts, this whole thing could become a little clearer. Except for the part about no motive for Charlie. *That sort of undercuts it, I'm afraid. Man'd have to hold a mighty big grudge to risk camping out maybe for days, in this kind of weather, on the chance he'd get a shot up close. And Charlie coud've just as easily found a rifle—army surplus thing'd be cheap—as that shotgun.*

But most of all, he just didn't have a grudge against the old man unless he'd really gone crazy. And I agree with Elijah: Charlie wasn't crazy, even if he wasn't the sharpest knife in the drawer. No, nothing about this whole business makes sense. To me or old Elijah or anybody.

Chapter Fourteen

Nate was, of course, shocked, torn by the news of Charlie's violent death. It would be long before he could come to accept that he'd never see his uncle again, even after the long periods he'd been gone before.

But his story mirrored Andy's in perfect detail, even to the question about the missing shotgun. They'd seen that it was gone along with Charlie that morning and decided that it couldn't be allowed to exist. *Aiding and abetting,* Nate had read somewhere. And Elijah had known about the Harlow family's leaving. Burgess questioned him for nearly an hour, but the boy's insistence on the facts as he gave them matched his aunt's. The boy knew absolutely that he could not admit to his uncle's having been there, and he couldn't let the modified facts vary.

Or they were all in trouble.

Nate even anticipated the sheriff's idea that Charlie could have hidden out somewhere till he could get Mabry outside. But like Burgess, he pointed out that his uncle had no earthly reason to hunt the lawyer. No gain in that at all, he said.

So the sheriff would have to leave with nothing solid here. He even went to his car, brought the shotgun in, had all three of them examine it. None of them recognized it, or else they were superb actors. *Which they could all b, with so much at stake. And I couldn't swear the gun was here last time I came: no reason to notice.*

Again Nate could see the four of them, from his imaginary, detached height: Burgess standing with the incriminating gun, Elijah, now in the armchair by the stove, shaking his white head. Andy, cool in her insistence of the facts, and himself, corroborating her account firmly, as if it were really the truth.

This was what he'd read was a tableau, actually a standoff. Just then, Hal Burgess was the enemy, as surely as a German soldier would have been a few years back or a Yankee officer grilling them as he would a Confederate family hiding a wounded Reb nearly a hundred earlier.

So they were liars, all three of them, deliberate, bald-faced liars, in direct opposition to the Bible they tried to live by. But just then, from his strange but somehow secure viewpoint, it seemed to Nate that the lawman was in the wrong, and this family, united solidly in its defense, was, in fact, innocent in the face of this accusation. *Is this the way Satan gets hold of folks? Helps 'em, then won't ever let 'em get away from his power again? Hafta talk to Granpa about what we're doing here. But no, he said a feller oughta protect his kin that other time.* Gradually, he came back down to where he still leaned against the wall opposite the sheriff.

And having learned nothing, Burgess, still unsure, left them, again expressing his regrets at having borne bad news.

So Mabry's insistence on the killing being self-defense would stand, it seemed. The community gossips clucked that poor old Charlie, who'd never done anything right, had finally gone crazy or something, and look what it got him. They also believed he had it coming for being the one who'd murdered Barry Mabry. What went around came around, they nodded sagely.

Mabry wasn't even asked to stand trial: the district attorney had more important things to attend to. Prime suspect in a murder got himself shot going after another man: plain and simple.

Case closed.

This troubled Hal Burgess no end; it just didn't fit, any of it. He'd just as soon suspect Mabry, since he had the motive, if he could somehow explain how the two met there on the killing ground. But self-defense was the law all over the world, and who was he to insist it hadn't happened that way?

Charlie's death did have a major adverse effect on the sheriff's relationship with Andy Millard. She remained bitter at Mabry's dismissal and aloof to any sort of closeness with Burgess. He had not only not found the real murderer of Barry Mabry, now he'd let Charlie's admitted killer off without even a slap on his wrist. It angered her, burning through her grief like a hot knife.

And the sheriff wasn't welcome at the Prescott place ever again. Unless he had law business to attend to there, he could make other people's lives hell, she decided. And she put him completely out of her thoughts this time.

Nate continued to be devastated at his uncle's death. He'd known the hiding thing couldn't succeed, but who could have predicted it'd end like this? There had to be some reason Charlie had taken the gun and run into Montgomery Mabry there in the woods. But even if Charlie had just wanted to go out, hunt, tramp around, get rid of cabin fever, how did Mabry know where he was? Could he possibly have learned Charlie was here, and somehow followed him well away, shot him, then twisted what happened to appear the victim?

No, too complicated. Too unlikely. No. But whatever was behind this, it would destroy something good inside Nate and change the way he viewed the world he'd been dropped into forever. Elijah told him that life just wasn't fair, and here was proof. Further proof, after the boy's losing his parents. But the old man also insisted that God had a plan for us all, and hard as it was to take this and those other undeserved deaths, we just had to accept it and keep the faith.

That hadn't been easy before, and it wasn't going to be easy this time.

Nate and his aunt had not agitated for a trial in this: with no witnesses and no contrary evidence, Montgomery Mabry would be acquitted, they knew. No sense getting everybody all worked up again. Charlie was gone, and nothing would bring him back. Even if either of them harbored secret thoughts of revenge, there was nothing he/she could do. The system had failed, and a killer was going free; that was all there was to it.

Again.

Neither of them had even the faintest thought that Charlie Millard had killed Barry Mabry, so the lawyer's avenging himself on the supposed guilty man didn't hold a drop of water. Both hoped and prayed that somehow the real killer could be found, and at least Charlie would be exonerated, albeit long after it would do any good. Well, they told each other, if that could happen, it would at least help remove the blackening they'd sustained because of his supposed guilt.

* * *

Christine Mabry noticed that her father-in-law wasn't enjoying what he'd called the justice he'd achieved. If anything, he was more distracted than before. Revenge hadn't exorcised any of his demons, it seemed. His legal work became sloppier, despite her increased help wherever she could give it. He was slipping, and it was obvious. *And maybe the story he's telling about Charlie Millard coming after him has some holes in it. I suppose that's disloyal, but why else would he mope around like this? It's all over, Pa, get on with your life.*

Christine was not an intellectual, but she had enough common sense to know that if Montgomery kept slipping like this, he'd start making serious mistakes. He'd always been cautious about his business deals, for instance, curbing Barry's wild schemes. But lately, the way he talked about investing heavily in the volatile cattle market, harvesting the timber using local, shirttail loggers instead of men with the right equipment, even considering selling off a big chunk of his land for supposed development, worried her. And there'd been that whole wild scheme of those detectives: wasted money. An old man's fantasy.

He needed her; that was for sure. So she pushed herself more into his dealings, cautioning him to think harder before making major decisions. He didn't really like this, but with her and his grandson his only family, he didn't openly resent it. *And hell, maybe she's right: got a better head on her than anybody suspected. And I don't want her wandering off, taking Giles. Wouldn't hurt to take her advice now and then, let her think she's helping run things.*

But it was true, the whole rural community saw: the old lawyer wasn't up to snuff. Well, anybody'd be shook up some, losing his only boy that way, then having to kill a man was after him. Some took such as that harder than others...

* * *

The assassin, for that was who this was after all, checked the target, seeing the close pattern of the rifle bulletholes. Getting this good with this weapon had taken a lot of time, a lot of ammunition, and it hadn't been that easy. Finding the time to get away undetected had been the hardest: too many people knew the killer's whereabouts too much of the time. But planning was essential to this task, along with attention to the most minute detail.

The telescopic sight helped a lot at these distances. It was expensive, accurate, a joy to work with. Its power brought these hardly seen targets into sharp relief, and with allowances for windage and elevation, the rest was easy.

The crosshairs settled on an even farther cardboard circle tacked to a tree, with its concentric rings around the bull's eye. By now the rifle felt as if it were an extension of the killer's body, a necessary added limb with its incredible reach. The finger put increasing pressure on the trigger, and the shot echoed through this hidden hollow deep in the woods.

Another shot. Then three more. The figure, in its hooded, bulky coat, strode confidently toward the target. *There, that's good: five hits within two inches, despite the breeze. This really is an art, a fine art. And at a distance like this, I'll be anonymous forever. And this one should be the last time I'll have to do this. Or maybe not: there's possibly one more, or even two...*

* * *

The winter wore itself out, punctuated sadly by the death of Elijah Prescott one cold February night. Andy found him lying peacefully in bed, his eyes closed, his hands folded across his chest. She'd known it was coming, of course, but no one is ever really prepared for death, and it grieved her. *He had a hard life, without much ease anywhere, any time. But I guess, when it's time to go, this is better than some people have it. Just went to sleep and never woke up.*

Nate bore the news well, externally. Inside, this further loss of his family cut him deeply. Now it was just Andy and him. *Yeah, against the whole damn world, looks like. My parents gone, Granpa gone, Uncle Charlie gone. An' both of us wanta make more of our lives than bein' dirt farmers. We don't have any friends here really, and nothing to look forward to. Granpa said to be thankful for what we have, but what do we have, really, when you look around? Not much of anything, that's what.*

With the new spring just ahead, it'd be only two more years till he could be ready to go off to college, let his aunt go to whatever she wanted. Yes, they'd sell the place, split the money. If he got a scholarship, that'd help. Or he could work his way, if he went to a college in a town big enough for there to be work.

Andy wanted to go to college, too, and it was a secret hope that, once through, Nate might help her do just that. He was big-hearted enough for that, she knew, and probably would insist on it. The plan to sell the place would help, but cut-over backwoods farmland didn't bring much. Still, it was something to look forward to, and to work towards.

So planting time came again, then Nate was out of school, and would be a junior in the fall. He was sixteen, tall, strong, and good with his hands. Any observer who saw them in the village would have to agree that they were a striking couple: the earnest young man nobody had ever disliked, and the dark-haired, attractive woman who, no matter her past, had shown her better side in raising him and caring for old Elijah. And folks couldn't really forget she'd just lost her only brother, almost the last of her kin, no matter he'd deserved it.

This was about as good as things were going to get for Nate and Andy they knew, driving the horse and cart back home this day. After just those two more years of this, their real lives would begin. Meanwhile, they'd just keep on, squeezing every dime, growing everything they ate, balancing a livestock sale with feed purchases, but also planting feed corn, harvesting hay. They turned the hogs out to salvage acorns in the fall and winter, calling them back at night with a little precious feed.

With no gun now, Nate couldn't go hunting the squirrels and rabbits that were about all that was available, and he missed this. He resolved to save any money he could make doing odd jobs this summer so he could hunt, come fall. He was living proof that a country boy just has to go out after wild things. But in this case, it was a real necessity.

He had come to like this place he'd inherited, with all the work they'd put into it, but the dream of getting away, moving up in life was more powerful. This would be just a step on the way, this interim of working the soil, running the farm, keeping the place up. He chafed at the prospect of those two years, not realizing how fast his youth would disappear. Forever.

Then Nate met Angie Mitchell. Her family had moved to the Arkansas mountains from wherever her ex-captain father had been stationed when he left the Army. They were originally from Vermont, a state Nate didn't know much about—he'd never been out of Arkansas. She didn't have a particular accent, having been raised on military bases around the world, but she was clearly different from any of the other girls he'd known.

Angie was his age and would be in classes with him that fall. The family had bought a farm up toward Elijah's old church, and her father was reclaiming the grown-over fields and the creaking house. Angie, as the oldest of three girls, was her father's helper. She was brown-eyed, freckled, and very outgoing.

They'd met at the high school, where the sports coaches were beginning training of the basketball teams for the coming school year. Nate liked the game, and being tall and agile, had been targeted by the coach for his team. Angie was five-foot-nine and had played at her last school.

Nate had been hesitant to go to the preseason gathering, not intending to try out for the team—too much time taken from his studies—but he'd gone, partly to get away from the steady grind of the farm work. And Andy had encouraged him, knowing he should get out among other young people as much as possible. She didn't want her nephew to be totally out of place when he went out into the world.

He was immediately taken with the newcomer. Where the local girls never bothered much with their hair, Angie's was glossy. Where his female classmates wore simple dresses, some homemade, and some jeans with blouses that didn't fit well, Angie's clothes looked tailored to her slim body. She laughed a lot, got along with everyone there, and clearly was the focus of all the young people's eyes.

At sixteen, Nate was coming into young manhood, and while he hadn't ignored the local girls, he hadn't spent any time with them outside school, either. Now he wanted to be around Angie Mitchell, experience that new tingling she elicited all the time.

So he gave the tryouts his best efforts, and the coach encouraged him. The designated center, at six-foot-three, was a powerful red-headed boy who broke horses for his spending money, a senior who would surely win an athletic scholarship to some college. The coach wanted Nate to be a backup center, but trained him to be a forward also. He had little experience but was a fast learner.

This would mean a lot of time spent with the team, travel to other schools for games, and late-night arrivals home. He talked this over with Andy, pointing out that if he did this, she'd have even more to do at the place. But he also felt he could do most of the late chores by lantern light and that he could handle it.

Andy had known she could never keep this boy at home once he neared maturity, and yes, as part of his growing-up, she would let him go, manage the place by herself if necessary.

"You go with the team, Nate. Do you good to get away more. Nothing here I can't handle. And I'll get rides with some of the parents to see you play. It's a good idea, and I want you to do it."

She'd also picked up on his mentioning Angie's name often and suspected rightly that there was more than the love of the game going on here. Which was okay: sooner or later Nate would meet somebody he liked, and if it came sooner than later, that was okay, too. *Or okay just as long as he doesn't make the same dumb mistake I made.*

Ridgeway High School didn't have a football team, so they played a double season of basketball, as did other rural schools. The superintendent, a balding example of the old-school model, believed in strict disclipline, keeping that leather strap in the drawer of his desk. He ran a tight ship and tolerated no troublemakers. But he was also a fanatic supporter of the ball team, even declaring Fridays off for the entire school after a big win.

That extended schedule meant more games, more travel, more time away from the farm for Nate, but this new double attraction had him excited. He felt he could tackle anything with that youthful sense of invulnerability, that bulletproof attitude of teenage optimism. Besides, with Angie on the girls' team, they'd play a lot of double games, which the small schools in the region scheduled. And of course he'd see her that much more.

He knew he'd have to move fast with this girl. There was Mark Reid, his old enemy, now as close to a friend as he had but also on the team. Mark was dark, part Indian, they said, and had piercing black eyes that gave him a predatory look. After their scuffle on back, he'd grudgingly accepted the fact that Nate could whip his butt, and yes, they'd become companions, if not close ones.

And there was the big center, Red Spaulding, who at eighteen had dated all the pretty girls in school and probably in the county. He drove his own pickup truck, into which he'd trained his palomino gelding to jump at his command and ride untied anywhere. He'd be real competition for Angie, Nate was sure. These two were among the boys who'd openly eyed the new girl from the first.

But how did a poor farm boy with no car make any time with a sophisticated girl who'd been everywhere, was well spoken, talented? She could sing, he'd heard, planned to join the glee club, work on the school newspaper. In her company, he felt like a clod of dirt the plow had turned up.

Wait, now: I've read more than anybody else here. I don't mangle the lan-

guage, thanks to Aunt Andy. Can't sing, but I'm not dumb: got the best grades in school. That'll be the way to handle this.

So he pushed himself into whatever situation presented itself to spend time with Angie. Talked to her about literature, asked her about places she'd lived. He'd heard stories from Charlie about towns, cities he'd been in, and could always drop a few words about these, at least.

She seemed interested. No doubt, presented with these young, half-wild hill specimens, an educated one had some appeal. Of course, like any girl would, she'd checked out the boys here, and nobody could miss Red Spaulding. She hadn't responded to any of his obvious, clumsy advances but that hadn't discouraged him.

Nate knew she could take her pick of any of them, and even with his determination to be first in her affections, feared she'd pass him up for somebody more exciting. Well, nothing he could do about that; he wasn't the least exciting. But he had plans, ambition, was going places, and that could work in his favor.

All this soul-searching, this post-adolescent fantasizing was universal with teenage boys, but Nate was sure nobody else had ever felt like this. And he'd forge ahead, turn his loner status around, become outgoing, try like hell to become this Angie's steady guy.

So, practical considerations: he needed transportation. Well, he could ride the horse to her house, for starters. He was no cowboy, but that'd beat walking. And he'd noticed that most girls had a thing for horses. Charlie, in his crude humor, had joked that every woman really wanted a hairy beast between her legs. Which had earned him a light slap from Andy and had made Nate's cheeks flame in embarrassment.

But how to take her anywhere? Like to the picture show in town, or even just for a hamburger at the roadside café? Girl like that, she'd expect to go out, matter of course.

It came down to money, like it always did. He'd have to earn some money, real money this last month of summer, and whenever else he could find work. He racked his brain for ways to find just what every other human being on earth wanted.

There were the other two prime white oaks down by the spring.

But even if he and Andy could cut them with the crosscut saw, haul them one or two lengths at a time on the cart, he'd probably have to fight old Mabry over them. No, too risky, and if that old fool accosted him, he'd want to kill him, with the battered 20-gauge he'd managed to buy.

Then Nate remembered: Elijah had owned his sagging cabin and a small plot up by his church and, of course, had left it to him. Could he sell that? Who'd want it? Well, Angie's dad had bought that old place from Miz Ed's uncle, so why not some other Yankee who wouldn't know the value of a piece of hillside? This seemed like a good idea.

Except that it didn't fit with his long-held plan to share every penny he earned with his deserving aunt. She was the one who'd taken the old man in, fed him, clothed him, nursed him in his last days. A wave of shame spread over Nate at the thought of wasting what little he might get for that place on running around with a girl who probably wouldn't even give him the time of day in the end.

He was aware that he'd been fantasizing about her, about what they could do together: have fun, maybe even get close, like the other boys were always bragging about. Even…no, he wasn't ready for sex, tantalizing as that was. He'd seen too many shotgun weddings around here, too many high school dropouts forced to the altar and miserable thereafter. And the thought of Angie's hard-eyed New England father actually chilled him.

Okay, then. He'd just have to settle for maybe long talks, a horseback ride now and then if he could borrow another one. Lunchtimes together. And of course the camaraderie of the basketball trips and games. If that didn't work, he'd just have to let this one go: he was just sixteen, and there was a world of girls out there, surely many as attractive as Angie Mitchell.

Still…

The girls' and boys' games with other schools were set up to occur one after the other, so they started early in the evening. Nate didn't have time to go home after school on game days, although he was there faithfully after practice, even if it meant walking from the school bus stop after dark, lighting the lantern and milking the cow, feeding the stock, getting in firewood, which he cut on weekends.

In the event one of the teams made it to regional or even state tournaments, the school would put them up in a motel wherever that was. This was exciting, since few of the players had been far from home. They all vowed to beat every team in the region, earn that prize.

And beginning with their first game, against the Tigers of Henderson County High, they proceeded to slaughter them, despite their own shallow bench strength. Ridgeway actually had a five-foot-seven player who could hit from anywhere this side of midcourt. When he was double-teamed, which was often, Nate or big Red would get open to receive a bullet pass from him, Mark Reid, or another of the wild mountain boys, and score.

It was a heady time for Nate, this being an important part of the team, this seeing his grades at the top, and most of all, having almost-stolen moments with Angie, maybe sitting next to her on the team bus, the regular schoolbus which they both rode, or those brief moments between classes.

She even invited him to her parents' house for dinner one Saturday night (they didn't call it supper). He wore his best clothes and rode the horse, hoping the unsaddled beast wouldn't leave him too smelly through the blanket. Angie's mother greeted him at the door, and her father, who resembled a chunk of New England granite, shook his hardened hand with his equally hard one.

Angie and her two sisters had helped their mother in the kitchen, and Nate noted the woman had what must have been arthritis in her hands. She clearly depended on the girls, as Angie had told him her father did for her own help on the farm.

The younger girls giggled a lot, casting merry eyes on Nate, who was, of course, uncomfortable. He didn't know what to talk about with the reticent father, who'd no doubt kept a firm leash on his oldest daughter. Nate had seen the family at home games but never met them. Now he searched his mind for subjects to break the ice.

"Do you hunt, sir?"

"Like to, but don't really have time, with all we're doing to fix up this old place. You?"

"About the same. I do get out some, always have. Nothing much but rabbits and squirrels around, now: deer all hunted out. Summers, I fish when I can, but again, with the crops and the stock, that's a luxury."

The father noted this boy's speech: he wasn't illiterate, which was something of a surprise. And he'd seen him on the ball court, seen him score well. *Hmm, this one's a bit of a surprise, here back of nowhere. I hear his aunt's someone special, too. Guess she's taught him, since the local schools are pretty backward.* He eyed Nate with something near appreciation.

After dinner, Angie's mother took him aside. She'd noted his threadbare coat, and like her husband, thought it was a shame he was so obviously poor. After a quick consultation with the girls' father, she offered Nate a coat he no longer wore.

"It'll just gather dust," she assured him, noting that he was about her husband's size. "We want you to have it, Nate." She smiled. He had the impression this woman was one of those innately kind people you sometimes met, that you just couldn't take offense at. And of course he blushed wildly, ashamed at being obviously ragged. He swallowed hard, tried to rise to the occasion.

"Thank you, ma'am. It seems I have always depended on the kindness of strangers." That quotation caused her eyes to widen.

"Why, that's out of Williams' *Streetcar Named Desire*. You know that play, Nate?"

"Read it, but haven't had the chance to see it."

"Angie, did you know Nate's familiar with plays, literature?"

"I did, yes. I told you, he's not your stereotype hillbilly, Mom." She surveyed her father's coat on him. "Looks good, Nate. Mom, you know you've embarrassed him beyond words." A reproachful look.

"No, I haven't: he's no adolescent, unlike some boys you've known. Right, Nate?" The eyes were warm, kind.

"No, ma'am, I'm not one to refuse a gift given with the best intentions. And again, thank you." He glanced at himself in a wall mirror; he did look good. And he'd learned long before that poor folks traded clothes among themselves, always had. A kid outgrew something, it went to a neighbor's smaller kid. Way of life where everybody barely subsisted.

"You're so welcome, Nate. But back to *Streetcar*: we saw it onstage in DC when Horace was stationed there, with Jessica Tandy as Blanche. I love the theater, but so many places, like here, there isn't any." He sensed that she hadn't been thrilled with her husband's packing the family off to this backwoods.

"Well, there's community theater and college plays over in Jonesboro. And down in Little Rock: productions at the junior college there. And I heard from a cousin of a lady down there she even has begun opera. At least operettas." Another bit he'd gleaned from Charlie's accounts.

"Really? Oh, we'll have to go, if I can drag Horace away from his tractor and chainsaw. He never takes time for any culture. Horace, did you hear that? Theater and even opera in Little Rock?"

"Yeah, I heard. Hey, Nate, that old coat looks good on you; glad you can wear it. Donna loaded up stuff for the move down here that'll be around when I'm dead. But did I hear you're actually a theatergoer?"

"Not really, being chained to the place all the time. But I read a lot, listen to the radio: the Saturday operas. Don't wanta be totally ignorant." Yes, he'd surprised Andy with that gift he'd saved handyman money to buy, secondhand, one of those battery sets. He was finding it easier to talk to these people. After all, Angie had gotten her easy manner from here.

"Well, that's...well, it's surprising, back here. Not to put down the local folks, but Donna's been moaning about being buried here. You'll have to swap stories with her. And of course, with Angie." He actually smiled, which seemed almost to split the rocklike face.

"I'd like that. My aunt and I try to keep up with what's happening in the world, much as we can. She's determined to get me educated, actually make something out of me."

"Oh, yes," Donna said, "we've heard about your…Andy, isn't it? Some of the neighbors seem to think she's well, acting too good for her station, I guess you'd say. Sounds like envy to me. I'd like to meet her."

"She hasn't been to any of the ball games yet, but she's promised, next home game. I'm sure she'd welcome being friends." *Yeah, the one-syllable locals aren't much intellectual stimulation: she's miles beyond them. Envy, that's it.*

"Well, she's certainly welcome here. And I'll try to get down, visit, if that's all right."

"I'm sure it is. It's been kinda lonely for her, staying home, raising me. And for awhile after she had to run her no-good husband off, folks talked her down, like they will." The memories still gave him a twinge.

"I'm sorry about that. Yes, people will gossip. Well, I see it's getting late, and I expect you've got a load of chores in the morning. We're glad you came, Nate, and do come again. Right, Angie?" She cut her eyes at her daughter. *Don't dump this one, girl; we like him.*

"I guess. Looks like you've survived the third degree, Nate, which a lot of my…acquaintances didn't. Or is this the last we'll see of you?" Her eyes were merry, along with that perfect smile, which warmed him to his toes.

"Guess that's up to you folks," he said easily now, including all of them. The sisters giggled, and Horace looked up from his newspaper, nodded. He said his goodbyes, wanting badly for Angie to walk him out to his horse, but she didn't offer. He untied the gelding, mounted, rode away with the feeling that he'd been more than accepted here. *Just hafta see where this goes, now. One thing to get in with the family, but sure another to shoot the other guys down. Red's got the edge here, and I wouldn't be surprised if Mark appeals to her, too. Both of 'em better-looking than me…*

Nate had that almost universal fear that he was inferior in many ways that teenagers have harbored since there were teenagers. He knew better, with Andy's tutelage always telling him how he didn't have to take a backseat to anyone, but among his peers, such as they were, he wasn't so sure. He desperately wanted to be a leader, to be among that select group in any school that got things done, that the teachers knew they could count on, that represented the best and the brightest.

Oh, what the hell; it's not that important. I'll outgrow Ridgeway. Couple years—less now—I'll be gone and never come back. But this is here, and it's now, and it's my world, for better or worse. Don't wanta be miserable while I'm here, be left out, even if being in isn't a big deal.

Andy had stayed up for him and eyed the coat with appreciation. This would get him through the winter nicely, and that'd be one more thing they wouldn't have to buy. The sale of pigs and a calf, plus some regular customers for their eggs, had given them a few hoarded dollars, and Nate had managed to find four short jobs during the summer to add to the total.

Again, they'd get by, even if barely. She was thankful for their good health; doctor's bills would destroy them, as had Elijah's funeral expenses, small as they'd been. *We've managed here for five years, and I guess we can do it for two more. That is, as Elijah used to say, "If th' Lord's willin' an' th' creek don't rise."* So far, He was, and no, it hadn't. Yet.

* * *

The dim light of morning filtered in through the motel window, rousing the truck driver from a restless nonsleep. He looked over at the inert woman beside him, trying to decide whether to wake her, or slip out and get on the road again. Cam Henry never stayed with a woman for long, and this one he'd met just the night before.

They were in Joplin, Missouri, where he'd unloaded steel beams the day before, and he was waiting for the dispatcher to call with his next pickup. He'd run into this peroxide blonde at what could only be termed a honky-tonk along Highway 66 just out of town. Too much dancing, too much to drink, and they'd ended up here, late. It was just one more mini-episode in the man's life.

As he studied the profile of this woman, smeared makeup, maybe forty, he was shaken anew by how much the opposite of his ex-wife these pick-ups were. *An' I let her go when we coulda had a good life t'gether. Won't never learn, I guess: next road, next town, next woman, till I git too old for enny of it.*

He dressed quietly as the old anger flared in him again, remembering the hell Andy had gone through, despite what had happened to her tormentor. And how he'd heard her brother had taken the heat for that deserved killing, disappearing for a year. And then foolishly coming back for that confrontation with the senior Mabry. *Biggest fool thing in th' world, doin' that. But she and Nate were th' only fam'ly he had left; guess he got t'missin' them too bad. But just what in hell wuz he thinkin', goin' after ole Montgom'ry that way?*

But I always liked Charlie, an' that wuz plain murder.

So, that ole devil's got it comin' fer that'n. He won't git away clean, though he ain't hadda stand no kinda trial. Money, that's what done it: anybody else, he'd be under th' jail b'now, er headed fer th' 'lectric chair.

Cam climbed into the cab of the White, headed for the café where he'd eat, call in and wait for the dispatcher's directions. Another load, another road. But the injustices done by the Mabrys chewed at him, and wouldn't go away.

Thought it'd be all over after Barry, but I guess I'se wrong. So, looks like somebody's gotta stand up t'th' ole man now, make it right.

***

The Ridgeway team's biggest, toughest rival was Harrison, over on U.S. 65, with its deep bench and perennially high-score wins. The first time they'd played them, it was a home game, and Andy'd attended. She met the Mitchells, who liked her immediately, even taciturn Horace. If they'd heard the gossip about her, they'd set it aside as just that, and maybe, as they'd suspected, there was a lot of envy behind it, anyway.

And to everyone's surprise, Ridgeway stomped the favored team, 68-57. It was close for the first quarter, then Red, Nate, and Mark found their opponents' weaknesses and exploited them. Little Ellis McEntire scored big, confusing the taller players, who despite his successes, didn't guard him closely enough. At his diminutive height, he was easy to overlook till his shots swished the net after arcing high over their heads.

Everyone congratulated the team, slapping backs, talking excitedly. Nate felt like a king, but he also credited the entire team with the cooperation, dedication that'd made the win possible.

Then the girls took the floor, and everyone's attention riveted on them. Angie scored frequently, and their center, a gawky, driven girl six feet tall, got every rebound. It wasn't even close at halftime and even farther apart at the end.

Nate thought he'd never seen anyone more beautiful than Angie, flushed at their win, sweaty, red-faced, exultant. And he wanted more than anything in his life to get his arms around her, feel that fast-beating heart next to his own. She ran to her family, hugged first her mother, then her father, both sisters, and finally, even Nate himself.

Andy watched this display with a mixed expression. *Girl seems okay, and so does her family. But you're sixteen, Nate: don't go thinking this is the end of the rainbow. And I do see the way Red Spaulding's looking at her, and Mark Reid, too. You've got competition here; hope she doesn't break your young heart.*

"Well? Nate asked his aunt after they'd reached home, after accepting a ride from the Mitchells, who'd dropped them off. And where he'd been delightedly squeezed in next to Angie, feeling her soft breast against his arm in the crowded car. "What did you think of her?" He clearly wanted her approval, as after all the only other person in his life.

"She's okay. Cute, athletic. Not dumb either, like a lot of nice-looking girls. Obvious you like her."

"Well, yeah, I do. We can talk about stuff: literature, politics, the economy. Nobody else around here, girl or boy, can do that. And okay, I realize we're just sixteen, and I know that things will change around us and between us, but for now, I'm glad we're friends."

"That's a good insight. Yes, there are millions of girls out there, as you'll find out.

College will open some doors for you in a way you won't expect. It'll be a collection of the best from all over, boys and girls. More like your peers, you know."

Nate didn't wonder how his aunt knew about college; he was aware that she'd always picked up on things others didn't notice. And his plan first to get into one, then someday after he'd graduated to help pay her way through, became more entrenched. He owed her everything, and he wouldn't forget that debt.

Chapter Fifteen

Montgomery Mabry looked forward to this hunt; he'd been inside too long, and the weather should be perfect. On top of that, the boy who mucked out the stables had reported seeing a rare eight-point buck the day before, headed across his fields toward the woods. Mabry aimed to bag that buck. His 30.06 was cleaned, oiled, and he'd zeroed in the scope the day before.

Now, before daylight on this December Saturday, he tramped determinedly across the first field, the frost crunching under his boots, leaving clean, purposeful tracks that would disappear as the air warmed. Christine had cautioned him to be careful; there would be other hunters out, and she'd made him wear a bright orange vest, one she'd sewn to fit him. *Girl worries too much, but that was sweet, like a daughter should be.*

Young Giles had wanted to go along, but both his mother and grandfather had told him he'd have to wait a few months. Which brought home to Montgomery that the boy was eight now, and it wouldn't be long till yes, he could take the .22 rifle out after rabbits.

The tension rolled off the lawyer's shoulders as he crossed his acres, noting the mown fields, the tight fences, the partially logged forest off to one side. A small frown creased his forehead when he recalled the sloppy work the locals had done with the timber, leaving good tops, letting some of the trees split as they fell, chewing up his land getting stuck. He'd made them sign a release in case one of them got hurt, but so far that hadn't happened. And yes, Christine had probably been right about insisting he use better-equipped crews for this, but well, he was just stubborn, he guessed. *My place, and I'll run it the way I want. Even if she was right.*

He neared the cut-over Prescott land, which was now grown up in brush and scrub, with an occasional red oak or hickory sapling reaching high for sunlight. *Shame that boy can't keep the place up better. Go down quick, like this. Well, not my worry how those people live their lives. Dave was the exception, but those Millards were and still are worthless.*

Mabry harbored not a single regret at his having shot Charlie Millard, totally convinced as he was that he'd simply rendered justice. The law he served had failed him and his family, and he'd done just what his ancestors had, back when this country was raw and new. A man had to right the wrongs to his family, and he'd done it. End of story, and end of that feud, too. He just wished it had brought him peace of mind.

He skirted this corner, worked his way into that part of his own forest where the big trees still stood, leaving open areas shaded out below. This is where the deer would bed down, after their nighttime grazing what was left of the grass where the mower hadn't reached. And if the big buck was here, there'd be does, too. Wasn't legal to hunt does, but who'd know the difference, once it was all venison? Again, his place, his rules, and damn anybody who didn't like it.

The lawyer moved stealthily from tree to tree, working his way into the woods about the distance he figured the buck would go to get away from the danger of the open land. He selected a big oak and settled against it to wait, a classic still-hunt in a calculated position with good sight lines. The odds were long with so few deer left in the region, but he knew he had as good a chance as anyone at this.

* * *

Andy Millard started awake. She'd had a dream about being hunted back on the Arkansas farm all those years ago. There'd been a shadowy shape with a sinister rifle, slipping silently through strange woods, stalking her. She'd tried to stay far enough ahead of him—it—and out of range, but every time she looked back, there it was, seemingly even closer.

Andy didn't dream often, and almost never here in her secure cottage in Virginia. *Probably that security has a lot to do with it: nothing to be afraid of now.* She'd taken control of her life just as soon as she could, and despite the fears, had charted her own course, once having seen to it that Nate was well on his way with his. Now, drowsily realizing the dream had been just that, she let her mind wander back over part of that old story.

It was so worn in her memory, all the events of their time in Ridgeway now read like a novel, or maybe a saga: circumstances crowding her and Nate, and before that, Elijah and Charlie. Well, even before that: the wasted years with loser Cam Henry, and the untimely deaths of her sister and Dave Prescott.

It was easier to be philosophical about all of it now, with the perspective of her many years, the experiences, even maybe the acquired wisdom. Her life wasn't over, but it had settled into a rhythm she enjoyed without all the stress and worry about survival. And of course without the suspicions, the accusations, the outright meanness she and Nate had endured.

They'd triumphed in the end, but it hadn't seemed they'd get the necessary breaks, back then. *Cards all stacked against us, for sure; just seemed like no way out for us. But Elijah's faith must've rubbed off on us a little, because surely God had a hand in it.*

But this dream bothered her: she had no idea where dreams came from, although she'd read they were usually just rehashings of recent events, impressions the brain was trying to organize into some meaning, in that near-awake state where they occurred. Of course she and Nate had been hunted, after a fashion, as had Charlie… *Or is this dream some crazy twist of the facts? Could I really be the hunter here?*

No, of course not. And I should never let myself go there. This is surely just some sort of flashback to how I felt at the time: do remember imagining powerful forces at work against us, like huge jaws. But why now? Both of us have had good lives, after all the bad stuff, so why should my subconscious or whatever it is take me back to old fears? I haven't been afraid of anything for a long time now.

She rolled over, saw that it wasn't that long till dawn, and managed to drift off to sleep again. *Yes, secure…*

* * *

An hour passed. Mabry's legs were growing stiff, and he shifted carefully, keeping quiet, knowing any sound would carry on this still, slightly overcast morning. He slowly massaged his arms, flexed his shoulders, feeling the familiar twinges from having hunched over paperwork too long. If nothing showed in the next few minutes, he'd move a few hundred yards deeper into the forest, set up again.

Mabry reflected that, despite the disappointments of the past few years, despite the searing loss of his only son, this really was about as good a life as a man could expect. He had this land free and clear, was a good steward of it, was profiting from its harvesting. He lived comfortably, had his grandson and the boy's dutiful, even loving, mother at home. And he was still able to practice his profession, although he knew he'd never, at his age, get into the political realm he used to dream of. *And even if they say I'm not as sharp as I used to be, I've still won most of my cases this past year. But yes, I guess I'll cut back, focus on deeds and paper law, take it slower.*

Yes, it was a good life, even with that damned Charlie Millard's barbaric murdering of Barry, and his thieving, underhanded ways. *Well, he's paid the price: I saw to that when the law I've dedicated my life to couldn't. And I'd do it again—will do it again—if anybody else threatens my family.*

He found himself thinking of that Andy Millard, a woman who could be capable of anything and probably had proven that before. He'd never been sure she hadn't planned the whole savage murder of his son, that elaborate trap Charlie couldn't have dreamed up on his own. *Well, all over now, that feud.*

He stood slowly, letting his muscles handle the changing position. Then he stepped quietly away from the big tree, paused. A slight movement caught his eye. Was that a glint of something off in the distance? And was that partial shape human?

He had no time to verify what he thought he'd seen before the shot thundered through the forest and the bullet struck the center of his forehead.

* * *

Once again the car, this time a long, low '56 Plymouth with its sheriff's star, rolled up to the Prescott place and Hal Burgess stepped out. He was alone, and for an instant, realized he was in the open, a target for anyone inside the house. He shook the feeling off, strode up to the porch, knocked. He knew Nate was away with the basketball team at a regional tournament this Saturday, and she'd be alone.

Andy opened the door to him, wiping her hands on an apron he noted was patched. No, things weren't any better for these people, he saw, same hardscrabble life.

"Come in, Mr. Burgess." Her tone wasn't welcoming. "What brings you here this time?" She hadn't asked him to sit, so he stood. Somehow the air in here was chillier than outside.

"Well, Andy, Montgomery Mabry's been shot and killed. He didn't return from a hunting trip this morning, and Christine sent their farmhand out to look for him." He waited for a reaction. Her hand went to her mouth.

"Oh, I'm sorry. Accident? A stray bullet, you think?"

"Possible, but it was a clean shot to the head. No tracks, with all the leaves underfoot, and nothing visible in the fields. And it's doubtful anybody mistook him for an animal because he was wearing a bright hunting vest. No, it looks like murder."

She regarded him for a long moment. *And of course he suspects me—us. Again. When in God's name will this…this feud, end?*

"So of course you're here again, obviously convinced again that I, or even Nate, is the killer. Isn't that what you're thinking? The logical suspects?"

"No, I'm not. I doubt very much if you or Nate has a high-powered rifle or could even get your hands on one. Or that you could target him from the distance we've figured. Surely used a scoped gun. No, what I think is, one of the enemies the man undoubtedly has made over the years stalked him and killed him. Andy, why are you so angry at me, so bitter?"

"I'm bitter because that man shot my brother down, believing in his twisted mind that Charlie had killed that worthless son of his. I'm bitter because he got away with it. And I'm bitter because my life's been corroded by his ruthless slandering, his insistence that I'm a slut and a whore. And that he and others have concluded that I'll never be entitled to be called a human being again. And that we're near starvation here. That enough for you?"

"Andy, I'm sorry about all that. And you've proven your worth ten times over, in the face of it. All right, I'll grant you neither Barry's death or Charlie's has been satisfactorially solved, but now the old man's dead, too, and surely it's finally over. And unless we discover some clue, some tangible evidence to the contrary, you and Nate are innocent. Please realize that. I came here only to tell you the news before you could hear some wild rumor." His eyes were steady on hers, those dark, inscrutable wells. Finally, she spoke:

"All right, Sheriff. I suppose I should thank you for that. But unless you do find that evidence that I'm sure you'll look for diligently, just please leave us the hell alone, will you? We're trying hard to survive here, get Nate through school and into some kind of a real life, and we just don't *need* this!" Her voice had risen, her face gone hard.

There was nothing else he could say. He nodded, replaced his hat, turned and walked down the porch steps. He heard the door close behind him, not slam, as he'd expected. *Damn this job. It's what's soured this girl, what's kept us from any kind of relationship. And now yes, I've got to keep digging, keep knowing every person around here believes absolutely that she's killed another Mabry. Help ruin her life even more. Nothing else I can do.*

The enormity of this revelation sank into Andy as she watched the sheriff's car back, turn, disappear. And she knew instinctively that no, the lawmen wouldn't find out who'd done this, just as they hadn't the other times. Well, at least they'd known who shot Charlie, little good as that had been.

So, old Mabry dead, and yes, she and Nate would be judged by the gossips, the upstanding people of the county, those who just couldn't wait to heap more scorn on whoever made a slip. Their self-righteousness was sickening: skeletons in all their closets.

Where had it all begun? Not with that desperate timber cutting, no, it went back farther. Dave and Becca had been upright people, admired for their grit, solid citizens, even looked up to, despite her Millard name. So yes, it'd been her own taking the initiative, throwing worthless Cam Henry out, the cheating devil. That had sealed whatever reputation she'd had, which she guessed wasn't much: people always resented a woman who spoke out, who dared break the mold.

Charlie hadn't helped, with his good-natured bumbling, his rubbing envious young Barry Mabry's nose in his popularity. And his carefree style, always broke, never fitting the mold either. And these years of her unselfish work here, taking care of Nate, Elijah, becoming proud of the young man, being almost his mother? That hadn't erased a thing, once she'd been blackened. *Divorced woman,* what a label, like the scarlet *A* on Hawthorne's Hester Prynne.

But yes, it was the killings that had pushed it all beyond salvation. At least half the community still believed she'd helped Charlie murder Barry. At least half of them felt Mabry was entitled to his revenge. And now more than half of them would believe she'd taken her own revenge on the Mabry patriarch, as what they'd think she'd seen as the source of all her troubles.

Damn, this made her sick. Sick of hypocrisy, sick of this place, this life, if you could call it that. Why couldn't she and Nate just sell out, go somewhere else, let him finish school in some civilized place, go on to college as planned, but away from this diseased pit now, today?

No, that'd convince the lawmen she was guilty. Have to tough this out.

Again.

She allowed herself to be overcome with self-pity for half an hour, staring out the window at the winter-ravaged, skeleton trees against the overcast sky. Her hands began to ache, clenched tight, fingernails digging into her palms.

Then she roused herself with a deep, racking sigh, turned back to the never-ending task of mending the fraying clothes she and Nate wore. *Okay, I've had my figurative cry; it's time to get on with this day's struggle. And tomorrow will be no different, but it's a day closer to freedom; I'll focus on that.*

* * *

As a matter of course, Hal Burgess and his deputies did try, and try hard all that day and later, to find out who'd been out hunting that Saturday morning, and of course there had been dozens. Maybe not so many on the Mabry place, but nobody would admit to that at all, having heard the news through the grapevine. It could have been someone from out of the area, come here just this once, making a tragic mistake.

But not likely he knew, with that red-orange vest clearly visible. No, this was murder, which didn't narrow the possibilities much. Too many people who'd lost legal cases to the shrewd lawyer had motives. He concentrated on the major ones of these, the ones dealing with loss of home places, bitter divorces, even yes, killings, still not that rare in the mountains. Who'd he defended, who put away, with that skill he had?

People went over the edge. People nursed grievances till they became obsessions. Uneducated people saw things in black and white, lived by outdated codes generated from the harshness of their lives. And did take revenge.

He was aware of the expected suspicion in general that Andy Millard had killed the lawyer. *Woman had it in her,* they'd speculate. *Kind of person would do whatever she thought she could get away with. 'Course old Mabry, he had enemies, but she was prob'ly number one.*

But with absolutely no evidence, once again the sheriff declined to pursue the idea that Andy was the killer. True, she had no alibi for that Saturday morning, other than that she'd been home, getting Nate ready for the basketball trip. But neither had anyone seen her out, and certainly not with a high-powered rifle.

On that subject, he'd let it be known that the killer had struck from a great distance, likely using a telescope-sighted gun, and had to be a good marksman. The 30.06 slug had lost a lot of its velocity, though retaining enough to smash Mabry's skull. That quieted some gossip, the community knowing how few among them could afford that kind of rifle and could use it well. And also had a grudge against Mabry.

So the investigation would stall but inevitably turn to Andy Millard as the only likely suspect. And again there was instant pressure from above on the sheriff, who steadfastly refused to consider her guilty.

"Hal, you're not doing your job," District Attorney Sam Blevins told him. "And you're not letting me do mine. Here maybe the most prominent man in the county's been shot to death, and you're not giving me anything to go on."

"There's nothing *to* go on, Sam," he replied. "Dead ends everywhere. Here's what we have: a long-range shot, despite the red vest he was wearing, clean shot to the head. That means a top shooter, and it means no accident. So far, no suspects among people he's angered." He spread his hands.

"Andy Millard was certainly 'angered' at the way he went after her, painted her as a loose woman, killed her brother. That's motive," Blevins pointed out.

"Where'd she get that good a rifle? And where'd she learn to shoot? I've asked around: woman never hunted, never owned a gun. And dead broke, how could she even have had somebody else do it? It won't wash, Sam."

"But how about before? With Barry? She had motive then, too. No, Hal, there's just too much adding up here to leave her out as a suspect. You have to bring her in for questioning, at least. If she's innocent, we'll find that out. If not, we've got our killer,of at least one of the Mabrys."

"Oh, my God, Sam. You're on a witch-hunt, here. You're letting the gossip about her, which the Mabrys did their best to pile on, affect your judgment. Be fair here."

"I'm doing my job, Hal. I can't have these unsolved murders piling up here in Everett County like this. Why, there won't be a single industry willing to locate here, reputation like we're getting."

"Is that what this is all about? You want to go after Andy Millard to help the economy here? I can't believe I'm hearing this."

"I want justice, Hal. And I'm going to get it. If she's the only suspect, we go after her. And if we find she's guilty of both murders, that cleans up the slate a lot."

This outraged the sheriff. He had to bite his tongue, leave this man before he said something he couldn't take back. Or did something. He'd so hoped the dead ends would have settled into the assumption that perhaps a stray bullet had felled the lawyer. Happened all the time, and with hunters in the woods, you just never knew when a ricochet might hit a fellow, with the shooter unaware of where his shot had eventually gone.

Like the killing of Charlie Millard, in this case, there were no facts to contradict an accidental death. No, that wasn't right: Mabry had deliberately shot Charlie. But the DA refused even to consider closing this case, getting on with whatever was next.

Burgess hadn't been cursory in his investigation. He'd sent every deputy out to scour the county. Even gone himself to Mabry's house, where the grieving Christine and her son had been in shock, confused. But while there he'd examined the lawyer's other guns, all of which were clean and oiled, all accounted for. He'd had a long-shot thought that someone could have broken in, stolen one of the fine rifles, killed the man. Of course he wouldn't have returned it: long shot indeed.

And now he had to bring Andy in, see her put on the rack again, see her life ripped open again, over something she couldn't possibly have done.

He hated this job.

* * *

It was after the boys' team's tournament win, after the bus had brought the players back to the high school that Nate received an unwelcome life lesson. The girls' team had also won, and the bus ride home had been a high celebration. Nate hadn't been able to get close to Angie with the other girls crowded around her, and even Red Spaulding among those hugging her, congratulating her on the twenty points she'd scored.

Well, that was all right: he'd get his chance on the ride on toward home. The anticipation sent a thrill through him.

Only, as they stepped down from the bus late that night, there was Red Spaulding's pickup truck. And he told Angie he'd drive her home. That was a disappointment, but with all the laughing, back-slapping, hugging, Nate just shrugged, let it pass. He was sure rustic Red was wasting his time, trying to get next to this sophisticated girl. He watched them drive away.

Later, the bus dropped off the few players who lived on the way to Nate's stop, calling farewells, still excited at the win. *Yes, we showed 'em. Undefeated, no losses all year, wow!*

He began the walk up the gravel road in the chill air, the warmth of the day's achievements filling his body and mind. Then as usual, his thoughts turned to the ever-present dilemma of how to make some money for now and for the future. It was a constant drag on his spirits, and it was there even now after the excitement of the two teams' wins.

Then he saw Red's truck, off the road behind some bushes. Had the thing quit on him? No, it was parked, and he heard voices inside it. He stopped, stared. Red's words were muffled, but they were urgent, insistent. A thought flashed: was he pushing himself on her? He took two steps closer, fists clenched. Saw the opposite door open.

Then he heard her voice, too, breathless, pleading.

"Oh, Red, yes, *yes!* Give it to me, Red, *now. Now!* Oooh…"

The truck began rocking, and Nate stared, slowly comprehending. The grunting, gasping continued, the truck's windows steamed, evidence of the awful truth of what was happening. *Oh. My. God.*

And Nate Prescott turned, ran blindly up the road.

* * *

Nate's secretary had left a note for him: the mysterious Giles Mabry had come down with a summer flu bug and wouldn't be able to come for the meeting after all. He'd call again when he was recovered, reschedule. And again, the man hadn't left any word what this was all about.

That was all right: Nate hadn't been overly curious about this visit anyway. So many years had passed, so much had happened, that the reappearance of a man who'd been just a young boy back when all the trouble had come couldn't be that significant. *Probably just wants to hash over old times, see what I remember, talk about some of the folks back in Ridgeway; that's what old people seem to do.*

He found himself doing just that, there in the half-empty office before leaving on errands and home. Yes, Giles had lost both his father and his grandfather those bad years, and nobody had ever figured out who'd killed them. Of course, they all knew old Montgomery had shot his uncle Charlie, but the man had gotten off.

And maybe sure, Charlie *had* stalked the lawyer, meaning either to talk to him, and possibly, in some of his imaginings, set things right between them. Charlie could have found out something about the real killer even, to erase Mabry's belief that he'd done it. Contacted the lawyer somehow, set up that ill-fated meeting in the frozen woods. And just didn't get the chance? Or hadn't been convincing enough? Who knew?

Or maybe even, as had occurred to Nate when thinking back on it, in a twist, Mabry had actually trailed his *uncle* with the specific purpose of killing him. Avenging Barry's death was certainly motive enough, after all.

Charlie'd had no motive.

Unless, in some imaginary, modern, hill-country version of an old-time feud, he'd wanted to wipe out all the enemy. Yes, before more harm could be done to the Millard/Prescott family? Nobody'd ever known what might have been in Charlie's not-too-complicated mind.

Nate and Andy had gone over all that so many times afterwards. It had become the elephant in the room that never went away. A blight on their lives at that time, one to be temporarily banished only by hard work, persistence, their absolute determination to get beyond it, beyond Ridgeway, beyond all the dirtiness of the place, the small-minded people.

Well, not all the people. Nate had always regretted that Andy had blamed Hal Burgess for much of the failed justice of it all. She'd frozen him out, a good man who'd done his best. Nate had never reproached her for it—her business—and if there ever had been a woman who knew her own mind, it was his aunt.

That she'd never remarried had astonished him. He'd always accepted the fact that she'd meet some good man, either in college or thereafter, to bind her life to. But as the years passed, he recognized that she just hadn't found anyone who measured up. And of course, the longer she remained single, the more she settled into her own ways and the less likely it was that she'd make room in her life for a man.

Andy had been the perfect great-aunt to Nate's and Audrey's children, always to be counted on for gifts, babysitting, and later, counseling for the teenagers. Like Nate, they had realized this forceful lady was a tower of knowledge and strength. The three of them almost worshipped her.

His recollections took him back to that junior year in high school and the basketball games. Their winning year, yeah. And of course he remembered the feeling of betrayal and actual disgust at discovering Angie Mitchell and Red Spaulding, going at it like two dogs in his truck. Now he just smiled and shook his head at that. A lesson learned.

Boy, was I naïve.

There'd been other girls, once he got to college. But he'd rarely actually dated, some he'd been just friends with. The male perspective of the time was that females were to be pursued, bedded, then forgotten. *You only married the one you couldn't screw. Treated like things instead of human beings. What blind fools we were, what pigs!*

Then he'd met Audrey, more than four years out of college.

There'd been no nonsense about her, and she'd reminded him at once of his aunt. Knew who she was and wasn't about to waste time with an air-headed loudmouth or a shallow predator. Whoever she chose would be a helluva man, he'd known, and he'd been intimidated for a while.

That she'd chosen him still amazed him. He'd considered himself a gawky backwoods specimen, despite his degree and his second engineering job. He'd still been shy, and maybe even a little gun-shy, from having misjudged several girls since Angie. But she'd seen something in him she liked, and after a few tentative near-dates, she'd seemed to make up her mind to be his woman.

And what a woman! She'd pushed him when he needed it, depended on him, made him feel like he could whip the world. She'd been a religion major, her father a minister, but she'd never put him down for his non-faith. And of course she'd eventually brought him around to just that reformation. They'd raised their children in the church, and the grandkids were being led on the same path.

Andy had approved of this young woman mightily after they'd met and approved later of Nate's faith journey, which coincided closely with her own. Yes, the more his aunt had been exposed to a reasoned Christianity, instead of old Elijah's fire-and-brimstone preaching, the more she wanted to learn about it and the more it made sense to her.

She still reigned as the matriarch of the extended family from the little house in Albemarle County. All of them made time to come visit; Aunt Andy was a joy to be around. She'd learned enough about so many subjects, she was on a solid footing in any discussion, from world affairs to economics to growing herbs, even to classic cars. She held her own with Nate's son, daughters- and sons-in-law, along with the grandnieces and nephews.

Nate drove to her house after his errands to visit awhile and tell her that Giles Mabry wouldn't be coming that Saturday after all. He could've called but always took any opportunity to see her. Even when he was away at college, and later when she was, they'd kept in close touch with letters, phone calls, visits.

"Well, I'll admit I've been curious about that fellow's wanting to see you. I'd about decided to ask if I could be in on it. So I suppose he'll follow up when he's ready."

"I guess so. I'd forgotten that bit about his mother running off after that man. That's why she decided to sell out, wasn't it?"

"Oh, yes. Christine thought she'd found the love of her life. I guess I'm gossiping here, but you probably didn't know she never loved Barry. Got pregnant and forced him to marry her, left college. Old Montgomery always liked her, though, and knew she'd be good for his boy, whether he liked it or not. Yes, they went to Texas, I heard, and then either she dumped him, or maybe it was the other way around. Woman never could keep her pants on."

"You shock me." He grinned.

"No, I don't. We all pretended to be so innocent back then, while everybody but the densest knew dirt on everybody else, and most had something going on the side whenever they could."

"I seem to remember Giles had to work his way to finish at some university. Not sure I remember how I heard that or maybe have the wrong man in mind. But I wonder: did he cut himself off from her, or did she die?"

"Don't know what happened there, but she was still around. Had no better sense than to team up with another worthless man, I heard, who expected her and the world to take care of him. Men're fools around pretty blonde women, always have been."

"There were men who were fools about you, Aunt Andy," he needled.

"The crop around Everett County were fools *and* dumbasses, Nate. I suppose I shouldn't have blown Hal Burgess off the way I did, but I just didn't have the patience for going through all the motions. Besides, he died of cancer not that long afterwards."

Her expression softened, and Nate could tell she was remembering the earnest lawman. But any man in her life at that time would've been just an impediment, he knew, a dead weight to slow her down, add to her troubles. *But it'd have been so great for her to've had a strong man to lean on, share with, help when she needed it. Her choice, though, her life, and don't you ever forget it.*

"And I never told you about the missionary, did I? I really thought I loved that man, but he wanted to plant me in some God-forsaken hole in Africa with him, so that didn't work out."

"No, that's a story I never heard. You'll have to fill me in on it, if you ever decide you want to share your colorful love life with me." She punched his arm playfully.

"I'll save that one for when I'm wheelchair-bound and babbling." But her eyes returned to some place far away. Nate waited a few minutes, his mind back in Arkansas.

"As I remember it, Giles got his degree, then went to Dallas, got a good job. Or maybe went to college there. Seems I heard that, or am I still confusing him with someone else?"

"Oh, yes. In the irony of the century, the very dude who did the snow job on Christine kept in touch with him later, had connections to that Texas company, and helped get him that job. He was a handsome, shallow fake, but maybe that was a bit of redemption. And it was Bobby Harcourt who told you about them many years later—he never knew where I'd gone. Anyway, I can't imagine what Giles has to tell you—us—but I do wanta hear it, okay?"

"Sure. Whatever it is, it can't be something you can't know. But it's just probably gonna be two old codgers comparing notes, getting the old stories all wrong. Bore you to distraction." He grinned again, knowing she would be there, no matter what.

"Well, Giles couldn't be that old, really. Let's see, he'd be…what, sixty-five or thereabouts?"

"About that. Retired, of course, maybe nothing else to do. Probably a company man, spent his life selling electricity or trying to make people happier about their electric bills. The kind goes to every high school reunion, tries to keep up with old acquaintances or something. Anyway, as I've said, what he's got on his chest probably isn't that important since he was so young when we left there."

"Maybe it is. Maybe he could know an answer or two that's been beyond our reach all this time. Or he thinks you—we—might know something that could clear up some detail that's been troubling him. That's really more likely.

"After all, I have to remember I was the prime suspect in his grandfather's death. But he probably doesn't even know I'm still alive, so that wouldn't be a motive." *Or maybe it is. Now that would be a real bite, wouldn't it? If, after all these years, he comes after me?* She went on:

"I do imagine he was thoroughly burned up at the way his mother frittered away her life, and apparently the Mabry fortune, too. He's surely had to make it on his own, which wasn't at all the future the old man would have planned for him."

"No, I guess there wasn't any legacy there. Sort of 'what goes around comes around,' wouldn't you say?" He realized, though, that so little of that old feud had seen the guilty punished.

"Well, we didn't—don't—know the man, and he certainly wasn't our enemy even if his crazy father and grandfather were. Shouldn't blame the guy for the sins of his family."

Nate thought about the events of his youth for a while, neither of them speaking. Then he decided he'd raise a question he'd kept to himself his whole adult life. *Maybe shouldn't, and she'll probably slap me down, but it's eaten at me for too long.* He took her hand, looked directly into those deep eyes.

"Aunt Andy, you don't have to answer this, and maybe I shouldn't even ask you, but tell me, this long after the fact: did you...have *anything,* no matter how indirectly, even innocently, to do with Barry Mabry's death?"

She returned his gaze frankly, never one to hide from any question, any time, from anyone. He could tell she was turning this over in her mind, and no, he couldn't guess what her answer would be.

"You're right, you shouldn't even ask, Nate." She sighed deeply. "I bottled up a huge load of rage toward that slimeball, kept it inside when I wanted to tear his eyes out, see him bleed out onto the dirt, plunge my hands into his blood where I'd ripped his heart out. Oh, I fantasized about that in ways that'd make you shudder. So much so that the obsession took me over, consumed me. I was just going through the motions there with you and Elijah, while my mind was plotting, completely in another plane.

"The only thing I'll tell you is that I've never done a thing in this world that I'm ashamed of, sorry for, or regret, except for Cam Henry. And that's all you're ever going to get out of me." Her face shut down completely, like a door slamming in his face.

"I'm sorry. Like Hal Burgess, I knew you didn't do it, but I just thought, somehow, something could have gotten…well, out of hand…"

"The subject's closed. And please put it out of your mind, Nate; it doesn't belong there."

Chapter Sixteen

"I want to leave this place, Aunt Andy. I want to leave it right now, get away from the filth, the poverty, the violence, the lies." His face was actually streaked with tears now since she'd told him the news about Montgomery Mabry's killing. But she'd seen the raw turmoil inside him as soon as he'd come in the door. Wordlessly, she held him to her now, let him stifle sobs, tried to gentle his convulsions of what, rage? Betrayal? Heartbreak? Didn't matter: he needed her, needed to talk about this, get past it. *Dear God, he's just sixteen.*

"You want to tell me?"

"No, I…I just want *gone.* Can't we just walk away, hitchhike somewhere, like Charlie always could? With this disaster, on top of…everything else, can't we just…disappear?"

"I'm afraid not, although I've had the same overpowering urge to do just that, most of today, Nate. I'm sick of it all, too. I'm afraid, with no other suspects, the law will come after me, sooner or later, and maybe it'll be sooner. Yes, we do need to leave here as quickly as we can, go away, make another start as far as we can get from this hole.

"But we'll need money, and the only possible prospect is to sell this place, and Elijah's, too. That'll take time, and that keeps us right here where neither of us wants to be. I won't ask you what's pushed you too far, but I know it's a culmination of all that's been piled on us. Let's go to bed now. Tomorrow's Sunday, and let's spend the day working on this. There's *got* to be a way."

She eventually got him calmed, sent him to bed. *This is more than I bargained for, whatever it is. But he'll run into more disappointments, those nasty situations that seem like they'll ruin his young life. Kids can be so cruel and hurt others to the bone. Well, so can adults. Maybe I ought to pray here, the way Elijah would.*

Maybe I'll try.

Next morning, after the chores, the two of them sat before the fire, and she told him more of the details of Montgomery Mabry's killing. His face went pale this time, and she could almost see the workings in his mind, the realization of what this could mean. *Yes, he can see what will probably follow this.*

"They'll think you did this." A statement.

"Yes. Hal said it was a rifle shot, that Mabry was wearing red, so no accident. And whatever they dig up in the way of motive with anyone else won't come near what they'll think of mine."

"But you couldn't...no rifle, no way you could've..."

"That's not the way the law works, though: they'll say I could've stolen a gun, borrowed one, even got some man to do it for me. I couldn't have paid for that, but with my 'reputation,' they'll think I traded sex for the assassination. What's the formula? Motive and opportunity? I'd have both, and that'll outweigh the detail of the gun. And with too many people's minds already made up about maybe my killing Barry, I won't have a chance. But tell me, am I overreacting, here? What do you think?"

He was silent for perhaps five minutes, during which he was using that mind of his to turn this over and over again. Gone was his own anguish that'd kept him from thinking of this all night, insignificant now: this had to be dealt with, and there was no time left.

So for the next hour they explored their options as they had so many times before. But this time there was the urgency, the immediate *need* to do whatever they could, right then. Andy felt as if a giant fist hovered above, was about to come down on her—them—and there was no way to avoid it. *If I'm tried, go to jail or worse, what'll Nate do? I can't take that chance.*

For his part, the little perspective he'd gained over the sleepless night hadn't changed the feeling of betrayal, the crushing disappointment he'd known. The high elation over the teams' wins, then the dirty revelation of who and what his fantasy had told him was the love of his life, had racked him. Now with the grim reality of Mabry's death, he just wanted to focus coldly on the way out, no matter the cost.

"I can just drop out of school, dumb as that sounds, Aunt Andy, go somewhere else, finish there. My grades are good, and if we can just get away from here, manage somehow, I won't lose a thing." He leveled his eyes on hers. "And I want to do this. You're right; it's all that's been building up, all the hatred, the violence, the injustice. And with this on top of it all, I just don't think I can take it any more."

She took his hand. This was, for all intents, her son here. So she hadn't borne him: her sister had. But she'd taken up the task of being his real mother. And now they were up against what seemed a certainty that their lives would be ruined even further if the law sent her away. Yes, they had to do something—and now—and finally she thought she knew the way. She spoke:

"I can write Bobby Harcourt, Nate, send him the deeds to both properties, ask him to arrange the sales. You own the property, and I'm your guardian. But it's really complicated now. I'm almost certain I'll be arrested for Mabry's murder. there's no one else, and Hal Burgess has got to be under more pressure to get this solved, even if it's wrong. I've the fear that he'll be here, probably tomorrow, to arrest me.

"Now, this is a little awkward to say, but last night I took your grandfather's advice and prayed my heart out about this. And just before I woke up a while ago, it came to me. Take that however you will, but it may just have been God at work.

"Anyway, I remembered that the Clemsons had asked, a few weeks back, if we'd sell them our horse and cart. Of course I said no; they were all we had to scrape out our living. Well, they're as bad off as we are, you know, with his eyesight going, even if they do have a telephone and electricity.

"But, and this is probably crazy, we could go down there, make some kind of cash deal for whatever they can pay. Or pay part of.

Should bring at least a hundred dollars, and we have maybe twenty saved. I'd like to sell the cow, pigs and chickens, too, but what you said last night and what I fear have decided me, if you agree: get away *today*, be gone when the sheriff comes, tomorrow or whenever.

"Leave it all, and just disappear. What do you think?"

"Wow. I guess I've been so confused and all, I haven't seen a way to do it, really. Just leave, just vanish like I wished? That's pretty radical. And how far could we get on a little over a hundred? And where would we go? But yes, there's no time here: 'If 'twere done, 'twere best done quickly,' to quote the Bard." He was pleased that the words came so aptly.

"Be sure you're okay with this. Leaving all you have here, and yes, just turning the stock loose. No time to try to sell them. Maybe ask the Clemsons or Miz Ed to come get them, but I'm not sure we should let anyone know we're going, leave any trace."

"There's that, all right. Okay, I guess I'm for it: total commitment, in for a penny and all that. So, you really think we can do this? I mean, it'll mean walking somewhere to catch a bus, try to stay out of sight, maybe wave one down. And that'll leave a trail surely."

"That's come to me, too, and it's funny, being sort of led to solutions. I say we head south, maybe toward Little Rock, first. Then we switch, go back north, different bus line. Now, I'll need another name, Nate, and I'm going to have to disguise myself. Maybe become a blonde?" He grinned at that, imagining what that'd make her look like. She went on:

"You won't have to do that, because you'll disappear, too, and shouldn't be a suspect anyway; you were on that basketball trip early. Just be you, but if they do find you, you'll have to deny any connection with me, say you have no idea where I've gone. And at first I won't tell you—make that true. Maybe hint at some distant relative in say, California, where Charlie used to say people on the run head for.

"Now, I know that little college, The School of the Ozarks up in Hollister, takes kids who haven't finished high school. You've heard of it: you work twenty hours a week for room, board, and fees. It's a

Presbyterian place, used to be a high school, but now is a junior college, and they're planning to make it the full four years. Like any school, they want achievers like you: makes them look good."

"What do the kids there do? I've heard it's a sort of farm…"

"From what I know, they have a dairy, beef cattle, crops to work. And some inside work, helping the professors with paperwork, kitchen help, whatever needs doing. The president is a man named Dr. Robert Good, who's been there forever. That's all I know, but he has a reputation for helping anyone in need, and for bending the rules when he sees it's best for them.

"If we double back to there, you can apply as an orphan. I don't know if I'll have to sign papers or not: just say your grandfather you've been living with has died, which is true, and that you couldn't make it on your own. That should get you in okay."

"And what'll you do then? You won't just walk out of my life; I know you wouldn't."

Or would she?

"I'll go on maybe to Springfield. Or if that's too obvious, maybe to Forsyth, or Joplin. Harrison is too close. Maybe even Fayetteville, university town, and maybe a job there. I'll get whatever work I can find, Nate, wherever I can find it. I'll muck out stalls, do housecleaning, scrub floors, anything. I'll have to keep most of the money, because the students at the School are all supposed to be broke, from penniless families: that's the requirement, and you won't need much. I actually know of a fellow who got into the junior college down at Little Rock with just fifteen dollars in his pocket.

"It can be done, Nate. I'm starting to believe God wants us to follow Him on this, that this is a way He's provided for us to go. You know we've never been religious, at least not in Elijah's way, but maybe…" her voice trailed off.

"You're maybe right about that, I dunno. Okay, this sounds like a good plan. Depends on selling the horse, though. Why don't you try to throw in the other stock, too? If they can't pay now, they can maybe send the rest of the money to Bobby Harcourt, and he can reach me, at least. I hear lawyers and their clients are…what's the word?

Privileged, some way."

"That'll tell the Clemsons we're leaving, but I guess they'll figure that, anyway. Okay, I'll try that. If we let ourselves lose money here, sell cheap, they may just go for it. All right, I'm on my way. They don't go to church either, so they'll be there. Wish me luck." She put on her coat, squeezed his hand. "Go ahead and hook up the cart; this is going to work."

* * *

Hal Burgess couldn't bring himself to go after Andy Millard on Sunday. He wasn't overly religious, but that just wouldn't be right: day of rest and all. Monday would be okay, nasty day as that always was. So he'd arrest her on suspicion, subject her to the humiliation of whatever interrogation was necessary, doing his best to exclude the taint of the past events, try to make sure she wasn't prejudged.

That would be nearly impossible. Not only the law, but most people in the community would want her to be guilty: finally get her comeuppance, in their eyes. And he thought of Christine Mabry; she'd want her pound of flesh from the perceived killer, the violent ruining of her and her son's lives. No, Andy wouldn't get a fair shake, no matter how hard he tried.

Public opinion was a bitch.

And then there was the nagging possibility that she might actually be guilty, and of more than Montgomery's death. Who else would have planned and executed that elaborate trap for Barry Mabry? That hadn't needed a high-powered rifle. And now, who else would have so improbably managed to kill the old man, left no evidence? And had she really somehow managed to get that good with a rifle without anyone knowing?

And there was always the barely possible, longest-shot idea that she could have enlisted some man to kill at least the lawyer. But how would she pay for that? Assassins for hire? Unheard of, in rural Arkansas. But maybe there *were* men so desperate, so corrupt. *But surely not anybody Andy'd know. And surely she hasn't been in touch with that worthless ex-husband of hers.*

All this surged around in Burgess's head, leading nowhere, as usual. But okay, he'd do his duty here. The fleeting thought flashed that he could always resign, run off with Andy, disappear. *That's nonsense: she's already slammed the door on that fantasy. No, I've gotta do my job, nasty as it is.*

* * *

Giles Mabry couldn't at first understand that his grandfather had been killed. He'd been closer to him than to his own father, even on back. The old man had doted on him, given him and his mother whatever they wanted, held them close, as his only family.

And now he was gone. Not for a minute did his mother think it had been an accident: she'd made sure he wore that red vest, after all. And so the boy's mind, once he'd accepted the horrible truth, turned to trying to figure who could've done this. He was eight years old, and his knowledge of violence, even after his father's death, had come mostly from comic books and radio shows.

But this was real. This was a repeat of that earlier horror. This had to be solved, the way the detectives did in the stories. The sheriff had to find out who'd done this, even though he'd never learned it about Barry's killer: Grandpa had solved that. So yes, Giles would figure this out, and justice would be done.

Who had a grudge against the Mabrys? Oh, that was simple: the Millards, those lowdown people the family was always talking about. And hadn't that Charlie come after his grandfather before? Good thing he'd shot that bad guy.

Giles had heard vaguely about feuds, those ongoing battles between families. Was this a feud? No, those were a long time ago, like so many stories. But maybe people did still hold grudges, did hunt each other down, even today. He'd have to think about this.

For her part, Christine insisted with ferocity that the Millards, and maybe even that Nate Prescott, had killed both the Mabry men. Who else had such a motive? That slut Andy was capable of any evil, and murder wasn't beyond her at all. Everybody knew what kind of woman she was, trying to snare Barry that time, and getting away with it.

And she swore she'd see Andy Millard rot in jail for what she'd done.

* * *

Slade Clemson came back to the Prescott place to examine the horse. Nate had just unloaded firewood from the cart, had it harnessed to the gelding. The neighbor went over the animal closely, nodding, muttering to himself.

"Nate's been accepted early to a college," Andy told him, "so we'll be leaving in a few weeks. I think I've got a job down in Little Rock, so we need to sell out, Slade. Hope you can use a lot of what's here, the other stock and all. If you can't, we'll advertise it in the paper, sell stuff off a little at a time." *No, we'll just have to walk away from it all.*

The farmer was a close trader. This horse was good; he'd seen that before on the road past his place. And the cart was sound; be good for hauling wood, other stuff. He moved down to the sheds, noted the fat pigs, the flock of chickens, the cow, bred to a good bull, Andy'd said.

"Give you two hunderd dollars fer th' lot, horse, cart, cow, pigs 'n' chickens," he offered.

"Worth more'n that," Andy countered, needing every dime.

"Wal, thet's all I c'n offer. Got cash, I'm sellin' thet good truck: eyes gittin' too bad t'drive it. Take it er leave it." He spat tobacco juice.

"We want two-fifty. Nate's got to have money for that college, Slade. You know he deserves the chance, has always worked his way."

"Hmm. Wal, I might go two-ten. Hafta scrape up butter'n egg money fer that, though."

"Two-thirty-five?"

"Oh, hell, Andy, I know y'need th' money. All right, two-twenty-five, an' thet's it."

"You're a hard man, Slade Clemson, but okay, two-twenty-five it is." They shook hands.

Nate had remained silent, leaving this trading to his aunt, who he knew would do better than he ever could. Now he stared in amazement as their neighbor pulled out a roll of bills and peeled off the agreed amount. You just never knew about these old farmers.

Then Clemson climbed into the cart, clucked to the horse, and drove away down the road toward home. They watched him out of sight, then turned, grabbed each other in a bearhug.

Back inside, they gathered the barest necessities, stuffed them into battered cardboard suitcases, one apiece. Nate rued leaving his shotgun, but there was no way he could disguise it or use it at the college. But Andy broke it down, crammed it in with her own possessions, along with cartridges.

"Never know what a woman alone might run into," she grinned. "The myth of chivalry among males in this world is just that: myth." He got the image of her running that drunken would-be lover off those years ago. *Yeah, man messes with her's gonna get a shock, all right.*

They knew the bus ran on Sundays and was due soon. There were three houses they'd have to skirt on the way to the highway, including the Clemsons'. So without a backward glance, they set out, leaving their shared life of the past five years, the necessary closeness the death of Nate's parents had created. *Try not to think about that* was Nate's determination.

He experienced that old levitation, observing the farm from above, its familiar contours, the fallow fields, the aged house, roof shingles clear and sharp, that he and Charlie had replaced. And this time he was looking down also on the two of them. Yes, two antlike fugitives, slipping slyly away through the trees, to become two other people entirely, somewhere far away. Like caterpillars, emerging as butterflies, flitting away.

They circled the three farms on the way, arriving at the highway shortly before the bus was due that would connect them to U.S. 65 and the route south to Little Rock. Andy worried that someone might see them, but it was Sunday, light traffic, and she hoped their luck, or whatever it was, would hold. But they waited out of sight among the trees anyway.

And it was just before a grateful glance up toward Heaven that she saw the approaching round-nosed bus, which they waved down and boarded. They settled into their seats, noting that the vehicle was almost empty and that no one they knew from Ridgeway was on board. They exchanged glances, smiled. They were on their way to whatever lay ahead. And the curving miles rolled past toward that distant, dim destination.

Going in this direction, there was no long layover at the junction store, only a two-hour wait. By now it was getting dark, and they ate sandwiches Andy had brought along, paid a nickel each for soft drinks. By now they felt it unlikely that anyone here would remember them, and it wouldn't matter if that happened. So both relaxed as much as was possible.

Eventually the bigger bus came, and they settled in for the false route that was the next step in their plan. Just where they'd stay in Little Rock was up in the air, but Nate decided to treat this as an adventure and savor every phase of it. For now, he was getting sleepy, and in time, leaned against Andy and drifted off.

There were stops on the way, and both roused from sleep briefly, then drifted back. Finally, quite late, the bus crossed the Arkansas River and pulled into the station. Groggily they stepped down, there in the heart of the city with moderately tall buildings all around them. The Grady Manning hotel was close, and they registered, taking two rooms. Andy knew she couldn't pass for Nate's mother, so grudgingly paid the extra four dollars.

Nate fell gratefully into bed, minor aches from the uncomfortable bus easing. He dreamed of a place that was a combination of South Sea islands he'd seen pictures of, and Western landscapes, with idealized cowboys chasing outlaws. Angie Mitchell came into these images, but he angrily lurched awake, then buried his face and her image in the pillow again.

Checkout time was ten o'clock next morning, so they cleaned up, went in search of breakfast, finding a café close by. Afterwards, Andy told Nate to wander around, see the sights, but be back here by two o'clock. She gave him five dollars, cautioning him unnecessarily to keep it for emergencies.

"Nate, I've a bad feeling about going back up 65," she told him. "I'll go to the train station, get us tickets. Be a longer trip, but we can stay away from where they'll look for us. Should be okay: the people at the junction may remember us going south, but well, let's be as safe as we can be, okay?"

"Sure. I wouldn't have thought of that. So what're you planning on doing while we're here?"

"You'll see. Be here at two now." She walked away.

And found the nearest beauty parlor, where a hair-coloring service was offered. She knew it would be a stretch to become a blonde but left it up to the woman there as to what she could do with her dark hair.

"Well, honey, I can make you ennything you want, give me time. But I'd say go for maybe auburn: won't be so hard. An' it won't take so long. Know you don't wanta stay planted there all day."

"Just don't want to scare my friends," Andy told her with a chuckle. "But I'm tired of black. Do what you can."

Nate wandered up Main Street, window-shopping. Then all the way up and left into a nearby park. He sat awhile, watching an old man feeding squirrels and pigeons. It was peaceful here, quiet. But he knew he was missing seeing things and headed back west to a street named Louisiana. Down it he passed a block-long arcade and wandered through it, then back, fascinated by all the little shops along it.

He was amused to note that this was a one-way street, coming his way up from the river, where he'd left Andy. He strolled along, noting the passing time in shop clocks. He'd never seen tall buildings before and saw that the tallest one in view wasn't all that high. He'd read about skyscrapers, but he guessed those were in really big cities like New York.

Later, seeing a stranger in the mirror, Andy was sure no one would recognize her. *I don't even know me.*

Still later, she saw Nate approaching the café rendezvous and deliberately walked past him, eyes ahead. He didn't know who that was and kept looking for his aunt. She turned, grabbed him, making him jump a foot high.

"Fooled you, Nate. This is the new me." A wide grin.

"Wow, it *is* you. I was sure some cop had me there. Hey, you look great! Like one of those mysterious Mata Hari types, a woman of international intrigue."

"Really? Think I should apply to the FBI?"

"Better not: they probably work pretty close with local law, even out in the boonies."

They caught the train that ran northeast with connections that would take them eventually back west to Hollister, Missouri. They'd overnight at the junction well east, on the line that met the one coming from Springfield, then connect south from there. It was a long, roundabout way, but that would be fine: safer. And Nate would see new country, albeit from the train window, but he was excited just the same. Andy had traveled some with her former husband, who it seemed wasn't comfortable unless he was on the road somewhere. Her concern wasn't the scenery, but finding work, preferably close to Nate's school.

In time, they left the train at the picturesque pseudo-English village of Hollister, built to attract tourists fifty years before, and walked up the big hill to the college entrance. A receptionist directed them to the admissions office, where an older woman in steel-rimmed spectacles welcomed them, looking closely at Nate. Andy introduced them.

"How old are you, Nate?" the woman asked, and alarm bells went off in his head.

"I'm sixteen, ma'am, halfway through my junior year."

"Oh, I'm afraid, without having graduated from high school, you'd have to be an adult to enroll here. At 21." She seemed truly regretful, then hastened to add: "But there have been exceptions. If you'd like, I can arrange a meeting with Dr. Good." She leaned forward, almost conspiratorially. "He's always open to alternatives."

They agreed readily and for the next hour, wandered about campus, their suitcases left at the reception area in the administration building. The school was situated high above Lake Taneycomo, and a narrow field lay off to one side between it and the cliff. There was a dairy barn and milking parlor opposite this, and various shops, with students and their supervisors at work everywhere. Nate learned they put in half-days, with classes the rest of the time. *This has to work out; it just has to.* Andy had reservations: what if the school was full? What if there was some sort of state regulation about under-age students working around machinery? Surely would be. What if…

Dr. Robert M. Good, the president of the college was thin, with a hawklike beak and kind eyes, pleasant, and obviously deeply involved in the activities there. He'd been largely responsible for its transition first from high school to a junior college, then a four-year degree-granting institution. He took a few minutes to explain how the Presbyterian Church had originated the school, down the White River at Forsyth. That building had burned, however, and a donated one re-erected on this site had replaced it. Others had followed as additional gifts had poured in, and today it was thriving.

"We're dedicated to educating young people who can't afford it," he announced matter-of-factly. "But we do have a board of directors and rules for applicants." He steepled his fingers, regarded Nate closely. *Oh, oh, here it comes: I'm gonna have to wait a few years.*

"High school graduates are admitted, despite their age, with their parents' permission. Now, our registrar tells me you are orphaned, is that correct?"

"Yes, sir, my folks died five years ago. My grandfather was my guardian, but he's dead now, too. My aunt here has taken care of me and wants very much for me to go to college. Well, so do I."

"Of course. But you've a year and a half to go before you graduate. Can't you go back home, finish?"

"Not really, sir. My dad cut all the timber to pay for the place, and we've had to sell all the stock, just to get by. And a couple of years back, our barn burned, and we lost our mules, wagon, and all the hay and feed." It sounded bleak, because, well, it was.

"I see. What kind of grades did you have, down in Ridgeway, Nate?"

"Always *A*s, sir. My aunt insisted I study all the time. She coached me in proper grammar, helped me all the way." He turned an appreciative eye on Andy, who dismissed the compliment with a wave of her hand. He was glad he hadn't mentioned her by name.

"Hmm. Do you think you could pass a high school equivalency examination?" He directed the question to both of them.

"I'm sure of it," Andy supplied her opinion. "He's been two grades ahead of the other students all along. Of course I'm biased." A dazzling smile.

"Well, then. This could be our answer. We administer such a test. When could you take it or would you need to prepare?"

"No, sir, I'm ready now. Clock says two o'clock. How long does it take?"

"Usually two hours. So why don't we set it up? I'll do it myself, or at least get you started. Lots to do around here, you know." He rose, smiled at Andy, ushered them out and Nate into an empty classroom. "You can wait anywhere you choose, ma'am," he told Andy, who'd given her name as Naomi Jenkins, supposedly Nate's mother's sister. Now she sat in a chair in the reception area, reading literature about the college.

It was 45 minutes later that a young assistant came from the classroom, holding Nate's completed test. The girl's eyes were still wide in surprise as she approached Andy.

"These are all correct," she marveled. "You must be very proud of your nephew. I'll take this directly to Dr. Good." She bustled away.

Damn right I'm proud, girl; this isn't your average hillbilly here. She allowed herself an inner glow: this would be all right.

And it was. The good doctor/president accompanied Nate to where she waited and announced that there was always room for a top student. And he even said he didn't have to send to Ridgeway for Nate's records: the test spoke for itself. *Yes! Bending the rules.*

"This is perhaps the best score I remember, Miss Jenkins. You've obviously spent a lot of time with this young man's studies. So if it's all right with both of you, I'll get the paperwork in order, and see that Nate is assigned to a dormitory room with a roommate, and to a work station. You seem familiar with farming, son, or would you rather do something else?"

"Well, I like woodworking, and anything mechanical. I'll do whatever needs doing, sir."

"Oh, and he's also a top basketball player, Dr. Good," Andy pointed out. "I hear you have a team here." She wanted Nate to experience as much as he could the next four years.

"Indeed we do. Forward or guard?"

"Forward, and I was backup center, but I know I'm not tall enough for that."

"You never know: we had a boy here who was under six feet who was a star. You're at least an inch over that, I see, and still growing." He was measuring his own height against Nate's. "One more question: are you a Christian?"

"I think so: Granpa was a preacher, but not a Presbyterian."

"I see. Well, we have regular chapel here, and you'll be expected to attend." He looked the question.

"Surely, sir. We've been talking about God a lot lately, the way He's taken care of us."

* * *

Hal Burgess was shocked to find Andy and Nate gone Monday morning. Had to've left yesterday. *Damn, this looks bad for them. Like with Charlie, the spotlight's on them now.* He knew they were dead broke: must've just walked away like Charlie had. So they'd still be close by surely if they hadn't hitched a ride, which was getting harder to do, especially for two people. He got a mental picture of the two of them, maybe carrying all they owned, on foot along one of the back roads they thought would lead them to freedom.

Okay, first he'd check with the neighbors, see if any of them had helped or even seen them leave. He called Cale Wilcox on his radio, had him go ask first at the three houses between the Prescott place and the highway, while he'd go on up the road the other way himself. *They could've reached the highway, got a ride, or maybe if they could, caught the bus. Well, start searching; it'll be worse for Andy—both of them—running like this. Not smart, and Andy's smart.*

Which could mean the worst.

He stopped at the first neighbor, who hadn't seen either Nate or Andy in several days. Then the next, a half-mile farther on. Then at the Mitchells, the new people with the daughter on the ball team.

"They're gone?" Donna Mitchell was surprised. "Why, Nate was with the rest of the team just Saturday at the tournament. He was one of the top scorers and such a nice boy. Surely they'll be back. You've checked the school, of course."

"Called and Nate's not there. This is a mystery. Livestock's all there, except for their horse. If you hear anything, please call my office." He hurried on.

Two miles farther, well past Elijah's empty church, no one had seen the fugitives. He radioed Wilcox.

"About to call you. These folks, the Clemsons, just bought all th' stock from them. Got th' horse and cart, goin' today for the hogs and chickens, cow. Said th' folks were leaving in a couple weeks, something about Nate going t'college. But no, they haven't seen them since around noon yesterday. And I don't reckon that boy could get into college, still in school."

"Good work, Cale. All right: they're on foot or at least set out on foot. Could be somebody in town saw them; might've caught the bus there or be planning to. Think it leaves around four."

"I'll go now, check that out. That'd be the westbound bus, so I'll ask at the station. Over and out."

Well, at least they have a little money. But just to leave this place, walk away? Andy must've figured there was no way to beat thi, with all that's gone before. I won't believe she killed either of the Mabrys, but this is redneck, to run like this. Damn, she doesn't trust anybody, least of all me. Wish I didn't have to hunt her down like this, like I tried with Charlie.

Subsequent questioning didn't turn up any sightings in the village, even at the bus stop. But figuring the time it would've taken to walk there anyway since the last sighting, Burgess thought it likely they'd flagged down the bus the day before. Or caught a ride. But why hadn't anyone seen them? Oh, they'd have skirted the houses surely. Andy wasn't dumb, and neither was Nate. Shame, now these two, several cuts above any others around, were reduced to being wanted suspects, and the pressure would be greater than it had been in the hunt for Charlie, now with the lawyer's death added.

He'd have to notify the state police again,and the sheriffs of surrounding counties. But first, he wanted to see if they'd caught the westbound bus: there'd be the short wait at the junction with U.S. 65, and maybe he could pick up the trail there.

He drove the miles to the little store depot, questioned the store clerk. Sure enough, he remembered the scruffy couple, just ordinary hill folks, nothing special about them. They'd caught the southbound ride to Little Rock. He hadn't paid much attention, figured it wasn't any of his business.

All right then. Get the word down there to local police, sheriff in Pulaski County, the state boys. That town's about a hundred thousand, and they could get lost in it. For a while. But it's likely they kept going. Maybe to Texas, Mississippi, or anywhere. I've gotta remember, they won't do the obvious: Andy will second-guess me here. If she wants to stay gone, she'll do a better job than her brother did, and we didn't find him; he found us. The hard way.

Burgess thought about all these two had left: not much in the way of possessions of course, but the farm? And Nate's school, where he was a standout on the team, the top student surely on the way to a scholarship? Just walked away from all that they'd built up? That sure didn't look like something Andy would have done, the way she'd always planned, made sure her decisions were the best they could be.

Of course they'd toughed it out before, against the gossip, that stupid trial, the barn-burning, crazy Barry's attacks. Even the accusations about that nasty pitfall killing. And okay, they'd do it again, no matter the odds against them. These weren't people who'd let even dire circumstances defeat them.

So this sudden flight, despite its implications of their guilt, had to be either the last straw or a desperation move when it looked like they just couldn't win, as he'd thought earlier. For a few minutes, he tried to imagine himself in their circumstances: what it'd be like, two people leaving a hardscrabble life, with no education between them, little money, no way to survive out in a hostile world. Bleak. So much so, he just couldn't put himself into their shoes. *And those shoes worn out from the rocks and hard places here in this hopeless place.*

And Sheriff Hal Burgess knew, deep down inside himself, that he'd never find Andy Millard or her nephew, no matter every lawman in the country would search for them.

And gazing up at the black, bare limbs of the winter trees, he felt the emptiness they embodied. The same emptiness that left him aching.

Chapter Seventeen

Finding a job wasn't going to be easy for Andy. She'd really felt she was being guided for a while, things working out for Nate almost ideally. Even if Hal Burgess or some other police found him, he'd say truthfully that she'd disappeared and he'd had no contact with her. She knew they'd go easy on him, with his airtight alibi, and being a minor with a good reputation: she'd be the one they wanted.

But now she was on her own and had absolutely no direction, no sense of things falling into place. *Maybe the Big Man's been looking out for Nate, not so much me. No, I don't really believe that. Don't know what I believe, actually. But best get on with it: finding work.*

She wanted to be some distance from the college in case some lawman did track Nate down and locate her. She didn't worry much about him, now believing he'd been taken care of. She had no skills, though, other than housekeeping, farming, and having been a creep's wife. *Maybe I should have been the one to apply to the college.*

The idea of working her way through to a degree now that Nate wouldn't need much money had an appeal. But that'd mean living near a college. There was a big one in Springfield, she knew, Southwest Missouri State, maybe 50 miles away from Nate. The Arkansas University was much farther, so she ruled that out. There was a college down in Batesville, but that was too close to Ridgeway. There was Arkansas Tech, at Russelville, also a long way off. One at Jonesboro: too far also, but a possibility.

So she'd try Springfield first. She rode a bus to the campus, went first to the reception area, asked about the school in general. She also asked what students could find in the way of work to pay their way.

"Well, there are always jobs in town," the young woman on duty told her. She was tiny, with eyes set far apart, which gave her a sort of surprised look. "What can you do?"

"Nothing specialized. I've worked on a farm, cleaned house, did finish high school, but that's about it. I can type, and I guess I could handle a secretary's job, but it'd have to be part-time if I took classes."

"Go to the state employment office then, and see what's out there. And sometimes the professors here need typing done on their research stuff. Oh, and you wouldn't have to pay out-of-state tuition if you were working here. Tell you what, I'll ask around about that for you. And my name's Cindy, what's yours?" She was outgoing, friendly.

"Elizabeth Wilson." She took the girl's offered hand. She'd realized she couldn't use the name Nate's college had: too easy to be tracked down. She also knew she'd have to get a Social Security number, something she'd never had, going off to get married so young and never having a real job.

"Well, Elizabeth, you just check back here tomorrow, and maybe I'll know something by then. I'm actually taking a few classes when I can squeeze them in, too. One at night this semester. Slow going, but I'm poor, too." Her smile was genuine, and Andy felt that here might be a future friend indeed. She didn't see a ring on the girl's finger. *S, she's right where I need to be.*

She walked the few blocks to the employment office, registered as Elizabeth Wilson, and talked to a counselor, a woman who used too much makeup to disguise the lines in her face, failing at the attempt. But everybody wanted experienced help, it seemed, and there were no part-time jobs just then.

"I can send you out for these three interviews, Miss Wilson, though it's almost closing time. Here are the addresses, contacts, if you want to go tomorrow. Just let me know what they say so I can update our records. And if nothing works out, come back next week."

Andy thanked the woman, walked outside. She went back to the college, sat on a bench on the grounds, read over literature Cindy had given her. The range of majors was wide, and she imagined fitting into one, then another. She really had not planned that far ahead, but these offerings intrigued her. She got the impression, a new one, that she could accomplish anything, go anywhere, succeed at her choice of careers, given just one break.

It was a good feeling.

She found a cheap hotel for the night but knew she'd have to get herself a room soon and, of course, money to pay for it. She was squeezing every dime, but the bus and train tickets, these hotels, were draining her. She bought a newspaper in the lobby, went up to her room. There she ate a sandwich of bread and cheese from a scant grocery store purchase, scanned the want ads, marked a few. She then tried to read a book she'd brought with her but couldn't concentrate much on it. She showered, went to bed. Tomorrow would be the all-out day, the day she *had* to find work.

But Cindy's digging hadn't turned up but one professor who was working on a dissertation and could use some typing in about a month. She seemed genuinely disappointed.

"And it only pays fifty cents an hour, which would've maybe been ten dollars a week. Room'll cost you at least five or six, and you'd starve."

"No, I can't do that, but thanks very much, Cindy; you've been great. I guess I'll go check out a couple places I heard about at the employment office. Wish me luck."

Okay, that dream's out. Chase these down, then just hit the streets one place at a time if I have to, and I guess I do. She left the campus with regret. It would've been so perfect…

The first company was a Caterpillar Tractor dealership that needed a receptionist. The position consisted of answering the phone, typing up work orders, filing, keeping track of the salesmen's paperwork. Andy knew she could do this.

"But you don't have experience, I see," the vice president, who was the owner's son, pointed out. "We'd be taking a big chance." He was looking her up and down openly.

"I can do this, sir," she told the balding, overweight man, noticing what could be his slight leer. "I'm fast at everything I do, and I'll have this down very soon."

"Well, I don't know," he said, his eyes still running over her. "The last girl we had spent all her time on the phone to her boyfriend. Wouldn't want that. You're not married?"

"No, sir. And business is important to me; you'll find I'm dedicated to my work." She could sense this was going nowhere but continued to radiate what she hoped was confidence. Apparently he was reading this wrong.

"Well, let's get this out in the open from the first: Sometimes I'd ask you to work late. Would that be a problem?" That *was* a leer. She began to feel like a target.

"Not if there's work to do. Who else would be here late?"

"Just me. My father expects me to do twice the normal amount of work, I guess to prove myself." He laughed, but it came out as more of a calculated chortle. *I don't need this predator: time to go.*

"Well, sir, if you don't think I'm qualified, we're both wasting our time." She rose, turned, and walked out, leaving him open-mouthed.

The next interview was more promising. At first. The personnel director at the paper cup factory on Glenstone Avenue asked her the usual questions, had her fill out an application. When it came to the Social Security number, she told the man she'd never had one, always done short jobs for cash wages. Which was true, or at least wasn't entirely false.

"Well, you'll have to get one. I think you can do this job, since the woman who's leaving will have a week to work with you, and I'm willing to take a chance on you. But you'll need the SS card. I think they only require a birth certificate. I'll talk with our department heads, show them your application. Come back tomorrow then."

That, she should have anticipated. Of course she couldn't get a card in her real name. And no, Elizabeth Wilson couldn't produce a birth certificate with that name on it either. And this was going to be a problem.

Okay, she could say she was orphaned, which was true, and that she'd been born at home with a midwife who kept no records. She actually knew several people like that, and maybe she could swing it. Surely there were ways for such undocumented people to get registered.

And that was the story she told the people at the Federal Building. Which did not seem out of the ordinary in 1957. After all, this town was full of former farm families who'd come to work in the factories from all sorts of places and backgrounds. After some additional questioning, she was presented with a form to fill out and sign and made to swear allegiance to the United States, and some other things she promptly forgot.

Eventually she was handed her SS card and walked out feeling more optimistic. She went to the third interview, a long walk west. This job would be running the office for a used car/garage outfit in the seedier west end of town.

The blocky owner, one Trey Collins, chewed tobacco, and he and his cheerful wife, who was, strangely, one of the mechanics, asked her about her background.

Somehow, she felt more at home with these almost-grubby people, and she opened up to them. *Can't appear too different here, and I'm not really.*

"Well, I had to throw my no-good truck-driving husband out for cheating on me, and since then I've been taking care of a nephew and his grandfather. We were dirt poor, and I still am. Old man died, and the boy got into college; will hafta work his way through. I've always worked, tried to help my husband work on his trucks, did all kinds of farm work, logging, making do. That's about it, and if you can use me, I'll do you a helluva job, whatever it is." *Yes, just get it all out there.*

The two looked a question at each other. Andy could see, out the grease-stained window, two men under a car that was up on a lift. The smell of oil and gasoline was everywhere. There was grit under her feet. She looked back at the owners. He was stubbled with arms that almost reached the ground when he stood. His wife was red-faced, with hair the color and texture of straw but with laugh wrinkles at the corners of her eyes. Andy thought she might like them.

"Reckon you could sell cars?" Trey, the husband, asked.

"Try me."

"Okay, you know how t'type, file, keep records?"

"I did that for my ex, whenever I could catch him, yes." That got a smile from the man.

"Gets a mite rough around here, with th' boys works for us an' all, an' guys comin' in t'get stuff fixed. That bother you?" Starr, the wife, asked pointedly. "Might sorta come on to you, you bein' nice t'look at."

"I've had to run more'n one man off, ma'am. Used a shotgun. No, I was raised amongst rough men, an' when I need to, I c'n be rough, too. Way I look at it, this is a place to work, not mess around." They could tell she meant it.

"Well," Trey confided, "th' last gal they sent, she took one look around, walked right out th' door. Not her kinda people, I guess." A question in his eyes.

"Always found folks all about the same, underneath: some mean-er'n others, is all." She was aware her speech was slipping more into the localisms she'd tried so hard to get away from. *My roots showing, I guess.*

The two exchanged looks again. Andy sensed that these two had that kind of silent communication some couples shared. She knew the jury was out on her, so to speak.

"You know a differential from a gearbox, Betty?" Trey asked.

"Give me two days, and I'll know every part of every car you've got here." A chuckle from both of them at that.

"You talk a good fight, honey," the woman grinned, slapping a heavy hand on her shoulder. "Whattabout it, Trey? Think she can hack it?" He thought for a beat, leaned, spat into a can.

"Tell you what, girl: we'll take you on trial. Two days, like you bragged. Starr c'n show you what's what in here, an' if you work out, we got a deal. Thirty dollars a week. Don't, we'll pay you for th' two days, an' we part friends. You sell a car, we give you a five percent commission. Fair 'nuff?"

Andy stood, grabbed the man's hand in her own hard one, wrung it, then impulsively hugged Starr, and set her purse on the desk.

"I can't start before…what's it, four-thirty? How about right now?"

"I like that, don't you, Trey?" Starr had a near-constant smile.

"Almost quittin' time, so let's make it tomorrow. Oh, you got a place t'live yet?" He'd noticed her battered suitcase.

"I don't. Find something I guess, but it's gotta be cheap. I'll want to watch the pennies, send whatever I can to my nephew; he's all I've got left."

"And you won't have a car," Starr mused. "Hafta be close, least at first. How about your sister, Trey? She's by herself, now."

"I'll call her. She's got a place out a mile or so, on west, little farm. Her man died last year; might want comp'ny." He dialed the phone, spoke into it.

"Susie. We just hired ourselves a girl t'run th' desk, here. Yeah, that job we been pesterin' you t'take. Well, she's new in town, knows how t'work, an' needs a place t'stay. Think you could put her up? She don't look sloppy or mean, but you never can tell," glancing with a grin at Andy. "Okay, I'm gonna bring her out, soon's we close up. Yeah, I'll bring Starr, an' you wimmen can talk each others' ears off. Girl's name's 'Lizbeth. Bye, honey.

"Susie's older'n me, keeps a house she won't hardly let me in with m'shoes on. But she's lonesome now. I'd say you'll get along. Whattya think, Starr?"

"I made th' suggestion, boss, remember? She'll sure like Betty here better'n you." She squeezed Andy's hand.

The house was an old two-story, fading white, like a million others on farms across America. It had big trees in the yard, a small barn out back, sheds. Andy didn't know if it had running water, but it did have electric lines running to it, which, of course, it would this close in. She could hear the distant hum of traffic faintly, back toward town. They walked up to the door.

Susie was maybe fifty with iron-gray hair, half-glasses. She was spare where her brother was a chunk, but her severe look dissolved into a smile of welcome. *She's really pretty; I'd never guess they were brother and sister. May have to watch my manners here, though.*

The woman looked Andy up and down, noting the plain clothes, the worn shoes, the reddened hands, the now-auburn hair. She nodded, smiled, stood aside to let them in.

"Well, Elizabeth, you really think you can put up with this wild old brother of mine? I know you'll get along with Starr 'cause she's all that keeps him human. Come on in, and yes, you're all staying for supper.

"Trey, how you can get away with working this good woman all day and then expect her to cook for you, I'll never know. Someday, she'll catch on and walk out on you." That smile again. Andy liked this woman instantly.

The others went to wash up, and she went to the kitchen to help. It was surprisingly modern, evidently remodeled recently. She remarked on that.

"Yes, this was the last thing my Tom was able to do as a present for me. It gave him a lot of satisfaction, tearing out all that old stuff. We still had a pitcher pump right here where this new sink is. Where you from, Elizabeth?"

"End of nowhere Arkansas, ma'am. I lived several places when I was married to my cheating truck driver; he was always running out of money but wouldn't let me go out and work. But I'm from Everett County down across the line."

"Well, my pa always told my brothers, 'if you want a good time, find a Texas girl, but if you want a woman can work, stick with you, get yourself a gal from Arkansas.'"

"Oh, I'd have stayed, fool that I was, if Cam could've kept his pants buttoned." Andy knew this was maybe too brash but Susie actually cackled. "I think he had another woman at every truck stop."

"You're lucky to be rid of him then, girl. My Tom stayed faithful, thank God, or I'd have been out that door, too, or broken a skillet over his head. Some of 'em seem to think their purpose in life is to grab every woman they meet." She shook her head, still smiling.

Andy's first impression was reinforced throughout the meal, with Susie obviously enjoying having them there. There were no awkward pauses, and she allowed a few more facts about herself to surface. Afterwards Susie saw her brother and Starr off, turned to Andy.

"Got two extra rooms, so take your choice. My man Tom also put in another bathroom upstairs, along with this'n. I sleep down here, so you'll have the run of the house up there. And I think we'll get along as long as you don't bring all those truck drivers around." Another smile.

"You can bet on that. But well, we should talk money here, shouldn't we?"

"Oh. Well, five dollars a week's about right for me, if that's okay?"

"It is, and thanks. I'll buy my own groceries, of course, and stay out of your way unless you want the company. I read a lot, and I'm thinking I'll maybe take a night course at the college."

"Why, that's fine, now. Probably be two nights a week, the way they set the courses up. SMS isn't far from here, so if you're not scared to walk it at night, that should work."

"I'll try to be always with another student, late nights. I don't fool myself that the city's any safer than out in the hills." She was thinking Nate's shotgun wouldn't do to carry with her.

"Smart girl."

Andy slept soundly that night, having felt in those minutes before dropping off a feeling of being taken in by people who liked her, here far from home. It was a good feeling, a warm feeling, a little like love.

* * *

Nate and his new roommate talked late that first night, about the college, about the work, about where each was from, what they'd done before coming here, and anything else that came to mind. According to this Harley, the students weren't expected to work too hard, there being more of them than there was work to be done. The place ran principally on donations, trusts, gifts. A big part of Dr. Good's work seemed to be fundraising.

He got his books the next morning and was assigned to the woodworking shop. He'd go to classes till noon, then to work after lunch in the big dining hall. The bustle of the place made him feel like part of a big machine, where he had to do his part to keep it running.

The course work was not strange or that hard. Nothing he hadn't experienced a little of, either in his high school classes or from his reading and Andy's tutoring. *This won't be tough at all.* His work supervisor explained that most of what they'd be doing was repairs and new construction on the buildings at the college. Now and then, he told Nate, they'd take on an outside job to help bring in money for the school.

There were electric saws here, a planer, bandsaw, jointer, drill press. Many hand tools also, most of which he knew. He was impressed with the quality of the work being done, since most of his experience had been with rough repairs and barn-grade building. He knew he'd enjoy learning the finer points of the carpenters' trade.

Nate had mailed the letter he and Andy had written to the lawyer Bobby Harcourt, asking him to take over the sale of both Everett County properties. If possible, he was also to see if the neighbors could keep an eye on the empty places so they wouldn't get looted. That wasn't going to be easy, and they'd both admitted that they'd lose probably all they'd left there. Nate had also requested that the lawyer not tell where he was unless he had to. He was to mail all correspondence to him at the college.

A few days later he received a reply that the lawyer would indeed handle the listing and sale, but he couldn't guarantee protecting the property. He'd be in touch with any further news and agreed to take his fee out of the sales.

Okay then. That's about wrapped up that part of my life, unless some lawman comes here after me, which I hope doesn't happen. He and Andy had agreed that he was to tell anyone who asked that she'd disappeared he knew not where. Without outright lying, he could say he'd come up from Little Rock, parting company with his aunt, who'd gone looking for work. Again, he didn't know where, which was true.

He knew she'd be in touch with him soon and was sure she hadn't gone far: would want to visit. He remembered her as a redhead and grinned. *With a new name, nobody'll ever find Aunt Andy. She'll build herself another life, and good for her.*

Then he set himself to excel at his classes, work hard toward that coveted degree, and in four years or maybe less, be able to go out into the world to seek whatever fortune was out there. And to help Andy go to college, too. Eventually they'd be able to get back together somewhere beyond the reach of the north Arkansas authorities. Unless, of course, Hal Burgess managed to find Montgomery Mabry's real killer.

Nate had never seen so many attractive girls before. He noticed pairings everywhere and remembered his grandfather's comment that a lot of young people seemed to go to college just to find life partners. For himself, he was determined to keep his nose to the proverbial grindstone and not let himself be deterred from his course. *Plenty time to go courtin' after I'm out of here. Get tied up with a girl, that'd throw a monkey wrench into all my plans. Besides, that experience with Angie Mitchell's enough of a snakebite to do me for awhile.*

That he was younger than the other students also served to keep Nate focused on work and study. He remembered how disdainful the high school girls had been toward boys younger, if only by a year. The standard had been for all the ninth- and tenth-grade girls to try to connect with senior boys, or at least juniors.

So okay, he was the new kid here, and he was just as glad; he'd watch and learn. And stay out of trouble. From the first he'd heard of after-hours escapades by daredevil students, some of whom were no longer on campus as a result. There was a lesson there.

Sometimes the memory of Angie Mitchell did come into his mind, but he shook it off impatiently. That was another world, another life, and thank God he was out of that mess. Maybe he'd overreacted, but the end result was positive, with him in college and his aunt, he was sure, securely working and opening new doors for herself.

He found he did have to work harder in his courses than he'd ever had to before. As Andy had told him, college had the best of the best from the high schools all over, so he wouldn't automatically be top of the class. That these others were poor like him didn't mean they were dumb.

* * *

Hal Burgess's attempts to locate Andy and Nate had of course come up dry. Nobody in Little Rock had noticed thc two, and law enforcement there had no leads. He knew that city had probably been just the jumping-off place to any number of possible destinations. Andy even might have zigzagged their route to make sure they left no trace to follow.

The Arkansas State Police had cooperated, as had those in surrounding states, to varying degrees. A detective named Howard Hardison had come up from Little Rock to aid in the case. He was a thorough investigator and went over the facts as Burgess provided them, adding his own speculations to those of the locals. With absolutely no results. The most likely suspect in Montgomery Mabry's killing had just disppeared with no trace.

So, unless something like Charlie Millard's mysterious reappearance occurred, Burgess knew he'd seen the last of the two. With a sigh of regret, he tried to forget his attraction to the girl, to that fantasy. *Guess it just wasn't meant to be, unless I'd quit my job, talked her into running off somewhere. Too many complications, though, and I'll have to put all that out of my mind.*

After Hardison left, the sheriff often went over the entire Prescott/Millard/Mabry feud details yet again, still trying to find whatever he knew they were missing. Somewhere he'd overlooked a significant clue, but it just wouldn't come to him. And the more time passed, the less important it became. *All over now, and yeah, I guess it ended the best way it could: Andy's safe somewhere, and she'll see to it that Nate gets an education, amounts to something. Better than being stuck her, with all that hanging over them.*

But news of the later sale of the Prescott place jolted him back to a realization: someone had handled that for Andy, Nate being underage. If he could find out who, that would lead to her; it had to.

He toyed with this revelation for several days. Did he really want to pursue this? The whole case was dying down in people's minds. Of course, others would figure out the obvious connection: the purchase money had gone somewhere, so where? Or could he ignore it and hope it wouldn't come up…

No, things just didn't work out that way. And he didn't need yet another accusation of going easy on Andy Millard, who, for lack of a better candidate, was the prime suspect in Mabry's murder. He'd have to follow up on this, he knew.

Inquiry at the newspaper office revealed that Bobby Harcourt, the lawyer he'd found for Andy, was the sellers' agent for the properties. Burgess knew of the lawyer/client privilege, of course, but a murder investigation trumped that. Or he half-hoped it did. He wasn't sure how hard he'd go on the lawyer if he should stonewall on this.

He called, then drove through Henderson County and on to the next one, looked up Harcourt. The lawyer was expected back in his office shortly, his secretary told him, unless court ran late. Burgess sat, waited, again not certain this was the right thing to do. *But Harcourt's a good lawyer; he'll cooperate. Then, God help Andy when we find her.*

Harcourt returned after twenty minutes, shook hands with the sheriff, invited him into his office. Of course, the lawyer had heard a lot about Mabry's killing and asked what the status of the investigation was.

"Well, Bobby, I'm afraid the logical suspect was your former client, Andy Millard. You probably heard about Mabry's shooting her brother, Charlie. The old man claimed he was being stalked, and he was defending himself. No witnesses, so Mabry went free. I was sure Andy was innocent: she had no access to a high-powered rifle, which was used in the killing. And as you knew, she's always just wanted all this to go away.

"Anyway, you probably also know she disappeared, along with her nephew a few months back. That, of course, makes it more likely she's the killer. I frankly don't believe it: I think I know the woman well enough to doubt it.

"But the Prescott property just sold, and I've learned you handled the deal. Surely Andy hired you, since Nate is underage. I'm bound by law to pursue this, and to get right to the point, I need to know where she is." He sat back, watching the lawyer's face.

"Wish I could help, Hal. And it's not an attorney/client situation: I'm not representing her. Fact is, I don't know where Andy is, and neither does Nate. He sent me a letter a few days after they left, asking me to handle the sale, yes. Said his aunt had left him in a good situation, and gone off looking for work. He hadn't heard from her then and hasn't since.

"Now his being a minor essentially means he can't make such deals. But he's asked me to act as trustee for the money received for the sale, which I've agreed to, until he reaches the age of twenty-one. At that time, he gets the money, out of which I've taken my fee. All legal, of course. So Andy didn't sell the property; it wasn't hers. But I have to ask: is Nate a suspect?"

"Well, no. Got the best of alibis: was at a basketball tournament. Nobody's pushing me to go after him except as a way to find Andy. But, of course, you know where he is."

"Now we *are* into attorney/client privilege territory. Unless he's charged with a crime, I'm not authorized to disclose his location. I haven't seen him or talked with him. I really don't know exactly where he is either, since all I have is a mailing address that could've come from any post office in the country. But I won't expose my client to anything less than a serious murder charge." He spread his hands. "Surely you'll have to agree this is right."

"Well, I guess you've got me there. But I doubt that he really doesn't know where his aunt is. They're too close, have been for years."

"Think about it: Andy Millard's no fool. Best way for her to be found would be to tell Nate where she is, knowing you or the state police would track her through him. No, I really believe she's disappeared from us and from him. You probably agree with me that this is a strong woman, one who'll do whatever's necessary and has in the past."

"Well, as I said, I don't believe she did it or killed Barry Mabry either. But with no other suspects, at least nobody with motive and opportunity, the higher-ups have leaned on me hard to bring them somebody. I won't see anyone railroaded here, and I'll admit I've had second thoughts about trying to find Andy. God, man, she's been through enough!"

"I'll forget you said that, even if I agree with you. But again, she's a dead end as far as I'm concerned. But really, has she been charged?"

"Not as such. Wanted for questioning is all, but you know the DA would go after her full force if he could get his hands on her. Told me as much when he demanded I arrest her on suspicion. She got the jump on me, by half a day, apparently."

"I told you she was smart. But it must've been hard, the decision to pull Nate out of school, leave everything they had, which wasn't a whole lot. Still…"

"Yeah, she could see the deck was stacked against her: nobody else around, she had to be the one. I know it was like a big trap to her, with no other way out. They sold the stock for enough to get away, but if you're holding the money for Nate, they haven't had anything else to live on."

"All I know about that is what Nate wrote me: she got him set up some way, somewhere. Then vanished. And just guessing, she'll stay vanished."

"Have to agree with you on that. Well, thanks for what you've told me. All we have is their trail down to Little Rock, and they could've gone any direction from there. I guess it's possible there was a distant relative around there or somewhere Nate could go to." He rose, put on his hat. "It's good to see you again anyway. How's your practice?"

"Growing, slowly. Trying to be an honest lawyer takes a huge amount of time, research. And, of course, you win some, lose some. But I'm up on the win side." They shook hands, parted.

So Burgess was faced with either getting Nate Prescott charged with murder, which would force Harcourt to reveal his whereabouts, which *might* lead to Andy. Might. But if Nate really didn't know his aunt's location, that'd be a pretty harsh thing to do to the boy. Who could very well have traveled to some other post office to mail and receive mail from Harcourt. And he was, after all, a minor. *Well, it'd just ruin his life, that course. So it's no course at all because I won't do that. Far as I'm concerned, from this moment, this case is closed.*

That is, unless we find Andy Millard.

Or the real killer, if they're not the same.

* * *

The walk was for Andy refreshing in the brisk air next morning, and she entered the concrete-block building grateful for the heat. Even the machinery smells didn't bother her. Starr began showing her the bookkeeping, the paperwork, which took an hour.

"There's more, but Trey needs me out back. Got a man comin' for a pickup he traded for, and it needs a transmission. I see they've got it up on the rack. You just go on with that stack of receipts, put 'em in the file there, and I'll be back in after a bit."

Andy glanced out the window to see the woman start helping her husband unbolt the transmission and drive shaft from an aging truck. This she recognized, but she'd have to ask about some of the other parts, pieces, and procedures. *Watch, ask questions, and learn.*

One of the other mechanics strolled in, got a soft drink from the machine. Then he sauntered over, grinned at her, offered her his not-too-clean hand.

"Hi, I'm Clayton Beal. You'd be th' new lady in th' office. Betty, is it?"

"Hello, Clayton. Yes, and I'm behind already on this stuff. Don't wanta shove you off, but I gotta get this done." She turned away, dropped papers into their slots.

"Oh, that's just paperwork: don't amount to much. Real work's out in th' shop." He was obviously going to hang around if she let him.

"Okay, and not to be mean or anything, but that's where you need to be right now, and I need to be doing this. Bye, Clayton." She tuned him out, despite his open mouth and offended air.

"Well, I just thought we oughta get 'quainted, is all…" He was backing toward the rear door.

"And we will, when we have time. Which isn't right now, okay?" He turned, left. *Hoped I handled that right: don't wanta make enemies, but I'm not here to waste time.*

And when Starr returned, wiping oil from her hands, she was nodding approvingly. Andy glanced out the window to see the transmission in place, and Trey lowering the truck to the ground.

"You handled Clayton just right, girl. He'll stand around on his foot all day if you let him. Doesn't mean bad, but time's what makes us a livin', and he just doesn't get that like he should."

"Hope I wasn't too hard on him, but you said do this, and I've done it. What's next?" She looked around for more papers.

"Well, we won't have all the bills together yet, so you just come on out with me and meet the other boys, learn your way around." She led the way out after Andy had grabbed her coat. Trey and Clayton had the hood up on the pickup, heads under it.

Another older man, lean, hair almost white, was seated on a rolling stool, putting brake shoes on a '50 Plymouth. His movements were rapid, precise.

"This's George Bascomb, Betty. He's worked here longer'n we've had the place. Betty'll be in th' office, George, and maybe sell a few cars when she's caught up."

"That's good. I git tired talkin' t'those folks ain't gonna buy ennyhow, jist lookin'. Trey says we's doin' good if one outta ten buys, but he ain't convinced me yit. An' you'll hafta put up with th' other nine, Betty, so good luck." He grinned, showing a tooth missing, then bent to his work again.

"Eddie Thomas over there is the helper, does the washin', greasin', changes tires, runs for parts. He's a good boy, tryin' to save money to get married. Which is good, way most kids nowadays just jump in, not knowin' what they'll live on."

"Yeah, afraid I did that myself, blind as a bat, and oh boy, was that a mistake. Hi, Eddie, I'm Betty, and I'll try not to give you a bad time." She reached out a hand, shook his. He was freckled with wild red hair that was more or less captured under a baseball cap.

"That's good: Miss Starr here, she thinks I gotta be faster'n a speedin' bullet, runnin' all around town, pickin' up stuff." He grinned at his boss, turned and went back to washing a newly acquired Ford. This was inside a bay with the door closed but it was still chilly, and his hands were red, chapped. Starr stepped over to a control knob, and the big hanging heater surged on, sending a wave of warmth over them.

"Don't freeze y'self, Eddie. You won't put us in th' poorhouse if you warm th' place a little. When you're done, rub some of that glycerin stuff on your hands. Sally'll slap you away, you go scratchin' her all up." The boy turned red, speechless.

"That's th' crew, Betty. Now, a lot of these are trade-ins, so we hafta watch or we'll end up with older and older stuff. Trey or I'll go to an auction when we need something shinier, and sometimes we even have to junk the hopeless ones. Take that '47 Dodge truck over there: somebody put another worn-out engine in it, and it came in smokin' like a stove. Trey took it on trade on a slick '53 Buick, but that truck isn't worth foolin' with.

"And that's what you learn first: figure everybody wants to trade what they got in on somethin' better. Well, nobody trades a car that's good, so all of 'em need work. Thing is, we price our cars high enough to allow as little as possible for the junk they bring, so we don't get taken bad. We c'n always come down on a close deal. You go with th' listed price, and when you get a live one, come to Trey or me to see if we can dicker. Somebody pays th' askin' price, you take it.

"Now, let's go in and I'll show you the listings on all these. And if we could get what we're askin', we could retire an' move t'Florida. These are just th' startin' prices, and most people know it. Gives 'em a boost to chisel us down even a little. I guess sellin' cars is a little psychology really."

So Andy learned that a $900 Pontiac could be sold for $750, bottom price. If it sat too long, it'd be marked down to $850. Starr explained that people bought on price, no matter what they said, and they would look only at cars in their range.

"Trey tried an experiment: when a car wouldn't sell, he'd go and *raise* the price, and a whole different bunch of people would come look at it. We've actually sold a few that way. And if we price something too low, they figure there's something wrong with th' car.

"Folks have their favorites. Chevrolet man might wanta move up a little in General Motors, but not to an Oldsmobile, so he'll buy a Pontiac. Plymouth owner might trade up to a DeSoto or just to a Dodge. We don't get many people want Cadillacs, Chryslers, Packards, but we like to keep a couple on hand just in case. People want cars they know they can get parts for easier, cheaper. You hafta rebuild th' engine in a V-12 Lincoln, you're gonna spend some dollars.

"Another thing: people have come to know we don't do sloppy work. We don't just stick a set of rings and bearings in a motor. Nossir, if it needs it, we bore it out, grind th' crankshaft, replace valve guides, camshaft bearings, th' whole works. Do it right, th' thing will outlast a new one. Costs, but we have a lot of repeat customers and a good reputation. That's worth gold, girl."

Andy was trying to take this all in. She knew she'd have to cram a lot of knowledge into her head very quickly to be able to talk intelligently with customers, both potential buyers and those who needed repairs. She wasn't about to have to ask one of the mechanics every time a question came.

Her idea was to study the repair bills in the files, learn how much similar jobs had cost, be able to come up with hourly labor charges, mark-ups on parts, profit. She found herself actually looking forward to this: it gave her a feeling of competence to have answers, even if they'd be approximate and need verifying by her two bosses.

Noon came, and she ate a sandwich she'd put together at her new home, spent a nickel on a Coke. She'd made three dollars that morning and had time to talk with two sales prospects. One had been for a $1,000 '53 Studebaker hardtop, a sleek specimen, deep black with little chrome trim. The man hadn't bought but said he'd be back. Starr had told her that usually wasn't true, but you never knew.

Idly, she figured the commission on $1,000. *Fifty bucks, wow. Now I've gotta perfect a sales pitch, here. Even a $600 sale would double my week's pay. Okay, that'd be about a '50, '51 Ford or Chevrolet, Plymouth, in good shape, which I expect is what we'll sell most of, from these records. Cheaper ones, I won't push so hard. And if I get a hot buyer for something higher up, I'm gonna lay it on thick, maybe even try a little charm, within reason.*

So, she'd focus on sales whenever the office work would let her. Trey and Starr encouraged her in this since they really didn't like having to stop in the middle of a job, clean up quickly, go talk to an often-just-looking arrival. Those people were the bane of the earth to old George, who could hardly hide his impatience with him. Not a super-salesman, George.

She'd made her point with Clayton, which had been reinforced by Trey's word to the wise not to bother the new girl. George got his business done quickly whenever he came into the office, which everyone appreciated. Eddie was in and out and in again, earning that greased-lightning reputation. He was a little shy, but friendly.

The end of the day saw her exhausted, with figures and procedures and plans crammed into her head, and she walked home hardly noting her surroundings on the way. She did stop in at a neighborhood grocery to stock up on food, planning a simple supper.

Susie surprised her, however, by having a meal already on the table. She also had a big smile of welcome, and Andy felt like hugging her.

"Figured you'd be 'bout worn out, first day and all. My brother, you've noticed, doesn't ever slow down, and Starr's the match for him. You'll be hopping to keep up, which I'm sure you already know. So, this's my treat. We can trade off after you've got your breath, okay?"

"You're an angel, Miss Susie. My feet feel like lead. I'll just put these away…"

They talked all through the meal, getting to know each other, finding out little things that made them both laugh. Later Andy reflected that okay, God hadn't forgotten her after all. *Have to maybe look into that more: Elijah always said it was a two-way deal. I won't get any free ride from Him. What was it? The Covenant, a sort of contract. Well, yes, I'll follow up on that, I guess. Susie hasn't mentioned church, but I'll ask her, offer to go with her.*

Next morning, the garage seemed like such a familiar place, she got right to work on tallying up yesterday's work orders, bills, estimates. The owners were taping off a '54 Ford convertible for Starr to paint, back in the far bay. They'd lightly sanded the car to remove the shine and hosed the place down first, so no dust would settle on it. They were both chatting away like teenagers as they worked. Trey had told her this painting was Starr's specialty, leaving the others free to do general work wherever they were needed.

"I don't have th' patience for paintin', Betty. 'Druther be bangin' on an engine any day, but Starr, she likes it. An' she's good at it. Me, I get runs, leave out spots. Drives me crazy."

"I've told you and told you, Trey, you just stop right before th' paint runs," she chided. Apparently a joke, but Andy didn't know enough to appreciate it, as both the others chuckled. But later she peeked in at the car with its masking off, and the vehicle shone. She could almost picture herself in it, flashing down some road with the top down, come summer.

That was always Cam Henry's dream, to have a new car all the time, fancy clothes, throw his money around. He just couldn't ever catch up, let alone get ahead enough for that sort of fantasy. And of course she now knew where he'd spent all that money his job was supposed to bring in: on other women.

Well, someday I'll try to get myself something cheap that runs, and by then I'll know what to avoid.

Chapter Eighteen

Andy had zeroed in on old George as her most likely ally at the garage. He was no-nonsense but not angry at anyone. *Sort of like me, I guess. But he'll be the way for me to keep this job.*

This second day at the place, Trey and Starr were going to an auto auction to replenish their stock and also to sell two cars that had sat on the lot too long. As soon as they left, Andy approached George, who had a '40 Nash eight-cylinder up on the lift, replacing its exhaust system. The car reminded her of a tank.

"George, could I talk to you a minute? I won't take you away from your work because I know you don't like to waste time." He turned to her, grunted, nodded. She took that as positive.

"Well, I like this job, and I want to get good at it. Problem is, I don't know much about cars. I'm going to have to talk to a lot of people about repairs, and if I'm gonna sell anything, I need to know what I'm doing. Could you maybe help me a little? Maybe at lunchtime give me some quick advice? I'd really appreciate it."

The mechanic hadn't stopped moving, and now slipped the multi-curved exhaust pipe up over the rear axle, twisted it into line, and threaded it forward to connect with the muffler. He already had the wrench in his hand to tighten the clamp on the pipe. He stepped forward, fitted the connection, began to tighten the clamp bolt.

"Reckon I could, yeah. But Clayton, he 'druther fill yer ears with stuff: jist lookin' fer a chance."

"That's exactly why I want you to help me, George: I don't want 'stuff'; I want somebody who knows what he's talking about. I can imagine Clayton taking an hour to explain a spark plug just so he could put off having to put it into a motor." She smiled at him, returning his grin.

"Wal, like I said. Okay, soon's I git this'n back on th' ground, I'll take a few minnits in th' shop t'point out a coupla things. Then yeah, noontime I'll run you through some more common-sense things. Be glad to." He was securing a tailpipe clamp to a hanger as he spoke. The man was a study in efficiency, never wasting a motion.

"I'll owe you, George, and thanks." She handed him a Crescent wrench, which she'd seen he'd need to hold the head of the bolt from turning. He took it, his eyes widening a fraction, nodded his thanks.

She went back inside, continued going over records. There were some diagrams showing where some parts went, and she would concentrate on these when she had a chance. George came in the side entrance and she met him in the garage.

"Now, you prob'ly know, that's 'n engine, six cylinder. See, thar's six wires comin' from th' distrib'tor, goin' to th' spark plugs. That's what lights th' gas, drives th' pistons down. Now over here's 'nuther one opened up. See that big crooked shaft? That's th' crankshaft, an' th' piston rods thar, they git pushed down when th' spark lights th' gas. Makes th' crankshaft turn, an' th' flywheel thar, it keeps th' thing spinnin', evens out th' jerkin'. Gear on that camshaft runs th' valve timin', makin' th' right one open an' shut at th' right time, which lets gas in one an' pushes out burnt smoke th'u th' other'n. Those are th' valves, an' they git pushed up by these bumps on th' camshaft, come back shut with these springs. All of it gits oiled by th' oil pump here, so t'won't wear out.

"Now, you think about all this awhile, git it in yer head, an' we'll go over how th' engine hooks up, come noontime, okay?"

"I think I'm getting it, yes. And I know those thin things are gaskets, that don't let joints leak. Yes, thanks, George, and here's the work order for that '48 Ford pickup that needs a water pump. I'm guessing that's what pushes the water through to cool the motor, right?"

"Right. Okay, I'll git on that now. An' when y'catch him, tell Eddie t'put this Nash in, git it washed. It's a right nice car, oughta bring some money." He went back out.

Wow, that was a crash course, but it makes sense, I guess. End result is to send the power back to the transmissio,n I know, and on to the back wheels. I got some of that from Cam, when he'd condescend to show me. Well, it's a start.

True to his word, George walked her through more of the power train details: clutch, transmission, driveshaft, differential, rear axles, wheels, brakes. He had a sandwich in one hand, a Dr. Pepper in the other, and gestured, moving quickly from one subject to the next but keeping it in a logical sequence. Andy could follow it since, as she'd seen earlier, it was logical. She could picture the first builders of cars working all this out: to get the explosion of gas and air to turn the driving wheels.

Then she showed George some of the newest work orders and asked him where this or that repair fit into the overall scheme of the vehicles. He explained and pointed out some of what they'd already covered, and how it all fit. She thanked him gratefully, trying to figure some way to repay him. He just waved it off.

By the time the owners drove in with a '55 Studebaker V8 and a Dodge three-quarter-ton pickup, Andy felt more knowledgeable about what she'd be dealing with. No, she wouldn't know it all, not for a year, but with luck she could show them she'd been trying.

"Any disasters, Betty?" Starr asked her, handing her the new titles to file. "I see Eddie's polishing the Nash. Looks good."

"Nothing earth-shaking. I did show a woman that '50 Plymouth. She's just learned to drive on one like it. Said she'd see if she could get it financed at the bank. I doubt she'll be back: can't imagine selling a car my second day."

"Oh, it might happen. New driver, she'll want something right now, and it's cheap. Last her a long time if she doesn't wreck it. Some of those Plymouths go for a couple hundred thousand miles, you keep the oil changed, don't expect too much outta them. Okay, I wanta get onto that engine I'm rebuilding. Machine shop bring th' block back?"

"Yes, it's on the big bench. Bored out .020, crankshaft turned .010, new cam bearings. Rings, rod and main bearings, gasket set's all here. Eddie brought 'em just before I got him on waxing the Nash."

"All right! Hey, sounds like you're catching on fast, girl. Okay, I'm onto that engine now. Come get me if you run into a problem." And she was off into the garage, the parts in hand, a gleam in her eye. Andy marveled that this woman seemed to enjoy this work so much. *What a team they are; she's better at the bodywork, painting, big stuff, and he's the best at tuning, carburetors, electrical. George can do it all, and Clayton's really not all that bad a mechanic. That is, when you can get him to concentrate.*

She began to feel like a necessary part of the operation too, since her work let the others get on with what they did best. And the books showed a healthy business, which she determined to make even better. To do that, she'd concentrate on sales, move as many vehicles out as she possibly could. And make her commission.

At day's end, Trey and Starr sat down with her in the office. Trey had a scowl on, but Starr couldn't keep from grinning. Andy knew she'd be grilled and regretted her brag of the day before.

"Okay, Betty. You said you'd know every part on every car here by now. What've you learned?" He tried to keep the sour expression on. Didn't quite make it.

"Well, first of all, I've learned to keep my big mouth shut better. But I've also learned what all the men did today, and why. George wouldn't stop working to talk to me, but he did fill me in on some things at lunchtime. I know how an engine works, I know how a drivetrain works, I know about fuel systems and cooling systems and electrical systems.

"And while you were both under that Packard awhile ago, the lady came back for the Plymouth, paid cash for it. Wanted to dicker, but I held out: it was a bargain, I knew, from newspaper ads. She's coming back in"—she checked the clock—"five minutes for the paperwork and title. Here's the $400." She produced the eight fifties.

Trey didn't say a word, just went to the cash drawer and pulled out a twenty. He handed it to her with the widest grin she'd ever seen.

"You're hired full-time," he announced, shook her hand, and Starr hugged her. "How you getting' along with my sister?"

"I want her for my new mother. We talk so much neither of us gets much sleep. And, of course, you know you're both her favorite people in the world."

"She's a dandy, all right. Ran me ragged growin' up: wanted me t'make somethin' outta myself. I always told her I'd do whatever I pleased and didn't find out that was just what she wanted me t'do, all along. Just pushed me t'do it better."

From then on, whenever she could steal a few minutes, Andy pestered George on mechanical details, and finally, another day the bosses were gone, she helped him put pistons back into a rehoned engine. It was still in the car, a '54 Chevrolet six-cylinder. She'd upturn a piston with its rings on in a shallow pan of oil as directed and put the ring compressor on, tighten it. Then slip the rod and piston skirt down into the cylinder, tap it with a mallet till it seated on the bearing insert George put on it. He'd put the rod cap on, tighten the nuts and locknuts while she got the next piston ready.

They were finished in a few minutes. He'd explained that older Chevrolets had babbitted bearings instead of inserts, and that instead of a full oil-pressure system, the rods had a scoop that picked up the oil from a trough at the bottom of their travel. This system was better, he told her: didn't loosen rods so much. *Okay, makes sense, the way he tells it.*

"Now yer all dirty, girl. Better mop y'self up b'fore you sell 'nother car. Oh, thar's a feller lookin' over th' Nash. Here, use this hand cleaner 'n go git him." His smile had some admiration in it. She could tell he liked her, and the feeling was mutual.

She walked through to the office, wiping her hands, got a smudge off her face with a tissue, and greeted the man at the big Nash. He had the hood up, admiring the clean engine, the long eight-cylinder with the double electrical coil and the sixteen sparkplugs. Starr had given her a ride in it that morning, and she knew this was quite a car. At that moment, Trey and Starr drove in, waved, and went behind the garage to work on a Model A Ford.

"That's a real car, now," she began. "Rides like a cloud, and it's solid as a tank. And look at all that room. If you want class, you've got it, and it'll outlast two Fords or Chevrolets."

"What kinda shape's th' motor in?" He'd looked around for the man, but shrugged, decided it was okay to talk to this woman.

"We've rebuilt the engine. Bored it out, stroked it, everything new inside. A good rebuild will outlast a new one 'cause the guys at the factories just throw them together. We guarantee our work for a year."

"I'd like to drive it. Wanta trade that old Lincoln in on it. This th' askin' price?" He referred to the white shoe-polish figure on the windshield.

"No, that's the real, bottom-dollar price. No room to deal on this one: it's like new. I'd have to ask the boss about what your trade-in's worth, if you're serious."

"Well, like I said, wanta drive it first, okay?"

"Let me get Trey; you'll want to ask him more about it, I'm sure." She stepped toward the garage, called out to him. He appeared, wiping his hands, came over.

"Hi. I'm Trey. Wanta drive this'n?"

"I think so. Your saleslady's told me a lot about it. I hate it that Nash is losing money on their cars: these are classics. Think I'll be able to get parts later on?"

"Oh, sure. Companies always keep a big stock of parts. We're rebuilding a Model A back there, and the last one they made was in 1931."

The two men drove away, and Andy went back to her paperwork. She noted what they'd bought the then-knocking Nash for and ran her eyes over the parts and labor sheet. If they lowered the asking price any, they'd cut deeply into the hoped-for profit, and she didn't think that was the way to go. She wrote a quick note to Trey, left it on the desk with the work order.

As they drove back into the lot, she went out, told Trey he was wanted on the phone, and that she'd take over while he was gone.

"There's a note for you, too." Then, turning back to the potential buyer, "Now, sir, I know you liked the ride, and you know your Nash cars. With this one, you'll impress everybody with your good taste like you did with the Lincoln. What do you think?"

"Well, you've sold me, depending on how much your boss will give me for the Lincoln. It's got some problems." Andy was checking the exhaust pipe on that car, which was black, so the engine was using oil. And she bounced the back bumper up and down, felt the worn shock absorbers, reached in and felt the slack in the steering wheel. She also noted the high miles on the odometer.

"Sir, you know you're getting another real classic automobile, one you won't see often, and none as good. Now we both know your Lincoln is about worn out and will need a lot of expensive work to get it in good shape again. I know you value fine cars, and this is your chance. Just so you know." She turned to Trey, who'd read her note, and winked at her.

She left them to their dealing, knowing her boss wouldn't get taken with the repair costs fresh in his mind. She busied herself, also checking out the window every few minutes. Trey was going over the Lincoln the way she had, looking under the hood, noting the tires and other things she hadn't had time to examine. He started the engine to a cloud of blue oil smoke, then shut it down, shaking his head. It was the older, flat-head V8, in its day a fine car, but its day had passed. As Elijah would have said, it'd 'been rode hard an' put away wet'.

They came inside, and Andy handed Trey the Nash title, then stepped out to let them get on with their man-talk. She went around to where Starr had a door off the Model A, examining the worn hinges that had let it sag.

"I see you had that feller goin' on th' Nash, girl. I told Trey not t'mess with fixin' that'n up, but he's bull-headed. An' he really likes th' old, big ones. I don't think we'll come out much moren' even, and if we take that broke-down Lincoln, we'll lose. Takes a special buyer to appreciate somethin' like that Nash, and they're rare." She shook her head. Andy took a few minutes to hold the punch in pliers while Starr drove out the rusted hinge pins, which they'd replace with new metal. Then she noticed Trey and the buyer outside again. The man got his possessions out of the Lincoln and put them into the Nash. They shook hands, and he got in, drove away, the motor purring.

"Well, looka what I got, Starr girl. Betty softened that feller up, got him wantin' that car so bad we got our price, an' th' trade-in just about free." He displayed several bills.

"Okay, I saw that, but what did you get? Don't tease us."

He counted out a total of a thousand dollars, which meant a profit of four hundred on the sale, discounting the Lincoln completely. Starr hugged him, then hugged Andy.

"I'da given that thing away! Wow, you two scored big! Betty, what'd you promise that guy? No, don't tell me; might embarrass me." She was laughing, and so was Trey.

"I could tell he was that rare type wanted quality, and he's old enough to sort of treasure the classic stuff, you know. His shoes were good, his clothes expensive, and I just kind of assumed he wanted that car more than we wanted to sell it. Glad it happened."

"Well, you get the commission; all I did was ride him around in it. And thanks for reminding me how much we'd put in it. I'd forgot half of it." He put an arm around her shoulders. "We've had that car so long I was about to take it to the auction, where it'd bring maybe a couple hundred bucks. Okay, here's fifty dollars." He handed it to her.

"Oh, but that can't be right: you had so much in it, the work and all…"

"Worth it, to get it off th' lot. Now, I gotta go over that Lincoln more, see if it'll be worth wastin' our time on."

"It won't be, Trey," his wife cautioned. "Just send it to th' junk-yard an' be done with it."

"Well, maybe, but let me think about it some, okay? No hurry, an' a good Lincoln's worth a lot, right buyer like that feller."

"That's a bad Lincoln, an' you know it."

"Well, maybe." He walked back to the lot.

"He'll talk himself into keepin' that thing, Betty, an' it'll sit here forever, with us puttin' money into it, just wait an' see." She threw up her hands, went back to the Model A. Andy looked at the money again, smiled broadly.

There was a '48 Ford convertible she'd been eyeing for weeks that had new paint and an overall makeover. The V8 engine wasn't badly worn, hadn't needed a complete rebuild, and the cylinders had needed only honing out, new rings, rod, and main bearings. She loved the sound of the flat-head 100-horsepower motor and had saved up money with the idea of buying it, paying for it a few dollars at a time. This $50 would go a long way toward the $450 price. That was above the average value, but she knew every part of this car and felt it'd last her for years. She also knew her employers wouldn't charge her the whole amount.

She sent money regularly to Nate at the college and had been down to see him one weekend, incognito as the auburn-haired Naomi Jenkins, meeting him off-campus. He was doing well, she saw, keeping his grades up, enjoying the carpentry. And making some friends besides his roommate Harley Black. These two were just a year and a half apart in age, and shared several interests.

Andy wondered at any girl her nephew might be attracted to, but he didn't mention one. There were several clubs and group activity pursuits that mixed the sexes, and she approved of his participating in these. He was, she was glad to see, becoming a well-rounded young man. Her pride in him remained high.

He reported that no lawman had found him, telling her that Bobby Harcourt had sold the property and put the money in trust till he was of age. That would be his nest egg, he told her, which he'd split with her, for whatever she wanted to do with it.

No, it's his money, from his property. And by the time he gets it, I hope I won't need it, anyway.

Andy had not given up her plan to take a college course whenever she could fit it in. As the spring semester ended, she looked at the summer night-school offerings, seeing one called *Introduction to Design.* Nothing else being offered interested her, so she enrolled in this one.

As Susie had said, it wasn't far from home to the college, and even closer from the garage. She figured she'd work late, then go directly to class the two nights a week it met.

And it turned out to be intriguing: the part-time teacher owned an interior design business, specializing in commercial buildings, banks, doctors' offices, car dealerships. The woman reported to the class her income from some of these jobs, and the figures astounded Andy. *Of course I'd have to build up a business, but wow, this lady's rich! I could do this. Have to finish college, though, have a decent résumé to show. Maybe I could work for somebody else for a while, like this teacher, get some experience.*

This would be a long way from the garage office work and selling cars, but she'd seen her current employment as a means to the desired end, whatever that might be. And yes, this goal might be the one. Or other avenues might open up, with other courses. This college thing was exciting.

And not that hard. She was used to buckling down to whatever she had to do and did it here. With the result that her grades were top, which inspired her more as the weeks went by. Come fall, she'd keep this up, with a wider range of choices.

Life was good.

* * *

Christine Mabry waited a respectable length of time before stepping out into the dating world again. She valued her position as mistress of the family domain, which was completely paid for and provided a steady income from the cattle, timber, and investments Montgomery had made.

She'd worried about some of these as her father-in-law had become less stable in his last months and knew he'd gambled on a few he'd lost money on. The botched timber venture was an example, and he hadn't seemed to care much. His killing of his archenemy Charlie Millard hadn't settled him down: quite the opposite.

But there were enough sound investments, like the AT&T stock, the General Motors and other Blue Chip shares that paid well. As a result of Montgomery's will, she wasn't merely young Giles's guardian in all this: she owned it, and she found that she could make all the decisions, and she did.

That boy, now only twelve years from his legal maturity, let his mother run everything, naturally, and didn't know much about what went on. Either with the money or in her private life. She'd employed a live-in housekeeper who watched Giles whenever she spent an evening out, and this gave her unlimited freedom. Which, she realized, was something she'd never had, marrying Barry and dropping out of college as she'd done.

Well, that wasn't exactly true: she'd had Cam Henry as a diversion, back when he'd been around. But then he'd had to drop out of sight after a cuckolded husband threatened to shoot him. And meant it: the man had actually tried it but missed. So nobody knew where the truck driver had gone. He sure wasn't coming back to Ridgeway ever.

So it was that she often drove up to Branson or to relatively distant towns to take advantage of whatever nightlife there was, away from Ridgeway. It would be important for her to keep her reputation intact here as serious mother and steward of the Mabry holdings. Which nobody outside her lawyer knew were really hers now.

Christine had also banked the money from the sale of her own home and of Barry's Hudson. She now drove a '59 Oldsmobile 88 convertible, deep green, the envy of half the people in the county seat. She liked to drive fast and could be seen flashing along the better roads of the area, blonde hair streaming, drinking in the summer air, looking forward to whatever excitement she could find. And, of course, knowing an attractive, unattached woman in a shiny car wouldn't have to look far.

It was in Forsyth, Missouri, that she met the salesman in a local bar where liquor was legal. The town was tiny, but far from home, and therefore safe. She'd stepped in alone, aware of every eye on her as she settled on a bar stool and ordered a Bloody Mary. And of course it wasn't but maybe half a minute until the salesman, a curly-haired six-footer with unnaturally white teeth and a lightweight maroon linen sportscoat, sat down next to her. *All right! Now things are starting to happen. Guy's probably hidden his wedding ring if he has one, and that's okay: I'm not looking to tie myself to anybody; I'm in too good a position at home to ruin that.*

She expected a standard line from this man and got it, right on cue. He traveled to exciting places, sold heavy equipment. Just today he'd sold two Caterpillar motor graders to this Taney County for a healthy commission. What did she do? Owned a big farm? That was obviously fascinating to him, and she knew he'd have been just as impressed if she'd said she was a housemaid. *So transparent. He's got a woman in every tow, or is working on it.*

I'm horny as hell, but I won't insult myself with this guy. She tuned out his patter, glanced around at the other men in the place. Nothing looked good to her, and she briefly returned her eyes to the salesman.

"Go home to your wife," she told him and walked out the door.

Well, that didn't go very well. I guess it's going to be a really big adjustment, getting back into the singles world. Gotta aim higher, though, and that isn't going to be easy, now I'm over thirty. So who was out there, anyway? Divorced men, mama's boys looking for replacements? Ugly ones the girls had passed up? Right then, she thought of this foray as a waste of time.

But in the next few weeks, Christine did drive to surrounding towns: Jonesboro, Springfield, even down to Little Rock on one occasion, to see what there was to see and, of course, to let herself be seen. She was approached several times, as she knew she would be, but mostly by men on the prowl, each of whom wanted another notch in his gun.

Then, in the unlikeliest of places, right there in Ridgeway, she literally ran into Blake Walker. She'd headed for the checkout counter, cart full of groceries at the local version of a supermarket, and collided with him as she turned a corner. She slammed into his cart and almost tipped it over.

She reddened in embarrassment, then looked up to see who was struggling to keep the thing upright. And saw the best-looking man she'd ever laid eyes on.

"Sorry…I…wasn't looking where I was going. Did I break anything?" He was, of course, looking her up and down, the expected reaction.

"No, it's okay. I wasn't looking either. Here, go ahead." He was perhaps forty, with slight graying at his temples, tall, casually dressed. No wedding band. She smiled her thanks, slipped ahead of him, feeling his eyes on her body as she began to stack her groceries on the counter. *Okay, now it's up to me to make the next move.*

"Your wife have you doing the grocery shopping?" she asked, turning back to him with a raised eyebrow, giving him her better semi-profile: the brown eyes, the casually arranged blonde hair.

"Oh, no. No, I'm not married. Or perhaps I should say I'm not *still* married. We parted on friendly terms, but that was awhile ago." He didn't look as if that had been a painful experience.

"Didn't mean to pry, but I guess I am: you're not from around here." A statement, the obvious, since she'd have known this specimen otherwise.

"No, I'm out of Little Rock. I'm with the power company, and I'm up here for a few days working with the folks on the development over on the lake. They're putting in all-electric houses, you know, and I'm in what we call the development division."

"Oh, I'd have expected you to have a big expense account, eat at all the best places, not buy groceries. That is, if we had any of the best places in Ridgeway." A dismissive half chuckle.

"I found that out first thing. And I'm getting used to my own cooking. I'm staying at a guest house the developer has, which has a kitchen I'm trying to figure out." By now Christine had paid for her purchases and the man was piling his on the counter. She noted TV dinners, cans of soup, dry cereal. Not very appetizing.

As they exited the store, more or less together, since she'd dawdled over the newsstand, he caught up, smiled.

"I'm Blake Walker," he said, extending a hand. "And you're obviously stocking up for your family." He didn't ask her outright if she were married, although she now wore no ring.

"Christine Mabry." His hand was firm and dry, and his eyes, light blue, were on hers. "And I'm a widow, with a young son. My husband was killed a few years ago, and I have the estate he and his father left us." *Yes, estate sounds better than farm, and it's not a ranch, either. Estate.*

"Oh, sorry to hear that. So it's what, a sort of ranch, farm? You certainly don't look like the typical farmer's wife." He meant it as a compliment, of course, and she smiled her best for him.

"I suppose it is a farm. We have cattle, timber, horses. It's too big for me to run by myself, so I have some hired help. My father-in-law was a prominent attorney here and had built up the holdings. He was devastated at his only son's death, of course, but was grateful that we had Giles. He's nine now." *There: vital statistics over with. I could invite him for dinner, but it's his move, and this is a game.*

Or maybe it's really not.

"Well, as I said, I'll be around for a few days, this trip. You ever get out to the lake? Or does running your holdings keep your nose to the grindstone, which I can't quite imagine, seeing you."

"Oh, we do, now and then. Giles's grandfather taught him to fish, and he likes that. We have a small boat we take out on good days." She glanced at the sky right on cue. This day happened to be a fine one, with the early October air warming and the leaves turning red and gold. That sky was an impossible blue, a deep color that hurt your eyes.

"Would you think it forward of me to invite you and your son on a fishing excursion? I know you've only known me for…let's see…ten minutes, and you probably have other…priorities, but you'd be welcome." *Woman this pretty's got a man in her life for sure. But, nothing ventured…*

"Well, okay, that would be nice, yes. And it's been a good ten minutes. Giles does get bored with school, and didn't we all? Saturday? Which happens to be tomorrow, isn't it?"

"It is. I was planning to hole up with electrical specifications all weekend, and you'd be saving me from death by details." His laugh was easy, his manner gentlemanly, and Christine felt a quickening of her pulse. Could this really be happening? It was, and she knew in that moment that this man would become a part of her life.

It was just too right.

* * *

Hal Burgess regretted Andy's having to disappear for more reasons than one. She'd have to stay hidden probably for years, fearing the law would track her down, drag her back to Everett County. What kind of a life could she have with that hanging over her? And she'd still be supporting Nate, who'd surely gotten into some college somewhere. She'd see that as her responsibility still, till the boy graduated, got himself a decent job somewhere.

But, of course, the real pain she'd left in his life, even though she'd rebuffed him, was the realization that never in this world would he see her again, hear her voice, even be able to fantasize with any hope about what a life with her could have been. *I could have handled all that better, been more completely on her side, the right side. Just too much the cop, I guess. Or too old, after all. Or maybe just never knowing what's in a woman's mind—any woman.*

Even after three years had passed with no clues as to the real murderer of either of the Mabrys, Burgess still went over the cases and over them, each time becoming more convinced that Andy'd had nothing to do with either. He still remembered the anger inside himself at the way she'd been treated through all of it: the savagery of Barry's attack on her, the unquenchable gossip, the shameful trial, the destruction of her life, really.

That anger had taken hold of him more than once. He'd soon realized that, with exonerating her seemingly impossible, he could still have made things right for her. Or at least achieved a measure of backwoods justice. Of course, if he'd taken the law into his hands, he would have crossed a line he could never return from. But wouldn't it have been worth it? The two of them would have been forced to run away together, the only logical next step, and looking back, he often rued his righteous decision.

Periodically, he'd slipped into an imaginary role as her avenger, in his unique position able to destroy her enemies. *I could've wiped Barry*

Mabry off the face of the earth, after what he did to her. An "accident" in the woods, stray hunter's bullet, or even what happened. And now I know I'd have done it without a moment's regret. Should have done it. There are just too many cases of the wrong person getting away with evil in this world. Somebody's got to act for the victims, when the legal system won't.

Oh, he'd gotten himself into a state of mind more times than was healthy, in which he could easily see himself picking Barry Mabry off from an unheard-of distance, never to be connected with the killing. And later his obsessed, driven, killer father. It was fantasy, but so real.

And sometimes lately Burgess found himself unable to distinguish between reality and this imaginary state he spent time in. And less and less, he jolted himself back to the real world. He couldn't have known this was due to the slowly growing pressure from the tumor inside his head: it happened over such a long period of time he hadn't really noticed it.

But he did realize he was forgetting things, like a really old person would. Sometimes when someone would mention an event he'd been deeply involved in, he'd have to concentrate to remember it. Had he always been this way? Surely not. And it didn't happen often at first, but yes, maybe this was something he'd better look into: see a doctor when he could wedge it in.

Only there didn't ever seem to be time. His job had always kept him running hard just to keep up, and he wondered if that constant stress had pushed him into that recurring, unreal world of his imaginings. Sort of an escape from the pressure, the grime of being a lawman, the stains of which never would leave him clean.

But why do I allow these scenarios to build in my mind? I've never knowingly gone over to the bad side; always kept control, been the good guy. Maybe shouldn't have—no, I know I shouldn't have, looking back—even though I knew it would've been the wrong thing to do. But Andy, Andy, we could have had a life, if I'd gone ahead and acted when I had the chance.

Or did I?

Chapter Nineteen

Andy did meet a young professor at the college who taught religion. She hadn't taken any of his classes but seemed to run into him a lot just coming and going. He was very handsome, reminding her of some movie star she couldn't quite remember from the few picture shows she'd been to.

She speculated about a possible relationship. *Might be nice, hooked up with a minister—I guess he's that. Professor's wife: has a nice sound to it. So maybe he'll start doing more than just saying hi.*

Or maybe I will…

She knew she had no time to waste on a dead-end entanglement and had successfully put the possibility out of her mind. She thought. But when this Reginald Cabot began stopping and talking to her, she found herself responding. Maybe she was just lonely, but she was flattered that he'd noticed her out of all the younger girls on campus. But he was well over thirty and probably saw them as green, maybe even a little silly.

So he eventually asked her to lunch for the next day, but she explained that she had to work, that she had a full-time job. He seemed disappointed, so she quickly took the initiative and pointed out that she had no class that evening. He jumped on that and changed the invitation to dinner.

"That'd be nice, thanks. But I've been meaning to ask you: are your courses just on Christianity, or do you include Judaism, Islam, other religions?"

"Oh, we cover them all, even some of the obscure ones. The idea is to give a basis for comparison, to show the parallels, of which there are more than the differences. So you're interested in spiritual values?"

"Well, I've had little exposure other than backwoods preaching. Sounds intriguing, though. Maybe I can work in a course since I see you teach nights, too."

"Yes. And I must say, you don't seem backwoods at all. Where are you from, Miss Wilson?"

"Just about the deepest hollow in the Arkansas hills, Mr. Cabot. Or should I say *Dr.* Cabot?"

"No, I'm still working on my doctorate whenever I can slip a course in. So tell me why you don't sound like the rest of our Arkansas students, if you don't mind."

"Well, our kinfolks were hillbillies, all but our mother. She decided my sister Becca and I should prepare ourselves for a better life, and she made it her priority to grind proper English into us. Also tried that with my older brother, but he was too lazy, God rest him."

"Oh, he died. I'm sorry. And your sister? Where is she now?"

"I'm sorry, too. She and her husband were killed in a car wreck several years back. I raised their son." She found she liked talking to this man, whose manner was gentle, not prying, although she guessed that's what he really was doing.

"Oh, that's sad. So you two were essentially alone? Forgive me; it's really none of my business, except that you are a truly intriguing young lady, if I may be so bold."

"I had help from Nate's grandfather the preacher until he died, too. A fine man."

"I'm sure. Well, thanks for agreeing to go to dinner with me. Where can I come for you?" She gave him directions to Susie's house, realizing that this would be the first date she'd been on since Killer Cam Henry had somehow snowed her with his rustic charm.

And that comparison got her remembering the early days with Cam, when she'd still been in love with him. He was an expert lover, which should have told her something, but she was so green… And she'd made the mistake of thinking she was the reason he was so seemingly devoted, that he'd found the perfect woman. It'd been a heady feeling, had made her glow, built her sense of self-worth immensely.

Lies, all lies. I was just another score for him. Okay, he was good in bed, and yeah, I've missed that, all these years. But I'm in control now, and I will be for the rest of my damn life. I'll take another man on my terms, not anyone else's.

The next day at work, Andy kept remembering this professor's gentlemanly behavior, his earlier hesitancy to approach her. She felt a touch of warmth inside at the prospect of getting to know him better, but also little warning bells. *He, or any man, represents a derailment of all my plans. Which I guess isn't the end of the world, if it's meant to be. But hey, this isn't an earth-shaking event; I'm just going to dinner, just going on a date. About time, too.*

Which is exactly what Susie told her when she shared her plans for the evening. This woman, like everyone else probably, just thought an eligible girl should pair up if the right man appeared.

"Looking forward to meeting him," she smiled. "I know you won't waste your time with just any man. So he's a professor; that's impressive. What's he teach?"

"Religion. We've just bumped into each other a few times, then got to talking. Yes, he's really nice. He's been to seminary, a Methodist, but his courses take in just about every religion, he says. Be good to discuss things with him, I hope. I'm pretty ignorant in that area."

"Well! A minister. Girl can't do any better than that, I'd say. Of course I'm not matchmaking here, first date and all. And by the way, you do look nice. I'm glad you're squeezing money enough out of my skinflint brother to buy yourself a few things." She inspected Andy's new outfit with approval. Hemlines were edging up again, after the late '50s ankle length, and Susie approved.

She also approved of Reginald Cabot, when he appeared with a bouquet of roses for Andy. He was well spoken, as she'd expected, but he also had an aura of kindness about him. Susie wondered why some woman hadn't grabbed him before this. *Or maybe one did, and he's second-time-around like Betty. I'm sure she'll find that out soon. She'll want to know what she's getting into, our girl will.*

Dinner was at a very nice restaurant, and Andy had to remember which fork to use and was a little intimidated at first. *Now you stop this! This is just another human being, and this is just another place to eat. You realized a long time ago that there's nobody in this world better than you, and a whole lot worse. Get over this, girl.*

The conversation never lagged, as each discovered more about the other. No, Reginald had never been married; he let her know without her asking. He'd made up his mind early on to pursue religion, either as a preacher or a missionary. Teaching had, as he phrased it, slipped up on him when a friend at SMS told him of a vacancy on the faculty and urged him to apply. He found he enjoyed imparting knowledge, even in this increasingly secular world. And yes, a few students seemed to *get it*, he said.

Andy told him some of herself, mostly about the hardscrabble farm life in Everett County, and more than she should have about her having married too young and discovering she'd teamed up with a cheating loser of absolutely no morals. She shook her head wearily.

"I can't imagine now what attraction that man had for me, Mr. Cabot. I guess my redneck side saw that marriage as a way to get out of the woods and into the world. Boy, was I wrong. And of course, *I* paid the price, not him, in everyone's eyes surely the one at fault for its failure."

"That's so unfair. But I can see that any man who wasn't blind would want to be with you, Elizabeth. I think we all make mistakes when we're young: part of growing up. And I believe we're destined to know pain as part of the test that this life is. The book of Job in the Bible gives us around forty chapters of that lesson. And by the way, it's Reginald, or Reggie, please. I get called *Mister* all day."

"All right. And I'm Betty to everyone. That's a new idea for me, that about the test. So if we keep the faith, we pass, right? And if we don't, death is all there is? That door just slams in our faces?"

"Exactly. Oh, I think you'd enjoy studying more about religion, Betty. Maybe next semester?"

"Maybe. I know it'll take years for me to finish college after all that time I wasted with Cam and spent raising Nate. Of course, I didn't begrudge taking my sister's boy in at all. He's a fine young man now down at The School of the Ozarks."

"Really? I know Dr. Good well. I've even supplied the pulpit a few times when their pastor at the chapel had time off. Dr. Good doesn't hold my Methodism against me at all." He laughed, an easy, quiet chuckle that Andy had come to like.

"Nate's grandfather, despite his fire-and-brimstone preaching, told us he really couldn't see much difference among the religions. Like you said last night, the similarities. For an uneducated man, he had a lot of insight."

* * *

"Do you miss Memphis?" Nate asked his aunt. He'd made it a practice to take her out for dinner every week or so, and they were in an upscale restaurant on the pedestrian mall in Charlottesville. The bricked-over and tree-planted former Main Street outside was thronged with shoppers, passersby, couples, families. It was a weeknight, but that didn't seem to matter; this was a prosperous town, and the people had time and money to spend.

"I did for awhile, yes. I had so many friends there, you know. For a Southern town, it had a lot to offer. You know, it drew from Mississippi, Arkansas, even southeast Missouri. It just sort of happened to be in Tennessee. Yes, there was a graciousness there I appreciated, which I guess came from all the money. You get culture after you get dollars."

"Well, you know we considered staying there, being close to you, but there was so much more history here in Virginia, and restoration was so much more exciting than building more look-alike houses. For people on the way up. And this place has been good to us: kids never lacked for stimulation, friends, that culture. Rare for such a small town."

"And Audrey liked it, I know. Memphis just wasn't her town: too

Southern for a girl from up north. This is the South, too, but it's got so much going on. Still listed among the best places in the country to live, I see."

"Which explains why it's growing so fast, eating up all those great plantations, spewing brick ranches and ugly subdivisions. I'm just glad I found enough work with good architects and all those great restorations. But, of course, I'm old and bitter."

"We all get that way, remembering the best of the old days. Of course, you and I didn't have any best till we left Ridgeway. Looking back, both of us were led on our ways. How likely was it that old Dr. Good would bend the rules, let you into The School, take such an interest in you? And how likely that I'd find that great bunch to work with, live with in Springfield? God had plans for us, Nate, didn't He?"

"He did. And my finding Audrey, the best thing that could've happened. You know, it's funny, the way we didn't go to church before, despite Grandpa's faith, and things eventually just happened right, anyway. Like our prayers were answered even before we asked."

"He does things on His own schedule for sure, and in His own way. And I guess all that trouble was part of what He was testing our faith with, like in the Book of Job. You pass the test, keep the faith, and He rewards you, in this life along with the real one to come." She was remembering the quietly dashing professor she'd talked so much with, spent so much time with, maybe even loved. Yes, back when she was still considering a man in her life. Some regret at that now, looking back.

Nate reflected that this sort of conversation would have been awkward, back a lifetime to the harsh, violent events of their youth. Now it was as natural as breathing, discussing the things of real importance. *That's what you do I guess, when you're old and no longer chasing success, dollars, recognition. All that seems pretty dead-ended now.*

* * *

Nate had graduated college with a degree focused on engineering, which he soon found wasn't that helpful. The school at that time had only a few introductory courses in the subject, being a liberal arts college, and he'd taken them all, excelled in them. But once he was out looking for a job, his scant background hadn't opened up doors for him.

"I've heard of that place," one interviewer in Little Rock told him, "but didn't realize they offered much in the way of engineering. And from what I see here on your application, it seems I was right. We really need somebody with more education. Sorry."

And another, who advised him to go to graduate school or get some real training. And, of course, at his first job in that field, his lack of experience hobbled him. He'd eventually made his way to Springfield,and gone to work as a draftsman for a big firm there.

It was boring, putting down on paper the work and imagination of others, but he learned, got proficient, stayed with it for four years. He built his résumé, being later allowed to take on more responsibility, work his way up a step or two. His bosses liked his work ethic, his devotion to the company, his willingness to spend as much time as necessary to do his work right.

Eventually, the position with Mid-South Engineering in Memphis opened, and he eagerly applied for it. And got it, competing with a dozen other applicants, with enthusiastic references from Springfield. He left his aunt, who was still working her way through college at SMS with his help, and headed to the river town with high hopes.

He'd liked the Southern accents there, the Mississippi drawl that bled into the town. He liked the generally unhurried way folks did business, although this was a thriving, commercial center. Barges, with their powerful towboats, plied the big river, railroads carried a constant load of goods, the highways were being widened, the interstates being built. Memphis was a hub, a destination, a port, serving a broad area from the rice fields of eastern Arkansas to the cotton plantations in the Delta to the mills and manufacturing in southeast Missouri to the farms in Tennessee and Kentucky.

It was exciting, this place, so far in every way from the Arkansas hill country, where the next ridge hid whatever was out there, hemming the ingrown people in. One of his professors had told him that people who lived on seacoasts just couldn't be as narrow-minded as mountain folks; they were reminded constantly that their world was tiny compared to that ocean and all it led to.

So Nate had settled in, spent long hours at his work, helping design civil engineering projects in that rapidly expanding decade of the Sixties, with all it entailed. His firm specialized in water systems for cities, reservoirs, wastewater designs. The Second World War had seen farm people rushing to the cities, and there was the constant need for upgrades, new systems. This era's firms were trying to stay ahead of that urban influx at full speed.

But as his twenties fled on, Nate began to feel as if he were missing out on too much of life outside the office. Some of the company salesmen urged him to visit the clubs they belonged to, get outside, have some fun.

It didn't take but a few such outings for him to realize their idea of fun wasn't his: he'd no desire for short-term relationships with seemingly desperate women hearing their biological clocks ticking. It was time to find a good woman, a partner, a life.

The dating situation in Memphis was unlimited, he found, once he'd become serious about it. There were soft-spoken girls from the Delta, some who'd come after high school to the city looking for work or mates, or both. There were Arkansas girls from the hills near his home territory, some with college degrees, but mostly a bit awed at the city.

There was a spirited Texas girl he'd encountered, up from the University of Mississippi for a Saturday football game he'd gone to. She was with other students but happened to be sitting on the bleachers next to him. They talked. She was twenty-one, in her senior year. She was tiny, but her outgoing personality filled any space she found herself in. She liked a good time, he found, evidenced by her impulsively detaching herself from her group after the game, asking him forthrightly if he'd show her some of Memphis.

This took him aback somewhat, since girls of his acquaintance just didn't ask men out. But he took her up on it, and they had dinner at a decent restaurant and ended up going dancing. Andy had taught him the basics, and this wasn't the first time for him on the floor, but never with such a lively partner. He had trouble keeping up with her.

The question of how she was to get back to her dormitory 80 miles south hadn't come up, and Nate just assumed she'd get back with her friends for the trip. But no, she had written permission to stay with an aunt here in town overnight, and could catch a ride with returning students Sunday.

Only, as the evening progressed and she imbibed beer, it turned out that there was no aunt at all. And since Nate had joined her for a drink of bourbon—he didn't like beer—that sounded fine to him.

The girl, whose name was Drew, was quite pretty, and Nate was sure she had at least one attachment at the college, but if so, where was he? Right then, that didn't matter much.

Four of her group actually showed up at the little basement bar they were in, and joined them. Drew hugged both the other boys, kissed the girls on the cheek. She introduced Nate, with a proprietary arm through his. *Girl's sure outgoing. Maybe a little fast for a redneck like me, but seems nice.*

The six of them went to another bar the others had heard of for more dancing, more drinking, more fun. Nate was sipping his few drinks, not wanting to get crazy with these away-from-home young people.

Then, much later, it became obvious that they'd rented hotel rooms and were going to sleep there, leave late the next morning. Drew was odd-man-out, and it soon was apparent that she considered him, her new best friend, her partner for the night. He found this a little disturbing.

Because as the evening had worn on, this girl had confided in him more and more, as people often do with strangers, about the fact that her steady boyfriend had cheated on her, and this was why she'd come alone to the game. *So, I'm just a substitute here: her way of giving what's good for the gander what's good for the goose. This has the makings of a one-night stand.*

Now, Nate was a normal, healthy young man of twenty-six, and Drew was fun, attractive, and clearly available. He debated the obvious next step in this situation, thinking ahead to its aftermath.

And decided this wasn't for him. Perhaps it was Andy's bringing him up with fairly solid values; perhaps he wanted more than a fling. Or perhaps deep down, his sense of what was right and what wasn't was tapping him on the shoulder.

He bade the group goodnight and walked out of the bar, to their collective open mouths.

Other times, other situations, Nate sought a serious companion. It was time to settle down, and this dating was too much of a game for him. Too many girls began to look alike to him; too many of their stories were the same. He didn't consider himself a prize, but he knew what he wanted. Or thought surely he did.

He found Audrey one Monday morning at the receptionist's desk as he entered his building for work. He'd heard the other lady was leaving but hadn't given it much notice. This girl was quite attractive, with brown hair, green eyes, around his own age, and he could tell she was efficient, answering the telephone as she sorted papers, giving him a bare glance as he paused.

He waited till she hung up the phone, then introduced himself.

"I'm Nate Prescott, one of the engineers. Are you to be permanent here or just filling in?"

"I suppose I'm permanent. I'm Audrey Krauss. Hi." Her voice was a bit clipped, and he guessed she was from up north, maybe Minnesota, Michigan? She was reaching for another stack of papers, clearly not interested in him or in continuing their budding conversation.

"Well, see you," he promised and walked to the stairs, intrigued by this girl. *A Yankee, and she doesn't have horns. Krauss, probably German family. Well, a little variety around here. And it won't be long till the sales guys and the other single slide-rule pushers start moving in on her. And of course, I'll be one.*

She hadn't responded warmly to his greetings, always seeming busy. But he noticed she didn't to any others, either. The salesmen were the first to start trying to hang around her desk, but she shooed them off impatiently. Maybe even a little rudely, it seemed to Nate.

"Not to seem mean and nasty," he overheard her tell one of them, "but I know you have work to do, and so do I, and it's not quitting time."

"So what do you do after five o'clock?" the persistent fellow had asked.

She'd fixed him with an appraising look, no smile, and told him:

"Church work. Every day." The man had slunk off, obviously put off by this reply. *Church work, the complete opposite of what that guy had in mind. Well, I can do church work, too. Maybe I'll try that approach.*

He did. But not till after a lot of mentally trying out ways to bring the subject up. Not being that religious, he knew he'd put his foot in it for sure. *Well, she isn't wearing a ring, I'm single, so here goes…*

"What church do you go to, Audrey?" he asked innocently one day they were both leaving for lunch. He wanted her to think he assumed she was religious, and hoped she hadn't noticed him overhearing the earlier exchange with the salesman.

"Oh, I'm Presbyterian. I go to First. You?"

"I'm actually looking for a church. My grandfather was a minister, backwoods, a real firebrand. I've heard your denomination is strict. Is that true?" He desperately wanted this conversation to continue.

"Depends a lot on the pastor. People have the idea that we're all frozen into the concept of predestination: you know, we're chosen and everybody else isn't." She continued walking briskly.

"But you're not, I take it."

She stopped, turned to look at him. What was this guy after here? And was this just another pickup line?

"No, I'm not; we've all got a long way to go, as my father the minister says." A pause. "So now that we've broken the ice, what's next?" A sort of challenge in those mesmerizing eyes.

She's no fool, knows bullshit when she hears it. Well, here goes again…

"What's next is you agreeing to have lunch with me and we can cut through all the meaningless patter, and you can really give me some guidance, if you will, on my faith journey. How about it?"

"Okay, I guess maybe I can do that if you're sincere. I like the sandwich shop next block over, but I'm paying my way. Don't assume anything on short acquaintance. Oh, that didn't come out right…" She covered her mouth.

"Hey, I'm the one pushing. Because you're attractive, smart, and being religious puts you in a category apart. And my assumptions I'll keep to myself." He felt almost equal in this verbal skirmishing. New feeling.

"All right, we understand each other. You have to know, I'm so tired of the predictable come-ons by the married men—and the single ones—wherever I've worked. It's as if, having a pulse and being unmarried, I'm a target for predators, a chance for them to put notches on their guns."

He laughed at that, remembering Andy's saying that more than once when asked about men. No, he could get serious about this girl, and he wouldn't do anything out of line to jeapordize his chances.

"Part of the current culture, I'm afraid. Guys in the bullpen upstairs come in with tales of their supposed conquests every week, probably for my benefit, since I'm the only single one there. Whatever happened to morals, I wonder?"

"So you're gonna tell me you're pure as the driven snow; your mama taught you to respect all women and you've done it to the letter, right?" That rankled.

"No, unfortunately, both my parents died when I was eleven. My aunt raised me, and being divorced from a real creep, she had the undeserved reputation that a woman with that label still gets in rural Arkansas. But yes, she did aim me in the right direction. I hope." They were at the sandwich shop.

"Oh, sorry. Hey, I'm not trying to be ugly here: just want the ground rules set, okay?"

"Ground rules. All right. I'll start by telling you frankly that I'm going to court you, Audrey, and do it the old-fashioned way, in my backwoods naïveté. Yes, respecting you, sharing with you everything I can, including our faith, and I'm serious already. To me, dating isn't a game."

"Wow, that's up-front. What if I don't want that?" She cast a sidelong glance at him. "What then?"

"Then I crawl back into my hole and stay out of your life. Hey, I'm offering, not trying to persuade." *Oh, yes I am.*

They continued this conversation throughout lunch and on the way back to their building. If Audrey was put off by this directness he'd learned from his aunt, she didn't show it. But it was clear she wasn't about to climb onboard with anybody else's agenda. Audrey Krauss would clearly run Audrey Krauss's life the way Audrey Krauss wanted it run.

He learned that she'd been a religion major in college, had planned to become a missionary. But her mother developed a serious illness, and she'd stayed near home in Traverse City, working part-time as she had during college as a receptionist. And after her mother had died, she'd just gone on with that, while considering her options.

Nate had the usual stereotype of the foreign missionary woman: dowdy, passed up by all the boys, wanting to serve God, but taking this work as second choice. Audrey certainly didn't fit the image.

She left him to go on his way upstairs to work, after agreeing that he could yes, come to church with her Sunday. He couldn't help feeling that he'd made the correct moves, and his anticipation started a feeling inside him of…*rightness.*

The word had gotten around the bullpen that Audrey Krauss was on the God Squad, as the men termed it, and therefore off-limits to red-blooded sporting men. So of course they made her the subject of the office gossip.

"Woman like that," one wag insisted, "you manage to give her a good screwing, she'd follow you around like a dog." Chuckles. This attitude angered Nate, but he kept his counsel. Hell, it might even be true, but for him that was to find out on the honeymoon.

"What about you, Nate? Gonna try for that iceberg?" He decided not to make an issue of this.

"With you studs around? Hey, I'm an amateur; get my little ears burned off, I make a move on that one."

"Aw, they're all alike underneath all the pretense," another engineer volunteered. "Just wanta stick their feet under some man's table, forget all that career stuff, and I bet you've chased your share up into the haylofts back in Arkansas, haven't you? Audrey's no different." *Small talk, that's what she is to these creeps, in a small-talking place. If half the stuff they brag about ever really happened, they'd all be Don Juans. Get their morals out of Playboy magazine.*

Nate met Audrey at the church steps that early spring Sunday morning. She was dressed conservatively in a dark skirt, white blouse and gray-green jacket, which highlighted her eyes. He'd wondered what to wear for the occasion, but he'd been in three church wedding parties and had settled on slacks, a jacket, and tie. They looked good together he was sure, but that wasn't the point here, was it? They took seats in the center of the congregation as the sanctuary filled.

The bulletin listed the sermon as "Christ in a secular world," which he thought was so broad it didn't tell you much. One thing his high school English teacher, Mrs. Mann, had impressed on him was to keep your subject narrow and explore it thoroughly. Well, he'd see what the good reverend had to say here.

Audrey seemed right at home, speaking to several others as they passed. *Preacher's kid. Everybody knows they're the meanest. Maybe where she gets that touch of acid. Or is that just her pre-emptive strike? We'll see…*

There were familiar hymns, and some totally strange to Nate. He dropped two dollars into the collection plate when it was passed. Stood with Audrey when it was called for. All in all, this service wasn't much different from ones he'd attended with his mother at Elijah's church early on, just a lot quieter.

The minister read Scripture, then launched on a long-winded discourse on the evils of modern society, and how none of it fitted with the pastoral life God had intended people to pursue. Nate wondered how dedicated the good man was himself, remembering seeing his gleaming Packard in its reserved space outside. And envisioning the portly man with his distinguished gray, swept-back hair in a hut with sheep and goats in the desert setting of Israel. Or for that matter, in a rough-board farmhouse on a cut-over hill farm in Arkansas.

It went on too long, with a lot of repetition, the same message pounded home: God didn't like all this mechanization, technology, this loose lifestyle, this worshipping the works of human hands. Nate let his mind drift a lot, aroused only by the occasional shout from the dark-robed figure up at the pulpit. He hadn't known Presbyterian pastors shouted.

It was finally over, and amid greetings and hand-shakings, he and Audrey made their way out the door. He didn't want this day to end this way.

"I'm sure you walked here, but may I offer you first a ride and second, lunch, this time on me? I don't know about you, but that message didn't resound with me, I'm afraid. I need enlightening of a different kind."

"I might consider that." There was a definite twinkle in the green eyes. "And I must confess, I set you up. I came here at first but couldn't stand that man's pomposity. Now I go to a little church across town, with about fifty people and a down-home pastor. You'd like it, I think." She smiled up at him, mischievous laughter in those deep eyes.

"I've been had. You're cruel. And of course I didn't suspect a thing. You know I've been practically flagellating myself, pretending I'm on your level here, determined to make a good impression. I guess it's hopeless."

"Oh, sure it is. You've definitely failed to impress me, sweep me off my feet. But let's continue this soul-searching over that lunch, shall we? Is *this* your car?"

Nate, taking advantage of his aunt's acquired expertise regarding automobiles, had determined that if he were to spend his money on a set of wheels, as the other engineers termed cars, he wanted fine engineering, good design, something he'd be proud of. Thoreau had said a man's clothes said a lot about him, and Nate figured a man's car did, too.

So he'd bought a Studebaker Hawk, with its small but powerful V8 engine, sleek silhouette, and superb handling. Unfortunately the merging of Studebaker and Packard hadn't worked out well, and he knew this would be one of the last of these great cars. Even the Avanti, a futuristic, expensive offering, would be doomed.

"Yes, like it? It's one of those Satan-inspired mechanical contrivances designed to lure me away from the spiritual life. I figure if I'm gonna have a car, I want one I'm not ashamed to be seen in. And one that won't leave me stranded in a ditch somewhere."

"Wow, this is leather: feels good. I don't have a car, though not from automotive celibacy, just shortage of funds. I like this, air-conditioning and all. They must be paying you too much at the company."

"Not a chance: I'm still the rookie. But I don't spend my hard-earned bucks chasing women, doing drugs, swilling alcohol, or gambling. I'm plodding, predictable, boring, but not broke."

They turned heads going across town to find a place open on Sunday, eventually settling on the dining room of the Peabody Hotel, the watering place of the visiting Mississippi planters since forever. It was said the famed Mississippi Delta began at Catfish Row in Vicksburg and ended in the lobby of the Peabody, words coined by some prominent writer. Hodding Carter? He couldn't remember. It was famous for its indoor fountain with attendant splashing ducks. Nate had heard the tale of a drunken Ole Miss fraternity boy who'd jumped into the water, grabbed a duck, wrung its neck, and fled with it just ahead of the law.

"This is nice, but not in keeping with your thrifty lifestyle, Nate. Come here often?"

"Only one other time, and the boss paid. But I'm still out to impress you, Audrey, so let me keep on fantasizing. Besides, the money's part of what the good reverend was so down on, so let me get rid of it before it corrupts us."

"A philosopher; how'd I get roped into this?"

"A backwoods philosopher, at best. Let me jist clean th' manure offa muh boots, ma'am." She laughed, a sound like silver, and gave him a dazzling smile. She never actually looked severe, despite the chill the men at the office saw, but when that smile appeared, it was genuine and wholly captivating. Nate thought he would drown in it, and in those sea-borne eyes.

* * *

The budding romance with Reginald Cabot had progressed to the point at which Andy seriously considered what a life with this man would be like. If he continued teaching, it would mean settling down here or in some other college town, becoming a faculty wife, admittedly several cuts above what she'd known before. Not the worst fate for a woman, she knew.

Or perhaps he'd take a church somewhere, and she'd become the typical cookie-baking pastor's wife, the ever-present smiling pillar that supported the holy man. *And I guess that wouldn't destroy m, either.*

But he'd talked more and more about mission work as the weeks passed, recounting his experiences in Central America and even Africa as part of his religious training. At these times, his eyes would look beyond her, telling her that he really missed those times, places.

Before this observation, she'd also considered that they might both even make a change from all of this, move to some other profession, perhaps as a team. Or that each of them might pursue his/her own career, still together. Which would preserve her goal of independence while sharing her life with this good man. *Now that'd be just ideal: good life, too, the best.*

She enjoyed her time with Cabot. He wasn't a zealot nor was he skimming the surface of his calling. And she soon saw he was a dedicated man of God, through and through. Which began to cause a tiny doubt in her mind. Would he really just want her to follow him to some hidden primitive jungle somewhere to help him minister to the natives?

She'd read about the ill-fated South American efforts by a group of young missionaries who'd tried to reach out to a semicivilized tribe of natives. Five of them had been murdered, despite their peaceful intentions. She still shuddered to think of that situation. She even marveled that the widow of Jim Elliot, one of them, had stayed with her young daughter, Valerie, there near where that bloody business had happened. Later, she was to learn that the mother, Elizabeth, would become a powerful Christian writer, speaker, active all over the world.

That's just not me: I couldn't do that, not even for the right man or the right cause. That kind of dedication does fit Reggie, I can see. But I really don't think it's for me. Maybe it should be…

And this did indeed appear to be Cabot's eventual aim. He hadn't said much about this calling at first, maybe, she thought, knowing it'd probably scare her off. So yes, he'd waited till their relationship had built, till they both wanted to spend time together, looked forward to seeing each other, talking, sharing. Seriously.

So was she about to walk into a trap here? Well, not a trap as such, but a situation that'd stifle her, make her a virtual slave to her husband's however sincere aim in life? She'd have to think a lot more about this.

On the one hand, they seemed a perfectly matched pair. Both intellectual, she liked to imagine herself, both forceful, albeit his way was more subtle, more restrained. Everyone they knew evidently thought they looked and acted like the ideal couple. She detected this, even felt this way herself often.

And she recognized, despite their all-proper relationship, that she really wanted this man. Wanted his arms around her, wanted to be in his bed, discover the joy she knew they could share. *God, how long has it been? I've denied myself all these years, so betrayed by that bastard Cam. Isn't it time for real tenderness, real love, with all that goes with it?*

She found herself fantasizing about Reggie's body: what he'd look like, feel like, naked in bed with her. *Might have to teach him a few things.* And a hunger built in her, a desire that she knew could/would drown her if she gave in to it. *And really, why the hell not? Won't be a better man out there, anywhere.*

She found herself smiling a lot, humming at work. Everybody knew what that was all about, and her co-workers, schoolmates, friends were all glad for her. Susie even caught herself planning the wedding she just knew wouldn't be far off, the way things were going. *And nobody deserves a man that good more than our Betty. Life's not been good to her until now, and this'd just be the best ending anybody could imagine for her.*

But to toss everything she'd planned for herself all these years, go off to a life of unselfish service to a place and a situation much worse than her own poverty-stricken early surroundings? That didn't appeal. It didn't appeal at all. *But am I just being selfish here? A good man obviously wants to spend his life with me, and I'm flattered, thankful, even aroused. He's more than I deserve. And I think I do love him; can't think of anyone else I'd rather be with. He obviously loves me. Or thinks he does.*

But in the stark light of day Andy had to admit the whole package now didn't seem right for her. Maybe it would, given more time. But she also knew she could be talked into this life Cabot obviously had planned for her. She knew enough of human nature now to realize that. Especially with the sordid example of her mismatch with Cam Henry the Clod.

So, back off this while she still had her priorities set? Or, having found the right man out of the billions on the planet, should she jump at this? Was this truly her destiny? As she'd begun to understand, and told herself repeatedly, she'd have to think hard about this.

Only the more I think, the more time goes by, the deeper into this relationship I get. Or fall. Or sink. No, I'm going to have to make up my mind very soon, stay as clear-eyed as possible, as objective.

Only emotions aren't objective.

* * *

Andy had worked full-time at the garage until Nate graduated from college and found the Springfield job. She'd taken one class every semester and one in summer. She'd amassed some thirty credit hours at that point, equivalent to her first year.

She'd gone to his ceremony using the Naomi name again, and they'd had a serious discussion afterward. Nate had picked up their original plan for her: he'd insisted she drop her job and enroll full-time at SMS.

"I can't do that, Nate. Trey and Starr depend on me. With my running the office and my sales work, they're doing a great business. Anyone else, and they'd go back to just surviving. And I'm only thirty: plenty time to keep working my way through."

She'd told him nothing about her relationship with Reginald Cabot. That had come to a head one summer day at a picnic, when she'd had to tell him regretfully that she just wasn't the woman for him. He'd been stunned, taken totally aback, unbelieving, even. Here he'd thought… But she'd been firm, not wanting to hurt him, but not about to mislead him, once she'd realized clearly what she still wanted for herself. And she'd reproached herself for that stand many sleepless nights but stuck with it.

And shortly afterward, he'd resigned his teaching job and joined a missionary group going to Ethiopia. He'd asked her to write to him, which she'd agreed to.

"I'm completely with you, Reggie, but I honestly think I'd do you more harm than good in your calling."

"I don't see how that's possible, but I'll honor your decision. And I'll keep you in my heart forever, Betty." He'd kissed her goodbye and gone out of her life. Over the next two years, they'd corresponded, more as friends than soulmates, until inexplicably, his letters had stopped. Hers were returned. She never heard what had happened to him.

Her thoughts returned to her nephew's insistent reasoning.

"But they don't offer what you'll need for your major at night." Then he remembered who this was he was talking to. "Oh, okay, you win: so work part-time and concentrate on sales because you're terrific at it. Let them get a secretary, which they can afford with you bringing in the bucks selling. But don't overload yourself with too many courses. I found that out from the first; wanted to jump on everything that sounded good."

"My nephew the counselor. Okay, you can help, since we agreed on that way back. I can finish in three years, even with the work. You'll want to stay here until then, I know, keep an eye on me. But when we're both free and you've got a good résumé, let's plan on going somewhere exciting, as far from Hillbilly Holler as we can get, okay?"

"Just not New York or Chicago. I don't want us to get mugged or run over by a taxi. Sure, let's plan on that. The drafting part of this job doesn't pay a lot, but I know I'll move up. And you say you've got savings?"

"Yes, from all those sales to unsuspecting, gullible buyers I convinced that they just *had* to have all that shiny iron. And you'll get your farm sale money, such as it is, next year. I'll try not to bleed you dry."

"Oh, that. Yeah, the only connection to Ridgeway and the life I wanta forget. So, come fall, you'll register, okay? No putting it off." He shook a mock finger at her. "Promise me now."

She laughed, a sound he always loved and hadn't heard often back when he was growing up. What a woman this was! Why hadn't she found herself a good man, these years out in civilization? Well, it was her life, and she'd do that whenever she was ready. He imagined a distinguished executive, or a judge, an architect, for his aunt. She could still have a family; sure she could.

* * *

Christine Mabry and her son, Giles, had a wonderful time with Blake Walker at the lake. The weather had warmed a bit, and the day was ideal. The two adults got to know each other more, and it was obvious their liking was mutual. Giles caught two fish big enough to keep, and with the three Blake caught, Christine fried them up for dinner.

Afterwards, saying goodbye at her car, her new friend took advantage of Giles's snuggling up in the backseat to go to sleep, and leaned in, kissed Christine quickly. She reached, squeezed his hand, smiled at him. As she drove away, she felt a tingle inside. *This is gonna be the start of something good; I just know it.*

Walker was scheduled to leave for Little Rock that Tuesday, so Christine had invited him to dinner at her place Monday. She cooked, helped her housekeeper clean, readied the place for its first eligible male visitor in a long time. As the hour approached, she found she was as nervous as a teenager on her first date. *Now stop this! I'm in charge here, and this is just a guy: nothing special. Well…*

He arrived right on time, with flowers. She hadn't received flowers since college, or was it high school? This was good: an old-fashioned visit by a handsome man. Or did she dare call it a courtship? *No, not yet*, but the idea stayed with her.

The evening went well, with Walker playing games with Giles, a good wine she'd brought from Missouri with dinner, and no awkward moments. Christine was filled with anticipation as to whether he'd make a serious advance toward her later when Giles was asleep. *Second date: that's the formula, isn't it? As if I gave a damn about the rules.* She wouldn't hurry him off: give him the chance, of course. Just where that would lead remained to be seen.

So after her son was safely tucked in for the night, Christine got them each another glass of wine and they sat on the sofa in front of the blazing fireplace. She'd put several albums on the record player, soft music as background for their conversation. Then she'd told him she liked the firelight and turned off the lights. *Now, if this isn't the perfect scene, there just isn't one.*

Christine had been the object recently of two of the local eligible men's attention. The new lawyer in town was single, but he was a round little fellow, three inches shorter than she. And the doctor who'd succeeded old Aaron Blake had been twice divorced and was rumored to corner his nurse at the clinic regularly, as well as any other attractive woman he came across. *At least the men who're interested in me aren't drunken rednecks like those that bitch Andy Millard supposedly had to run off and probably didn't.*

Now, here, Christine believed the right man, the man she'd dreamed of meeting, was at that moment with her in this most ideal of situations, and she also believed her life was nearing a fulfillment she'd only dreamed of. Fleetingly, she remembered that drunken night back in college when Barry Mabry had torn her clothes off her despite her hazy protests. He'd actually raped her, in the sense of numbing her to the point of little resistance.

And she'd become pregnant. In 1948, that was the ultimate destruction of a girl's reputation, the damning seal on her life. No matter the circumstances, the truth, what stuck was the condemnation: *loose, immoral woman.* While the man was allowed to walk away with the admiration of his cohorts, having "scored."

She hadn't known which way to turn. She couldn't confide in her mother, any of her friends. She wasn't about to search out and undergo an abortion in those primitive back-alley desperation moves that were downright dangerous. And expensive. No, she'd have to take control here, shift her priorities, face this head-on. Barry was a clod, but seen objectively, she knew she could handle him.

So when she, in a highly practical but in reality desperate move, had revealed what had happened to her to Barry's father, the old man, against all odds, defended her. After, of course, the initial shock and predictable reaction. He raged at his son, decreed an instant marriage, made it right in his eyes. *Shotgun damn wedding, but what else could I expect from this boy: never going to grow up, so maybe this will help make that happen. And he could've done worse, I guess. At least she's not ugly or stupid.*

She'd often marveled at Montgomery's standing up for her until she'd realized that he'd seen in her the strength his son lacked. And the real possibility that she could and would try to give him the backbone he'd need as heir to the Mabry fortune.

And she'd accepted this role, despite the complete absence of any real love for her husband. This represented a big chunk ripped out of her life, this playing the role required of her, but she'd done it.

And now, after all the anger, the violence, the deaths, the desire inside her was about to be fulfilled: she was on the verge of plunging into the real, the living, the vibrant *woman* she knew she was. She had but to reach out, touch this man, and he would respond. He would belong to her. The absolute certainty of it swelled inside her, demanded that she take him.

Her fingers brushed his cheek so lightly, as a soft breeze in summer. She touched his lips, traced a provocative line down and across his strong jaw. She looked deep into his eyes, and the two faces drew together, magnetized in a powerful destiny that refused to be denied.

Chapter Twenty

Giles Mabry called again to make a date for his arrival from Dallas for the next Saturday. He did say the subject of his visit concerned Nate's uncle Charlie, but that was all he'd tell him.

Uncle Charlie? That's mysterious. What can this man know that he'd surely just have seen, heard when he was a little kid? Now he's got me hooked. So Nate speculated on this, casting about for any connection between his uncle and this boy. Was there something they'd all overlooked? Had wily Charlie, who'd left a trail of broken, or at least bruised, hearts like Cam Henry, somehow had something going with *Christine Mabry?* No way: that was beyond insane.

Yet the unanswered question had remained, this entire lifetime, of how Montgomery Mabry and Charlie had, of all the places in the world, met in those woods where the young man had died. All right, Nate now knew Christine had never loved Barry, knew about the college rape, the forced marriage. So had she been cheating on her husband? With *Charlie?*

That was so farfetched that Nate tried to put it out of his mind. Tried to. *Well, that could've explained Barry's murder, if Uncle Charlie had done it: get him out of the way. And the old man had his motive: no-brainer there. But who shot him then? Was there another killer besides Montgomery? Or one with some hidden agenda? Well, of course: Barry's killer.*

This is all too complicated. Maybe this Giles has gone senile, mixed things up in his memory. And any way you slice it, my uncle wouldn't have gone up against a rifle with just that old shotgun: couldn't have gotten that close.

So the secret, if there was one, had to do with his good-time uncle. Everybody'd known Charlie was harmless, just a sort of arrested-development case who wanted a fun time. And found it wherever he happened to be. So, *could* he, in the most bizarre of circumstances, have met up with Christine somewhere, somehow appealed to her? The man could talk his way into and out of just about anything, true, but *that* ex-cheerleader? She wouldn't have deigned to speak to him. And the way the Mabrys had put the Millards down, especially Charlie, just wouldn't allow that speculation.

But Nate dimly remembered part of some philosopher's observation about the things he could never understand. One was the way of a lizard on a rock, and there were a couple others, ending with "the way of a man with a maid." But no, this was beyond crazy.

Or could Giles possibly have seen Charlie setting that trap? Again, highly—no, impossibly—unlikely. A five-year-old? Across the Mabry fields and well into the woods on a crisp fall day? Or night even, though that complicated a pitfall could hardly have been carried out so convincingly after dark, even with a flashlight. And no, his father or grandfather wouldn't have taken the boy on a nighttime 'possum or coon hunt. And of course, they'd have seen the killer, too.

More questions. No more answers. Fruitless speculation. Well, the man would be here in ten days, so all this would just have to wait. That is, if what he had to say even threw any light at all on the multiple mysteries. Nate doubted it.

Andy was more curious when he told her. He had the idea his aunt knew more than she let him in on. That had been reinforced when she'd sort of dodged his question of whether she'd had anything at all to do with the killing(s). *She admitted to being obsessed with plots for revenge, and if she'd wanted to keep even something that drastic hidden, she could have done it.*

Omigod, does Giles know something on her? If so, what could it be? Far as I know, he doesn't even know she's still alive. Nobody but me knows she changed her name, is keeping Wilson here, too. But no, he said it was about Uncle Charlie. And like I said, he's probably got stuff mixed up in his head after all these years.

But the speculations continued, filling Nate's mind all the following week. He tried every scenario he could imagine, most of which were so fantastic they embarrassed him, thinking back on them. And he began to doubt his own memory of those long-ago events, the sequence, the details.

Well, just hide and watch, as his grandfather used to say.

* * *

The romance between Blake Walker and Christine Mabry caught fire after that night at her place. It was followed by her leaving Giles with the housekeeper and driving down to his apartment in Little Rock for the following weekend. After her forced abstinence of so many months—years—she about ate the man up. She'd never imagined such abandoned sex, such soaring to new heights every time they made love.

She knew she should take this slower, keep some perspective. After all, she had responsibilities: Giles, the properties to look after. And she'd do that, but just now, just here with this fantastic man, she'd let herself go completely. Time enough to get her feet back on the ground Monday morning.

For his part, Walker felt he'd finally met the woman who could fulfill his every fantasy. Whatever either of them proposed, the other was ready and eager to try. It seemed all they needed was each other, and they both nearly drowned in this new, fabulous love.

Then he had to go back to work, and she had to drive back to Everett County. All the way there, her head was up above the treetops, her mind replaying their time together, and a smile was permanently on her lips. *Plans. I need to make plans for this—us—for our future together. This is the real thing, and I'm being given a second chance at life, the life I was cheated out of the first time. Oh, God, this is terrific! This is…*

She swerved going down the switchback hill to the Buffalo River as a tractor-trailer coming up cut across the centerline. The Olds righted itself on the shoulder, and she fought down the momentary panic. It'd been close, and she realized she could lose this precious gift at any careless moment. She blared her horn in futility as the truck lumbered away in her rearview mirror.

The rest of the way home, Christine's mind was filled with plans, but she drove carefully, mindful of the other sharp turns on Highway 65, then off on the road to Ridgeway. All right, first she and Blake must find a way to be together more. He traveled almost all of Arkansas for his power company, so he'd be in this area some, but not nearly enough. And how often could she slip down to Little Rock, or to wherever he might be spending the night out on his territory?

She frowned, something the cheerleading coach back in college had told the girls never to do: *keep your face smoot, always; don't get wrinkles before you have to.* A lifetime ago, but only a little more than ten years actually. Ten years out of her life, and most of it spent with Barry. *What a waste.* But taking stock, she realized all the pain, all the violence had somehow worked to set her up as she was today.

Yes, all that productive land, the cattle, the timber, the investments left to her in Montgomery's will. It had been a hard decade, but very, very worth it, with her future now looking like paradise.

But I've got to keep this man. I know how they can stray, seeing pretty faces every day, away from home. I've got to chain this Greek god to me, keep him happy, or what good are the damn farm and all the money? And Everett County? There has to be a way to get out of there, too.

So Blake Walker probably never suspected it, but his newfound love was laying plans for his future despite what he might think he wanted. Top priority: be together. Next: get him in off the road. Then: get them out of Ridgeway and the backwoods.

He had no children, she'd learned, so it would be only Giles. He'd soon be ready for some good boarding school on his way to a fine college and wherever that led him. And they wouldn't have any more kids: a woman was a fool to go through that ordeal more than once.

And no, she wouldn't have to wait long for this: to hell with what people might think of her selling out and leaving their narrow-minded redneck haven so soon. Her business, all the way. Okay, she'd talk this over with Blake, let him think he was making some of the decisions. *Men are so blind, as long as they've got a warm bed, a warm woman who makes them proud, good cooking, and no chance to slip off. And I'll see to all that.*

At that very moment, the man in question was going over his own options. Here the perfect woman had dropped out of the sky into his arms, and he was going to make the most of it. Big farm, surely investments: he could leave the damn company, go live up there in the mountains. He liked her kid okay: could handle that. And clear streams, good hunting, no mortgage or money worries, a house right out of a magazine spread, and all he had to do was keep her happy. Which he knew how to do.

Remember to take her places, buy her things, show her off. And maybe most important, let her make some of the decisions. And I'll have to go slow about the place, the money. Plenty time to slip myself into the right position there. Do it right: big wedding somewhere, be the perfect husband. Hey, I'm being handed the ideal situation, so I can't blow this. He drove happily toward that new power plant location, down out of Helena, and the boring meeting with those branch guys.

Six months max, and I'm out of here, you losers. Maybe sooner, if she's on board, and I think she is. And on that note, I've gotta see to it I stay the man in her life. Woman that good-looking, with all that going for her, I can't let some slick salesman get in ahead of me. Okay, she's gonna see a whole lot of me, every time I can bend a trip in that direction.

* * *

Andy often thought of her situation as one nearly perfect, even with that lingering regret over Reggie. But a tiny doubt had begun to creep into her consciousness, in essence the idea that when things seemed to be going well, something might come along to wreck it.

Well after the missionary had left, she'd accepted the occasional invitation from an older graduate student or young professor, on a rare date. *Don't need to be a hermit here. And despite the growing independence movement among women, this equality thing, the guy still pays.*

So it was that she and a mid-thirties accountant, back in college working on his Ph.D., had gone to dinner at an upscale restaurant near the Springfield hub of Sunshine and Glenstone streets. The man was, of course, single, well off, drove a Chrysler Imperial of which she approved. They'd met a few times on campus, sometimes in the library, once at the cafeteria, just around.

Tom Hutchison wasn't handsome, with his thick glasses and receding hairline, and at first Andy had stereotyped him as the green-eye-shaded bean counter of movies and TV shows. But he'd turned out to be witty, intelligent, and a good conversationalist. She found she liked being with him, although never could she imagine him as a lover. His hands were soft, but at least they weren't stained green from handling money.

This wasn't their first date, but Andy had sort of rationed their times together, not wanting in any way for Tom to become a habit. And, of course, she couldn't help comparing him to absent Reggie. *No, just friends who enjoy spending time together.* Or that's the way she'd keep it, whatever else he might have in mind.

It was while deciding not to indulge in dessert that she saw them, and it was a shock. Christine Mabry with a handsome, middle-aged man, being escorted by the maître d' to their table. She started, visibly. Tom noted her wide eyes, followed her fixed stare.

As was her custom, Christine's own eyes swept the room, noting the well-dressed patrons, the elegance of this favored eatery. And there was something about that auburn-haired woman at the table with the ordinary-looking man that seemed familiar.

Now that's a bad hair dye job, but probably nobody else would've spotted it but me; wonder what the original was? Hmm, I should I know that face. Shouldn't I? The intense eyes, nowhere near right for the hair. Old college friend? About the right age. No, I don't think so… She allowed Blake to seat her, smiled up at him, basking in the realization that they were the best-looking couple there. *Well, that woman with the wrong hair's attractive, but the guy with her's a troll. Now why would she do that to herself? Dude want a redhead?* She allowed herself another quick look at the couple. The woman was actually staring at her.

Rude. But yes, there's something about her… She tried to concentrate on the menu, searching her memory for that face, trying to discount the hair. *A blonde? Don't think so, with those eyes. Probably mousy brown, and she's trying for anything better. Not working, dear. Even black? Hmm.*

"What was that, honey? Oh, yes, the red, if it's not something awful and sweet. You choose. I once heard a woman I respected say 'Good white wine is the result of skill, but a fine red: that's love.' She gave him a smile that she knew warmed their part of the room.

Andy wanted out of there. But a hasty exit would draw the woman's attention to her. She could see Christine was trying to place her: the abstract look, not really seeing the menu before her.

"I'm going to the ladies' room, Tom. Meet you at the front door, okay?"

"Sure. And no, I guess I don't need any more calories." He stood with her, signaling the waiter for the check. *Now that's odd: she's recognized that blonde woman over there, or her escort, but it's not a welcome sight. Well, we all have our people we'd rather not speak to.* He sat again and risked a look at the couple who were by now chatting, smiling, absorbed in each other. *Striking pair, all right. Maybe Andy thought she'd seen a movie star or something.*

Once outside, Andy had herself under control, at least outwardly. But when Tom suggested a late movie, she demurred.

"Like to, but I'm behind on a couple assignments, and I know you're facing that awful professor, the slave driver. Let's call it a night, okay?"

"Oh, okay. But let's don't let it be so long till we do this again." He opened her car door for her, closed it with the satisfying thunk of the Chrysler's heavy body. She did seem preoccupied on the drive back to Susie's house but managed to respond to his attempted conversation. *Whoever those people were, they meant something to Betty. Well, she's right: gotta hit the books tonight…*

Andy lay awake much of the night, newly aware that this woman from Ridgeway might have recognized her, or be trying to remember who she was. And that would mean discovery, and probably very soon. One call to the sheriff's office, and Hal Burgess, if he were still there, would begin a search.

Unless he's found Mabry's real killer, in which case I'm okay. Or maybe that's why Christine didn't push it: I'm in the clear? Can't take that chance. But maybe I can find out about that, write Bobby Harcourt, mail it from somewhere else.

Springfield was over a hundred thousand population in the early sixties, and Andy knew the chances of anyone's finding her at the garage or even on campus were, or should be, slim. But she couldn't think that way: no statute of limitations on murder, and with increased digging, her anonymity factor would shrink, narrow dangerously.

Could she uproot from here, leave her good job, her coursework, friends, all she'd gained, to disappear? Have to start over again far away? That would be wrenching. Elizabeth Wilson should be safe here, with no one close to her knowing her real name, or that she was a wanted fugitive. *But there's always that chance…*

So, choices: drop everything and run, the way they had from Everett County? Ahead of any searchers, whether real or imagined? Or stay the course, count on remaining invisible, push her luck. Or both: stay for now, search out another place to hide, lay the groundwork, plan, the way she'd almost always done. She'd have to think hard about this. And yes, pray about it.

* * *

"You've got your mind on something," Blake Walker observed on the late drive back toward Arkansas. "I saw you sizing up that other couple, the redhead and the nerdy guy. Know them?"

"Not sure. The man, no. But I know I've seen that woman before, and something tells me it's important. Been tugging at my mind all evening."

"Looked to be about thirty. Somebody from college? Surely not from around Ridgeway, or you'd know her for sure."

"I don't know. She's dyed her hair, I could tell, so that makes it harder to remember her. But Ridgeway…no, I don't think so. Or maybe years ago. Now who…"

"Well, it'll come to you, give it time. But you said it was important. So, have something to do with the farm? Or maybe your late father-in-law's practice? One of his cases?"

"Could be, but I didn't go to but a couple of his trials, see his clients or their opponents till later on. I'll think about it but not right now, okay?" And she snuggled up to her man, seeing the miles melt away before the purring Olds.

* * *

The men at the engineering firm teased Nate about Iceberg Audrey, as they referred to her among themselves. They told him not to waste his time on that one: plenty girls in Memphis sitting home painting their toenails. The truth was, they envied his being single. Most of them managed to play around on their wives when they were out of town, or claimed they did, in that early Sixties macho culture.

This may have been the decade of rebellion, of hippies and free love among the young, but in the corporate world, it was still the postwar pretense of propriety and rampant chauvinism. And these self-styled "swingers," as they termed themselves, had to keep these affairs very, very undercover. "Pun intended, Nate," his own boss chuckled.

In fact, Nate was to discover that this very man, with a doting wife and three children, had been involved with the stunning red-haired secretary to the president of the company for almost a year. He was shocked. *Right here under everybody's noses? How could he pull that off? And why would that girl, with guys running after her, hook up with a married man? Wow, I've got a lot to learn about what makes a woman tick.*

He needn't have worried about Audrey. It became evident that this girl would choose her own mate if and when the right one, the right time, came along. Nate suspected that dating for her wasn't a game either. Audrey was, he thought he could tell, the kind of young woman who knew who she was, knew what she wanted, and there wouldn't be any cute games about her choosing.

And I've gotta be the man she picks. Ignore all the advice from these studs. Be honest with her like I've been, let her know how I feel, which I've done, and just stay the course. My experience with dating hasn't been too successful so far, and I won't find another girl so right for me.

But, of course, he worried that some other insightful man might swoop in and get ahead of him. Not these randy types he worked with, not the playboy predators, but yes, he was no Romeo, just average-looking, nothing special about him. Except for that honesty, that dependability he knew he could give her. They'd have to become a team, and he remembered something his grandfather had told him about marriage: "It's whut they call a 50-50 deal, Nate, but t'keep it agoin' right, each one's gotta do 90 p'cent of th' work." That hadn't made sense to him at the time, but with this girl, he'd do it, willingly.

So his courtship moved ahead, albeit slowly. Sometimes she said no, she had too much to do to go out. Sometimes she said she just wanted to go to the library and look up a list of things she'd made that she wanted to know more about. And sure, if he wanted to join her there, that'd be okay, and yes, they could talk then. Some.

Of course Nate wanted their relationship to go into overdrive, but it was clear that wasn't going to happen. And he found he enjoyed, as she evidently did, digging deeper into subjects that interested him. He even enrolled in a night class at Memphis State as a possible step toward a future M.S. in engineering. *Can't hurt.*

And if he were to keep up with this intelligent girl, then yes, he'd read more, study more, learn more of what made this old world function. He'd been a good student in school and college, and there was no reason not to continue. So, of course, the two of them often met at the library or went to lectures. Or concerts. Or theatrical productions. With the result that neither of them owned a television or wasted time fitting into the lively young adult scene of the river town.

This went on for a year, until it became obvious to both Audrey and Nate that it was time for the next step. Nate took the plunge, bought a diamond ring, and made a date with her for dinner at a good but not expensive restaurant. This would be the night, and despite his believing he knew so much about her, he was obviously nervous.

So much in fact, that the men in the office noticed and ribbed him about it.

"Whassa matter, Nate? You slippin' out on Audrey and afraid she'll catch you? I say good for you, boy. Wondered when you'd give up knockin' on that locked door." And even "What's eatin' you, guy? You got PMS or somethin'?. Haw, haw." He managed to ignore all this but didn't get much work done that day either.

It rained. He'd planned a stroll in the little park high above the Mississippi after dinner to a quiet place where he could propose, just the two of them. So that was out, but he was determined to go ahead; he'd think of something. And miraculously, during their meal, the rain stopped and the setting sun came out. *Maybe this'll work out after all; I'll just get my knee wet.*

Audrey picked up on his case of the nerves but didn't remark on it. It was clear there was something on Nate's mind, and he'd just have to handle it. So as they left the restaurant, she surprised him by suggesting they go for a walk in the park in the twilight, watch the lights of the city come on. *Does she know what's in my mind here? I think she must, so here goes…*

"Audrey, I've been wanting to ask you something for a long time now," he began, forging ahead. She looked at him, the question on her face. Damn, he loved those eyes.

"Okay, ask away. We've only been talking each other's ears off for a year now, and I thought you knew all my dark secrets." She had that gay laugh, the total opposite of the sober expression she greeted everyone else with. Nate still thought it sounded like silver.

"Well, I hope so, but there's one more thing"—he took the ring box from his pocket, opened it, while sinking onto the wet grass—"will you…will you…marry me?" And saw those eyes widen like the deep pools of the Ozarks rivers. He realized he wasn't breathing as he waited.

She looked him up and down, kneeling as he was there in the near dark for what seemed like a long moment. Then she reached, hauled him up and hard into her body, kissed him deep and long. There was a singing sound in his ears, and he felt as if he were being drawn up off the ground into some rarefied atmosphere, where his entire universe held only this woman. And yes, now he could see the two of them from up there, as if alone in this teeming world. And the rest of the river town didn't exist just then.

"Took you long enough," she said when their lips finally parted. "Sure will, yes." And she kissed him again.

They set a date two months off, at her father's place up in Traverse City, preferable to there in the middle of Memphis summer heat, and neither of them wanted to wait any longer. That'd give them time to prepare, let their people know, and make arrangements. Audrey's father would officiate, and Andy would, of course, make the trip. She'd met the girl earlier on a visit to Nate in Memphis and had told him if he didn't marry her, she'd take a switch to him.

* * *

Andy had finally made up her mind, left the garage job reluctantly, but would try to keep Susie, Starr, and Trey as best friends, if at a distance. She'd called Nate in Memphis, told him she was coming to that city, would pick up her college work there, find a job of sorts. She didn't say why.

He was delighted at the prospect. There'd surely be places she could work, big a city as Memphis was. And he was in a good position now to help, along with that nest egg he'd added to, which she hadn't wanted to take there in Missouri. It'd be like old times, only better. And she, with Audrey, would be a family.

She'd said she'd see him the next day, so surely something had come up, and he dreaded finding out that some lawman had located or was about to locate her. To drag her back to Everett County, trial, and jail. At least. *Yes, get here, please, and fast. They'll never guess where you've gone.* Or maybe she'd just made the decision to be close to him and Audrey after the years apart...no, they'd seen each other often since his graduation. But whatever the reason, Nate looked forward to Andy's being here.

She boarded a bus the next morning, a Saturday, not dreaming a

Wanted for Murder poster with her picture had been posted that very morning all over post offices in Springfield and surrounding villages. Cale Wilcox, now the Everett County sheriff, could not keep the news from his deputies, one of whom had answered a call about a sighting of Andy Millard. Reluctantly, he'd set the wheels of the law in motion.

The bus rolled east toward West Plains, then down toward Jonesboro through the flat non-vista of the Mississippi bottomland. In Springfield, post office patrons saw the new poster up, with its raven-haired fugitive with the piercing eyes.

And even with the stops on the way, every mile put Andy farther from discovery. It was late afternoon when she arrived, to be met by Nate and his fiancée in his shiny Hawk. She hugged them both hard, the pent-up worry and fear subsiding, the feel of them saying: *safety*.

* * *

"That's it! Blake, I *knew* that was the woman!" It had been the weekend after their Springfield dinner, and Christine had driven down to Little Rock to see him, stay over. What had triggered the recognition she didn't know, but it had come like a bolt of lightning. She was visibly excited.

"What woman?"

"Okay, now get this: that redhead at the restaurant in Springfield I knew I'd seen? That was, *is* the murderer of my husband, Blake. *And* his father. She ran before she could be arrested, but that's *her;* I know it. The dyed hair: hers was black. Surely got a new name, thinking she could hide in that town. I've got to call the sheriff or the state police."

"Wow. You're sure? A lot of people look alike."

"No, I watched that bitch through that trial, after she tried to seduce Barry, got him beaten up. I'd know those eyes anywhere. She's a predator, a hawk. They've never found her, but now they can narrow the search. Springfield's not that big." She began looking through the phone book there in his apartment.

"I dunno, Christine: no name to go by and looking different. But yeah, this could get 'em closer, I guess. God, from what you've told me, she'd have to be a heartless, cold-blooded killer. What brought that all on anyway? What started it?"

"Goes way back. My no-good husband had actually thought he wanted her, clear back when she was in high school. She was white trash, had the gall to put him down, ran off with a worthless truck driver. Then, after she'd divorced him, or maybe it was the other way around, she went after my husband. Her loser brother had cut timber on our land, and Barry went to confront him. Andy—that's her name—tried to seduce him, or maybe he encouraged her, fool that he was. Anyway, this old preacher in their family walked in on that, beat Barry, broke his wrist, fingers, knocked him out.

"The trial was a sham, but the judge ruled against us. Woman had a nasty reputation, but somehow got off. Then she, or that brother, laid a kind of primitive pitfall trap for Barry, who fell onto the sharpened spikes, died horribly." She winced at the vivid, remembered ghoulishness of it. She'd insisted on going out to the site and had always regretted it. The blood, the obvious agony he'd surely endured, dying slowly. She shook her head to clear it.

"The brother ran off, and the cops sort of gave up trying to find him. But for some reason, the fool came back a year later, and somehow my father-in-law and he shot it out in the woods, and Charlie, his name was, died. Pa was convinced, like everybody else, that this scum had killed Barry."

"Good God, that's like an old-time feud! You told me a little of it, but this's heavy stuff."

"And that's not all. Later, Pa got shot in the head, high-powered rifle, while hunting. Despite wearing the red vest I made for him. Andy was, of course, the main suspect: motive and opportunity, but she ran, just ahead of the sheriff. No trace at all for these five or six years.

"But now that'll all change. She won't know I recognized her, and the police can surely find her, even in that big a town. I know she had no skills, so probably cleaning houses or maybe working as a waitress somewhere. They'll find her."

"But she was with that guy in that posh restaurant. Doesn't sound like an illiterate backwoods woman."

"Oh, she could put on airs. Could use the King's English like an actress, pretend to be this do-good guardian of her sister's kid she took to raise. Probably after that guy for his money."

"What was the kid like? Could've been in on the killings, or was he too young at the time?"

"Well, I'll have to admit, he was the best of the bunch, which isn't saying much for that redneck family. Always top grades in school, athlete, everybody liked him. No accounting for that, but he disappeared, too, even though he had an airtight alibi: was at a basketball tournament. But yeah, maybe someway might've been involved in Barry's death…"

She'd picked up the phone, got long-distance, then the Everett County Sheriff's Office.

Chapter Twenty-One

Eventually, Andy had the opportunity to go to work for a small design firm, mostly as a secretary, and had decided to pursue that vocation. She did this for four years, working in as many courses at Memphis State as she could but also building a résumé, enjoying a completely new perspective, that of a learning, experiencing employee of a respected profession she knew she'd love.

And finally, after her graduation, her job became full-time, with the aging owner of the firm promoting her to the creative staff. With what she'd already learned of this business, her degree now seemed almost an afterthought. *But I'd have been the* secretary *foreve, without it.*

Only this newfound, exciting position soon lost some of its attraction. She had to have her boss's approval for everything, and the woman wasn't always ready to give it. Andy knew she had to prove herself and worked hard to do so. Gradually, the owner had to admit that this young woman had talent, creativity, and gave her more complex assignments. That was what kept her from sending out her résumé, searching for another and better job.

Sometimes she almost regretted leaving Springfield, with her friends there, the smaller, less frenzied pace. But she knew there'd been no resolution to the Mabry shooting; her discreet inquiry to Bobby Harcourt had revealed this. She'd trusted him as a contact to some extent, but always drove to other towns where she had mailboxes to mail the few letters she'd sent. His replies also allowed her to keep track of what was happening in the region.

Hal Burgess had died of cancer, but she had no idea how aggressively Cale Wilcox would pick up the old case. *Okay, I'm still the prime suspect.* Harcourt had told her he thought the case, apparently unsolvable, had been abandoned, but not to count on that, so get on with her life, but maybe relocate farther away.

So that had added to the shock of seeing Christine Mabry that night, leading to her decision to flee. And she did like Memphis, and not only because Nate and Audrey were there. It was the hub of so much territory, its own culture, and a flavor of the Old South that appealed to her. She'd made two trips there to visit, and decided that, if she didn't stay in Springfield, she'd go to Memphis. Still as Elizabeth Wilson the redhead, though, since all her references would be in that name. Although she did wish she could stop torturing her hair.

Then after two more years at this job, the owner retired, and Nate and Audrey helped Andy buy the firm, with that now much-grown nest egg. She was suddenly the boss, albeit of a small business. The owner.

It was a new sensation, this being the one clients came to with their commercial design needs. Doctors, opening clinics, offices. Business executives planning their new headquarters. Even, in a twist of fate, the local Caterpillar dealership president, telling her his business had outgrown their old location, and he wanted something upscale. Andy couldn't help watching out for a predator son, discovering with relief there wasn't one here.

She expanded the business to become eventually one of the leaders in her field. Memphis was growing rapidly in the Sixties and early Seventies, and she soon had a lion's share of the commercial design business. She often compared this heady position with her beginnings back in Everett County as a penniless farm girl, and was content.

Life was good.

* * *

"Oil," Blake Walker told his wife, Christine. "That's the biggest thing in the world right now. Railroads are drying up, and big trucks are taking over, going to towns the rails don't reach. And with the interstates, we're gonna see a spike in gasoline and diesel prices like nobody's business. If we invest in oil, we can't go wrong."

Sounded good to her. This new man of hers seemed to know a lot about a lot of things and was surely miles ahead of her late husband, Barry, with his crazy schemes.

At first Blake had been happy to stay on the farm, which she was not, wanting more out of her life. But he'd eventually become bored with the sameness of the routine: managing the cattle, continuing with the timber operation, producing the crops of corn and soybeans. And the whole daylight-to-dark grind that was a farmer's lot, even a wealthy one.

He just wasn't cut out for this life. So the two of them talked long about their options, all of which required selling this place and moving where the action was, as he put it. Christine was with him all the way, since it seemed he'd researched every avenue they'd considered, and he was playing right into her plans. And she was certain this man could do no wrong: he was perfect in her eyes.

She compared Walker with her late father-in-law in his prime: solid investments, shrewd business deals, on top of every situation. But then of course the old man had later just about gone to pieces, over first Barry's death, the whole Charlie Millard manhunt, then his killing the man. His judgment had eroded, and she'd actually admitted to a degree of relief when that worry had been taken care of, no matter how it'd happened.

She was just sorry that the police hadn't found that Andy Millard, after she'd given them her general location. She wondered how seriously they'd taken her tip but had learned they'd tried, at least. *Hiding in plain sigh, with that bad hair job, which nobody'll look beyond. Well, I can put all that behind me, I guess, though it galls me she got away with it.*

Because now life was great, and the prospects for a cosmopolitan existence in some civilized location appeared a certainty. So yes, if Blake wanted to go to Texas and get into the booming oil business, then sure, they'd go. But they would also be sure to get a top price for this model Mabry operation. They'd advertise it in the *Wall Street Journal,* the *New York Times,* the *Chicago Tribune,* those places with retiring executives eager for a retreat in the mountains.

Eventually, a couple from Rochester, Minnesota, bought the place. The wife had been a nurse at the prestigious Mayo Brothers clinic, even after her husband had made his fortune in insurance. Now they just wanted to spend what they called their golden years in these scenic mountains, collecting antiques, horseback riding, enjoying the lakes and streams. And compared with other locations they'd considered, the price of even this paradise was astonishingly low.

The Walkers were off to Dallas and a future in the oil industry, armed with the proceeds of their sale. What could go wrong?

They soon found out that, compared with other budding oil entrepreneurs, they were sadly underfunded and underinformed, and all Walker's research had actually been mostly talk. On top of which, they invested heavily in a new start-up corporation that eventually turned out to be mostly a shell, for its executives to fleece the stockholders and send the company into bankruptcy.

It all seemed to happen so quickly: one moment they were new in town, eager to move into its newly rich society, convinced that they could compete with the best. The next, they were broke. Giles had to drop out of his prestigious prep school for a public high school. The family had to sell their elaborate house and move into a cramped apartment.

It was all unreal to Christine, this financial whirlwind and sudden downward spiral of their fortunes. She kept hoping some miracle would rescue them. It did not happen, and it wouldn't.

Walker was able to find a position with the local power company, albeit several rungs lower on the ladder than he'd hoped for. Dallas was not a cheap place to live, however, and it looked as if Christine would have to find work, too. For which she was woefully unequipped.

She remembered dimly an approximate quotation from a high school reading assignment in Dickens regarding the successful marriage: "Income greater than outgo: happiness. Outgo greater than income: misery."

And the fire of her relationship with Blake Walker suffered from exactly this. She began to see all her years of devotion to the Mabrys, her certainty that this man was her salvation, the glitter of this new place with all its promise as a lie, a pack of lies, a further waste of her life. She'd been used, despite her careful planning and all the effort she'd put into doing what must be done to ensure her eventual happiness and that of her son.

Christine was understandably bitter. And here she was, now past her prime, no longer a saleable commodity among these young, long-legged Texas women whose goals matched hers exactly. She brooded, went about her days in a resentful, frustrated fog. And found herself drinking more and more.

Finally, she filed for divorce from Walker to stop this downward avalanche. He'd just been fired from his job, she was horrified to learn, for becoming sexually involved with a company vice president's *wife*, for God's sake. Was that his way of trying to get back on top? If so, it'd blown up in his face. Christine wanted out. Better to struggle on her own than to let him pull her down farther with him.

Giles was by then in college and somehow had been able to work his way as a cameraman and then assistant director in a local television studio at night. The boy worked hard, kept his grades respectable, was determined to succeed, rise above the chaos his family represented.

Just maybe, his mother hoped, her son could somehow rescue them from this different but more dire pit they'd fallen into. They were living partially on her at-best-sporadic alimony settlement from Walker, barely paying the rent, just marking the days until Giles could collect his inheritance, graduate, find a decent job. The question was, could they hold on that long?

* * *

Nate and Audrey's wedding was a sort of revelation to him. He'd never ventured outside his work environs much and never traveled, really. That part of Michigan was a delight of lakes and forests, and Audrey's relatives and old friends were welcoming to this Southerner. They all liked Andy, too, whom Nate gave credit for raising and educating him.

Reverend Krauss gave a heartfelt homily at the ceremony, ending with a charge to the couple to draw strength from each other in times of trouble, to work together as a team above all, and to touch frequently. He instructed them to hold hands as long as they lived. *Nice bit,* Andy thought.

If this happy union made her regret not having found her own soulmate, she didn't let it show. She was just supremely happy that her nephew had come from such an unpromising beginning to this joyful pairing. She wished her sister Becca and Dave Prescott had been able to witness this wedding. *Another time, another generation. They missed so much, leaving us so soon.*

The newlyweds spent a week at a remote inn east in this lake country, a location they managed to keep secret. And both explored each other intimately, learning delightful surprises, imagining that their joy would last till the end of time. And it would, for forty-five years.

Andy's move to Memphis made her the couple's only relative there, among many friends they both had made. These were mostly from church, neither of them anxious to include the freewheeling engineers, salesmen, and others from work or their harried wives. The members of the little nondenominational church were a mixed group, from Delta farmers to business people, truck drivers to carpenters, secretaries, and teachers.

Life in the house they'd bought south of Memphis, toward the Mississippi line, was pleasant, and both were happy. They did, however, discuss where they wanted to raise their family and began looking into other parts of the country they might like better. Not that Memphis was a bad location, but Audrey particularly wanted a smaller town, or even a country place with space for the children to grow.

* * *

At first, the two men from Arkansas seemed to Nate just locals from some small town in the market for engineering for back home. An upgraded sewer/water system, to be paid for with a small tax increase matching government funds, recently become available.

Then, after being assigned to them along with a senior man, he learned they were from Ridgeway in Everett County. *Don't know either one of them, but one's checking me out, looks like. Oh, sure: they'll know my name, even after fifteen years.*

So, did he ask to be taken off this job? For what reason? Well, there wasn't one that'd hold water unless he got into details with his boss, and he wasn't about to do that. So again, just do the job, hope these guys didn't make any connection.

And what if they did? He wasn't wanted for anything, never had been. Okay, he'd take this on, a good project that'd make the company money. *Yeah, do the job.*

Mel Purvis was on the town council in Ridgeway, and Bill Yates was the local civil engineer there who'd worked with that body before, so he'd been the logical second man to send to this Memphis firm for their eventual bid. They'd already gone to Little Rock, Springfield, even St. Louis for the right company, and this would be their last call. The council would review the qualifications of the interested parties, their recommendations, then entertain bids.

Yates had a college degree, but Purvis was a shrewd cattleman who'd been involved in most of the doings of the town for the past ten years. They'd already formed their opinions of the firms they'd visited, but of course it'd be up to the other council members.

Purvis was red-faced, stocky, and out of place among these businesslike engineers. Except for this young one, who had an accent like his own. After their interview, both men needed a break before heading back to Ridgeway, so they took a hotel room, where they could further compare notes on the soon-to-be-competing companies before they presented them at home.

"What'd you think of that young feller Prescott they had workin' with that gray-haired guy, Bill? Reckon he knows what all he's doin'?"

"Seemed to. These new ones are all hot t'use all the latest tech stuff, and that can't be all bad, I guess. With the other one on it, too, I think it'll be okay. They stack up pretty good against the others we talked to, dontcha think?"

"Guess so. Been thinking, that young 'uns' name: oughta know that. Usta be Prescotts in th' county, on back, an' he's plain a country boy. Seem familiar to you?"

"No, but I've been there only nine years, you remember. Think he could be local?"

"Could be…there wuz a kid, few years back, was on th' basketball team, orphan boy b'that name. He'd be 'bout th' right age,' now. Reckon he coulda got into college, could be th' same one?"

"Not impossible. Might've got a scholarship,' if his grades were good. No money, I guess. Who raised him?"

"Wal, after his folks got killed, mother's sister took him in. She was d'vorced, not real popular 'round town, but way I remember, she did take care of th' boy, 'long with his old granpa, wuz a preacher. Yeah, an' she had that brother y'might of heard of, got hisself shot by big lawyer, Montgom'ry Mabry."

"Seems I've heard about that. Then somebody shot him."

"Shorely wuz th' woman: only one had reason to. Yeah, Andy Millard. Law never caught up with her. If this boy's th' same one, he'd know fer sure whar she's at, dontcha think?"

"Maybe so. Well, we can tell Cale Wilcox we may be working with him. And sure, he'll have to come to Ridgeway to be able to prepare their bid. But we don't know if it's the same man, really."

"Naw, guess not. Jist seems maybe we oughta help out th' law when we kin."

* * *

So it was that Nate and Todd McCaskill, the older engineer, were asked to go to Ridgeway to examine the situation there, to prepare their bid. Their company had made the cut and would compete with only the one from Little Rock. Nate put aside his reservations about revisiting his native town, telling Audrey only that he supposed the place had changed a lot.

"You've told me all about the trouble there, hon. Sure you wanta have all those bad memories surface again?"

"Well, after all these years, I don't think anyone will even know I'm the same Nate Prescott. And if that does happen, I'll just be the local boy who made good, now helping the town with its infrascture problems. And we lived pretty far from where I'll be, so no, I don't think any ghosts will show up to haunt me." He grinned, gave her a kiss. "But thanks for worrying about me."

He and McCaskill made the trip, met with Purvis and Yates to inspect the existing water and sewage systems. Both were woefully inadequate, even with the quite modest increase in the population of the town. Its out-of-the way location hadn't made it a destination like the towns to the east and north nearer the White River lakes.

These installations just hadn't been done right in the first place, was the conclusion Nate and his partner reached. So, upgrade wasn't to be the way to go: completely new installations would be their recommendation.

"Think they'll spend the money?" Nate asked.

"More like do they have the money. Matching fund thing, and it might take a big tax hike to pay their share, no more people than live here. But we can't recommend a patch job on either system. Boss wouldn't approve that, and it'd torpedo the company's reputation. No, we'll tell 'em we'll do it right, or not at all."

"And from what you just said, maybe we'll have to pass this one up: sort of a hopeless situation, this town. Always has been." So far Nate hadn't seen anyone he knew here, their visit having been limited just to the systems in question, although he'd sort of expected that. *Fifteen years: lotta people died, maybe moved away. And Bobby Harcourt did write us that the Mabry woman sold out, went to Texas or somewhere. Let's see, Giles would be what, well out of college by now, surely past being any threat to Aunt Andy. And certainly not to me. His mother sure hated us, though.*

His musings, a mosaic of memories and experiences of the past, intensified as he wandered the streets that evening. So long ago, but not really. Just the same, and so very different. The place did seem much smaller, the way he'd seen revisited locations after time had passed.

The next day, the engineers presented the town council with their findings, making it clear their company would not consider anything less than new, efficient installations. That would include drilling additional wells, larger storage tanks, new main pipes. And the latest in forced-air aerobic bacteria sewage treatment, using Caterpillar natural-gas engine pumps to replace the old slow-moving methane-driven pumping system.

Two of the five councilors winced at this plan: Mel Purvis and a matronly schoolteacher. The other three nodded gravely, not dismissing the proposal. Yet. Then they called Bill Yates for his evaluation of Mid-South's plan.

"Makes sense, folks: if we're gonna do this, let's do it right."

"But where'll we git th' money, Bill?" from Purvis.

"Put it this way, Mel: we don't do this, no matter what it costs, we'll have to shut down the entire system. Got corroded pipes, pumps coming apart, not enough water to run the place. Might as well abandon the whole town if we don't fix it and fix it right." He sat, end of discussion as far as he was concerned. There was a general buzz among the councilors, and it was clear the schoolteacher and Purvis were on one side, with the others opposing them. Or more accurately, in favor of the proposal.

Finally, the council chairman held up his hand for quiet. Clearly, they needed more time to consider this.

"Well, thanks, Mr. McCaskill, Mr. Prescott. Looks like we're gonna have to dig into this more: weren't prepared for nearly this big a deal. We'll think hard about this, and be in touch within a week, okay?" The engineers gathered their papers, spoke briefly to Yates, shook hands all around.

Then, on the way out of the room, Nate saw Cale Wilcox. An older, leaner Cale Wilcox, but the same man, now sheriff, he'd learned.

"Nate Prescott. How y'been, all these years?" He extended a hand.

"Well, Mr. Wilcox. Good to see you. Oh, I got myself an education, got on with this Memphis engineering outfit, been doing okay. This's Todd McCaskill. You probably know about the water, sewage deal. How about you, and your family?" *Now, what's he doing here?*

"Mostly good: holdin' down the sheriff job now, kids about grown, wife's working part-time. All of us gettin' older, of course." He was walking with the two engineers toward their car. "And how's that aunt of yours?" He asked it casually, as if it didn't matter. But of course alarm bells went off in Nate's head.

"Well, after we left here, she got me into college, and we said goodbye." He turned to his partner. "Todd, could the sheriff and I have a minute? Be right along. Would you mind waiting for me in the café over there? Order me coffee if you will." Nate didn't want any of whatever this was to get to his employers. McCaskill nodded, left them. *Catching up on old acquaintances, sure.*

"Y'say you haven't seen her, all these years?" Wilcox was incredulous.

"She knew she was surely the top suspect in lawyer Mabry's killing, sir, and knew, long as you all didn't find any others, she'd never get a fair trial. You'll recall half the county or more was down on her, believed she'd done it: motive and opportunity. So she told me she wouldn't let me know where she'd gone or leave any connection between us. That was hard: only family I had, you know. Do have a wife now." Nate gazed over the sheriff's head, as if in painful remembrance. "Only way she could see, I guess."

"Oh. Well, that's sad, all right. Well, you have t'know, th' case was never solved. Burgess an' me, we knew she didn't do it, but he was under so much pressure, y'know, from th' DA an' on up, all th' connections Mabry had. And of course, we looked hard for her, for a long time. Figured she and you coulda gone anywhere from down in Little Rock."

"Well, she probably changed her name or something; Aunt Andy was about as smart a lady as I've ever known. And surely married, got a family of her own by now somewhere." *Just wait for this, although I know where it's going.*

"I'd say so. Y'gotta know, Nate, I always admired your aunt, pitchin' in, raisin' you, and takin' care of your granddad. Can't say th' same for your uncle: sorta made it harder on your family, way he acted. No offense."

"He was a case, all right, God rest him. But if you're asking if I have any idea where Aunt Andy is, I just don't." *I do happen to know where Elizabeth Wilson is, but you didn't ask that.*

"Well, far's I'm concerned, that's okay. But there was a state police dectective in th' office on somethin' else when Mel Purvis came by th' other day. He heard you'd be one of th' team down on this water thing. Been on th' case since on back, and he was keen on findin' first of all, if you were th' same man, and second, wants bad to talk t'you, try to find Andy. Told him I'd ask you, but he doesn't wanta let it go. You stayin' over?"

"Hadn't planned to: we have a heavy workload and want to prepare our bid, depending on whether the council still wants to work with us. How serious is this guy?"

"He's a by-the-book type, hates loose ends. Now, I wanted—still do—to find Mabry's killer. Well, his an' Barry's, too: prob'ly th' same man since I really don't b'lieve Charlie did it. But like I said, Andy's not on my list, whatever anybody else thinks.

"Anyway, if you go on back to Memphis, you c'n expect th' state boys to follow up. If you stay over, I can call this Hardison, an' maybe he c'n come up from Little Rock, satisfy himself you can't help him." He looked a question at Nate.

"Okay then. Let me check with my partner, maybe call in to our boss. Wanta come with me, or I can stop by your office? Still the same?"

"Is. Sure, come on by, soon's you know. I'm not there, just leave word." Wilcox shook Nate's hand, and they parted. He joined McCaskill, sipped coffee.

"Old friend?"

"Not really, but yeah, we knew each other. Sheriff before him was a good guy, was a friend; this was his deputy. He was asking me about folks lived here when I was a kid." Nate realized that if he asked to stay over, it'd create suspicion in the company as well as with his partner. Didn't need that. *So, let 'em come to Memphis; no chance they'll find Aunt Andy there. Be looking for a black-haired country woman, not a top design firm president.*

They talked for several more minutes until Nate figured Wilcox was back in his office. Then he seemed to remember something, asked to use the phone, which was in the back of the cafe.

"Mr. Wilcox, we're gonna have to rush back to Memphis, I'm afraid. Anybody wants me, here's my home number. Rather not have any hassle at the office, you know. Or, if we get this job, I'll be here a lot. Tell your man that, would you please?" He gave his number, and they hung up.

"Well, I told the sheriff about one other person I'd forgotten, and that appears to be that. Ready for the drive?"

"Sure. We can be there before dark, easy." They paid, walked to their company car, hit the road.

Wilcox turned the situation over in his mind. *D'rather let this go, but that state man seems to wanta follow it up. So, I'll cooperate, but damned if I'll try hard to find Andy, even if I could. Nate's right: sharp woman. If she wants to stay hid, she will. Of course, he may be covering for her: didn't give me a really straight answer, or maybe lying. Couldn't blame him for that really.*

Wilcox would call the state detective, tell him what he knew, give him Nate's number, and just let him take it from there. No need to get involved since he'd considered the case unsolvable years ago.

Chapter Twenty-Two

The first thing Nate did back home was to walk to a drugstore and use the phone there to call Andy. It was after supper, and he'd told Audrey he needed toothpaste, which he did, and could he get anything for her? No, she told him, so he used what he knew was a safe phone.

He doubted that any police agency would or could tap his telephone that quickly, but didn't want to take the chance. Or even of someone following him if he went to see her. *Wreck her life, after all this time? I don't think so.*

"Gotta tell you, I've been to Ridgeway, Aunt Andy, on an engineering job. Don't know if they can afford us—water and sewage thing—but seems Cale Wilcox heard my name, first of all wanted to know if I was me, then told me stuff."

"What stuff? As if I didn't know. What a coincidence."

"Yeah. You may know he's sheriff now. Anyway, somehow a state police detective got wind of me and hasn't let the old case go. Wanted to meet me, but I was with another engineer and didn't want to stick around for that. Wilcox said to expect him to come to Memphis to talk to me."

"How'd you handle that?"

"Let them have my phone number: can't try to hide any of this. I told Wilcox just what you said to me when we left Arkansas: we'd have to separate and you wouldn't let me know where you were. True at the time."

"And of course, he didn't believe you. Or the detective won't. I'm curious: did Cale act like he thought I was guilty?"

"Opposite. Said both he and Hal Burgess had known all along you weren't, but that the pressure from above pushed the investigation. Don't know whether to believe him or not."

"Oh, I think Cale would've backed off, like Hal, if he could've. Well, seems my trail isn't as cold as I'd like it to be. Not likely they'll be able to find me now, though. New woman, new career, disguised, totally unlike the description they'll have of their supposed fugitive. Just hope they don't give you a lot of grief. You and Audrey don't deserve that."

"I'm a stone wall: don't even remember what you looked like in that other life. But you'd better not come visit or call for a while. Dunno what kind of phone taps, surveillance they may set up."

"There's that. Okay, maybe we can meet in some basement somewhere, wearing trenchcoats and dark glasses."

"Audrey'd love that: likes adventures, you know. But this'll be temporary, I'm sure."

"Don't count on it. But I'll find a way to contact Audrey if I get to missing you all too much: send a go-between, carrier pigeon or something. Well, give that girl a hug for me, and don't worry, okay?" They hung up, Nate thinking she was taking this news lightly. Well, he guessed he should, too. At least not let it interfere with their lives, since it was all so long ago, and Andy's identity was securely hidden.

* * *

About their proposed move, Nate was okay with whatever his bride came up with. He was confident he could land another engineering job most anywhere but did point out that a small town might not offer that. And he'd realized he wasn't wedded to the idea of sticking solely to this vocation, either.

And the more he thought about it, the more he remembered how he'd enjoyed the carpentry and other woodwork at School of the Ozarks in Missouri. He also liked the idea of being self-employed. The work he was doing now often involved many extra hours in order to fulfill contracts, design and fabricate systems, install them and modify them. He could foresee this demanding schedule cutting too much into time he wanted to be able to spend with his family. And he and Audrey were planning a family.

So now he might have to be gone from home to Ridgeway for weeks on that installation if Mid-South's bid were accepted. *Maybe a good time to think more about moving.* More so if the law came sniffing around after Andy.

They had agreed they weren't in a big hurry to relocate but also had already explored places that sounded good. Audrey definitely wanted to stay South, and so did Nate, so they'd begun to look more seriously into what was out there. And every vacation they'd already traveled to at least two places that sounded interesting: Natchez, north Georgia, Chapel Hill, Charlottesville, Hilton Head.

Some of these and others had been disappointments: too many mosquitoes, land too flat, no obvious culture. More and more Charlottesville seemed the best option, with its storied university influence, its horse country, the Blue Ridge, and the Shenandoah Valley. Then there was the Eastern Shore and the ocean, not that far away. And history, which both Audrey and Nate had become interested in, abounded there.

* * *

The Arkansas detective, Howard Hardison, called Nate shortly after that visit to Ridgeway. He politely explained that Cale Wilcox had told him that yes, this was the same Nate Prescott who'd lived there, raised by his aunt, still a wanted woman. And that Wilcox hadn't seen pursuing Nate as important.

"In fact, he told me you hadn't seen your aunt in fifteen years. But I'm sure you know there's no statute of limitations on murder, and she's still the prime suspect in at least Montogomery Mabry's killing. I need to come talk to you about that, sir."

"Sure, but I can't tell you anything. We parted just after we left Arkansas, and she knew I'd be the link to her whereabouts, so she regretfully insisted if I didn't know, nobody could get it outta me. Been that way ever since." *Well, she did say that.*

"I still want to talk with you. Why not Saturday, so it doesn't interfere with your work. I know you're involved with the proposed systems for Ridgeway."

"Like I said, come ahead." Nate gave him his address. Then told Audrey what this would be about.

"So your devious past is about to catch up with you?" She kissed him lightly.

"Not mine, but I don't want them finding out a thing about Aunt Andy. She's been through enough, clear on back."

"No problem, really. We just won't contact her, and she might as well be on Mars. How long do you think the bloodhounds will stay on the trail?"

"That worries me: been almost fifteen years, and Wilcox says this detective seems to be obsessed with the case. Apparently's been on it from the time we disappeared; won't let it go."

"I'm seeing Inspector Javert here, relentlessly dogging Jean Valjean. But seriously, since you're their only link to Andy, maybe we should expedite our move, just go undercover?"

"Surely it won't come to that. But yeah, I guess we could go ahead and move somewhere, not leave any clues, forwarding address. Of course if they really wanted to find me—us—they could, with all the tech stuff they're getting now. And I'm sure I'm in some huge database somewhere; Big Brother, you know."

"I'm trying to think the way the police would: figure she'll be close by, your only relative and all. So even without anything concrete to go on, Memphis will be their target area. And if they watch you long enough, you'll lead them to her."

"Umm. Well, why don't we just see how serious this Hardison is when I talk to him? If he seems to see me as the dead end, we don't sweat it so much. I've never been a suspect, after all. But if he's hot to find her, maybe to round out his career of successes, we do plan our vanishing act."

The guy was balding, wisps of gray hair clinging, red face, big gut.

Yeah, not the healthiest specimen: career guy. Surely been on the case all this time. He was polite at first, but clearly believed Nate knew where to find his number one suspect and was going after that information. Nate had insisted Audrey be absent for this grilling, assuring her he could handle it.

"When did you last see her, sir?"

"Told you, we parted in '57, after she got me into college."

"No, you didn't mention college. Where was that?"

"School of the Ozarks, near Hollister, in Missouri. Work college. They let me test in since I was underage." *Easy enough for him to find out.*

"I see. And where did your aunt go after that?"

"I honestly don't know. She was adamant that I not know that so I couldn't tell." *Well, I didn't know, for a while, and not just where in Springfield either, at first.*

"Okay, I need to remind you that aiding and abetting a fugitive from justice is a crime."

"I'm aware of that but since I didn't aid and abet, that doesn't apply here." *No, she handled it all on her own.*

"You must also be aware that we'll assume she's stayed close to you, her only family, so we plan to search Memphis thoroughly."

"Well, I'd say she's probably remarried long before this and has a family of her own by now. She was quite attractive, and several men I know of wanted to court her, back then. So no, I doubt if she's pining for me now: had her hands full raising me on the little we could scrape up back in Everett County. I could tell she wanted a life of her own, first chance she got."

"Hmm. Maybe. So you're certain she never contacted you? Letters, phone calls? Visits?"

"She was, and I'm sure still is, a very forceful and determined woman, Mr. Hardison. When she made up her mind to a thing, she saw to it that it happened. No, giving in to any desire to contact me would be the last thing she'd do. Do you know *anything* about the woman you're hunting?"

"We know enough to keep her as our prime suspect in at least

Montogomery Mabry's murder. That's enough for me."

"Even though Sheriff Hal Burgess was certain he was killed with a clean shot to the head at a great distance with a high-powered rifle, and that everyone who knew her told him she'd never owned a gun, couldn't have afforded such a rifle, or knew how to use it? Pretty thin, wouldn't you agree?"

"She could easily have hired an assassin. She had motive and opportunity."

"With what? We were worse than broke. And where does a poverty-stricken woman find a hired gun in back-of-the-boonies Arkansas?"

"Well, not to insult her memory, but a good-looking woman could've found a man to do it for her, for certain…favors."

"Not her, and that *is* insulting. Again, everybody, including me, knew she'd run off men, vowed to stay single until she could build herself a real life. Those five years we lived in that house, I knew where she was every single day: working hard to survive, keep us fed, clothed. No man anywhere except that pervert Barry Mabry, who attacked her, which I'm sure you also know about."

"Which makes her a suspect in his killing, too."

"Hey, everybody agreed that my uncle Charlie Millard was Barry's killer since he ran off. And when he was shot by the old man, that closed that case, Sheriff Burgess told us."

"This isn't getting us anywhere close to Andrea Millard's whereabouts. I don't think you're being honest with me, Mr. Prescott." The man's eyes were hard: no more Mr. Nice Guy.

"You can think whatever you want to, sir. I don't know where my aunt is, so I can't tell you. *Hey, she could be at the grocery store, dry cleaners. I dunno, do I?*

"Can't or won't?"

"Can't. If you can find her, assuming she's still alive somewhere, go to it. I hope she's got that life, and I can't help you locate her and tear that life apart. And this conversation is over, as of right now. Goodbye, Mr. Hardison."

"We're not through here, Prescott. You're a suspect, too, you know..."

"No, I'm not, and that's a cheap threat. You've already questioned me, I've answered your questions, and that's that. If there's anything I can really help you with, I'd be glad to do it in the interests of justice. But where my aunt is, after fifteen years, I just don't know." *Okay, outright lie. But as Granpa said, I've gotta protect the famil, above all else.*

"You'll hear from us again."

* * *

From then on, Nate and Audrey just assumed they were being watched, that their telephone was tapped, and that any slip would lead the authorities to Andy. It was a strain, and they planned to go ahead with relocating as soon as possible. Of course, it was obvious they couldn't do this without Hardison knowing about it if he *were* tracking Nate, but as long as they didn't contact Andy, it shouldn't matter.

For her part, Nate's aunt, despite her assurances to him, felt the jaws of the law again beginning to close down on her. Except for that encounter with Christine Mabry those years ago, she'd grown certain she couldn't be found.

She'd never know how close that sighting had come to her capture. But now she began to see discovery as a possibility since the case was still open. *But I can't let this ruin the life I've built. Just have to be careful, stay away from Nate and Audrey till they move, then there'll be no reason for anyone to search for me here.*

That'd have to do. Of course she'd miss her only family until she, too, could round off her career and surely retire to Virginia eventually. Meanwhile, she doubted that visits to them from the head of a Memphis design firm would be suspect.

No, not to trouble trouble till trouble troubled her, she decided, another of old Elijah's remembered credos. She loved this place, loved her work, and until or if a man came into her life, she'd go on with it. Let the bloodhounds of the law sniff around wherever they wanted; she'd forget them entirely.

If it could just be that easy.

* * *

Howard Hardison was not to be dismissed so readily. He suspected strongly that Nate Prescott was lying to him about Andy's whereabouts, and he was determined to stalk the man till he found her. Unfortunately, it turned out that state police headquarters did not agree with him that a fifteen-year-old case was that pressing, with all the recent crimes requiring solution. But of course, he was told, if he wanted to pursue the Millard/Mabry matter, he could do it on his own time.

He pondered this. The feeling had grown in him that he was close to finding the probable killer, bringing her to trial. But do it on his own, with no expense account, no car, no support? Another thing entirely.

Hardison was sixty-three, overweight, with high blood pressure, an ulcer that felt like a brick being continually torn out of his stomach. With just two years to go till retirement, his wife, Millie, had begged him to slow down, coast the rest of the way, be able to enjoy hard-earned years together. Certainly not knock himself out over a case from the '50s that everyone else had given up on. She'd tried to enlist their daughter Kathleen, a nurse, to convince him he would drive himself into an early grave, working the way he did.

"It's what he's all about, Mom," she'd shrugged. "You and I both know he'd be miserable sitting at home."

"He's driving me crazy, bringing it all here, pouring all the gruesome details all over me. And now he's tearing around, hot on the trail of a suspect from when you were a kid, just because the woman's nephew shows up. I guess he wants to wrap this one up as his grand finale or something."

"What kinda case is it? Big one?"

"Oh, some lawyer got shot up in Everett County after killing another guy he was sure had murdered his son. Sort of a feud, and it was all over the news for a long time. Howard was called in by the locals up there, worked hard on the case back when it was hot. Never found the top suspect, woman who was the brother of the one the lawyer shot. Messy, and there was a lot of prior stuff mixed in with it.

"Anyway, the woman and her teenage nephew disappeared, and Howard's sure the nephew knows where she is. He's gone to Memphis, grilled him, but it's a dead end."

"And of course, he thinks the nephew really does know and won't tell…" Kathleen was well aware of her father's bulldog approach to his work: never gave up, and to be fair, had solved more than his share of hard cases.

The detective himself was nearing a practical conclusion. He'd just had an ulcer attack, one of those nasty ones that had him vomiting blood. *Damn, maybe they're right: gotta get away from this tension.* And he wasn't blind (yet) and did realize he couldn't drive himself to a coronary over this Millard thing. He wanted to be able to play with Kathleen's kids, after all, spend some quality time with Millie, maybe take a few of those trips they'd always talked about.

And he knew mounting the kind of necessary search in Memphis for Andy Millard, surely with another name now, would be hard: big city, with thousands of places the woman could hide. And now, having been warned, Prescott would make sure to stay away from her, cut any connection, protect her. Even manage to send her away into deeper hiding.

That is, if he really knew where she was.

But of course he did.

It was in this undecided frame of mind Hardison received a call from Everett County Sheriff Cale Wilcox. Surprised, he'd thought the man had dismissed the whole Millard/Prescott case.

"Wilcox. What's going on, man? Got something for me?"

"Not exactly, sir. But you got me thinking, with the Prescott boy showing up. I've been going over the old files, and you may be onto something here. With the firepower you've got there, maybe we should team up, go after this some. I forgot to mention that a woman here reported seeing what could have been our suspect, some time back in

Springfield. Bad timing for me: up to my ass in alligators, and she wasn't really that sure. I turned it over the the boys up there."

"Springfield. I found out that Prescott worked for an engineering outfit there before Memphis. How long ago was this?"

"Oh, maybe nine, ten years. Woman was Christine Mabry, daughter-in-law of the lawyer, who I guess shoulda recognized Andy Millard if anybody could. Said she was disguised, though."

"Could I talk to her?"

"Married some guy, sold out and went to Texas, I think, not long after that. Dunno where…oh, his name was Blake Walker, if that helps."

"Long shot. But I'm glad you called, Wilcox: been thinking this over, and it looks like it'll be a big deal, whether the woman's in Memphis, or maybe even there in Springfield. And I gotta tell you, headquarters here won't commit to this cold a case, won't even support me if I go after it. Now, the wife's been after me, doctor too, to slow down. Only got a couple years to go till I hang it up, anyway.

"What would you say to you and me working together on this? It'd be on my own, and you'd be in charge…"

"Hadn't thought of that. Out of my jurisdiction, of course, unless we could get the Memphis or Springfield guys on it, too. Let me think about it."

"Well, another thought. Maybe I should just give you everything I've got, let you take it on. I may hafta go into the hospital for awhile with this damn ulcer, and you're a lot younger'n me. And it did start out as your case, y'know."

This was exactly what Cale Wilcox had been hoping for. He'd thought he needed Hardison on this, but if the detective couldn't offer any state assistance, that wouldn't help, and it'd mean he'd have complete control. And yeah, he'd been thinking more about the Memphis connection: Nate Prescott had gone to Memphis from Springfield, so why not Andy, too?

"Okay, maybe. I've probably got everything you have, but send me whatever you could get outta Nate, and yeah, I'll see if I can work this in. Oh, how hard d'you think it'd be to get his phone records, numbers he's called? Say, for the last year."

"That was gonna be my next step. I can get my bosses to okay that, I think, get the Memphis boys' cooperation on it. Sure, get that to you soon's I can."

"Thanks. We just might be able to wrap this, fifteen years after the fact."

* * *

Eventually Nate and Audrey sold their house at a decent profit, left their jobs, bade Andy goodbye through a note left with their mutual pastor, leaving as little a trail as possible. They moved east to a piece of land a realtor had found them a few miles northwest of Charlottesville. The Blue Ridge was beyond, and a clear stream wound among towering white pines and poplars.

They rented a cottage while Nate began building the first part of their house, largely from recycled materials he got free from dismantling old structures. It was the first time he'd been able to work with the old-growth heartpine he was to grow to love.

They still had the Studebaker, and Nate's one real extravagance, an early Jaguar sedan he'd bought in pieces at a Memphis garage. Andy had urged him to grab this, knowing it would be a good restoration project for him and would grow more valuable as the years passed. "If you don't buy it, I will," she'd challenged.

This car, now restored, might have to go, he realized, if their savings got low. He really had no idea how long it'd be till they had an income again. Audrey was sure God would provide, as old Elijah had always believed. And sure enough, as it turned out, they were able to keep the Jaguar.

He learned quickly that the preferred woods used early on here were that heartpine and chestnut, now available only by recycling. The pine was mostly heartwood, beautiful and rot-resistant, some wood showing several hundred years' growth rings. The chestnut, now extinct, was a fast-growing softer wood of bold grain that was all heartwood, and it didn't rot easily, either. By now there was a thriving business in resawing old pine beams into flooring and chestnut cabin logs into wood for furniture and paneling.

First on their list of necessities was a pickup truck, which would be a veritable workhorse for hauling everything from gravel and sand for concrete foundation work to roofing material. Again, Andy's shared knowledge helped Nate find one several years old that had been kept up well by its retired owner. It was a classic '53 Studebaker, which he knew would be worth more as time passed and it became rarer.

He put together a ladder rack for the truck to carry long lengths, and of course, ladders. A hitch allowed him to pull a trailer, which he constructed from junkyard parts, much as he had with his grandfather when a teenager.

Counting their dollars, the couple often worked together tearing down old barns, sheds, even dilapidated houses for this prime wood. Nate acquired secondhand machinery: table saw, planer, jointer, bandsaw, and a good new hand circular saw and drill to begin with.

The older structures were either rough-sawn, or in some, timber framing of handhewn beams, mortised and pegged together, and could be reused or cut into boards. He made friends with a local sawmiller for this, who was also a mechanical genius at keeping small engines, like his necessary chainsaw, running.

He built an open shed for storing this material, on racks out of the weather, until he figured he could start on the real construction. First he acquainted himself with the applicable building codes in this civilized region, most of which were just commonsense. Then he set to work in earnest, determined to have the structure, or at least the first part of it, habitable in six months. That was about as long as they could go with no outside income.

The design they agreed on was a traditional two-story, the core of which would be of hewn logs from two cabins they'd bought cheap and dismantled. This would be added to as they could afford it, with a recycled timberframe. Further additions could follow, as their planned family required the space.

Speaking of which, Audrey informed her man not that long after the move that they could expect a child maybe two months after the target date for the finished first section. Nate was overjoyed, and also realized that he had to finish before then—no leisurely pace for him.

He'd always dug ditches by hand, but figured a day's backhoe rental would get them farther quicker, to go the depth below frostline here for their foundation, which was 18 inches. This done, he got the required inspection, then ordered pre-mixed concrete for the footings and the foundation itself. He planned to cover this visible concrete with stonework later, so built up forms of castoff boards. He'd done this at the college often, and by scheduling these subcontractors, was able to begin the log section soon, which began to resemble a house after the first few days of log-raising.

He'd read in a crafts book how to construct a three-legged lifting device using a boat-trailer winch and pulley to lift the heavy logs from inside on the subfloor. With Audrey maneuvering the logs into place by a guide rope from a safe distance, he was able to place them back in their original order. The few that were decayed, he'd found replacements for in a tumbledown barn, free of charge for removal.

Nate loved this work. He wished he could just go on forever, building and/or restoring historic houses, and never have to go back inside an engineering office. Which became more of a plan as the work proceeded.

Even though their house was back in the forest, they soon discovered that people who'd heard of this unique project would drive in to watch the progress, offer to help, ask about the whole process. And while they didn't want to waste time humoring these visitors, both realized that this curiosity could lead to future jobs of this type.

At one point, the local alternative newspaper in Charlottesville sent a reporter/photographer out to interview Nate about this recycled structure. There was a renewed interest in log cabins now in the early Seventies, and anyone who restored or rebuilt one was of interest to readers.

And viewers. The local television station eventually sent a crew out to record the project, which by then was under roof. Nate and Audrey obliged, explaining, answering questions, some of which were almost ridiculous (Are the logs heavy? Believe it. How does a woman do this work? Same as a man.)

And sure enough, before they met their self-imposed deadline, an older woman who'd seen the work asked Nate if he could restore a slave cabin on the remains of the plantation she lived on for a rental house. A visit showed a one-room structure with a loft that probably housed an entire pre-Civil War family, now rundown, but not beyond hope.

Based on his own time-and-materials experience with their house, he and Audrey figured a 20 percent profit as a cost-plus estimate. She'd cautioned him against assuming that the visible decay was all there was, so insisted on this formula, to be added to if/when more work became necessary. And she also urged an additional 20 percent, just in case they'd figured low.

Nate had heard of that before, back in Ridgeway. In fact, it had been the old blacksmith Silas Greene who'd told him confidentially that he often added that 20 percent for wealthy customers. "Not fer you'ns really needs m'work, though." Nate had asked him what that added percent was for.

"I call it my *jfthoi*," he'd gleefully explained.

"That doesn't spell anything. What's it mean?"

"Jist fer th' hell of it," the smith had cackled.

"From what I've heard," Audrey now told him, "when you're self-employed, you have to be sure to pay yourself first. I know of small business owners who figure the costs and then just hope there's enough left over to pay themselves. Some of the builders' wives I've talked with say that's pretty much standard. We can't afford to do that."

And as it turned out, there wasn't much hidden damage on this job, but the owner kept adding extras to the contract. Audrey saw to it that they figured these additional costs into change orders, along with their estimated costs, which the owner had to sign ahead of time.

"That way, there won't be any of what they call sticker-shock," she told the woman. "You'll get just what you pay for, and you'll know what to expect." Nate was sure his bride was exaggerating, but no, her cautionary measures let them make that profit. He was newly appreciative of her common sense.

Audrey also figured that as Nate and his growing crew got more experience, they could estimate closer and even be able to give flat costs, guaranteed.

"People want to know just how much a job is going to cost, no surprises. So if we figure close, and add the blacksmith's *jfthoi*, we can do that when necessary to get the job. Of course then, we'll have to be sure to come in under, or we lose. If we're efficient, we get to keep whatever's left over after our costs, overhead, and profit. But let's not try that right at first: I'm thinking get good first, then get fast, then get rich." She grinned, poked her man in the ribs.

He was continually proud of this woman he'd chosen—who'd chosen him—and her good business head. He often shuddered to think he might've linked up with a backwoods hill girl, who'd have been totally intimidated at the prospect of starting a new business like this. Maybe that wasn't exactly fair since sharp women were everywhere, but like most people, he was prone to stereotyping. Notwithstanding the example of his own aunt.

Additional hands had been needed for this contract job, and Audrey screened the applicants. Nate had learned that carpenters are itinerant, drifting from job to job, and he wanted dependability as his top priority. To get that, he offered two dollars an hour above what he'd determined most contractors paid. He left the actual hiring up to his wife, whose shrewd judgment proved sound.

"If one out of three of these guys works out, we're ahead of the game," she told Nate. "I've talked to other builders' wives who tell me they don't get that many good people. I'm insisting on the best out there. We may not be able to work as cheaply per hour as others, but if we're fast and good, the customer saves using us."

Sounded right to Nate. He'd rather be cutting mortises or dovetail joints than managing, but some supervision was necessary. Not every carpenter could make the switch from two-by-fours to logwork, or work with the often-out-of-plumb walls, but that's what people wanted, were willing to pay for. Character, it was now called, although in Nate's youth, it'd been called sloppy building.

And with that prevalent mindset, he'd seen many log cabins back in Arkansas bulldozed to make room for modern, one-story brick ranches, the owners of the land glad to be rid of those "old shacks." So those relics were still disappearing, despite what they'd been: solid shelter, the results of sweat and skill and working with what you had. A pioneer legacy, and one he aimed to preserve.

But here in 1970s Virginia, these remaining were now being sought after, and their prices going up rapidly. A cabin he got free, or for two to six hundred dollars, would in ten years cost well over ten times that as the demand grew. And that demand would, as newly affluent seekers of Americana in their houses were able to pay. He was glad to get in on the beginnings of this phase of the restoration movement. Now, if he could just make a living at it...

Chapter Twenty-Three

"I've gotta go to Memphis," Cale Wilcox told his wife Gracie. "That old case about the Mabry killing: state detective's back on it, or still on it, and they've got me roped in, too. Wanta go with me? Could be a coupla days?"

"Oh, I can't get off work, Cale. Durn, it would be nice, goin' to th' big town an' all, but you'll be workin' all th' time of course, so no... Oh, I might could get Jessie May to let me switch off, but I'd be lost by m'self that way. C'n we go on a weekend, maybe?"

"No, hafta be able to find people during working hours, connect with other lawmen. It's all a hassle, this long after it all happened, but it's my job, I guess." He hadn't really wanted her to come along with all he had to do, but they did try to do things together, even little ones.

So with Nate Prescott's telephone records in hand, the sheriff drove down out of the mountains, across the river into Memphis. He rented a motel room and set about marking any calls that could possibly be to Andy. It'd be a huge job, even just this last year, with Nate and his wife no doubt calling friends, coworkers, all the people average Americans talk to in fifty-two weeks.

He used a code mark for repeat calls, any showing up between every week and every month. He figured that should be about as often as he'd check in with his aunt. Of course, she'd call, too, probably more than he would. Wilcox remembered how unselfishly Andy had denied herself to raise the boy.

Fortified with coffee, the sheriff first scanned the entire list for repeats that fit his criteria. That took hours. Then he noted the first three digits, knowing the telephone company allocated these to certain areas in and around cities. He'd have to get these locations from the company itself but had checked in with the police here and been assured they'd cooperate in this, a murder investigation. He also knew not to ask too much.

Then it occurred to Wilcox that he could just check his scaled-down list against the phone book itself, with its names and addresses. Of course, that'd mean going down every page of the voluminous book looking for matches: too big a job. *Okay then, back to the first plan: hit the company with what I've got.*

What he had was a relatively short list of numbers in each of several prefixes. Surprisingly short. So he expanded the time frequencies by 50 percent and went back over them. This actually didn't increase the number of prospects by much. He felt that Andy Millard's telephone number was somewhere in there, and the certainty grew inside him that he'd find her, if indeed he could get the company to give him those names, addresses.

Then it'd be a matter of calling the female names, even those with just initials for first names, since it was common for single women to list their phones that way. He'd never even considered that Andy would keep her real name but knew that people often kept some part of their original names in the assumed ones. Either out of simplicity in remembering them, a necessity until getting used to the new one, or out of some need to anchor their new identities to the old ones.

So, any derivative of Andrea, or Millard, or even Prescott? Probably not that one, since it'd never been her surname. Henry, then? Although she'd certainly have no fond memories of slippery Cam. Maybe Miller then. Or Anna, Agnes, or… *Can't remember her middle name, but it'll be in the old files.* He finally decided to go for matching initials first then when he got that far: any *A-M*s.

If anybody'd asked him why he was so intent on finding Andy, going so far beyond the normal search and this long after the fact, Wilcox couldn't have given a convincing answer. Well, there was Hardison's fixation, but that was out of the picture, now. Just doing the hard digging that went with police work, he guessed. *It's what I do. Here in th' other man's town, but th' case was and is on my turf, so I gotta give it this last try.*

* * *

Andy had regretted Nate and Audrey's leaving Memphis but wisely had realized that this new life belonged to them, not her, and although they'd have no family or friends in Virginia at first, she'd be able to visit, and they'd come back periodically. Besides, her workload was increasing, she was having to hire more design people, and with this established following, she knew she should stay where she was.

It was 800 miles to their new place, which wasn't insurmountable. A day and a half by car, or even less with the new interstates, could be managed whenever she or they could get away. She was at first concerned about Nate's finding a good job there in the crowded East where the competition was surely greater. But she had faith in her nephew and now also sent her prayers with him and Audrey.

For the first time in years really, with her only connection gone, Andy felt free of the cloud of violence, the feud between the Mabrys and her people back in Arkansas. And despite that bit about the Arkansas detective questioning Nate, she didn't really feel hunted any longer. She often speculated about what her chances would have been if she'd allowed herself to be arrested as the most likely suspect in Montgomery Mabry's shooting. There'd been no evidence against her whatever, but she knew the prejudice against her (divorced woman, funny-turned, too independent for her own good, sure capable of anything, grudge against all th' Mabrys) would have doomed her.

She thought back to Hal Burgess and his lone belief in her. She suspected his crush on her back then, which wouldn't have helped at all. *Good man really, but no, it'd never have worked out.* And she'd have lost him too soon, anyway.

She also remembered the dedicated missionary Reggie Cabot, disappeared in the African jungle, with a shudder. Whatever had happened to him? Killed by natives, like those in South America?

Felled by disease? Maybe met another missionary woman there and living happily in their version of unselfish paradise? She liked that scenario better and wished them well.

A small chapter of her life, closed now.

And what of the future? She was still just over forty, surely past childbearing age, and that hadn't been a priority. But what could lie ahead now? Not another impossible relationship that'd demand she give up her own identity, complete some man who'd probably not be able to stand on his own. No, she wouldn't play mother to anyone. Although she had done just that for Nate. And she was more convinced than ever it had been worth every moment of it.

In her role of successful business executive, Andy had even decided to stop torturing her hair and had let it grow. She'd been surprised to discover it had grayed, and when the dye was completely gone, she looked entirely different. *Well, it's still a disguis, then.* Probably hadn't been that necessary after just the first few years, she mused.

But right now she had to put together this proposal for the college conference center design. And she had to make time to work more closely with that new graduate from Virginia Tech, the girl with the fresh ideas who'd been among the first to break into the all-male design field.

And there was that conference with the telephone company executives, where there'd be competition from New York and Chicago firms. Multiple regional center designs, a lot on the table. They'd have their big guns present, of course, ready to squash this upstart Memphis woman with their cosmopolitan creativity. Well, she could hold her own with the best of them: had proven that again and again.

Bring it on, people. I may lose, but it'll be after the fight. And I'll bloody some noses before it's all over.

And maybe by week-after-next's end, she could shift things around to plan to take a few days off to go see Nate and Audrey in their new home. Surprise them with her new look.

* * *

The children began to arrive. First Andrea, a dark-haired little thing with her mother's green eyes, named, of course, after Nate's aunt. This child taught both her parents the art of coping with sleepless nights, feedings every two hours, and had a tendency to stay up late.

Audrey had the first-time mother's anxiety about her baby that had her starting wide awake at the slightest sound from the crib in their bedroom. She nursed the child at those bi-hourly awakenings and had trouble going back to sleep. The other mothers she knew advised her to let the baby cry a little, hoping she'd settle down. Audrey couldn't bring herself to do that.

So after many months of this, one night Nate put his arm across his wife's body firmly at the first whimper. Audrey looked a question at him in the dim nightlight glow. He shook his head.

And Andrea went back to sleep for four more hours.

They took turns at tending to her whenever Nate could be there. He and she waked up early, and he'd let Audrey sleep while he took his daughter quietly away, bathed and changed her, and the two made breakfast. That first winter they'd eat at the raised hearth of the fireplace Nate had built, the child watching the sparks and the flames, entranced.

When it was time for him to leave for work, he'd waken Audrey who, grateful for the needed sleep, would take over. Of course, the little girl became the center of their lives, a radical change from all they'd known. She was outgoing, laughed a lot, was curious about everything, but didn't want to go to sleep at any reasonable hour.

Nate would walk the floor with Andrea for what seemed like hours to get her to drop off, and after a day's work, this became a strain. This child just wasn't interested in missing out on a thing and would fight to stay awake as long as she could. Finally, they let her stay up until their own bedtime, when she'd close her eyes from sheer exhaustion. Both were sure they were doing exactly the opposite of what was recommended. By this time, neither cared.

But the early morning awakenings ceased, and Audrey and her

daughter got onto the same timetable. So after a few months, the Prescott home routine seemed salvageable. And Nate's business grew, which soon meant he kept more or less regular hours.

Then after two years, Eli made his appearance, bald as a marble, with his father's blue eyes and a voice that seemed to shake the house. But he slept well, ate well, was miles easier to deal with. And his big sister adored him. For some reason, there was none of that resentment first children have for the next baby. From the beginning, Andrea and Eli were inseparable, and this would continue until college.

Next was Barbara, named after Audrey's deceased mother, who looked like neither of her parents. Her own little person, Aunt Andy declared, seeing her for the first time on a flying trip to Virginia. Barbara, as the youngest, got perhaps more attention than she should have but wasn't overly spoiled. With no other kin close, she and the others weren't bombarded with toys and too many clothes they'd grow out of rapidly.

Which was not to say that Aunt Andy didn't do just that on visits, and grandfather Krauss was guilty of that as well. But all three children preferred the simple wooden toys their father carved for them: toy trucks, tractors, dolls, little kitchen things. The contraptions that lighted up and shone in plastic were pushed aside in favor of Dad's gifts, which gave him the big head, Andy often told him.

As the children grew, Nate would often take one of them onto his construction jobs. He'd bought a classic Series Land Rover station wagon, into which would fit a crib. First Andrea, then later Eli or Barbara would go with him on nice days to play in the crib, watch through the vehicle's windows whatever Dad was doing with those other men.

Of course, each got bored, and Nate would take him/her out, carry the child around, show things of interest. All three got initiated into construction work from an early age. Naptime was sometimes a problem, but he discovered he could drive the Rover around for a few minutes, and the rocking motion would put the current little one to sleep. And he usually planned these as short days for him, being able to leave some of the work to the crew.

That none of the children— with the exposure he gave them to this work and the actual time they spent working with him as they reached teenage—wanted to take over the business disappointed him somewhat. Audrey pointed out that the kids had to live their own lives, just as she and Nate had, *so don't mope, Dad.*

* * *

Cale Wilcox was reelected to the sheriff's job in Everett County for many more years. And then somehow his children were suddenly grown, he and Gracie gray-haired, and then there were just the two of them again. He'd prided himself on picking up where Hal Burgess had left off, trying his best to be fair, using his judgment instead of being pushed by the lawyers, DAs, the political pressure that always went with elected positions.

Cale had regrets: miscarriages of justice he'd been powerless to correct, complaints by battered wives he couldn't right, downright corruption he couldn't expose. Over time, he realized all this was part of the job; he just had to swallow some of it, do his best each time, try to stay sane, inject all the integrity he could into his office.

As he grew older, he harbored one situation he still wished could have worked out differently. He could at any time recall Andy Millard's face, hear her voice, imagine how life could have been different with her. *If only I'd pushed back at the beginning, made sure she saw me there among all the others. Back in school, before she met that fool Cam Henry. Or later, after she'd run him off, maybe…but no, that was after I'd married Gracie. Or maybe I could've left Gracie, and Andy and I could've just run off somewhere…*

No, my wife's been good to me, good to the kids. This's the best it could have worked out, I guess. And yes, all that hell Andy had to go through, it did get taken care of, most of it.

Yes, it most certainly did.

Cale Wilcox's smile was grim, even as he remembered that day in Memphis, and the promise he'd made. But there'd been so much more to it all.

Buried.

* * *

Christine Mabry Walker finally met another man who seemed sincere in his attentions toward her. He, too, knew how to make his moves slowly, respectfully. And he knew how to thrill a woman.

They'd met at a bar, a place she couldn't help going, even knowing how much the little money she made needed to go for important things for her and Giles. *But dammit, I've just got to have a little time for me, a little relief from the grind. Couple drinks won't break us: just gotta watch it close. Can't let myself become a hopeless drunk here.*

Ben Courtney was also divorced. Twice, it turned out. But he insisted he'd learned to appreciate a good woman and just knew Christine was that woman. She recognized this as just another line, but with nobody else on the horizon, she figured she needed the company, if nothing else.

That they both drank too much didn't appear to be a problem for her if maybe they *could* team up, have two incomes. Ben had a decent job with a public relations firm, and managed to show up each morning seemingly sober and ready for work. He was good at acting and had that touch of charisma necessary for such a job.

"It's basically making people happy with our company, I guess you'd say," he explained to Christine. "The sales guys bring in the bucks, but we can't afford a bad image. Come across as an outfit that cares, that gives a fair deal to its customers, and you've got 'em in your pocket."

She didn't care much what he did for a living as long as he brought home a paycheck. That he had to set some of it aside for one set of child-support payments presented something of a problem, but he assured her the kids would soon be grown, and that would stop.

"I think we're meant for each other, Christine baby," he almost slurred. She rolled her eyes but happened to catch sight of herself in the mirror over the bar. What she saw wasn't the Christine she knew any more. No, this woman had lines in her face, a certain haggardness, too much makeup. This wasn't by any means their first date, and she wondered fleetingly what Ben saw in her.

So okay, maybe I better grab this. While I can still grab at all. Yeah, it probably doesn't get any better at my age. But handle it right this time, the way I used to, before I managed to blow it all over that other fool.

They married. Giles came to the wedding with misgivings. He loved his mother but had seen her start to crumble and had watched in frustration early on, knowing he couldn't help. Yet. *But if you'd just hold on a little longer, Mom, you and I could still have a decent life. I could...* But he knew, even after he'd found a good job, he couldn't orchestrate his mother's life: she had to be in control, or as much as she still could manage.

Her drinking worried him most. He was aware that it was a symptom of her depression, her not being able to cope with what life had thrown at her. But he saw even young people all around him falling into that pattern, that addictive state, accompanied by denial that led to ruin.

And he saw that Ben Courtney was a drunk, no matter his seemingly being in control, his outward façade. He suspected his mother saw that, too, but was ready to take the chance on the man. And well, if it didn't work out, he'd just have to step in and pick up the pieces. Which he could surely do, now that he'd earned that magic degree and was using it.

Giles had spent some off-time investigating potential employment while in college. He was majoring in electrical engineering, which at that time was where the action was. These new computers promised a limitless future in which all the math he'd studied would be valuable. And there were the electric power companies, those firms his stepfather had worked in. Electricity was vital now, not just a convenience as it had been earlier, when country people just wanted a few lights, refrigerators, the first televisions.

And ironically, it was that same ex-stepfather (since he now had another one) who'd kept in touch with him, even sending him a few dollars on occasion, who made a contact for him there in Dallas. It seemed that even a failure had connections. And while Giles hadn't wanted to continue any closeness with Blake Walker, he was smart enough not to let this stand in his way.

He'd interviewed as a rising senior. There and at other potential companies. Recruitment was the order of the day, and representatives from promising firms visited his campus regularly now, eager for the best and brightest of the ambitious soon-to-be graduates.

But it was to prove his best choice to follow up on Walker's contact. Several of the companies that interviewed him were in Chicago, even New York. These people evidently kept their eyes on college classes across the country, always seeking new blood, no matter where it came from. But he'd eventually chosen to stay in Dallas, at least near his disintegrating mother.

* * *

The long-ago murderer often thought back to the necessities of the Mabry killings. The bottom line had simply been*: this must be done.* Wrongs had been perpetrated and would be again if these men had been allowed to live. That none of the lawmen had ever been able to find any clues or get on the trail of the killer was still a source of pride to this assassin. It had been too cleverly executed (good word), too well thought out, with too little left to chance. *Nothing left to chance, actually, not even the possibility of a missed shot on old Mabry. No, becoming in essence an expert sniper ruled that out.*

And before that, the seeming long shot of leading Barry Mabry to that death-pit was really not that much of a chance thing. Sure, he might *possibly* have spotted the trap, but he'd have been a dead man anyway. Because yes, the killer had been hidden nearby in the ruins of the old settler's cabin as backup, with a shotgun loaded with buckshot, deadly at that close range. Of course, it wouldn't have qualified as a possible accident that way, which had at the time seemed essential to the plan.

So, looking back, so much had changed, just in these few short years. The Mabrys dead, Charlie Millard dead, the sheriff dead, old

Elijah Prescott dead. New people on the Mabry place…all changed, including the lives of all who'd survived. And all of it now just a memory, and one that didn't matter any more, really.

But it wasn't just that it seemed like a good idea at the time: it really was *a good idea—the only good one—at the time.*

* * *

Andy Millard, too, often thought back those many years on those hard times with so little money, so little comfort, and on top of it, violence, gossip, prejudice, death. Now she could go anywhere she chose, if she'd just taken the time away from her career. Do anything anybody else could. She was educated, experienced: she'd proven she could compete anywhere, against anyone, be it in a small town or in a place like maybe even Paris, if she'd wanted. And now even that was behind her, in retirement.

Nothing intimidated her now and wouldn't have if she'd kept on working. She guessed she'd developed that self-assurance early on, really. Since her foolhardy alliance with Cam Henry, Andy Millard had never acted, or even felt, inferior. *I'm as good as the best, and I always was, despite all the cards stacked against me. And I not only pulled myself up by my bootstraps, I raised a fine man who made it out there in this hard world, a success in every way.*

But of course, the regrets were still there. First, there'd been her distancing herself from that good young man Cale Wilcox, her seeming to ignore him back in high school when he'd obviously been above the crowd. Went on to be a good husband, father, lawman. *What'd it have been like, marrying him instead of that bastard Cam? I'd have been stuck in Ridgeway, of course, but without the reputation I got. And logically, even if we'd taken Nate in, I probably wouldn't have gone to college.*

Or maybe I would've. Cale was really educating himself, reading a lot, trying to catch my attention; he would've supported me, I'm sure. But fool that I was, I let that liar, that slimeball, steal my youth. Well, nobody to blame but myself for that one. And really, it probably turned out for the best.

Except for the violence, the killing. But looking back on it, it was really necessary in the overall scheme of things. It escalated, all of it, from that stupid timber cutting. But I guess I needed that assault, that near-rape, to make it clear what had to happen. Poor Charlie, I know without doubt he didn't kill anyone—couldn't kill—even knowing it would have been justified. But what if he'd lived? Would he be an aging drunk, still leeching off me or Nate now?

It just got so out of hand, and so quickly. Cause and effect, a snowballing, out-of-control madness that engulfed us all. And the survivors: still victims, all of us, no matter the end results. The scars have remained, will remain. And the hidden facts will continue to burn inside.

Nate wants to bury it all, forget it. Put it away and never touch it again. He doesn't really want to hear what Giles Mabry has to say, if anything: it'll just open it all up again, and he—we—don't need that now. It's long over, long buried, long a closed, multilayered case. So maybe yes, Nate's way is the right way. He can shove it aside now, let it die. He can, unlike all the rest of us.

Most of all, unlike me.

* * *

It had been a typical Memphis day for Andy, a chaos of hurried meetings, designs half-finished, deadlines, huddling with her staff over whether this or that commission could be salvaged. *Of course it can: just have to work harder on it, put more into it.* So, at approaching dark, she'd driven her '66 Ford Mustang to her semi-elegant house toward Germantown, east of the city proper. A good, long soak in the tub would slide the cares and tension of the day off, then a leisurely glass of wine, some decent food…

The doorbell rang. *No, no, office hours over. Go away, whoever you are.* But it could be important: some client invading her privacy with a problem, and you didn't ignore those. She opened the door.

"Hello, Andy." Cale Wilcox stood there, and her life collapsed upon her.

* * *

Giles Mabry had misgivings also about bringing up the details as he knew them of what had become in his mind the Millard/Mabry feud. He speculated on what Nate Prescott might actually know of the facts. Surely the man had gone over it all many times, just as he himself had, trying to make sense of it.

A feud, that's what he'd called it back when he was a child. He'd been scarred by losing first his father, then later his grandfather.

And the fragments of events he'd heard, the absolute condemnation of Charlie Millard as a murderer and a thief and a worthless drunk. The towering anger of his grandfather, the shock to his mother, the dizzying pile of events mounting, smothering, whirling. All these bits had only added to his confusion, his uncertaintly of what was real. *Yes, I guess* scarred *is the best definition of what all that left me with. And of course, I wasn't the only one. The innocent ones were stained. The guilty weren't punished. Or maybe some of them were, actually. But so much was left hidden to fester, corrode.*

He shook his head. So long ago, all of it. Was he doing the right thing, tearing it open again for Prescott? Probably not, he realized, but well, he'd wrestled with this dilemma long enough, and with the years now running out for all of them, he knew this chance to have it all out, thrash it over, pick each other's brains must be taken. No, in the end he'd go ahead, and just let the proverbial chips fall where they might.

Giles Mabry had prospered at the Dallas power company job. He'd been able to set his mother up in a decent little house after her ill-fated hiatus with Ben Courtney wore itself out. Much good that had done. He hadn't moved back in with her because he realized he had to make a life for himself. She could never see that and lamented his absence constantly.

But Giles had met Celine not long after taking the position with his company. Celine was a Texas beauty, off a cattle ranch farther west, come to the city to make her mark. She was pursued by every eligible male in Dallas, it seemed, and a lot of those who weren't. She could have had her pick of Texas oil, Texas cattle, Texas finance, any Texas industry, or even some huge inheritance via whichever suitor had this to offer.

She could become a trophy wife, to be displayed all over the globe, an ornament for other men to salivate over, try to seduce, maybe kill for. Celine Abbot had been in the supremely coveted position of having her absolute choice of a Greek god mate, a gilded future, anything her big Texas heart desired.

But she chose young Giles Mabry as her soulmate to the wonderment of her world. What had she seen in him? Unglamorous job with a power company, ordinary looking, nothing special about him, and most of all, no fortune? Was this woman out of her incredibly beautiful head?

In fact, Celine Abbot had grown deadly tired of being fawned over, pursued, and of the blandishments of aging rich men, the big-buckle Texans who wanted to add her as a notch to their guns (double entendre intended). After their chance meeting at, of all things, a back-country rodeo, she realized that this earnest young man was just what he appeared to be: a hard-working, artless, honest human being. A breath of fresh air.

Celine had been raised on that ranch and could ride anything with four feet. She'd been a tomboy, and early on had seen the panting boys who gathered around her as plain silly, much less intelligent than she, and poorer riders. Her family wasn't exactly rich but not poor either. Her mother had connections to Dallas society, which she'd hardly taken advantage of herself, but kept for her daughter.

So the girl stormed that bastion of semi-bluebloods and fortunes without even trying. College was four years of football games, to-die-for vacations wherever her admirers vied for inviting her. She studied hard, partied hard, had fun at school and wherever she went. Through it all, though, she remained at heart a country girl who loved horses and anything outdoors.

Celine and a girlfriend named Sandy were at the rodeo without escorts, their current significant others not being into the dust, violence, tension, and broken bones of the sport. It also happened that Celine was to ride in a barrel race, and she wanted to concentrate. A lot of Texas cowgirls were good at this, and the competition was fierce. A bewildered beau would've been out of place and probably literally lost in the dust.

It was afterwards, after she'd won second place, when she and Sandy returned to the bleachers to watch the bull riding, that she noticed Giles next to her. And he didn't appear to be star-struck, offering only a quiet congratulations on her ride. *Okay, now let's have the tired old pickup line, guy, since I'm not at the moment taken.*

Which didn't follow. Giles seemed entirely absorbed in the exploding action in the arena, the charged seconds the bull had to dislodge its rider, and perhaps get a chance to gore him before he could run to the fence. After several riders, none of whom stayed on the required ten seconds, Celine actually found her curiosity piqued by this young man. And Sandy was clearly interested.

"So, you a rodeo freak?" Celine finally asked him.

"Not really, but I've been to a few." Blake Walker had taken him as a boy to several such events. *This girl's used to blowing men away at a glance. She's incredibly beautiful, but the formula says she's also either a snob or spoiled, has the homecoming queen complex, with all the football boys after her.*

"You're not gay, are you?" was the next shocking question. Sandy rolled her eyes, and Giles almost stammered, but recovered.

"No, are you?" he managed, with what he hoped was sufficient cool.

"No, and I'm here without an escort because I get so damn tired of the usual suspects. Your girl stand you up?"

"No girl at the present, and I don't find it necessary to snow-job a girl in order to complete myself. How about you?"

"Sandy and I came because we both like horses, excitement, the whole grit-and-bone experience. I'm just sorry I didn't win first place: must be off my game. And a guy trailing along would water it down for both of us."

"I guess so. Well, I've got a humdrum job, live a colorless life, and didn't see this show as a place to drag a girl to. But I'm glad you both came, and glad I did, too." He'd been told he had a nice smile, and he turned it on for them.

"Well, okay, now that we've skirmished. Wanta team up afterwards? Or am I being forward?"

"You are, and it's refreshing. Yes, I do, although I'm quite certain you're accustomed to more flashy male friends." A question in the raised eyebrow.

"Flash I don't need just now; I'm flashed out. So whattya do for a living?"

"I do boring things with electricity. Or maybe I should say I do new but equally boring things with it. Create new gadgets so people can buy them and use more of the stuff we generate. How about you?"

"I'm a dental assistant," Sandy volunteered, getting onboard now that this had become a group. She shrugged, as if *that* took the prize for boring.

"And I'm—you guessed it—a horse trainer. My life consists of communing with the monsters and getting them to do what their dumb-ass owners want. Like 'Okay, Fido, sit up and beg.'" She laughed and Giles had never heard a sound as entrancing as that.

"You realize that's pretty exotic, of course, to a non-horse lover. Although we did have some pretty good ones back when I was growing up." He was remembering his grandfather's stables, the smell, the regal mounts his father, Barry, had been so proud to ride and show off. But he'd been no real horseman, preferring to ride that old paint everywhere.

"I guess. It's a living, and sometimes I think I like horses better than people. Especially the pretty boys who seem to crawl out of the woodwork wherever I go." They'd reached her car, a dusty Ford Bronco, one of those '60s square-cornered ones: practical, tough, just right for a cowgirl. Giles had parked his rusting Dodge several cars away. "Okay, mine or yours?"

"Body parts might fall off mine, I'm afraid. I'm actually saving up for something in one piece right now. You like this Bronco?"

"It likes me. It'll pull a one-horse trailer if I don't speed, and it'll take me places I shouldn't go. Yeah, Dad wanted to buy me a Camaro with loud pipes, but this one doesn't mind the horseshit on my boots." That laugh again.

They drove to one of those ubiquitous Texas roadhouses, where the sounds of the local four-piece band drifted out onto the parking lot. The sun was slanting long by then, and Giles offered to buy the girls something to eat.

"Nah," Celine told him. "That'd make this a date, wouldn't it? Let's go Dutch."

"Whatever you say, and call it what you like; I'm easy."

They ordered steaks, and Giles was again glad that he'd inherited that cash from his grandfather at twenty-one. He'd split it with Christine, of course, which hadn't lasted her, predictably. He'd hoarded his part till he'd graduated college and was just now beginning to feel he could spend a little without feeling guilty. *Yeah, maybe finally buy that car if I could get interested in it.*

"So, you don't speak Texas," Sandy accused. "Where you from, Giles?"

"Backwoods Arkansas till I was twelve. Then here, but the die was already cast. My mom and I lived with my grandfather back there till she remarried, so I guess I'll be a redneck forever." He shrugged that off, which was about all it deserved.

"Arkansas doesn't have the corner on rednecks," Celine observed. "We've got 'em in spades all over Texas, and I'd guess every state in the Union's got its share."

"Just what defines a redneck, anyway?" Sandy asked. "I've always wondered. It's isn't just backwoods."

There followed a lively and sometimes hilarious pre-Jeff Foxworthy discussion on the attributes of the species, with Giles enjoying both girls' take on it. The definitions got farther and farther out from all reason, and everyone had fun. Sandy got top marks for her "They get it from necking too hard." Followed by Giles's redneck's last words: "Bet you fellers cain't do this."

"Okay, okay," Giles finally sobered up. "The origin of the term came from farmers being out in the sun so their necks sunburned. But a lot of rednecks aren't farmers. We've got 'em in our office, pale as ghosts. And like we've been saying, to qualify you have to be totally unaware of how completely inept you are socially."

"And they have to be chauvinist pigs toward women," Celine declared. That term had become popular by then.

"And love their trucks and dogs more than life," from Sandy.

In all, with the dancing that followed, it was a great evening. Of course, the men there moved in on Celine, and she did dance with a couple of them. Sandy had a grand time with all the shared attention. Giles knew he'd have to compete with half the world for this girl and had no illusions.

* * *

Andy managed to step aside, despite not being able to utter a word. Wilcox hadn't taken his eyes off her, now came inside, closed the door after them, with a sort of bemused half-smile. Still dumb, she automatically led him to an easy chair, sat at the end of a couch.

"Well?"

"Well, how you been, all these years, Andy? Besides havin' to hide out?"

"That pretty well sums it up, I guess. I won't ask the obvious: how you found me, because that doesn't matter. So, how've *you* been?" She was thinking there was no way, no way at all out of this trap. *All the clever covering my tracks, all the work, the education, the success. Won't be worth a damn when I'm in jail.*

"Mostly good. Gracie and I had twin boys, then one girl. She's in college in Batesville, but th' boys are in th' army. We're prayin' they don't hafta go to Vietnam. Gracie's workin' part time at th' café where I met her, and I'm sure you know I've been re-elected as sheriff, since Hal died, ten years ago."

"Yes, I learned that from Bobby Harcourt, the lawyer we had that time. And I do remember Gracie: sweet girl. Sounds like your shared life has worked out well." *What the hell is he doing, with this down-home stuff? Well, no hurry to put the shackles on, I guess: keep it civil.*

"Can't complain. We try to do things together, much as we can. She's a good woman, good mother. Guess I'm lucky."

"Well, you didn't dig this hard to find me just to pass the time of day, Cale. And I doubt very much that you've found Mabry's real killer."

"No, we haven't. And Hal'd closed that case entirely and I'd kept it closed until this bloodhound detective named Hardison from Little Rock heard Nate was workin' with th' town on th' utilities thing. Pure chance. He was assigned to th' case early on, but like th' rest of us, had t'give up on it. Only apparently he never quite did. Old guy, nearin' retirement, serious health issues."

"So he came after me? Like what, his last big score?"

"Maybe. He turned what he had, which wasn't much, over to me after askin' me to take over th' revived case. I'm sure you know he grilled Nate, tryin' to find you. Was sure he was stonewalling, really believed he was close to findin' you." He waved a hand. "Which doesn't matter now."

"No, since you *have* found me. Okay, so what's next?" *Time to get on with it.*

"My curiosity, mostly. What're you doing for a living, now? I've always wondered how you'd manage, even though I was sure you'd come out on top."

"Well, I got Nate into The School of the Ozarks, found myself a job, took night classes at SMS in Springfield and later worked part-time here, finished college. Believe it or not, I now own a prosperous architectural design firm here in Memphis." She spread her hands.

"And never remarried?"

"Not really time for that, although I didn't become a hermit. Almost did hook up with a missionary, who I hope is still alive somewhere in Africa. If I'd done that, you'd never have found me."

"No. Well, Andy, I know you're on pins and needles with all this reminiscing and catching up, in spite of how cool you're managing to keep. Right?"

"Yes, I've already asked you what's next, although it's pretty obvious. I'm still Suspect Number One, I know, with no statute of limitations on murder."

"Well, that's more or less true, all right." Wilcox was looking around the well-appointed room, and he'd registered the tasteful house when he'd driven up to it.

"More or less?"

"Okay, like I said, not only did Hal consider the case unsolvable. I did, too, until this detective thing. Pretty much had t' dig into it again, y'know..."

"You sound like you don't believe I did it."

"I know damn well you didn't, Andy. Never believed a bit of it. No way you coulda done it, Nor Barry, either. And if ever a snake deserved what he got, he was th' one. So..."

"You must do your sworn duty, then, right?"

"Find Mabry's killer, yeah." The faint smile was back.

"Where's this going, Cale?"

"Well, like I said, this detective wanted to come after you, but first of all, his bosses at th' state police headquarters told him no way were they gonna dig up a dead case fifteen years later, but if he wanted to, he could, but he'd hafta do it on his own dime. That's when he came to me. So, far's th' law establishment, I guess you could call it, the case is still dead." He spread his hands again.

Andy wasn't sure just where this was going, but there appeared a glimmer of hope. *If he's so convinced I'm innocent, what's going on here?*

"But this...Hardison, is it? Won't let it go?"

"Wouldn't have, no. But, Andy, he died of a perforated ulcer last week."

"He...did? And you said... But why'd you come after me, Cale? Is this your quest now?"

"Not really. But I've gotta tell you somethin' I shoulda told you back when we were in school, girl..." He looked around again, nervously now. "Y'see, I tried hard t'make you notice me, give me a chance t' spend time with you back then. Schoolboy fantasy, but y'gotta know, it never wore off."

"I did notice you, Cale, but you were so shy, and I didn't realize what was going on till long afterward. And you might as well know, just yesterday I was thinking how different things would have been if somehow we had paired up. Then of course, that ass Cam Henry showed up, and fool that I was, I let him snow me with his lies."

"Somebody shoulda shot that bastard. Well, b'fore you ran him off, I met Gracie, figured we were as good's it was gonna get, both of us. Or I'da come courtin', Andy, I swear I would, afterwards, even if you'd blown me off."

"I was so obsessed with survival then. We had nothing, Cale, and less than nothing after Barry burned us out. Charlie helped when he could, God rest him, but he was like a little kid: needed taking care of. So I sort of raised two boys, along with taking Elijah in. I couldn't see beyond the next garden row, or the next patched coat, or the next floor to scrub for money to buy shoes. No, romance was the last thing on my mind then. And when lawyer Mabry was shot, everything just came crashing down on us. I knew I wouldn't get a fair trial, so we ran. Which, of course, made it certain I was guilty."

"But you weren't."

"You and Hal apparently were a minority of two on that."

Neither spoke for long minutes, memories, speculations, thoughts tumbling around in both their minds. Then Wilcox stood, retrieved his hat.

"Goodbye, Andy. I had to see you one more time, and be able to tell you nothin's ever gonna come back on you about any of it. You got my word on that." He started to turn toward the door.

But Andy grabbed him, pulled him close, in a hug that lasted seemingly forever.

"That's for what we missed, Cale, both of us.

"And thank you. You're a helluva man, Cale Wilcox."

* * *

A lot of Celine's work with horses required her "unbreaking" them after some macho type had mistreated them. She held these obviously inwardly angry men in about the same esteem as rattlesnakes. Every time she encountered one, her comment about liking horses better than people came to mind.

And for the most part, her four-footed charges could sense that here was a human who really could understand them, wasn't out to beat them into submission, and they usually tried to please her. The ones she'd raised herself on the ranch were devoted, anxious to do whatever she wanted. She'd point out to the people who brought their horses to her how her own behaved, and they were sold, if they hadn't already been.

The Monday after the rodeo, she reflected on this new guy she'd met. *Plain as a feedsack, but he was fun. Sandy thinks I should spend more time with the executive types, plan my future. Well, right now my future's right here with my horses, but I guess that's gotta change someday.*

Or not. I suppose, biology being what it is, I'll sense the clock ticking in a few years, decide to join the ranks of the suppressed wives of the world. She thought back to girlhood, when she'd vowed never to give up her own desires, plans, for any sort of silly boy. Of course, the fantasy every girl has of the knight on the white horse riding into her life sounded like fun, but she'd outgrown that quickly.

The reality had, of course, been acne-faced adolescents and conceited football players either trying to grow up or convinced they didn't have to. It was all such a game, this sparring, daring, skipping away, with her determined to keep her independence at all costs.

Well, this Giles Mabry didn't seem to want to play from what she'd gathered so far. He was…earnest, she guessed was the term. Not bad looking, as if that should be a criterion (but yes, it was better to wake up next morning with handsome than mud-ugly, if one had the choice).

Celine often observed how many really beautiful women ended up with downright repulsive looking men. And conversely, the real hunks often paired up with girls who'd been overlooked. *Says something for taste for sure, or maybe insight. Luck?*

Anyway, there was more to life than hunting for the right mate, she was certain. Sandy made no bones about being on the prowl, and her experiences would make an adventure book. *But I think I've outgrown that phase—no, I'm sure I have. Oh, I like a good time as well as the next girl, but it does all get to looking the same. Guys all alike, just with different labels. Horses now, more stable, more dependable, and just more fun, really.*

But when Giles called her that night after a good day with the horses, she agreed to a Friday night date. He even asked her what she'd like to do.

"Surprise me. I like surprises, okay?"

"I'll do my best." On his end, he was already surprised—that she'd actually go out with him. On hers, she shrugged. *Worst thing would just be a wasted evening, and I've had those a lot lately, seems like. What? Am I becoming a recluse? After all the Dallas glitz I've been through? Well, maybe.*

Or maybe Giles had just come along at the right time in Celine's life: not the knight, not even a well-heeled scion of some oil or cattle baron. Enough of whom she'd spent time with, and set aside. Anyway, this might be a welcome break, even fun. She found she was looking forward to it.

And it *was* fun learning about this straightforward guy with no pretenses, no efforts to snow her with how great he thought he was. Of course, this didn't mean anything serious.

She'd already promised a real-life cowboy the next night, a fellow she'd also met on the rodeo circuit. He had a dark, hawklike face, coal-black hair, piercing blue eyes, in that Black-Irish heritage. She supposed he'd had girls hanging off him like a wide receiver, and she was right.

She and this dude talked horses. And talked horses. After awhile, it was only he who talked horses because she was bored out of her mind with his one-track, one-way conversation. So when he, having in his mind established himself as the ideal man for this knockout blonde, made his move, she almost had to break his arm. She couldn't help comparing this wannabe Marlboro Man with Giles Mabry.

Or Mabry with the young lawyer whose principal client was his oil-tycoon father. Who just assumed she'd be *so* impressed with his boasting of paving the way for Dad to make more millions, despite those nasty laws.

Or the up-and-coming country music marvel who wanted to add her to his string of wide-eyed groupies. That one didn't even materialize into a date.

Celine took her time deciding whether or not to let this tentative relationship with Giles go any farther. He wasn't her dream man, period. But then, nobody'd been her dream man. And did she really *have* a dream man? And was a dream man really even necessary? *Well, you only go around once in this life, so better aim high, or you'll regret it. Might regret it anyway.*

In the meantime, between young and sometimes damaged horses, group outings, the few boring social things her mother insisted she attend, she did manage some time for Giles. Just not much. She wasn't playing hard to get or any other game, she just wasn't bowled over by him. And he didn't seem that way about her either. Which was a new reaction.

Until she began to realize, after six months, that she'd cut out almost all other suitors somehow. And that she'd come to expect his calls, look forward to them. And really feel incomplete without his steady presence.

Was this love? Surely not, since Giles didn't represent any of the usual to-die-for traits a girl like her was supposed to insist on. No, it was more of a getting-used-to relationship; he was comfortable, like a worn shoe. *Not very flattering, that.*

A friend, that's what Giles Mabry was to Celine. Well, maybe even a good friend. That was unusual for her: a man friend. Girls had always been her friends, her confidantes. And too many of those had envied her, attached themselves to her, or secretly resented her. The boys, the men in her life had always come with baggage. She'd been a quarry for some, in their little minds, to be pursued, bedded if possible. To others she'd obviously been a trophy. To yet others, an object to be admired at a distance.

All of it, while early on seemingly to be enjoyed, had become...well, tiresome. And Celine didn't want to waste her time on tiresome.

But she did date a couple other eligible men during those next few months, mostly comparing. But not enjoying. She'd always come back to Giles, whether for something fun out on the town or a quiet evening just talking. They found they did a lot of that.

So while Giles's courtship of Celine didn't exactly parallel that of Nate Prescott's in Memphis, which had gone on not that much earlier, both men knew they'd found incredible mates. And were both almost overwhelmed at what they'd termed their good fortune. *If I can just make this happen,* Giles thought.

Eventually he did propose, one night under a nearly full Texas moon, with the smell of horses from a nearby paddock wafting through the open windows of his old Dodge, which he'd put off replacing. He knew this wasn't the setting sophisticated Celine would have expected, but by then he'd read the girl right: down-home to the core.

She thought about this for a few seconds, still not ready to say goodbye to…whatever, while he waited, not showing the anxiety that was consuming him. *No, this is it, girl: grab this, and never let it go.* So she said yes, got all over him for half an hour, and they started for her parents' house that night to share their joy.

The car broke down halfway there, and Giles got all black and greasy trying unsuccessfully to fix it. *Maybe should've studied mechanical engineering?* They ended up walking two miles for help, which consisted eventually of a ride in a rattly pickup to the Abbot spread with a man who knew her father.

The parents were roused from bed, now at one in the morning, and told the news. Giles was embarrassed, not the least by his appearance. Celine's mother hugged them both notwithstanding, and her father pounded him on the back, offered him a shot of bourbon. That was exactly what he needed just at that moment. And everybody talked away most of what remained of the night.

Chapter Twenty-Four

Saturday dawned, a bearable summer day in central Virginia, and Nate again checked the time of Giles Mabry's plane. He'd offered to pick the man up at the little Charlottesville airport, which wasn't far from where he still lived in the house that had been his first construction project that he'd shared with Audrey. *Two o'clock arrival, got almost all day. So, do I bring him home, have him stay over? Or surely he's made reservations somewhere. Just play it by ear. I guess a lot will depend on what his attitude is, really. I hope he isn't carrying any grudges from back in Ridgeway all these years.*

No, that wouldn't make sense: Nate had been too easy to find, and if there were some imaginary score to settle, Giles could have done it any time. *And I don't have any axe to grind, not with somebody who was just a kid at the time.*

He had projects in his workshop, mostly wooden toys for the youngest of the grandchildren, and the usual Saturday puttering around. If Audrey had been there, they'd have been watering plants, clipping the grass, keeping the place up. Now he let a lot of this go, just tackling it on the odd Saturday when he felt the urge. Well okay, he'd at least mow the tiny yard among the trees they'd let grow for forty years. Make the place look presentable, anyway.

Nate had a housekeeper in two days a week, who cooked, cleaned, did the laundry, and fussed over him. This woman had been with the family part-time since the children were small, Audrey spending parts of each day in the company office, holding the business together. So the house was neat, not the shambles Nate often left it in. He'd never been careful about where he'd put things, and Audrey had given up on civilizing him that way.

After lunch, he speculated on what Giles Mabry would look like now, surely so different from that family's men he wouldn't recognize him. Would he be healthy, tall, unbent? Only sixty-five or so, he figured, so maybe not beaten down like so many men he knew. In fact, Nate knew two ninety-two-year-olds at his church who were still active, one a farmer. And he himself wasn't decrepit, although there were aches from old construction injuries still with him.

At last he drove the few miles to the airport, early as was his habit. He sat in the waiting room, watching out the glass doors for the plane Giles would take from wherever he'd had to change. Maybe Chicago, Atlanta, Pittsburgh, since there weren't many direct flights from distant cities to Charlottesville.

He amused himself by trying to guess the careers of the several passengers who were milling around. The university generated a lot of travel to and from, employing around 20,000 staff. Only summer classes were meeting now, but that huge sprawl had to be maintained, remodeled, added to, and seemingly reinvented constantly. So that distinguished gray-haired lady was perhaps a professor? And the dark-skinned man maybe from India, a doctor at the university hospital?

And the tanned, T-shirted twenty-something guy in jeans, surely in construction, or maybe even a modern-day farmer. They all had stories to tell, lives they lived as complex as his had been, or more so in this electronic age. About half the people he saw were talking on cell phones, something he couldn't have imagined sixty years ago in Ridgeway.

Watching for Mabry, Nate took only passing note of the erect, almost-regal couple who came through the glass doors, looked around, then headed for the luggage carousel. The stream of passengers from the plane didn't contain anyone he thought might be Giles, so he concentrated on those standing around the carousel. He walked over to get a closer look and focused on each man as he grabbed his bags and walked out.

Okay, only a few left. The portly dude with the owl glasses? No, no resemblance at all. And he's headed out the door, too. So, the stooped, white-haired man in the polo shirt? Has to be, but he's surely past Giles's age. Maybe not well.

He started toward this man, who was just reaching for his luggage, skirting the couple. A woman's voice stopped him. He turned, saw that it was the tall lady, who was blonde and smiling. At him.

"You'd be Nate Prescott, right?" She extended a manicured hand, and Nate glanced from her to the man beside her. No spark of recognition at all.

"Yes, and could this be Giles Mabry? And you perhaps his wife?" He was taken aback, having expected the man to come alone, but he quickly grasped the situation.

"I am, Nate, and this is my bride, Celine." Giles shook his hand warmly, the eyes that now looked vaguely familiar, on his. "She doesn't let me out of her sight much any more."

"Well. You're both very welcome. Sorry I didn't recognize you, hard as I was trying. Almost sixty years, though, so I guess that's to be expected. Here, let me take that bag." He reached, retrieved a leather suitcase. They got the others. Then he motioned them toward the front door, refraining from the tired old question of how their flight had been. He couldn't help thinking how much he needed Audrey just then. *Okay, no crisis. But I'll take them to the house, of course, and maybe even invite them to stay over. Depends.*

His car was in short-term parking and quickly reached. It was his favorite, the meticulously restored '47 Jaguar 3.5 litre Saloon he enjoyed driving so much.

"Wow," Giles marveled. "Some car. You a collector?"

"Not really, but my aunt learned a lot about cars on back, and she advised me on the classics. Never could afford a collection, but I have a few I've kept till they're antiques. Celine, you ride up front with me where there's legroom, and we'll let Giles have the back where he can turn sideways for more space if he has to." He stowed the luggage in the trunk, which opened to a space featuring green felt with original tools nestled in their respective cutouts. They settled in, and the engine came to life at the touch of the starter button. Nate had learned to tune and maintain this and his other vehicles, and actually had time now to do that.

"It's like new," Celine praised, inhaling the scent of leather and polished wood. "There are men in Dallas who'd sell their tarnished souls for this car." Her smile was genuine, and she even stroked the walnut dashboard. "Most people just take these only to shows."

"Well, I don't belong to any car clubs or anything, except my church. I like tinkering, now that I've finally shut down my business. I'll leave the cars to whichever of the children wants them."

"Oh, how many do you have? Children, I mean." Her interest was real. *Surely a mother herself, and I hear it's incurable.*

"Just three, and now five grandchildren, all scattered over the country. How about you all?" He'd noticed their accents, pure Texas, and he guessed he'd never lost his own.

"Four actually, and yes, scattered. One daughter still single at 38, in LA teaching drama, directing. One married to a geologist in Montana. A son outside Dallas who inherited his grandparents' ranch. And an engineer still in Massachusetts, where he stayed after MIT. Where are yours?"

"A son, also an engineer, down in Blacksburg, where he stayed after Tech. A daughter in DC, married to one of those thousands of lawyers there, a lawyer herself. Don't see how they stand each other. And the other daughter in Alaska, where she and her husband have an earth-moving business. Don't see them enough, but the other two are close, and they all visit as often as possible." They were following the twisting road west of the airport through the tiny non-village of Earlysville toward Nate's place.

"This car rides like a cloud," Giles complimented. "All this recent technology hasn't really added anything important, has it? Is it pre-WW2?"

"Not quite: it's a '47, originally owned by a professor over in Oxford. I got it sort of in pieces after the Memphis lawyer who imported it couldn't find parts for it. It's been with us since the '70s.

And I agree with you: I don't miss the electronic stuff, the power steering or other gadgets. You see it has a sunroof, telescoping steering column, a 12-volt system. Ahead of its time, probably, but built to last."

"Any trouble driving it with that right-hand steering?"

"Not really. We went to Scotland once, rented a Peugeot, and I was the only one who would drive on the left side. With a lorry coming at you, it wasn't hard to get into the habit. Of course, nobody but me drives this now."

"Can't wait to see your others. What are they?"

"Well, I still have the Studebaker Hawk I courted my wife, Audrey, in, and the pickup I started in construction with. A postwar Dodge Power Wagon that was my winch truck, a Series Land Rover, and a Model A Ford. They're my main hobby now. I don't suppose keeping significant vehicles from one's past makes any sense to anyone else."

"Of course it does. I still have the '65 Bronco I had when I met Giles. He doesn't tinker, but I do: it's part of what provides me some respite from playing Dallas doyenne." She had a nice laugh, and Nate remembered Audrey.

"Well, I guess that means we can't be all bad." It was his turn to chuckle. *I think I like these people. See how it goes…*

They were approaching the woods road that led to Nate's house, and as he turned into it, he was struck by a sudden revelation. *Omigod, Aunt Andy will be there: the prime suspect in both Mabry deaths. What have I let happen here?* Then he remembered that anything public about his aunt would have been as Elizabeth Wilson, the dynamic commercial designer in Memphis.

The Mabrys shouldn't suspect who Andy really was, he consoled himself. At her eighty-three years, how could a man who hadn't seen her since he was ten possibly make the connection?

But I've gotta be sure they don't find out: don't want any fireworks. Not that she can't take care of herself.

The drive circled around in front of the house, with trees everywhere. A glimpse of slender porch columns, which they'd added later, showed through the greenery. And yes, there was Andy's gleaming '57 Thunderbird, where she always parked it. Nate shut down the purring engine and they got out, his visitors taking in the full-length two-story porches, the high dormers above, the stonework. To one side, a waterfall sounded faintly among ferns and mossy stones.

Andy came down the porch steps as they approached, her smile welcoming. Nate's stomach was tight.

"Well, this is a really nice surprise. You'd be Celine, I hope. Welcome, Giles, both of you. I'm Andy." She actually gave both of them hugs. Nate felt as if he'd been hit in the stomach. *Ouch, she's blown it.* He tensed as he watched for Giles's and Celine's reactions when it would inevitably hit them both. Or would it? No, these people weren't dumb…

Andy was still erect, her piercing eyes still forceful, her voice clear. Both women were as tall as Giles. Nate, well over six feet, was afraid Giles would feel dwarfed. He got that old in-the-sky picture of the four of them, standing there in front of his house, beside the two cars. *Tableau. Or standoff?*

But he was completely at a loss just now as how to handle this looming disaster. *Can't pass her off as a friend: the name. They do seem surprised at seeing her; must've figured I'd be alone…*

"You'll be staying, of course," Andy invited. "Here, let's get your things." Thus forestalling any other options Nate might have had to hustle them away. Giles and Celine started to protest, but Andy shushed them.

"Now, none of that. If you've made reservations somewhere, just cancel them. This big old house needs you: Nate rattles around in here like a marble. Celine, you're clearly the most stunning lady I've seen, including Giles's mother. And who'd have thought you'd find a girl so tall, Giles? But of course Christine was, too."

Okay, this had clearly identified Andy to them, and Nate resigned himself to whatever this revelation would lead to. *The discovery of the long-sought Andy Millard, who's surely been painted as the killer of this man's grandfather, at least. Dammit!*

But neither still-smiling Mabry seemed to make the connection, or there was something else going on here. Nate was figuratively sweating bullets, still casting about for a way to save this situation. Why had Andy told them her name? Okay, maybe she'd figured this had to be faced finally. And with a controlled inner shudder, he acknowledged that they'd just have to deal with whatever happened. Celine noticed his apparently anxious expression.

"You okay, Nate?" No, he definitely was not okay.

"He's just worried about springing me on you, Celine. You couldn't have known who I was, or that I'd be here. But I'm sure you've already figured out I'm his aunt, the very same principal suspect in part of the feud that took Giles's father and grandfather and my brother half a century ago. So now we all know, and we can proceed from there." She, too, was still smiling, as always ready for anything.

"Yes, we were sure of that," Giles said easily. "There's been enough published about Nate's work, and recently some you did with him, to make that clear. After all, who else could that aunt the designer have been?

"And it doesn't change a thing. All that's buried and won't ever come up again after a little explaining, and it isn't going to be the elephant in the room, I can assure you." He took her hand warmly in both his. Nate felt like the only one of them in the dark. *Okay then, it won't degenerate into gunplay. Whatever's going on here, I'll play the gracious host. At least until we see where this is going.*

"You're off in another world, Nate," the insightful Celine observed.

"Oh, just looking forward to catching up on the last half century or so. I warn you, I'll bore you to distraction, but maybe Aunt Andy can keep me in line."

"No worries: I've been bored by Giles for more than forty of those years, and he by me. And both of us have to flee stifling Dallas to the ranch regularly to keep from smothering." Giles shrugged, grinned.

"She tells me I have a flair for the obvious, Nate. I've always been about as exciting as a horse blanket."

"Oh, you'll do, honey, at least till I find somebody better." A playful kiss on his cheek.

The banter went on, and Nate began to relax, except for feeling he was sitting on a bomb. Surely with this beginning, the visit wouldn't deteriorate into any form of violence. But then he remembered Giles's father, whose adolescent outbursts had been completely uncontrolled. Of course, his mother had been the moderating influence at the Mabry place, and he knew old Montgomery had been grateful for Christine's presence, partly for just that.

Andy seemed to know much more about this couple than Nate did, and he realized she'd probably Googled them. That was something he'd never bothered to do: learn about computers. He'd always insisted he had too much crammed into his head to make room for this latest fad. That the fad had lasted a long generation and counting hadn't changed his mind.

"Now, after you have a chance to freshen up, I have lemonade, ice tea, with and without, and some goodies I baked. If I left it up to my nephew, he'd subsist on breakfast cereal." She led the way to the downstairs guestroom, a separate wing with its Jacuzzi, windows on the deep woods, its own porch. They thanked her, and she returned to Nate.

"How'm I doing, guy?"

"Well, aside from the fact that you've blown your secure cover for some reason, which probably wasn't anyway, you're being the epitome of the gracious hostess, which part surprises me not at all. But I'm hugely worried about this—my bringing them here—since it's finally dawned on me that Giles might be carrying a grudge. You don't seem concerned."

"Nate, I can spot sincere a mile away, and these two aren't on any kind of eye-for-an-eye trip, believe me. So let's be sweet, okay?"

"All right: I can do sweet, Audrey used to tell me. And I like them, so far. First impressions anyway. She's apparently a cowgirl, likes old cars. Don't know much about him yet."

"Oh, I got the whole package off Google. He's self-made: went all the way to the top at his company. Apparently Mom didn't help him much, blowing the family fortune. I do sort of wonder what genes from his idiot father might surface, but I'm sure Celine's taken any of that out of him. I'd say she's quite a woman."

The others rejoined them, and Andy led the way out to a backyard patio paved with broad stones, with cushioned stone seats. A swimming pool shone through more shrubbery. The visitors gazed about at the extensive plantings, vine-clad stone walls, yet another waterfall and pool.

"This is enchanting, Andy. May I call you Andy?"

"Of course: we're all past the generation thing. Yes, I pushed myself into Nate's and Audrey's lives to design most of this. I did commercial interiors till they came out my ears, and this place was a joy to work with. And so, of course, was Audrey. We miss her a lot still. She was a helluva woman, I can tell you."

"From what I learned on Google, she was from up North, right, Nate?" Celine, too, had done some research. *So, they already knew all about me, and about Andy, too, or could guess.* "How'd you two meet?"

"She came to work for the same engineering firm I was with in Memphis. Her father was a minister, and she'd planned to be a foreign missionary, but circumstances changed, and looking back on it, I don't believe it was an accident. Don't know if you folks are religious, and we never were before, but it's all so obvious now: being directed, watched over, despite the odds." Nate didn't push his beliefs on anyone, but he wasn't ashamed of them either.

"Well," Giles began, "the way things were going back in Ridgeway when I was a kid, it was hard to believe in anything. Celine's folks set me a good example, and she's managed to instill some spiritual understanding in me, despite the resistance. We did raise our kids in the church, and they've done well, maybe because of it."

"I'm sure of that. Yes, times were hard on all of us back then. And whenever you're ready to talk about that, which seems to be the point of your visit—not that we're not glad to see you anyway—just you fire away." Andy nodded in agreement, and Nate was glad he'd started the conversation on this path. *Let's get it out in the open: better sooner than later.*

Giles looked around again at this serene setting, here deep in the forest, a kind of oasis of charm hidden here. A man's house was his refuge, an extension of him, as Thoreau had written, and this one said a lot about his one-time neighbor/adversary. He'd thought often of how this meeting would play out, and here it was. Celine hadn't let him keep putting it off, and now he guessed he was glad: clear the air for all of them.

"All right." He looked to his wife for assurance, then began. "It all started—the feud, I guess you could call it, with your uncle Charlie, that timber cutting, and the property line. So let's look at that first, then take it in order. And right off, please realize that there're no hard feelings on my part about any of it: couldn't be, once the truth was known."

That assurance finally settled the churning inside Nate he'd been trying to mask, and he closed his eyes in brief thanksgiving. Andy, as always, seemed completely at ease.

"When my mother sold the place to follow my stepfather to Texas where he planned to become an oil baron, we had it surveyed. And sure enough, the old records mentioned the line right through that spring beyond and below your house, which everyone in the community remembered.

"But our survey didn't show that. And there was a little confusion for a while, till the surveyor's retired father, who'd gone along just to observe, remembered a similar situation. Seems some springs, over many years, move back into the hill as erosion washes soil from the banks of the spring branch and is carried away in heavy rains.

"So he checked with an old member of the Putnam family, who'd owned your land for several generations, and the fellow—he was about ninety—remembered some of that happening. The conclusion was that, over the more than a hundred years since the land was first settled, the spring had retreated from the actual line.

"Now, in some states, like here in Virginia, I found, property lines are what's called "metes and bounds," going from a tree to a big rock to a stream, to maybe an iron rod set by the surveyor. But in Arkansas and most places west, the land is divided into townships, which I'm sure you already know. So Stark Township was then divided into square miles, 640 acres each, then further split into 160, 40, and on down. Your folks had 80 acres, defined by a straight line on all four sides. So in reality, the legal line didn't move, as it could in some states, but was no longer through the spring. I think that's where the trouble started, because your uncle, knowing the spring should be the line, assumed those trees were yours. Am I right?"

"You are. So that's the original mistake. Okay, I owe you five stave-bolt quality white oaks, Giles, and I'll be happy to give them to you now with my apologies, speaking for him, Aunt Andy, and myself." This was meant to be funny and got a grin.

"Thanks, but they're a belated gift from me to you. Unfortunately, that misunderstanding started the bad feelings between our families..."

"Not quite," Andy interposed. "They started long before that, when I dumped your dad for a worthless truck driver in a spate of blind teenage foolishness. He never got over that. Not to insult the memory of your late father unduly, but he was looking for an excuse to get back at me, and our 'stealing' your grandfather's trees gave him just that. You've heard about the rest I'm sure, the assault, the trial?" Andy wasn't going to varnish any of this history.

"I have, and I'm heartily ashamed of how my father treated you. But of course, Grandpa insisted you'd...invited the attack," he held up his hand, "which was patently untrue. But I now know how that whole thing blackened your reputation among the prejudiced gossips of Everett County, and it became clear you could never get a fair shot at any kind of justice or have any kind of a life there."

"And I know how, back then," Celine put in, "the label *divorced woman* carried such a taint. Like the bastards who beat their wives, cheated on them, degraded them until they just had to leave weren't seen as being the least at fault. I've seen that often, and still, recently."

"Right you are," Nate agreed. "It didn't matter that this good woman gave up any life she might've had to raise me, provide for me and my grandfather, Elijah, and even Charlie: nobody was going to cut her any slack."

"Yes, and I know of the other insults, threats, the barn-burning, all of it. My father was a mental adolescent, I'm afraid, propped up by his father's hopes for him, which were totally unjustified and undeserved. But to move on.

"My mother died two months ago, Nate, Andy. She'd made a mess of her life, going from one worthless man to another, drinking herself nearly to death, wasting away. Amazing she lived up into her eighties. She let my stepfather, the first one, lose all the money from the farm sale, which was considerable, and went downhill from there. I don't fault her for that part, however: none of us is perfect." He took a deep breath, looked again at his wife for support, who put her hand on his arm, smiled wanly, then summoned the strength to go on.

"What I'm not sure I can ever forgive her for is that, so very fearful of my father's getting his hands on Grandpa's money, and seeing him starting to ruin the family, so certain he'd leave her and me destitute, she believed she had to act to save us.

"My mother killed him."

There was a silence like a thunderclap there in that afternoon air, as if a heavy cloud had blotted out the sun. Nate gave a sharp intake of breath, Andy's eyes widened in shock, and tears appeared in Celine's beautiful eyes. Giles seemed to have shrunk, somehow, at this revelation.

"Yes, she planned it carefully, to look like some bizarre hunting accident that could never be traced back to her if it went wrong. She told me, literally on her deathbed, that she'd considered just shooting him, but she wanted it to look like an accident. And she really knew little about guns, and feared she'd only wound him, or lose her nerve, with disastrous results…"

"But what if he hadn't fallen into that pitfall, hadn't even gone that way…?" Nate was incredulous, his mind sifting all the other things that could have gone wrong.

"She was hidden right there, behind the collapsed chimney of the old cabin, not thirty feet away, with a shotgun. Even she couldn't have missed him at that close range. Buckshot.

"And she'd known Grandpa had to leave that morning, that he'd ask Dad to go after that bull. And of course she was the one who'd let the bull out, led it past the trap. She'd gotten ahead of him while he saddled his horse, you see.

"For the past two months I've been tormented by the vision of my father's body impaled on those sharpened stakes, writhing in his death throes, far from any help, with my mother right there, surely hearing his screams. She even walked over, looked down to make sure he wouldn't get free, then just left him there. I can't possibly imagine any human being doing that, but she did.

"She knew the truth of that assault on you, Andy. She knew he carried such a grudge against you it became an obsession. She knew he'd burned your barn, with your mules and practically all you owned in it. And she knew he'd go even farther next time. So, despite the cold-bloodedness of the act, she must've seen some twisted justice in it. She didn't go into that part with me."

"The incriminating ladder," Nate remembered. "She left it at our place to point to us."

"Yes, capitalizing on Charlie's record of drinking, never keeping a job, himself the brunt of the region's scorn. She didn't have to do that but knew it'd take the pressure off her, which never materialized anyway. That was compounding the evil, I know, but I have to admit that my mother was an evil person, despite always meaning so well as far as I was concerned.

"She never loved my father. Some people knew he'd raped her and she'd forced him to marry her, with Grandpa's help. Killing him ensured her—our—survival in her mind, especially since she went on to make herself indispensable to the old man. No one in the world saw through her dedicated performance in that. Finally, mostly to make sure that she wouldn't run off with another man, taking me away with her, he actually deeded the place to her in his will, reserving a trust fund for me I'd get when I was grown. The loss of his son really must've unhinged him, something I later learned from what folks there remembered."

"All an act? That's hard to believe," Andy was astonished. "Everyone saw her as the ideal daughter to him, the ideal mother. She was so destroyed by Barry's death. It seemed."

"Yes, Mom could focus on what she thought had to be done and could go ahead with it, apparently without conscience or regret. Ends justifying the means, in spades. But I'm not saying Dad didn't deserve punishment for his sins. Mom told me he was sure he'd found a way to get hold of a lot of the family money, whether that was true or not, and had already made arrangements to invest it in some fly-by-night scheme. She couldn't allow that."

"And so," Nate said, "with Uncle Charlie the prime suspect, more so when he ran away, she was completely safe. You have to know, Giles, that his purpose there was deliberate, to erase any suspicion from Aunt Andy and even me, young as I was. That was maybe the most unselfish thing he ever did."

"I realize that now. But Grandpa was so obsessed with Charlie's guilt, he even hired detectives to track him, hounded the sheriff to stay after him, couldn't admit to any other possibility than that he'd murdered his only son. That's when it became evident that he was losing it.

"And this part nobody could ever understand: why Charlie came back, first of all. And then, how in that incredible coincidence, the two of them came face to face there in the woods that time. I've even speculated that your uncle might have actually contacted Grandpa to set up some sort of meeting, maybe to clear the air..."

"That's something I considered, too, Giles," Nate agreed, "but he could only have done that if he'd had proof that somebody else had killed your father. Obviously, that wasn't the case. If he *had,* he wouldn't have had to run at all. And he could have made all the rest of it go away if that were true, by just telling what he knew. What's hard to envision is how it all deteriorated into a Western gunfight, a short-range shotgun against a high-powered rifle." He shook his head as he had a thousand times before when trying to figure this.

"Well, I'm afraid, once I was grown, I never really believed it was a fair fight. I believe, in his obsession, Grandpa ambushed your uncle, shot him from behind that tree. And I further believe he then fired that shotgun at the tree, as if Charlie'd shot first. Too easy to stage that. And maybe I'm wrong. Certainly everyone believed Charlie had started the fight."

"A mystery, all right," Andy shook her head. "I knew Charlie hadn't killed Barry, but you're right: his reputation, unfortunately deserved, condemned him in everyone's mind. He was my big brother, but I'd always had to prop him up, rescue him, feed him, treat him like my wayward son. He could never handle growing up, despite his popularity back all the way to school, his likability. Which also led your dad to resent him early on."

"Mom pointed that out, too. Despite setting him up, she said she was genuinely sorry Charlie was unjustly killed that way, not that it helped, after the fact. And as I said, she was more in the clear then than even before, so that remorse obviously didn't last long.

"So everything should have been safe then, with both their killings unsolved, or at least Charlie's not prosecuted. You, Andy, of course were even then still a suspect, but not a serious one, with Charlie dead. And Mom didn't care anyway. She resented you too, you know: always inside, she really envied you."

"Me? She had everything, if not the ideal husband. Okay, I wouldn't have traded places with her for anything, but *envied* me? That's hard to believe: I was penniless, blackened, uneducated, with no possible future. And, of course, hunted like an animal in the end."

"That's what she told me, facing death as she was. And I guess she didn't just resent you: she actually came to hate you. Actually saw you, or someone she was sure was you, in Springfield once, reported it to the police."

"Yes, I saw her then. That's when I decided to leave everything there: college, my job, friends. But I didn't realize how deeply rooted her feelings against me were."

"Yes, none of us did. But we have to realize how much all this eventually ate at her, all that deceit, the violence, killing. Much too late, she acknowledged the enormity of what she'd done, how she'd made the wrong choices. She had to get it off her chest finally, for better or worse."

"But you said 'should have been safe.' What happened next?" Nate had an inkling but wanted to hear it spelled out. The whole feud was becoming clear at last, but there were still too many unanswered questions here.

"Well, Grandpa couldn't just accept that justice had finally been done after the law, in his mind, had failed him. This is further evidence that he was slipping, but he couldn't find any peace. That's a lot of why I think he shot Charlie in cold blood, but later he couldn't live with that after a lifetime of practicing the law. So…"

He paused again, took another long drink of ice tea, reached for Celine's hand. She had watched him intently, totally engrossed in this story of blood, hatred, wrong, suffering. She'd heard it before, of course, but this retelling so obviously wrenched her husband, she felt it deeply, too.

"He'd willed everything to her, as I said, but he still had total control over his assets, the place, cattle, timber, investments. And he began making irrational decisions. He'd already wasted money on those detectives, then hired ne'er-do-wells to harvest his timber, and they mangled much of it, didn't show up, slaughtered his woodlands. He was thinking about making other investments Mom could clearly see were ruinous. I've always been amazed she didn't see the same thing in Blake Walker, the second husband. Blinded by love, I guess.

"Anyway, she eventually saw no way out, in her mind facing ruin, but to kill him, too. I guess she had some idea that another murder wouldn't matter; she was beyond saving anyway…"

"But Montgomery was shot at long range and right in the head," Nate protested. "You said she didn't know anything about guns. Hal

Burgess insisted that was an expert shot. And from an incredible distance. That's also what refuted, at least for him, any idea that one of us could have done it."

"That was before. Grandpa had talked about taking me hunting soon—I was almost nine then. He had a fine collection of guns, right there: 22 rifle he'd bought for me, his hunting rifles. So Mom started going out to practice when he was gone. She'd always clean them carefully afterwards, oil them as she'd seen him do. She told me she'd regularly replenish the ammunition so he'd never suspect, and even if he had, he'd never guess what she was planning.

"She even hand-sewed him a blaze-orange hunting vest, which he thought was for his protection. It was actually to make it easier for her to see him when she went out to stalk him.

"So now at last, she was safe. We were safe. She had everything with no way to lose it. She wasn't dumb and managed the investments wisely, used her head with the cattle and timber, profited all around, learning from my grandfather's early success. With her secrets maybe in denial, but surely hidden away inside."

"While the lawmen hunted first Charlie, then me," Andy pointed out. "Collateral damage, I guess, which is an inhuman way to put it. So I realized that Nate and I had to disappear, with all of it stacked against us—me, at least. Leaving both cases unsolved, and yes, your mother safe. But what happened? With the man?"

"Right. Well, I'd never have imagined my mother so blown off her feet as she was by Blake Walker. I guess she was one of those people who mistakenly think that the right person, the one they search for, the storybook one, can complete them, fulfill every fantasy, provide the mythical happy ending. When all along, as I'm sure both of you know, each person has to become complete on his/her own, before being ready to take on a life relationship." He glanced fondly at his wife.

"Anyway, everything she'd…well…sold her soul for, I'm afraid, vanished, in one crazy scheme after another: Walker was so much like my father in that way. Oh, she was bitter. At him, at the world. That's when she started drinking in earnest. I was in high school, then college by then, working my way since my inheritance was still in the future. I couldn't help much, and the jobs she found didn't support her habit, or the men who attached themselves to her. It was all downhill for her, with the inevitable end in sight, but as it turned out, far in the future.

"She suffered a long and painful downfall, which I guess is some sort of retribution. I know the Bible says the enemy's evil should be left alone till Judgment Day—the parable about the thorns in the wheat—but I'd say my mother suffered her punishment in this life. Or at least got a headstart on whatever was to await her…afterward.

"So I guess there it all is, the mystery solved, the feud ended, the questions answered. You must know, I considered just leaving it hidden, but I wanted you to know, both of you, the truth. It's left its mark on all of us, and I hope we can put it to bed now forever. What do you think?" He spread his hands, completely drained.

There was a long silence, again. Nate's mind was whirling, as was Andy's. All this and all at once. In the end, the absolute *waste* of it all was overwhelming, staggering, rendering them both speechless. Their visitors' eyes were going from him to his aunt, still questions in them. *Sure, they're wondering how, deep down, we're taking all this. But that waste: seems we weren't the only ones to suffer from it in the end.*

Finally Andy stood, went into the kitchen, returned with more tea, lemonade, pastries. She sat again, took Celine's hand in one of hers, Giles's in the other. No one could have guessed what was going through her mind just then. *She never gives anything away, not even now.*

"I think, and I know Nate will agree with me, that we are both so very glad you've come to us. Despite the old pain, the old anger, the injustice of it all going so very far back, you've given us a precious gift. And I know it wasn't easy, realizing that your own mother was…well, so driven, so insecure really, so *forced,* I believe, into what she saw as the only way. Thank you, Giles. And I see a little of what you've seen, Celine, in this man who shared our hurt.

"Now come inside, it's time to start dinner."

"I'll help," Celine hugged her, and they went to the door, glad words pouring out of them like schoolgirls.

"Well," Nate observed, staring beyond his trees to a time and place dim with years, worn with rememberings, "I'd say we should maybe have a drink to our roots now, Giles, tangled as they are." He retrieved a decanter and glasses from inside, poured, touched the other's glass. And they said it in unison:

"To Ridgeway."

Epilogue

The rest of that evening, and the next and then the next, heard Nate's story, Andy's story, Celine's and Giles's. It also saw the foursome's visit to Jefferson's Monticello, the famed University of Virginia campus, and a drive along the Blue Ridge Parkway with its heart-stopping Shenandoah Valley vistas below. They also drove around in his and Andy's classic cars, mostly to Celine's delight.

It turned out that both men were fly-fishermen, and they sampled the waters of the Rapidan, Moormans, and Jackson rivers, although it was late in the season. Didn't matter, there being enough bonding between them even if no fish struck their flies. Both men savored the discretionary time their decades of effort had earned and enjoyed sharing it.

Andy took Celine to those special places she'd discovered in this cultured town and surrounding area. Her favorite pottery shop, unexpected in rural Stanardsville; an edgy modern theater offering at a downtown venue; all of them to a bluegrass festival down against the Blue Ridge at a custom brewery. And they lazed away two days just sunning, swimming in the pool, strolling along paths Nate and Andy had laid out through the acres he owned.

Unfortunately, there wasn't a rodeo within several states to go to, but Nate and Andy promised to make the trip to Dallas whenever the Mabrys told them the date.

About the Author

Charles McRaven is an expert stonemason, blacksmith, and restorer of historic buildings, with five published books on these heritage crafts. A native of Arkansas, he now lives near Charlottesville, Virginia. This is his second novel.

CPSIA information can be obtained
at www.ICGtesting.com
Printed in the USA
LVOW08s1543110417
530416LV00003B/735/P

9 781944 962289